STEVEN RIGOLOSI

THE HAUNTING OF KINNAWE HOUSE

Black Rose Writing | Texas

ISBN: 978-1-68433-935-8
PUBLISHED BY BLACK ROSE WRITING
www.blackrosewriting.com

Printed in the United States of America
Suggested Retail Price (SRP) $22.95

The Haunting of Kinnawe House is printed in Chaparral Pro

*As a planet-friendly publisher, Black Rose Writing does its best to eliminate unnecessary waste to reduce paper usage and energy costs, while never compromising the reading experience. As a result, the final word count vs. page count may not meet common expectations.

For Linda Konner, who believed

THE HAUNTING OF KINNAWE HOUSE

Guide to Gaelic pronunciations:

Bébhinn: BAY-vin

Kinnawe: Kin-NAW-vuh or Kin-NOW-uh

Léana: LAY-uh-nuh

Parthalán: Par-tah-LAHN

"Wounds heal in time, scars leave their signs—
Sewn up inside, sewn up in mind—They follow you."
—Siouxsie Sioux

"God plays chess and the Devil plays poker."
—Jeremy Massey, *The Last Four Days of Paddy Buckley*

Part I
Make Him Bleed

1

West 51st Street, Manhattan

It was one thing to seek followers on the internet, Matthew Rollins thought, but quite another thing to be followed.

That was how the Web worked, though. You searched for something on Google—a classic album on vinyl, a new power cable for your amps—and soon every sidebar featured ads for memorabilia and guitar equipment. This kind of stalking was different, though. Blocked musically, frustrated, he'd started looking at short-term rentals in inexpensive locations. A change of scenery might provide inspiration.

The email came from Bartholomew Dubh. The subject line: WELCOME TO AGAMENTICUS.

Dear Mr. Rollins,

Thank you for your interest in Kinnawe House. This historic home, built in 1746, sits on the Atlantic with spectacular ocean views. Whether you are looking for an elegant entertainment space or a cozy nook for composing or napping, Kinnawe House is the ideal retreat.

The house's builders and their descendants have occupied the house continuously since the eighteenth century. Now Mr. and Mrs. Forde, who spend most of their time in Europe, are willing to rent Kinnawe House to a tenant who will treat their home with care and respect.

When traffic conditions are favorable, a trip from Manhattan to Agamenticus, Maine, should take no more than six hours. Please click this link to learn more about this gracious home.

Sincerely,
Bartholomew Dubh
York Village Realtors

The message was both intriguing and unsettling. Matthew hadn't visited any New England realtors' sites—he wanted away from the snow, the ice, and the bitter cold of the impending Manhattan winter, so he'd looked at Florida, Arizona, South Carolina, New Mexico. He hadn't provided his name or email address on any of the sites he *had* visited. Nonetheless, Bartholomew Dubh had determined Matthew's identity and pieced together an accurate profile of his life, from his solitary existence in Hell's Kitchen to his (stalled) musical career.

Deep research on the Dark Web would not have been required. A Google search on "Matthew Rollins" would send anyone to Matthew's Facebook page and Twitter and Instagram accounts, which were plastered with photos of him performing "Silver Horses" at small, but not tiny, venues in the tri-state area. His banner photo on Twitter showed him sitting, guitar in hand, on the hood of the tired Honda Civic in which he hauled his equipment between home and gig. Kellyce, his girlfriend but not quite fiancée at the time, had snapped the pic, insisting it would increase his street cred. No fancy wheels for him, the photo implied. He was an indie singer-songwriter without a contract from a major label who'd nonetheless managed to get a song into rotation on all the major New York stations. And, the last time he checked, the views of "Silver Horses" on YouTube had exceeded 500,000.

He clicked on the link in Bartholomew Dubh's email, and his MacBook didn't blow up with malware, as far as he could tell. Instead, the screen filled with a slideshow showing Kinnawe House and its property in glorious detail. Vast, panoramic views of the Atlantic. A sundial entwined with ivy. A picturesque church in the distance. A bi-level living room with a piano and harp. A bookshelf-lined, ocean-facing library dominated by a portrait of a stern-looking New England preacher, an unsmiling but handsome man dressed in black.

The house was imposing, impressive, almost familiar. Matthew had almost no memories before his first day of kindergarten, but sometimes lightning bolts of déjà-vu sent a shock through him. That sensation zapped him now, and for a moment he was convinced that he'd been in Kinnawe House, really *inside* it, at some point in the past.

Agamenticus. Native American? Definitely New England-sounding. His mother had never mentioned the name of her hometown, but he knew she'd grown up in Maine and that his father was a native of Maine, too. What had happened between the Maine years and the Pennsylvania years remained a mystery that Rose of Sharon refused to talk about.

Matthew allowed himself a brief fantasy: In the pre-kindergarten days he could not remember, he'd lived with his mother and her wealthy, aristocratic family at Kinnawe House, their New England estate. His mother had entered the world as Rose of Sharon Kinnawe, not as Rose of Sharon Rollins. She'd embarrassed her family (by getting pregnant?) and they'd disowned her. The Fordes, or the Kinnawes, were the grandparents he'd never known, their name never mentioned, their existence never acknowledged. Or ... Rose of Sharon had married the Kinnawes' son, Matthew's unnamed father, and his mother had suffered her in-laws' disapproval and cruelty before fleeing the house with only the clothes on her back and Matthew in her arms.

It was as good an explanation as any. Among his mother's many cruelties, refusing to name his father was by far the cruelest, and he'd compensated by indulging in flights of fancy, grasping at small coincidences and exaggerating imagined connections. He'd been told he resembled a B-list actor, a silver-haired Irishman with a thrilling, Shakespearean voice. The actor was about the right age, so it wasn't impossible that he was Matthew's father, but he was from Dublin, Ireland, not Maine. At unexpected moments—walking along West 51st Street, performing at a Long Island club, buying comfortable used clothes at a secondhand shop—Matthew sometimes sensed a shadowy entity lurking in his peripheral vision. Was it a guardian angel? The embodiment of vengeance? The benevolent, or malevolent, ghost of his father? Anything was possible in Matthew's idiosyncratic spirituality, which he would have described, if asked, as "open to the forces of the universe."

His heart sank when he saw the rent on Kinnawe House. The paid downloads of "Silver Horses" had helped him save a few bucks, enough to get away for maybe a month in an inexpensive locale. But his entire savings account wouldn't have rented Kinnawe House for a week.

Matthew typed a quick response.

Dear Mr. Dubh,
I'd love to rent Kinnawe House if I could afford it. But I can't.
Sincerely,
Matthew Rollins

That should have been the end of it, but within an hour, Matthew received a second email from Dubh, this time with an offer. Dubh had emailed the Fordes, he said, and the Fordes had Googled Matthew, found the "Silver Horses" video on YouTube, and fallen in love with the song. Proud patrons of the arts, they were happy to provide Matthew with a quiet retreat and a small stipend in exchange for some basic caretaking duties.

New England in the winter? So much for getting away from the snow and ice, but being housebound would force him to write new music and help him catch up on his sleep. And hadn't his mother's boyfriend, Ray Lonegan, mentioned having family in Maine? If he was still alive, Ray would be in his sixties by now, and older people often want to live close to their families. With a good internet connection and plenty of time on his hands, Matthew might be able to track down Ray and ask the question that had haunted him all these years: *Why did you leave us, Ray? Why?*

Matthew grabbed his phone and scrolled through his contacts. His finger hovered over BRODY, JOSH as he pondered whether his closest friend would prefer not to be bothered. If this opportunity had come to him a year ago, he would have touched the CALL icon without hesitation.

A week earlier he'd mentioned to Kellyce the idea of getting out of town for a month, and she'd been supportive, vaguely promising that she'd figure out a way to visit him, somehow.

As he scrolled to her name, the chorus of "Silver Horses" announced an incoming call from a 914 area code. The Caller ID said BED HILLS INST, and his heart started thumping.

"Hello?"

"Hi, am I speaking with Matthew Rollins?"

"Yes, this is Matthew."

"Hi, Matthew. This is Patricia Symons at the Bedford Hills Institute. I'm sorry to tell you that your mother passed away three nights ago. I've been trying to reach you, but this is the first time I've been able to get through."

And all the feelings of guilt, regret, anger, and sorrow came flooding back.

2

Much had changed since Jonathan Edwards preached the sermon in Enfield, Connecticut, five years earlier. In the early 1740s, no man instilled more fear of God in the people of New England than Reverend Edwards of Northampton. But in the intervening years, "Sinners in the Hands of an Angry God" had inspired a backlash. Longtime friends began choosing their words in Edwards' company. Most of his ten legitimate children—all except Jerusha—had become a touch wary of their beloved father, who spent long hours writing impassioned responses to his detractors.

Edwards looked to the future and weighed the possibility that his congregation might remove him from the pulpit. Already he was being asked to account for his expenses; some members of his parsimonious community considered his silver shoe buckles extravagant and unbecoming to a man of God. And Bébhinn's behavior had become bizarre, erratic. If she broke her promise and revealed him to be Parthalán's father, he would be exposed as the greatest hypocrite in New England.

Jonathan Edwards had not risen to his prestigious and influential position through meek and humble piety. Rather, he had pursued advancement whenever and wherever favorable circumstances presented themselves. Edwards lived by a verse from Proverbs: "A little sleep, a little slumber, a little folding of the hands to rest—and poverty will come on you like a bandit and scarcity like an armed man." God had spoken to him, had decreed that he was to lead the people of the Colonies back to the faith they had forsaken, for God required more from His people than grudging attendance at weekly services. The enemies of the faith—the lazy, the sybaritic, the greedy—would block Edwards at every turn, the Father warned. Edwards must therefore seize every opportunity to gain advancement. Only by doing so would he accomplish the mission that had been assigned to him.

Edwards was an opportunist not only in his clerical duties but also in his personal life. Always attuned to circumstances that might benefit him, Edwards saw a heaven-sent opportunity when Gregory Brautigam approached him after the early-morning Sunday service. Brautigam had been a successful Boston merchant, but he'd had no desire to remain in the city after his wife's death. He'd relocated to Northampton to live with his unmarried sister, Lotte, who'd helped him raise his two children.

Brautigam and a dozen others wished to start anew in the burgeoning Maine district, he said. He sought to join the growing number of fishermen, farmers, and merchants who'd purchased cheap land on the northern frontier from a government trying to pay off its war debts. The residents of the Maine district were a people without a faith, Brautigam said, settlers in need of a community. Brautigam would brave the frontier with the help of several close friends, all hearty men not tied to Northampton by wives or children. Would Reverend Edwards, Brautigam asked, sponsor the building of a new meeting house, and the formation of a new congregation, on Maine's southern coast?

Edwards was well acquainted with all of the would-be pioneers, as no man or woman joined his congregation without a thorough vetting. They were a varied lot who'd come to Northampton from other parts of New England. Michael Ayers, a fisherman known for his strength and his willingness to brawl, had run afoul of the law in Newburyport and had received an ultimatum: Leave, or rot in prison. Ayers had no difficulty finding work in Northampton as a blacksmith's assistant. Sebastian Collinge III, a respected farmer whose seedlings were much in demand, had grown weary of sowing and reaping another man's fields in Springfield, and had purchased acreage on the Northampton outskirts. Charles Meer, well schooled in animal husbandry, had come from Worcester: He needed more land to raise and slaughter goats, pigs, chickens, and cows. Now Brautigam and these three ambitious men wanted to settle on the Maine frontier. "Our chances of success will be much greater if we have your, and the Lord's, support," Brautigam said.

Edward did not hesitate to promise his assistance. If he aided the men in their endeavors, he reasoned, they would be in his debt and would provide a warm welcome to his family if, or when, he was no longer able to browbeat his Northampton critics into submission.

Here, too, was an opportunity rid himself of Bébhinn and her bastard.

Clapping Brautigam on the back—a rare gesture, for Reverend Edwards did not like to touch people who were not members of his family, or to be touched—Edwards agreed to talk with the leaders of neighboring congregations and attempt to acquire the land for a new meeting house.

His efforts were successful. A wealthy scion donated 1,200 acres in Cape Agamenticus along the shore road connecting the villages of York and Wells, where wealthy Bostonians spent their summers frolicking on the beaches.

•   •   •

For more than a decade, Bébhinn Mac Conshnámha had served as an unobtrusive assistant to Jonathan Edwards' maid, Léana, running errands and helping Edwards' wife Sarah with sewing and childcare. In payment Bébhinn received a small salary, three meals a day, and a tiny attic room to share with her son. In recent months, however, Bébhinn's behavior had become unpredictable, even menacing, and Edwards had begun to fear for his family's safety. In addition, Bébhinn's boy, Parthalán, had become surly and disrespectful.

Before she'd begun slipping into dementia, Bébhinn had warned Edwards to leave Parthalán alone. "He is sometimes taken by an inexplicable anger, Jonathan," Bébhinn confided, daring to use Edwards' Christian name, as she had on the night she'd seduced him, a week after taking up residence in Edwards' house.

"A boy needs a father to direct his energies," Bébhinn said. "Parthalán does not have one."

A reproach, yes; but undeserved. Edwards had faced his congregation's disapproval when Bébhinn could no longer hide her pregnancy. He'd paid a large sum for forged papers proving Bébhinn's marriage to a sailor who'd been lost at sea, the nonexistent man who'd supposedly sired Parthalán. In the sweeping oratory that had catapulted him to fame, Edwards had harangued his congregation into sympathy for the widowed Bébhinn, quoting Proverbs 19:17: "One who is gracious to a poor man lends to the Lord, and He will repay him for his good deed."

Once Bébhinn extracted Edwards' oath that he would feed, house, and clothe her and Parthalán in return for her eternal silence, she receded into the background as Sarah Edwards gave birth to one child after another. Meanwhile, Edwards spent many sleepless nights begging God to forgive his weakness.

The dark-haired, black-eyed Parthalán looked nothing like his father. The lack of any resemblance should have been a relief, but Parthalán's handsome face and athletic physique tortured Edwards. With his cleft chin and thick curly locks, Parthalán had inherited the brooding Black Irish features of the Mac Conshnámha clan instead of the long face, stringy hair, and bony arms of the Edwards family. Edwards often averted his eyes when his illegitimate son was near. He could not bear to contrast Parthalán's doe eyes with his own squinty, disapproving myopia; did not like to compare Parthalán's robust olive complexion with his own sallow pigmentation; did not want to envy Parthalán's muscular legs and then look with disgust at his own knobby knees, sharp shins, and slender calves.

His other, legitimate, boys were unimpressive at best, an embarrassment at worst. Timothy was a sickly adolescent, Jonathan the Younger a pudgy glutton. But Parthalán—the one boy he could not acknowledge having created—was magnificent. Timothy and Jonathan the Younger were pallid, anemic specimens, while Parthalán was the greatness within Jonathan Edwards made flesh. Parthalán should have been the son trained to take over Edwards' pulpit when he entered his dotage. Instead, Parthalán was the guilty secret whom Edwards did his best to ignore.

Never did Edwards say Parthalán's name; to him, Parthalán was always "Bébhinn's boy." Upon returning home, Edwards would embrace his daughters and sons but say not a word to Parthalán. As Parthalán grew older, Edwards noticed the change in the boy's response. In his youth, Parthalán seemed hurt and confused. By adolescence, the hurt had turned into anger and scorn.

It was a blessing that Parthalán's twin brother had died shortly after birth. The tiny body lay buried in a far corner of the yard in an unmarked grave.

•   •   •

On a spring afternoon a couple of months before Gregory Brautigam approached him with his plans to settle in Maine, Edwards heard a knock at the front door. He continued working on his sermon as his maid, Léana Mac Concradha, answered the door.

"Is this the home of Parthalán Mac Conshnámha?" asked an unfamiliar voice.

"Yes, it is," Léana replied.

"Would you please see that he gets this package?"

Edwards watched through his library window as Léana approached Parthalán, who sat alone underneath a tree, using a quill to annotate a thick tome. Though Bébhinn was uneducated, she was not illiterate, and she had taught Parthalán to read.

Parthalán took the package from Léana. The window was closed, so Edwards could not hear their conversation, but their faces spoke volumes. Léana smiled as she handed the parcel to Parthalán; she'd always been kind to the boy. As a toddler he'd hugged her knees as he'd hugged his own mother's. Parthalán's mouth was now set in a more-or-less permanent frown, but he bestowed a dazzling perfect smile on Léana, putting Edwards in mind of his own yellow, crooked teeth. As Léana walked back to the house, Edwards returned to his sermon.

From the corner of his eye, Edwards saw a shadowy man materialize as Parthalán removed a book from the parcel Léana had given him. As Edwards turned toward the two men, Parthalán's companion vanished into thin air. Parthalán turned and caught Edwards' eye. A jolt of adrenaline traveled from the base of Edwards' spine to his brain, where the pulse exploded into an electric shock that sent a violent tremor throughout his body.

As Edwards sat paralyzed, unable to blink his eyes, Parthalán placed the book into a grimy rucksack. He stood, turned his back on Edwards, took three steps, and disappeared.

The accidents began the following day. Edwards' wife Sarah fell down the staircase. His daughter Mary developed a raging case of scarlet fever. Timothy almost drowned in the Mill River. Edwards himself was nearly thrown by a horse that had been spooked by a pedestrian who, Edwards thought afterwards, bore a resemblance to Parthalán's unknown companion.

After a near miss with a poisoned tankard—not filled with water, but rather with a corrosive acid that did not damage the tankard itself—Edwards told Léana to bring him the next package that arrived for Parthalán. A fortnight later, Léana carried a box, posted in New Orleans, into Edwards' library, where he used a pair of scissors to remove the twine that encircled it.

With the first snip, Edwards' left foot started to throb. With the second snip, the pain traveled to his ankle, knee, and hip. By the third snip, Edwards was lying on the floor of his library, gripped by a gout flare-up so agonizing that he lost consciousness. He awoke three hours later in his bedchamber, surrounded by Doctor O'Hara and his concerned wife and children. When he returned to his library the next evening, after the household had gone to sleep, the box was gone.

•   •   •

After securing the land in Cape Agamenticus, Edwards summoned Bébhinn and her son.

"Bébhinn and Parthalán," Edwards said, "God has called you. Four weeks hence, a party will leave Northampton. They will build a meeting house 200 miles to the northeast, in the Maine district, on the Atlantic coastline. Bébhinn, you have been a loyal servant in this house. You will now serve as housekeeper to the minister, Einar Koskinen. Parthalán, you will accompany your mother and aid in the construction of the meeting house. You depart three days hence."

"You send me away to die," Bébhinn said, her eyes on Edwards' shoe buckles.

"I have not made this decision, Bébhinn," Edwards said. "Our Father has. You must not resist His will."

"Let us make preparations for our departure, Mother," Parthalán said, staring directly at Edwards. "Perhaps you will sleep better alongside the ocean."

"Parthalán, I will never sleep again," Bébhinn responded, shaking her head. "It is our family's curse."

3

Bedford Hills, New York

Matthew drove the Honda south on Interstate 684 on his way back to Manhattan and his apartment on West 51st Street. The carton on the passenger seat held his mother's meager possessions and a lavender-colored urn filled with her ashes. Patricia Symons, the administrator of the Bedford Hills Institute's South Wing, had explained that state law required the facility to "effect final arrangements" within two days of a patient's death, and cremation was the preferred method when the staff was unable to reach a family member.

Matthew had checked his missed calls, but there'd been none from the Bedford Hills Institute. But why would Patricia have lied about trying to contact him? She seemed genuinely sympathetic. After promising to email Matthew a copy of the death certificate, she gave Matthew a list of websites that offered good advice for coping with grief.

"Was she in pain?" Matthew asked. "Did she suffer?"

"Heart failure usually happens pretty quickly," Patricia said. "I hope that's some consolation."

In repression lies madness, Matthew's Shakespeare professor had decreed, not considering the possibility that repression may preserve the veneer of sanity. Repression would help him push back thoughts of the asylum in which his mother had lived her last deranged years, shackled to her bed, a threat to herself and everyone around her. But as he drove, the maniacal newsreel in his head played snatches of the past on an endless loop.

She'd deserved better. She'd loved him with all her being—until the madness descended and he became the Enemy, an adversary to be destroyed. Her wild and gruesome accusations had accurately predicted the future, and he became the selfish, ungrateful child who'd destroyed her life.

How sharper than a serpent's tooth it is to have a thankless child.

Back in his apartment, Matthew removed from the carton a jar filled with leaves, twigs, and dead spiders and insects. Cautiously, as if fearing the lavender urn would bite the fingers off his hands, he moved it to a smaller box. After sealing the box with duct tape and placing it on the top shelf of his linen closet, he began sorting through the contents of his mother's jewelry box. Its two small drawers and three larger drawers were packed with Rose of Sharon's homemade jewelry: bracelets crafted from twisted string, necklaces pieced together from chewing-gum wrappers, rings made from plaits of hair, anklets of dried mimosa seeds.

He seemed to remember that the jewelry box had a hidden drawer. As a boy, hiding in his mother's bedroom closet, he'd watched her accessing the secret compartment. How exactly had she done it? She'd pressed the diamond on one side of the box ... No, the other side ... Yes, that did it. A tiny drawer popped open.

Using two fingers, Matthew extracted the thick, slightly sticky item crammed into the compartment. It was a Polaroid Insta photo of two newborns, covered in afterbirth and lying curled together like a yinyang symbol. A man's disembodied face hovered over the infants. On the white tab at the bottom of the photo, where the original developing chemicals had been stored, someone had written a date. August 8: Matthew's birthday. The letters RIP were scrawled in permanent marker beneath the infant on the left side of the photo.

Examining the photo more closely, he noticed the birthmark in the shape of a jagged star on the other, presumably alive, baby's right forearm. Matthew had a scarlet-red star-shaped birthmark on his right forearm. People often mistook it for a tattoo.

Matthew lowered himself onto his thirdhand couch as the truth sunk in. He'd had a twin who'd died at birth, or soon afterwards. His sibling was another secret his mother had taken to her grave. Another family member she'd denied him.

Angrily digging a tear from the corner of his eye, Matthew squinted to focus on the face hovering over the two babies. Though it was hazy and out of focus, Matthew thought he recognized the face of the black-garbed minister in the portrait hanging in the library of Kinnawe House.

A drop of blood from his longest scar—the one on his upper-right torso, to the right of his aorta—soaked through his T-shirt. From force of habit, he reached for the stone hanging around his neck. It felt warm and reassuring as it throbbed like the beating of a tiny heart, and within a few seconds the blood adhering to the T-shirt had sealed the scar.

He checked his phone: no voice mail, no text from Kellyce, who hadn't volunteered to go to Bedford Hills with him.

The day had been exhausting. He'd nap for half an hour on the couch—if he could, which he doubted—and he'd call Kellyce after thirty minutes of not sleeping.

.　　.　　.

Neither awake nor asleep, he heard the footsteps. His heartbeat accelerated as a wave of terror rippled through his body. *Wake up, Matthew*, he commanded himself. *Wake up*. But his eyelids would not respond to the signals sent by his brain, and through the tiny slits between his upper and lower eyelids he watched a broad-shouldered man, dressed in black, disappearing into his bedroom.

Matthew's paralysis broke, and he grabbed the stone around his neck. The apparition disappeared, and Matthew's eyes sprang open. His heart pumped wildly. Hell's Kitchen had long since become gentrified, but burglaries were still common in the neighborhood.

Matthew forced himself to think rationally. An amateur burglar would see him sleeping on the couch and exit the same way he'd entered, but a junkie in search of a fix might be more determined to find cash or something pawnable. But Matthew heard no sound coming from his bedroom.

The only logical conclusion: The man in black must have been a dream.

His heart still thumping, Matthew tiptoed to his bedroom door. The room was empty, the window closed and locked.

Matthew gazed out of the window at the worst that New York has to offer: three rats ripping open garbage bags in a dumpster, a drunk taking a long piss in the alley, and a bird impaled on the razor wire surrounding the parking lot next door. From out of nowhere, a possum appeared on the fire escape, bared its teeth at him, and hissed.

Two hours later, after a dozen unsuccessful attempts to get Kellyce on the phone, he gave up and went to bed. Waiting for his phone to ring, and fearing another phantom invading his bedroom, he slept not a wink.

4

The house, much larger than planned, would be ready for the new minister by September. Gregory Brautigam had advised against building so close to the water. A nor'easter or hurricane, he said, would drag the house into the ocean, leaving behind only the foundation built from the stones gathered during the excavation.

Parthalán, Reverend Edwards' newly appointed foreman, overrode Brautigam's protests, and construction went forward.

As work on the house progressed, Parthalán rode on horseback each day to the York Village Inn, where he collected Reverend Edwards' letters containing instructions for refinements. A few of the builders wondered why the size of the minister's house had expanded so much beyond its original scope, but only Brautigam questioned the orders from Northampton.

"The house is immodest," Brautigam said to Parthalán. "It will now be much larger than Reverend Edwards' own house."

"The extra rooms will house the ill and the elderly," Parthalán responded.

But Brautigam would not be brushed off. "And what of the meeting house, Parthalán? It is too ostentatious. We are not Papists."

Parthalán handed Edwards' latest letter to Brautigam. "Read the Reverend's letter yourself, Gregory."

Brautigam scanned the letter and nodded his grudging assent.

• • •

As Gregory Brautigam returned to his labors, he decided there was no benefit in quarreling with Parthalán. Besides, Brautigam had claimed a plot of pristine oceanfront property on which to build his own house. God would not look favorably on one who preached humility and modesty but who lacked those virtues himself.

Still, someone had to build on the site, and why should it not be Gregory Brautigam? Gregory had suffered the loss of his wife, Eliza, without complaint and without recrimination. It was he who had approached Reverend Edwards with a plan for establishing a congregation in Maine. He deserved an ocean view no less than any other man.

Perhaps, too, the land was a sort of compensation for his wounded pride. Reverend Edwards had decided to transfer authority from Gregory Brautigam to Parthalán Mac Conshnámha, the inexperienced and overconfident son of a housemaid. *You are too busy, and your time too valuable, to waste in correspondence with me,* Edwards had written to Brautigam. *Henceforth I shall send instructions to Parthalán, who has proved himself worthy of increased responsibility. Send all requests, whether for funds, information, or advice, through him.*

All would be set right, Brautigam thought, upon Einar Koskinen's arrival. A close friend of Edwards, Reverend Koskinen had trained at Yale but returned to Finland to care for his ailing father. According to one of Edwards' recent letters, Koskinen's father had died a month earlier. After settling his father's affairs, Edwards wrote, Einar would begin his journey across the Atlantic, arriving in Boston and traveling thence to Cape Agamenticus on horseback.

Einar Koskinen would waste no time in reminding Parthalán Mac Conshnámha of his rightful place: stable boy, ploughman, fish gutter. Gregory Brautigam took some satisfaction in that.

Parthalán knew that Edwards' original conception of the meeting house had been a basic New England house of worship, with a simple pulpit, boxed pews for families, and a balcony for single people and servants. An observation tower was to provide a view of the Atlantic and the countryside, and at ground level three doors would provide entry—one door for men; one for women; and one for the minister, his family, and his guests.

The plans did not call for a cellar, but soon after the builders' arrival a letter arrived from Reverend Edwards directing them to excavate for a crypt to run the structure's full length. After the cellar was dug and the foundation laid, Reverend Edwards provided additional changes to the design. A transept was to be added, and the entry doors were to be moved to the rear of the building. The observation tower was not to be built. Instead, the second story was to accommodate a large stained glass window to be installed by glaziers from Boston.

Despite the changes, the original footprint of the meeting house remained unchanged. Thirty-six pews in twelve rows of three would be enough to hold the congregation.

The workmen, about a dozen in all, accommodated the evolving plans with few complaints. After the meeting house and the minister's house were complete, Parthalán knew, most of them intended to disperse to the Maine interior. They had become enamored with Maine's night sky, filled with stars, and the mild ocean breeze that carried the scent of freshly laundered linen. But a few chosen men would remain behind. Already several of the best men had agreed to join Parthalán: Charles Meer, an expert in animal husbandry; Michael Ayers, whose catches at sea had become legendary; and Sebastian Collinge, a farmer able to coax seedlings from dust.

Soon Parthalán would demand Gregory Brautigam's loyalty, too.

* * *

At Parthalán's feet lay the head of a fawn that he'd killed. He lifted a cudgel, prepared to pulverize the head, and stopped his swing in mid-air.

Someone was crashing through the wooded landscape toward Parthalán's small cliffside cave. Sniffing the air, Parthalán identified the man before he saw him. The mixture of sweat, sawdust, sand, and cider was unique to Samuel Mason, a curmudgeon as inflexible and dogmatic as Reverend Edwards himself.

Mason stumbled out of the woods and pointed a finger at Parthalán's face. "The meeting house you build is an abomination, Parthalán. I've held my tongue long enough, and I'll hold it no longer."

Parthalán tossed his cudgel to the ground. "Your drunkenness disgusts me, Samuel Mason. You are dismissed. Be gone by tomorrow."

"Oh, I'll be gone, you creature o' Hell. But not 'afore I have my say. By the morn, you mayn't have more than a handful of men to finish your Devil's work. You'll damn your own soul, but I'll not allow ye to damn mine, nor those of misguided men."

Parthalán stood rooted to the ground, drawing strength from the earth. In the gathering dusk, a scarlet glow rimmed his pupils.

"You are deluded, Mason, but I nonetheless wish you the best," Parthalán said. "Now let us shake hands and depart as friends, as Reverend Edwards would wish." Parthalán extended his right hand and took Mason's.

With a single tug, Parthalán ripped Mason's arm from his body. As the maimed man lay writhing and whimpering on the ground, Parthalán grabbed Mason's other arm, twisted, and ripped it from the torso. He used the second arm to smash Mason's skull to bits and to crack open the fawn's head. He scooped out the animal's brains and tossed them aside. Grabbing Mason's right leg, he twisted until it separated from the man's trunk. He did the same with Mason's left leg, using the fawn's head as a chalice in which to collect the blood pumping from the artery.

Parthalán raised the fawn's head, tilted his head back, and drank until the skull was empty.

The next morning, Parthalán dropped two heavy bags at his mother's feet. For the next three days, the workers enjoyed a rare treat of Bébhinn's hearty Irish stew.

"I wish you'd brought me the bones of these possums," Bébhinn said to her son. "I can make a fine soup with good bones."

"They were old animals, Mother. Their bones were dry and brittle. I burnt them."

He hadn't burned the bones. They would be buried, along with the bones of the other traitors, around the foundation.

Over a late meal, Parthalán announced that Samuel Mason had decided to return to Northampton. A prayer was said for him, and work resumed at sunrise.

5

Alphabet City, Manhattan

After storing his mother's ashes in his linen closet and lying around for most of the afternoon, Matthew began the long trek to the far East Side, Alphabet City, and Kellyce's apartment on Avenue C. As he walked, he remembered the summer nights he'd lain alongside Kellyce in her bed as the neighborhood's noises and odors drifted through the open window: exhaust fumes from cars crawling along the FDR drive, blasting their horns in a futile effort to speed the bumper-to-bumper traffic; the fish-emulsion scent of the East River, two blocks east, after the City had gone too long without rain; the greasy reek of burnt sesame oil from the Chinese take-out on C at East 4th. A homeless man leaning against a deserted, boarded-up storefront asked him for a couple of bucks. Matthew gave him a five-dollar bill.

He hoped Kellyce had moved beyond the funk in which she seemed to be mired. He'd spent the day hoping she'd show up at his apartment with a sympathy card or flowers, but she hadn't. Instead, she'd invited him to dinner somewhere in the East Village, venue to be determined.

Matthew used his key to unlock the building's front door. He stepped over the glossy menus that had collected in the foyer and climbed the three flights to Kellyce's strangely apportioned apartment, with its oversized eat-in kitchen and tiny living room. He knocked his signature knock, a quick *rat-a-tat-tat*, before using his keys to unlock the door's three locks.

A distinctive scent—a citrusy unisex cologne—wafted from Kellyce's bedroom as she emerged from the bathroom, her hair dripping and her skin pink from a hot shower. He moved to embrace her, but she pulled back.

"We have to talk, Matthew. Sit down."

We have to talk: four words that rarely preceded good news.

"Is everything OK?" Matthew asked, lowering himself onto the lumpy loveseat that they'd rescued from a curb on trash day.

Kellyce crossed her arms over her chest.

"I'm pregnant."

To say the news was unexpected was an understatement. He was always careful about using condoms, and Kellyce never missed a pill. But Matthew's shock quickly turned to pleasure, even delight, at the prospect of starting a family.

"Wow," Matthew said. "That's awesome. I mean, I know we didn't plan it, and we haven't set a date yet or anything, but maybe it's the universe telling us it's time to ..."

Kellyce's arms remained crossed over her bosom. "I can't have the baby, Matthew." Tears the size of large raindrops began rolling down Kellyce's freshly scrubbed face. "All the tests say it isn't viable, and I've been advised to terminate. My appointment is at the end of this week."

Matthew repeated the words that his brain couldn't process. "Not viable? What does that mean? Is there something wrong with the baby?"

"It won't survive. I can't lose a child, Matthew. I'm not strong enough."

Matthew stood and tried to take her in his arms. She backed away, as if he were a leper.

"Matthew, I'm sorry, but I can't be with you. You're broken. Your seed is rotten."

Matthew felt as though he'd been punched in the face. "My seed is rotten? What does that mean?"

"I'm sorry, Matthew. I know what I want for my life, and it's not you."

Matthew couldn't believe his ears. "Are you saying we're over? The end?"

"Yes."

"You're not serious."

"I'm completely serious. I don't want to see you, or talk about this, ever again. I'm sorry about your mom, and I'm sorry it has to end this way. It'll be easier on both of us if you just go."

After Kellyce closed the apartment door behind him, he removed her keys from his key ring and slid them under the door, one at a time.

As he descended the staircase, five of his scars popped open. His T-shirt absorbed the blood, allowing just a small trickle to drip down his right wrist and into his palm. He sat on the building's front stoop, his hand curled into a fist, until the bleeding stopped.

He stumbled along Avenue C in a near-daze. Kellyce had inspired him, kept up his confidence when self-doubt plagued him. Rubbed his back and his feet when he couldn't sleep. Made him laugh with her made-up words, like *fabulosity* and *douchery*. Managed his social media presence so he could focus on his music.

At the corner of 4th and C, he stopped at a deli, where he bought wet naps to wipe the dried blood off his hand. Suddenly ravenous, he also purchased a pint of fresh blueberries, which he ate as he walked.

Strange. He'd never liked blueberries.

He passed the homeless man again, still sprawled against the door front, and gave him all the money in his wallet.

As soon as he entered his apartment, Matthew typed an email to Bartholomew Dubh, accepting the offer to serve as the caretaker of Kinnawe House until spring. Between his absent muse, his mother, and Kellyce, he'd had enough signs from the universe that it was time to get the hell out of New York City.

6

Einar Koskinen, chosen by Jonathan Edwards to lead the new Maine congregation, enjoyed a reputation as the strongest man in Porvoo, a medieval town on the Gulf of Finland about two days east of Helsinki. According to local legend, he could hurl a boulder with one arm and swim the gulf, back and forth, without missing a breath.

Einar's source of strength was his faith. As a young man studying at the Royal Academy of Åbo, he had pored over every word written by John Calvin. The more he read, the stronger his calling became. The Academy sponsored his voyage to the Colonies, where he trained at Yale, engaging in philosophical and theological debates with Jonathan Edwards and his other classmates.

Einar had been living in rural Connecticut when the letter arrived from Porvoo, telling him that his elderly father had only months to live. A devoted son, Einar hastened back to Finland. Soon after the elder Koskinen's death, the missive arrived from Edwards, asking Einar to minister to a new congregation on the northern frontier.

Einar accepted the invitation without hesitation. He packed a small travel bag with his Bible and some personal effects—mementos of his parents; a small charcoal drawing of his brother, sister-in-law, and their children—and set sail for the Colonies. While most of the ship's passengers lay below deck, green and vomiting, Einar hobnobbed with the crew and dined with the captain. He set foot on the docks of Boston Harbor filled with holy fervor.

The trip along the colonial roads was long and arduous, but Edwards had provided a spirited horse, Augustus, and a list of colleagues who would offer a good meal and a comfortable bed during his overland journey.

Einar grilled his hosts for information about Cape Agamenticus. Most had heard vague reports that the town was thriving, but they were unable to offer specific information. The Reverend Henry Hawley, a man of God with an ear for gossip, sounded a note of caution: "The house built for the minister is much too large, 'tis said, and the residents are a witches' brew of vagabonds and scoundrels: men for whom nothing is more important than a good hunt and the day's catch, and who care nothing about the word of God."

•   •

As Augustus trotted along the shore road, Einar caught his first glimpse of his new residence. The grandiose house alongside the ocean, with its high stone foundation, was indeed ostentatious, flamboyant. Conceited.

Einar turned Augustus's head toward the smooth dirt road leading to the house, but the horse, which until that moment had been an amiable travel companion, refused to place a hoof on the path. Einar used the reins to encourage cooperation, but Augustus remained immovable.

Believing that all God's creatures are entitled to an occasional bad mood, Einar dismounted, tied Augustus to a tree, and completed his journey on foot. As he approached the house, he saw a path connecting it to the meeting house. Einar was puzzled. He hadn't seen the meeting house from the road, but a meeting house should be at the center of the congregation, visible and welcoming to all, not hidden behind a thick screen of scrub pines, oaks, and black birches.

Einar weakened with each step. It was as if the entire journey from Porvoo had caught up with him in a few hundred feet. A metallic, charred odor mixed with the briny air to press on his lungs. By the time he reached the house's rear door, he was on the verge of losing consciousness.

A heavyset, unkempt woman with wild red hair opened the door in response to his knock.

Einar leaned against the doorjamb. "I am Einar Koskinen. Forgive me ... I fear I am taking ill after my journey."

"I'm Vivian Forde, your cook and housekeeper. Let's get you to bed."

"My horse ... he's tied to a tree at the end of the road ..."

Einar collapsed against the sturdy Vivian, who half-walked, half-carried him to a gloomy, cramped room, no larger than a storage closet, at the rear of the house. Before fainting, Einar thought it must be a quarantine room in which the sick were isolated.

• •

Einar Koskinen woke the next morning feeling no better. Above him loomed a dark young man, rather handsome with curly hair, a swarthy complexion, and a cleft chin.

"I am Parthalán, Vivian's son. I oversaw the building of the meeting house and now tend the grounds."

"The meeting house has been built according to Reverend Edwards' instructions?" Einar asked, eager despite his illness to begin fulfilling the responsibilities with which Edwards had entrusted him.

"To the letter," Parthalán responded.

"Does Reverend Edwards continue to correspond with the community? I have had no word from him since my departure from Finland." Einar had expected to find Edwards' letters awaiting him at every stop along the road to Cape Agamenticus. But whenever Einar asked his hosts if a letter had arrived for him, the answer was always "No."

"When construction of the meeting house was complete, all correspondence with Northampton ceased," Parthalán said. "As Reverend Edwards has appointed you the leader of this community, it is now your duty to ascertain his wishes."

Einar had expected a warm welcome in Cape Agamenticus, not the cold words of an angry groundskeeper. Perhaps Parthalán resented his demotion from builder to groundskeeper. In Finland, and in the Colonies, builders were proud men many rungs higher on the social ladder than gardeners. The loss of status might explain Parthalán's attitude toward him. In time, Einar thought, he would find a way to befriend his housekeeper's son. First, though, he had the more pressing task of restoring his health.

"I hope to be on my feet within a few days," Einar said. "In the meantime, would you please ask Vivian to bring me a cup of tea and perhaps some broth?"

"Vivian is your servant. I am not. You may make your request to her directly."

"My horse? Is he stabled and fed?"

"His leg was broken, and he was put down last night. He will not be wasted. My mother makes an excellent stew that will feed many members of the congregation."

•

A week later, Einar had still not left his fetid sick room. By night, as fevered hallucinations dominated his dreams, animals whimpered and scratchy human voices whispered in the attic above him. By day, when his fever dropped a few degrees, he was aware of activity in the cellar beneath him. Why, he wondered, had not a single member of his congregation visited him, inquired after his health, or sent a doctor? Had Parthalán chosen not to tell the congregation that their minister had arrived and now lay, close to death, in a dank corner of the house?

After a fortnight had passed, Einar decreed that sick or not, he must meet the members of his flock. Parthalán took him on horseback to the meeting house, where the townspeople gathered to welcome him. Einar heard their Christian and surnames as their owners stated them, but they disappeared from his mind as soon as the words dissipated into the peculiar metallic air.

I shall become better acquainted with every member of the congregation when my health returns, Einar vowed, making it back to the house seconds before collapsing.

•

During his first two months in Cape Agamenticus, Einar was unable to offer a single sermon. In the space of eight weeks, he'd transformed from a man in the peak of health into a shivering cadaver. During his more lucid spells, he stumbled along the rear hallway to gaze through an east-facing window at the meeting house, where activity was greatest after dusk on weeknights but nonexistent on Sundays. The source of the multicolored lights penetrating the darkness was a mystery. If the meeting house had been a Catholic church, stained-glass windows would have explained the glow. But such Papist ornamentation was impossible in a house of worship commissioned by Reverend Jonathan Edwards.

One Friday night, Vivian found Einar sleepwalking. She helped him back to his chamber, where he fell onto the bed, awoke, and asked the time.

"I don't pay much attention to time, Reverend. Morning, afternoon, night, they're all the same to me."

"But Vivian, they could not be more different. We sleep at night and work during the day." This was the natural order everywhere, except Cape Agamenticus, where nightfall seemed to rouse the townspeople.

"I work all day *and* all night, Reverend. I don't sleep, not during the day and not at night, either."

The heavy purple-black rings under Vivian's eyes seemed not only to reveal a profound exhaustion but also to hint at a heavy burden of pain and sorrow.

"Is your soul troubled, Vivian?"

"There's an old saying, Reverend. 'No rest for the wicked.' Well, I'm wicked, so I get no rest."

"Isaiah 48:22: 'There is no peace, says the Lord, for the wicked.' But all of mankind is wicked, Vivian. You must pray for forgiveness and give your soul to our Father, who will lead you out of the darkness."

Vivian sighed, and in the creases of her face Einar saw the remnants of the striking Irish beauty she'd once been. "As sure as I stand here, Reverend, there's no hope for me or my soul. What's bred in my bones is a curse that no Mac Conshnámha man or woman has ever bested. I have no reason to live, but I refuse to die, because Hell is my destination, and I'd rather be the walking dead on Earth than a sinner roasting in the fiery pit."

Vivian pushed a strand of red hair from her forehead. "I apologize for all that will happen to you, Reverend. I am to blame. If I'd made the correct choice, all would have been different. You would not be here. Nor would I. Now rest, and pray that the end comes without pain."

Einar fought to rise from his bed, and in doing so lost consciousness for the longest period yet, four full days.

•   •   •

When Einar awoke around midnight after four days and nights of torturous nightmares, the house was silent. The usual scratching noises from above were absent. Sensing that he was alone in the house and summoning his strength, he lit a candle and struggled to his feet.

He walked through the house's main corridor, a stranger in his own home. In the darkness, the waves of the Atlantic crashed against the rocks. In the center of the parlor wall was a door, perhaps leading to the second floor. Further down the hallway on the left, a large, luxurious bedchamber overlooked the ocean. Across the hallway, away from the ocean, was a smaller chamber. At the end of the corridor was a library. Its bookshelves were lined with leather-bound volumes and unlabeled glass jars filled with dead insects, spiders, leaves, and twigs.

Einar placed his candle on the library desk and reached for a slender volume on the bookcase. He was so weakened that he doubted his ability to lift one of the thick, heavy tomes. His chosen book reeked of decay and putrefaction, as if it had sat at the bottom of a poisoned well for centuries. No title was stamped on the cover or spine.

Einar turned to the first page, on which a pentagram was inscribed in thick strokes of purple ink. He turned to the next page, on which the scribe had drawn a two-headed goat and scribbled in a language unknown to Einar—not English, Finnish, Gaelic, Latin, Greek, Hebrew, or Arabic. The next page featured an ink drawing of a bear standing on its hind legs, displaying eight human breasts. Underneath were more words in the unknown language.

Scrutinizing the scribbles, Einar perceived that the writing was organized, not haphazard. Each line began with a small blob of ink and ended with a dash.

In a flash he understood the book's purpose. It was a manual instructing readers in the creation of abominations.

Einar closed the book and returned it to the bookshelf. His hand, once strong and steady, quivered with palsy.

If Parthalán and Vivian kept such filth on the house's main floor, what would he find in the attic and in the cellar? For the good of the congregation, he must find out. He returned to the parlor. The door to the second story was locked, with a key nowhere to be found.

Candle in hand, he exited through the house's rear door. Following the foundation around to the ocean side, he located the cellar door. It was closed but not locked. He used his shoulder to push it open and entered. In the distance, three black-tallow candles glimmered. He threaded his way among dozens of rancid-smelling oak casks as he approached the flickering candles.

Getting his bearings, he realized he stood beneath his sickroom. The candles burned beneath his bed.

He tried to blow out the candles but could not gather sufficient breath to extinguish the flames. Not caring if he burned his hands, he cupped each flame until the lack of oxygen snuffed it.

As he extinguished the third candle, air filled his lungs. His strength doubled, tripled, quadrupled. For the first time since his arrival in Cape Agamenticus, Einar Koskinen was the man who'd left Finland for the Colonies.

Exiting the cellar, he perceived dancing lights and a chanting murmur in the distance. Cupping his candle's flame to conceal his presence, he crept toward the meeting house. He lifted his head and gazed in horror at the stained-glass windows on the second story. Like the pages of the grimoire, the windows depicted unspeakable perversions.

Einar tiptoed to the rear of the meeting house—which faced the road, unlike the rear doors of all other meeting houses in New England—and peeked through the door.

Lying on the altar was a naked, fleshy woman with wild red hair. A man, naked except for a ram's head mask, approached the woman, a dagger raised over his head. Einar noticed a black star-shaped mark on the man's left buttock.

"Vivian Forde, this is the price of your betrayal," the ram said. "Never will you find a home, not with our Great Father below nor with the Great Filth above."

The man plunged the dagger into Vivian's heart. Then, after removing the ram's head mask, Parthalán lifted his head and stared straight ahead.

The whites of his eyes had turned black, and the irises had transformed into upside-down silver crosses.

All of Einar's worst suspicions were confirmed. Parthalán Kinnawe was in league with the Devil. The house, the town, and Parthalán Kinnawe were causing Einar's body to eat itself.

7

Midtown West, Manhattan

It was Matthew's last night in Manhattan, and he'd arranged to meet Josh Brody, his closest friend, at a local hangout that Josh had recommended. Now Matthew sat in Café 862, one of those tiresome, trendy Hell's Kitchen boîtes where all the women have hair extensions and all the guys overpay for food and drink. The music was loud, the décor faux-chic, the patrons horny and social climbing.

Matthew squinted at the bar menu, unsure whether his eyes were playing tricks on him. $22 for a chocolate martini. $16 for a 14-ounce bottle of water, said to be imported from Finland. $32 for three tiny "bison burgers" that wouldn't have fed the mice that scampered around Matthew's apartment at night. He would have been happier with a beer at a dive on the West Side Highway or a burger at the Moonstruck Diner, followed by a few games of pool at the Mob-run billiards hall on Twelfth Avenue. But Josh wanted to meet at Café 862, so Café 862 it was. It was the least Matthew could do. He hadn't made much time for Josh after "Silver Horses" became a minor hit, and their relationship hadn't quite recovered.

After their dinner, Josh planned to meet his new girlfriend, the latest in a long string of New York career women. Matthew hadn't caught her name, but it probably didn't matter. She wouldn't last longer than any of Josh's other girlfriends. The average was about two weeks, give or take a weekend. Matthew briefly wondered why Josh hadn't invited her along—he hadn't been shy about doing so in the past—but he was happy that Josh hadn't.

As Josh tapped away on his smartphone, leaving Matthew to gawk at the overpriced menu, Matthew wondered how exactly Josh had become a full-fledged Manhattan player. The gradual transformation away from borderline geek had started in college and now seemed to be complete, perhaps with the help of Botox, steroids, and hair plugs. No other explanation was possible. Josh's once good-looking but undistinguished face had become chiseled. His cheekbones, once hidden by a normal layer of fat, could cut glass. His biceps and pectorals distended his too-small-in-the-chest and tight-around-the-slender-waist shirt. Once thinning at the crown and temples, Josh's hair was impossibly lush and shiny. The dark beard that framed his face contrasted with Josh's piercing blue eyes. Contact lenses? Josh's eyes used to be a bland baby blue, not two shimmering sapphires. Matthew felt puny and pig-faced in comparison.

They'd been besties since they were schoolboys in Bala Cynwyd, Pennsylvania, a tranquil town on the Philadelphia Main Line. They'd both scribbled the same words to each other in their middle school, high school, and college yearbooks:

I'll always have your back.

But times had changed. Over the last couple of years, their lives had diverged as Matthew followed his muse and Josh followed the money. Still, they would always have a shared history and an unbreakable bond. Each was the brother that the other didn't have. They were growing in different directions, Matthew thought, but that didn't mean they had to grow apart.

Josh interacted with his phone through most of the meal, frustrating Matthew's attempts at a continuous, focused conversation. Matthew wanted to talk about Rose of Sharon and Josh's parents, Toby and Kathryn Brody. It was Toby who'd saved Matthew's life after the accident, and Matthew sometimes felt guilty about not staying in closer touch with him. Until a couple of years ago, Josh had never failed to invite Matthew to the Brody house for Christmas, but the invitations had stopped, and Matthew had never found the courage to ask why.

When Josh put down the phone, Matthew seized the opportunity.

"Hey, Josh, do you remember Ray Lonegan, my mother's boyfriend?"

Josh nodded. "Yeah, he disappeared, right? Probably couldn't take your mother for another second. She did have that effect on people."

Josh's words were needles that pierced his heart. Rose of Sharon wasn't even dead a week, and Josh still hadn't offered any condolences. Quite the opposite, actually. When Matthew texted him with the news of her death, Josh had texted back, "Good riddance."

"I think I remember him saying that he's from Maine," Matthew continued, pushing through the hurt. "I thought I might do some searching up there, see if I can find him. Maybe get answers to some questions. My mother was born up there, and supposedly, so was my father. I wanted to go there so badly when I was a kid, but my mother would never take me. This gig feels like fate in a way. A homecoming, sort of."

Josh's phone rang. He picked it up, looked at the caller ID, and answered. "Hi. Yeah. Now's not a good time. We're having dinner. I'll call you later. Don't worry. You'll be OK, honey."

Honey. Josh called all his girlfriends *honey.* Or *sweetheart.* Or *doll.* They ate it up and, for a while, refused to accept reality when Josh stopped responding to their calls, texts, and emails.

Josh placed his phone face down on the table. "This break-up has been really rough on Kellyce," he said.

"Wait," Matthew said, wondering if he'd misunderstood. "That was Kellyce on the phone?"

"Jeez, Matt, relax. I'm just trying to be a friend. If you have a problem with it, I'll block her from calling me."

"No, it's OK," Matthew said, in a small voice. Josh and Kellyce, friends? They'd never been particularly fond of each other. Kellyce had once described Josh as a "greasy Gordon Gecko," and Josh had mentioned, several times, that Matthew could do a lot better than a girl who carried around twenty extra pounds. "It's just so soon, you know? She won't return any of my calls, but she'll call you? It doesn't make sense. None of it makes sense."

Josh leaned back and crossed his arms over his chest. "Matt, listen. Forget about her and get on with your life. I mean, there's no way you're getting back together, right? And who needs a fucking kid, especially a mongoloid? You're a musician, for Christ's sake. Women throw themselves at musicians. So stop moping around and start having some fun."

"Yeah, I guess you're right," Matthew said, but as they pulled out their wallets to split the check, a voice in Matthew's head whispered, *With all the women in New York City, you have to befriend the one who broke my heart? The one who never liked you—until now.*

Outside the restaurant, they exchanged a quick bro-hug. As Matthew walked home, he reached for the stone that hung around his neck. His mother had given it to him shortly after Ray moved in. It was a security blanket in the form of a stone with a rune carved into it.

He wished he knew the rune's meaning. He'd spent hours on occult-oriented websites but hadn't found any image even remotely similar to the one carved into the stone. Even the reference librarian at the New York Public Library had given up. And if a reference librarian at the NYPL couldn't find something, then it didn't exist. It was as simple as that.

In his apartment, the garish neon signs on Tenth Avenue created a stained-glass effect as they filtered through the living room window. He stepped into the light, expecting warmth in the room. Instead, a chill traveled through him.

As he lay in bed, he thought about the questions he'd wanted to ask Josh about Ray, about Rose of Sharon, and about the accident. The unanswered questions buzzing in his head kept him from falling asleep.

After a couple of hours of tossing and turning, he grabbed his laptop from the nightstand. From the York Village Realtors website, he pulled up the photos of Kinnawe House—his home for the next six months. He copied the image of the library, expanded it until the minister's imposing portrait filled the screen, and compared it to the Polaroid he'd found in his mother's jewelry box. The two bore a distinct resemblance to each other. Ancestor and descendant?

Matthew had spent the last two decades wondering why his father had never tried to contact him. Maybe, Matthew thought, his father had wanted to wait until Rose of Sharon was dead, or until Matthew was an adult. The portrait in Kinnawe House and the hidden Polaroid in the jewelry box didn't prove anything, but the coincidence made Matthew's heart skip a beat and his fingers shake. Someone, or something, was reaching out to him, calling him. He simultaneously welcomed and feared it, whatever it was.

8

Cape Agamenticus, Maine
Fall 1746

Einar Koskinen watched from the rear door of the meeting house as Parthalán sawed through his mother's breastbone with the dagger and pulled her heart from the chest cavity. The congregation tore apart the corpse, raising the dripping limbs to their mouths and slurping on the blood that pumped out. The dismemberment complete, the people of Cape Agamenticus ripped Bébhinn's flesh from her bones, chewing the sinew and gristle.

Parthalán held the still-beating heart over his head. "Great One," he said, "we offer you this filthy soul, which has betrayed You and us. We ask your wishes. How do we dispose of this heart?" Using his right foot, Parthalán kicked open a trap door on the floor and tossed Bébhinn's heart into the crypt.

The heart floated over the space, as if buoyed up by a breeze. The rising air transformed into four burnt-orange fingers before igniting into flames.

Parthalán dropped to one knee. He looked downward, into the crypt. When he looked up, a voice pushed itself through his throat.

This is rejected.

The fingers of flame curled around the floating heart and thrust it through the stained-glass window over Einar's head. The window shattered, and as flaming shards rained down on him, Einar ran back to the false sanctuary of his sickbed.

After Bébhinn's disappearance, Parthalán brought Einar watery broth with chunks of tough meat each morning. To Einar's question regarding Vivian's whereabouts, Parthalán answered that his mother had gone to live with her sister in Concord.

Plans for escape occupied all of Einar's waking thoughts. He had no chance of getting out of Cape Agamenticus alive if he did not restore his strength first. So, when he was certain that Parthalán was not at home—Einar had fought sleep to track the minion's comings and goings—he crept from the house and tossed the broth and meat into the Atlantic. The meat shriveled into a hardened clump as it hit the water, dropping like a stone to the seabed. The broth, which smelled of urine, turned into ropes of thick black seaweed. The currents carried them away from the beach and deposited them on the rocks that were visible only at low tide.

Next, after extinguishing the candles beneath his sick chamber and gathering a small amount of their melted wax, Einar went foraging along the western cliff for the wild blueberries that had become his sole source of sustenance. Before Parthalán returned each evening—at about six o'clock, according to the sundial behind the house—Einar crept into the basement, relit the candles, and returned to his chamber, where he drew small, inconspicuous wax crosses on the wall behind his bed. He was weakened and vulnerable, but he still had the ability to ask the Father to bless the wax, to protect him, and to help him escape. An hour after the nocturnal hissing and whispering from above and below ceased, he returned to the basement and extinguished the candles again, rising before dawn to relight them.

Within a fortnight, much of his spiritual and physical strength returned. God had sent him across an ocean to eradicate a town founded on sacrilege, debasement, and blasphemy, but he had to accept the fact that he could not defeat an evil minister and several hundred Satanists by himself. He had but a single option: to make his way to Boston, there to call on the assistance of old friends—those with whom he'd trained at Yale—in destroying Cape Agamenticus and sowing the ground with salt.

In the meantime, Einar wondered what Parthalán had planned for him. A sacrifice on the altar? No; or at least not in Einar's current state. The dark lord would not permit Einar, a man of God, to cross the threshold of his church. First, Parthalán would have to succeed in destroying Einar's faith and convincing him to renounce his Father above. Only then would Einar be permitted to enter the church and have his heart ripped from his chest. Or perhaps Parthalán had decided to use Einar, to keep him ill but alive, to increase Parthalán's influence and power in Cape Agamenticus and beyond. Einar had not studied the occult in detail, but he knew that Satan's followers took a special pleasure in enslaving priests and ministers, transforming them into monstrous perversions of their former selves.

Two weeks after the sacrifice of Bébhinn, Einar felt strong enough to attempt escape. He would work with the crescent moon and slip out in the small hours of the morning, when darkness would provide cover.

He climbed out of bed and tiptoed down the hallway to Parthalán's library. Ignoring the hissing in the corner, Einar searched for and found paper, a quill, and ink. Then he returned to his chamber and composed his letter:

> To the good people of Cape Agamenticus,
> And to Vivian Forde and Parthalán Kinnawe, who have cared so well for me,
> As a man of God, I never expected to take my own life.
> But my body weakens more each day, and I wish to end my suffering.
> By the time you read this letter, the tides will have carried me far away.
> I know your next minister will serve you better than I.
> Godspeed
> Einar Koskinen

He hoped to be in Boston within a fortnight.

• • •

Scudding clouds obscured the sickle moon as Einar pulled open the house's rear door. Earlier in the day he'd spread candle wax on the hinges to prevent them from creaking. With only the clothes on his back, the shoes on his feet, and the small sum of money he'd brought to Maine, Einar crept toward the shore road. Once on the road, he ran with all the strength he could muster.

He'd been on the road about eight hours when he became aware of heavy breathing behind him.

It happened in a matter of seconds. Two men on horses appeared on either side of him while a third brought up the rear. A cat-o'-nine-tails lashed his back a dozen times, ripping his shirt off and removing nine layers of his flesh in parallel lines. He blacked out from pain as the horses gazed at him with their glowing silver eyes. He'd seen those silver eyes before, through a slat in the stable next to Kinnawe House.

Einar awoke in his sick chamber, surrounded by Parthalán and three other men.

"Leave us now, but return tomorrow to dig the trench," Parthalán said to the townsmen. "Collinge, have Brautigam call on me after eleven but before midnight."

The men filed out of the room, leaving the true minister alone with the false one.

Einar spat in Parthalán's face. "This was built as a Christian minister's house. You defile it."

Parthalán used a handkerchief to wipe the spittle from his cheek. "This house belongs to me. *You* are the defiler. And you are living proof that only fools worship as you do."

"You are the fool, Parthalán, believing that your reward will be anything but eternal damnation."

"Tell me, Reverend Koskinen. Has your God saved you? Here you lie, at the mercy of the men you sought to betray. But we will show no mercy."

Einar knew he would not live through the night. He would not betray God by making a deal with the Devil. When he awoke, having been torn apart and burnt to cinders, he would stand with the martyrs in heaven.

"I expect no mercy from a man who would deliver his own mother into Satan's hands," Einar said.

"You are not worthy to speak his name. As *she* was not worthy. *She*, who betrayed this community by writing to our sworn enemy."

"Do you think you intimidate me, Parthalán? You do not."

"I do not seek to intimidate you, Einar. Rather, I seek to eat the flesh from your bones and feast on your heart. I will leave your entrails to the men, who have a taste for such parts. Holy men are a delicacy in these parts."

"May my blood act as a poison that rots your innards."

Parthalán smiled. "Reverend Koskinen, you are the only man of God I have ever respected. Unlike Jonathan Edwards, who is a fop and a hypocrite, you act in accordance with your stated beliefs. It is the rare minister who cares more about his God than his own comfort and privilege."

"You dare to speak thus of Reverend Edwards?"

"Jonathan Edwards is a dung beetle. He will meet a different end than you will, but I *will* take him, when the time is right. In the meantime, I find your idle threats wearisome."

With his left hand, Parthalán reached out and ripped the Adam's apple from Einar's throat.

• • •

At ten minutes to midnight, Gregory Brautigam entered Parthalán's library.

"You know why I have asked you here, Gregory," Parthalán said.

Brautigam stared at the floor. "Yes."

"Look at me, Gregory. I must have your answer."

"I cannot do it, Parthalán." *I will not pledge my soul to you or your master. My faith is not strong, but it is not nonexistent.*

"You have built a fine house for yourself here, Gregory."

"I will donate it to the community upon my departure."

"As you wish. Before you leave, however, I ask you to read the clippings I have circled in red." Parthalán opened a desk drawer and removed half a dozen sheets torn from the pages of New England newspapers.

All the articles described the brutal rapes and murders of young men and women. In all cases, the rapist-murderer had eviscerated his victims, gouged out their eyes, cut the hearts from their bodies, and stripped layers of skin from their chest and buttocks.

"What is to be learned from these gruesome stories?" Brautigam asked, knowing the answer and sick in his heart.

"They are cautionary tales. You have a sister and daughter in Northampton, I believe. And a son in Boston. I do not wish such a fate to befall them."

"All the more reason I must return to Northampton, to ensure their safety."

"Do you believe that you can do so? Your best option is to remain here, Gregory. I will insist on your complete loyalty. In return, I will not require your children to join the congregation."

Brautigam remained silent.

"I take your silence as assent," Parthalán said. "You will not regret your decision, Gregory. Joining the congregation brings many benefits. The men say you miss your late wife. I promise you a new woman, as soon as you are ready for one."

Brautigam nodded his head once and took his leave. Entering the house he'd built in happy anticipation of a new life, Parthalán's words echoed in his head. *You will not regret your decision.*

As if he'd had a choice. As the congregation grew, men who disagreed with Parthalán—many of them younger, bigger, and stronger than Brautigam—had found themselves stricken with mysterious conditions: diarrhea, leading to dehydration and blindness; almost-constant bleeding from the nose or anus; thigh bones snapped in two while the men slept, followed by leg amputation and death. And after each death, the two deaf-mutes, James and Elias Featherstone, conveyed a large sealed cask to the cellar of Parthalán's house.

Gregory knew what those casks contained. By agreeing to join Parthalán, he'd prevented his children's remains from being dumped into one of them, and that was the most minuscule of consolations.

9

After a few hours of fitful rest, Matthew woke up before at 4 A.M., long before sunrise. He wanted to be on the road by six o'clock, before rush hour started. More than that, he wanted to be away from New York City, away from Kellyce, away from Josh.

He shuffled into the bathroom to brush his teeth and comb his hair. As he turned away from the mirrored door of the tiny medicine cabinet, an inky black hand tattooed with a star reached out through the mirror, as if to caress his cheek.

He reacted without thinking, smashing his fist through the mirror. The remnants of the black hand faded in the bloody shards that had scattered in all directions.

Matthew used gauze—always at the ready—to wrap the deep gashes the mirror shards had carved into his fingers, palm, and wrist. As he sat on the edge of the bathtub, his hand throbbing, he consoled himself that a few more scars wouldn't matter.

He'd just experienced another hallucination. First, the dark man walking into his bedroom from the living room. Now, a ghostly hand reaching out from a mirror.

Stable, mentally healthy people did not hallucinate. Unstable, insane people like his mother did.

He had a few hours to kill before the long drive north, so he spent the next hour researching genetic testing on the Web. Some of the services were reasonably priced, though the user reviews were decidedly mixed. Still, it was worth a shot. Any information that the test revealed about his heritage would be more information than he had right now.

In Maine, he'd have plenty of time to consider his options.

10

While their leader sat brooding in his cliffside cave, Charles Meer, Michael Ayers, and Sebastian Collinge III left their modest homes, which they'd joined forces to build, and met in front of Gregory's Brautigam's house. All sturdy men, they'd become stronger since throwing in their lots with Parthalán. Collinge, who'd begun wearing spectacles two years earlier, no longer needed them. Meer, who'd walked with a slight limp as a result of a vicious horse-kick, had awakened one morning to find his gait returned to normal.

All of them had been single when they left Northampton. After their houses were built, Parthalán wrote to Boston, New York, and the other flourishing cities of the Colonies. Within three months, the women arrived, and soon all the men except Gregory (who declared himself still in mourning for his late wife) were married to young, pretty, obedient women who kept a spotless home and whose abilities in the kitchen matched those of the finest Parisian chefs. They were skilled musicians, too. Rebecca Collinge did justice to Corelli and Vivaldi on her flute, Leah Meer played the harp like an angel, and Abigail Ayers was more than a match for her husband on the fiddle.

Happily for the men, their wives were sexually voracious. These were not modest, prim, Protestant ladies, but rather experienced women who seemed to have learned every technique practiced in the lewdest brothels.

"Good morn," said Meer, the youngest of them, to Ayers and Collinge. Upon his arrival in Maine, Meer had been a tow-headed blond, but his receding curly hair was now tinged with red, and a thick auburn beard covered his weak chin. His eyes, once a sparkling blue, had darkened into a muddy brown.

"And to you, Meer," replied Michael Ayers. While working at the blacksmith's in Northampton, Ayers had a lean, fit physique and lush, flowing locks. He was now bald and muscular, almost twice the weight he'd been a year earlier. The men of the village joked that Ayers must not be permitted on any fishing boat, lest he capsize it. In truth, Ayers was welcome on any vessel because his presence guaranteed a large catch. His wife Abigail, who had miscarried twice, was pregnant for the third time, hoping to give birth to the boy they so desperately wanted.

Brautigam exited his house through the back door—the door facing the road rather than the ocean—and joined his friends. Parthalán's inner circle, the other four points on the pentagram, was complete.

"We welcome you to the congregation," Meer said, shaking Brautigam's hand. Ayers clapped Gregory on the back while Collinge tipped his cap.

"The sooner we begin, the sooner we're done," Collinge said.

At the minister's house, the men retrieved pickaxes and shovels from the cellar. Wasting no time, they began digging a trench around the house's perimeter. Breaking up the dirt and removing the large stones from the earth was slogging work, but they labored without complaint.

They completed the digging by late afternoon. After a break for cider and the tasty mini-cakes baked by Leah Meer, the men returned to the cellar and rolled out six casks with a five-pointed star inside a circle burned into their staves. As they broke the seal on the first casket, an overpowering stench of ordure assaulted their nostrils.

Ayers dumped the cask's contents, a combination of thick brown liquid and human bones—skulls, femurs, tibias, rib cages—into the trench. Then the men rolled the next cask twenty feet further along the trench, pried off the wax seal, and repeated the process. After dumping the contents of all six casks, they donned gloves, climbed into the trench, and began arranging the bones. Parthalán had said the bones must form a complete, unbroken circle.

Their labors complete, the men climbed out of the trench and examined their work from above. As Brautigam walked the perimeter to conduct a final check, an acrid scent of urine-soaked pine trees assailed his nostrils.

Parthalán had materialized behind him. "Let this trench be finished before the sun sets," he said, "and we will celebrate tonight."

Parthalán opened the rucksack he was carrying and dumped Einar Koskinen's bones into the trench. The last item to fall from the bag was the holy man's skull, which perched on the edge of the trench but did not tumble in. Parthalán stomped the skull with his boot. The five men then stepped forward and spat on the skull before Parthalán used his boot to grind it into dust.

Brautigam took no pleasure in pulverizing Einar Koskinen's skull. In that reluctance he was alone; but appearances must be maintained. Ayers, Meer, and Collinge had no such qualms.

Brautigam had wondered why three good men had, with so little apparent cost to their conscience, agreed to join Parthalán's community. The promise of wealth, prosperity, and an elevated position in the community would entice any man. But to exchange one's mortal soul for a full belly and an accommodating wife? No, the men's decision had gone much deeper than their desire for comfort. It had touched on their resentment against Reverend Edwards, his iron-fisted manner of dealing with his congregation, and his insistence that they were all just one step away from eternal damnation anyway.

•   •   •

Spring 1747

Gregory Brautigam had left his native Boston after the death of his wife, Eliza. His spinster sister, Lotte, had invited him to live with her in Northampton, where she helped him raise his two children, Tobias and Emma.

A year before Brautigam began his journey to Cape Agamenticus, Tobias was apprenticed to a Boston bookbinder. Tobias would be permitted to remain in Boston, Parthalán now said, but Gregory must send for Lotte and Emma.

Brautigam's sister and sixteen-year-old daughter arrived in Maine two months after receiving Gregory's summons. Lotte kept their oceanside house immaculate and well stocked while Emma did not do much of anything beyond deflecting compliments about her apple-cheeked, slender beauty and her thick ringlets of chestnut-colored hair.

Lotte's skills did not go unnoticed. Since Bébhinn's execution, Parthalán had needed a housekeeper, and he chose Lotte for the role, leaving Brautigam without a woman to look after home and hearth. Parthalán wrote to New Orleans, and one month later Naomi Thibodeaux, a statuesque Creole woman, arrived in Cape Agamenticus.

"I will hear no refusals, Gregory," Parthalán had said. "You must take a wife. The women need guidance and watching, just as the men need a leader. Naomi will serve well in that role. She was raised by devout parents."

Parthalán had promised that Gregory would have no regrets. That prediction proved inaccurate for two reasons. First, Naomi and Emma disliked each other at first sight. They concealed their underlying, omnipresent hostility when Gregory was at home, but it erupted in snippy flare-ups while he was out. In a close-knit seaside village, voices carried, and the other wives needed something to talk about. Brautigam was aware of the rumors: Naomi called Emma a prude, while stepdaughter accused stepmother of being a whore. Busy with the duties Parthalán had assigned him, Gregory chose to ignore the gossip, and to allow women to be women.

Second, Gregory was not always able to suppress his conscience. Life on earth was short, damnation eternal. But that was true only if one believed in God above, and, as Parthalán's power increased and his reach expanded, Gregory began to have his doubts.

Part II
Leave a Window Open

11

Kinnawe House
Agamenticus, Maine

After twenty minutes of driving north on U.S. 1 through Summer Tourist Country, Matthew cut off to the right and linked up with the road that ran alongside the ocean. At one point the road was so close to the water that Matthew felt he was driving *through* the Atlantic. He had the sensation of being baptized, of the briny air exfoliating the Manhattan grime from his face and sucking it out of the Civic's window.

Bartholomew Dubh, the realtor, had instructed him to make a hard right after passing the white clapboard church that sat back from the road. Kinnawe House's official address was 99 Agamenticus Cliff Road, but the road wasn't marked with a sign. According to Dubh, the locals didn't want tourists invading their neighborhood in search of ocean views or beach access.

Matthew didn't miss the turn only because he was looking for it. As Agamenticus Cliff Road twisted and turned, the lavender-painted façade of Kinnawe House briefly came into view, disappeared, and reappeared.

The photos on the website had shown the house at its best, with perfect landscaping and a fresh paint job. The reality was somewhat different from the Photoshopped images. The rear door into the house was almost invisible among the twisted willow trees and thin, reedy weeds. But the house itself! It made everything surrounding it seem tiny and insignificant. Since moving to Manhattan, Matthew had lived in a 400-square-foot box. Compared to his apartment on 51st Street, Kinnawe House was Buckingham Palace.

The fierce winds off the Atlantic buffeted the Civic as Matthew pulled into the gravel driveway alongside a cherry-red BMW. He climbed out of the car, and as he stretched his back and legs, most of his scars began to throb. This throb did not presage a splitting open. *That* throb was sharp and painful, as if a box knife was trying to slice him open from inside. This was the excited, nervous throb he experienced before he walked on stage to perform. Adrenaline-induced, and generative of energy.

To the left of the driveway was a path between the house and a small, freestanding garage. Matthew peeked through the garage windows. Household detritus was piled from floor to ceiling—stained mattresses, beat-up furniture, boxes of clothing.

Matthew followed the path through shrubberies and suddenly, there it was: a breathtaking view of the ocean. The house and the ocean seemed to be welcoming him. The salt air scrubbed his lungs and cleared his sinuses. Scrub pines swaying in the ocean breeze replaced the frightening apparitions that had haunted his closed eyelids for the past week.

The Atlantic did not sit in the distance. Rather, it came within a few dozen feet of Kinnawe House. A deck stretched across the rear the house, providing points of entry into all the ocean-facing rooms. Above him, a second-floor balcony promised an even more magnificent view from a higher vantage point. A dock with a small rowboat tethered to it extended about thirty feet out from the narrow beach into the ocean.

The rear deck was low to the ground, only three steps up. As Matthew placed his right foot on the first step, he encountered a strong resistance, as if cinder blocks of spongy air had been placed on the stair.

As Matthew grabbed the railing for support and tried to move through the mass, the blocks of air seemed to become thicker and more gelatinous.

The door nearest him opened. A 50-something handsome man with thick, dark curly hair appeared, his hand extended for a shake. Matthew recognized Bartholomew Dubh from their Skype calls, but Skype hadn't given him an impression of the man's size. Dubh was tall and broad, with a Hollywood physique that Matthew could not have achieved even with a Josh-sized injection of steroids.

Matthew reached for Dubh's hand. As soon as their hands touched—Dubh's hand was as cold as a block of ice—the air blocks disintegrated. Matthew ascended the stairs with ease and followed Dubh through the door into the kitchen, trying to shake off the shiver induced by Dubh's arctic handshake.

Dubh decreed that a tour of the house was the first order of business. He led Matthew from the combination kitchen/dining room into the living room, which was built on two levels. The lower level, two steps below the upper level, was informal, with an overstuffed couch and loveseat, recliner, coffee table, occasional chairs, end tables, lamps, and a black-and-white spotted area rug. The upper level was more formal, with a few straight-backed chairs, a brocade-covered sofa, an oriental rug, a coffee table, a harp, and an upright piano. Antique musical instruments were mounted on the wall alongside the piano: a trumpet, a horn, a thin fiddle, a flute. Kinnawe House was clearly owned by music lovers—a very good sign.

The room was perfect, both cozy and elegant. As Dubh engaged in a running monologue, Matthew imagined long, rejuvenating naps on the couch with the waves as a background melody.

A hallway connected the living room to two bedrooms. On the ocean side was a master bedroom with a king-sized bed from which sleepers would awaken to a view of the Atlantic. Across the hallway a smaller bedroom held a queen-sized bed. To the left of the smaller bedroom, at the end of the hallway, was a large bathroom with black-and-white matte tile and a claw-foot bathtub. A tangle of plumbing and a handheld showerhead promised a simulated shower-stall experience. To hell with showers! Matthew planned to take a long, relaxing, luxurious bath every night, emerging wrinkled as a prune and bursting with lyrical and melodic hooks for all the songs he planned to write.

Matthew followed Dubh to the rear of the house, which served as its service hub. A storage room was packed with linens and other household necessities. A small, dark room with empty shelves served as a pantry, and a closet-sized utility room held the electrical panel and hot-water heater.

Back in the living room, Matthew noticed a door along the wall shared with the master bedroom. But he hadn't noticed a door on that wall in the adjoining bedroom.

"Is that a door to the library?" Matthew asked, pointing.

"No, it's a staircase to the second floor," Dubh replied. "Mr. and Mrs. Forde's bedroom is up there. It's a private space and off limits. But you're free to use all the other rooms in the house."

"Is the library upstairs?"

Dubh's eyes shifted to the right, to nothing in particular. "I don't know. I've never been up there."

"It must be there, I think. Your website had photos of the library. It faces the ocean."

"You must be thinking about another house. We rent a lot of oceanside properties. There's one up in Ogunquit with a big, fancy library."

Matthew had visited the York Village Realtors website at least a dozen times. Though he'd imagined/hallucinated that spectral hand reaching out of the mirror toward him, he knew he wasn't imagining the photo of the library. He'd even downloaded the minister's portrait and then run fruitless Google image searches trying to determine the man's identity.

The upstairs floor appeared to run the length of the house—a space large enough to accommodate not only the Fordes' bedroom but also the library. He'd have to find a way to sneak upstairs. Who'd know? One look would satisfy his curiosity, and by the time he left for home, the dust upstairs would have settled into an undisturbed layer.

After giving Matthew a primer on household basics—the septic system, the password to the house's wireless network—Dubh took Matthew on a tour of the exterior, pointing out painted areas that needed touching up. Matthew asked about the weathered wooden door in the stone foundation, a few feet below ground level, held tight with a hasp and a combination lock. Dubh explained that the door provided access to the cellar, which held the well pump and not much else.

"The pump was replaced about a year ago, so you shouldn't have any trouble with the water," Dubh said. The two men shook hands again, and Matthew was alone in Kinnawe House.

As Dubh's Beamer turned left onto the shore road, Matthew realized that he'd neglected to ask the most basic of questions. Where was the nearest grocery store? Where could he grab a decent cup of coffee? Might any local restaurants or bars welcome the services of a New York singer/songwriter, who'd be happy to perform his quasi-hit song, along with other crowd-pleasing favorites, for free?

But no matter. Answering such workaday questions was the internet's job, and he had nothing but time. He would get acquainted with York County, Maine, day by day, town by town, using his ample free time to dig for answers to the questions that had been haunting him far too long.

In the meantime, he was eager to explore the environs. Agamenticus Cliff Road continued along the cliff to the west. He was curious to see if other houses were located on the road, as none of the mapping programs displayed either Agamenticus Cliff Road or the local real estate, including Kinnawe House.

As Matthew crossed the threshold from the living room into the kitchen/dining room, his nostrils were assaulted by the odor of ... Moss? Mold? Rot? His stomach cramped, and for a second he thought he might vomit. A scar on the back of his neck split open, sending a trickle of blood dripping down his back. But within a couple of seconds the reek was gone, the nausea passed, the blood coagulated with the help of Matthew's T-shirt, and the bleeding stopped.

The car had to be unpacked, the Fordes' dressers filled with his clothes, those musical instruments liberated from the living room wall and played—but all of that could wait. The sun was high in the sky, and the western reaches of Agamenticus Cliff Road called to him. He locked the door of Kinnawe House behind him and began his stroll along the cliffside road.

12

Reverend Jonathan Edwards sat composing his Sunday sermon, trying to distract his thoughts from his 17-year-old daughter Jerusha, who lay burning up with fever. She'd caught the disease from her fiancé. The fever had killed him, and it might kill her, too.

As Edwards dipped his quill into the ink bottle, Mariah entered the room and placed a mug of cool water on his desk. Edwards nodded his thanks and continued his scribbling. Mariah, forever grateful to him, always seemed to know when he needed refreshment. Fifteen years earlier, in Newport, Rhode Island, he'd saved her from the brutal whipping of an innkeeper who would have murdered her if he hadn't interceded.

"If you want the useless bitch, she's yours," the innkeeper had said. "I've no use for a girl who refuses to earn her keep."

"How can you treat your own child thus?" Edward had demanded, enraged. "Are you a Christian man, sir? Do you not live by Psalm 127? 'Behold, children are a heritage from the Lord, the fruit of the womb a reward. Like arrows in the hand of a warrior are the children of one's youth. Blessed is the man who fills his quiver with them!'"

"You insult me, sir, by implying she is my own. She is the daughter of a filthy sailor who was set upon and murdered after leaving a whorehouse. And this is how she shows her gratitude—by refusing to work, and by back-talking my wife. If you'll not take her, I'll give her to the next man who walks through the door. I'll no longer suffer her spite and laziness."

Edwards was well acquainted with the matrons who ran the Northampton orphanages, stark buildings where the children began working almost as soon as they began walking. But they were well fed and clothed. All had beds in which to sleep, and most of the boys were apprenticed out when they came of age. The orphans who grew to adulthood in Northampton spoke of a childhood of hard labor and frequent sermons, but none complained of cruelty.

"How old are you, lass?" Edwards asked the girl, who cowered in a corner.

"Fourteen, sir."

Not too old for the orphanage; and with a good washing up, she would be presentable, though her looks were a bit exotic for Northampton. Her dark brows and Mediterranean complexion would stand in stark contrast to the pale skin and flaxen hair of the townspeople.

The girl looked sturdy, capable of doing more difficult physical household work. An assistant would allow his current maid, Léana, to spend more of her time minding the children. "You will return with me to Northampton," Edwards said. "Gather your belongings, and meet me in the stable yard."

The girl ran out of the taproom. A glowing golden light in a strange but familiar shape lingered in the corner in which the innkeeper had cornered the girl. The light's shape, if light can be said to have a shape, matched the carving on the three stones that never left Jerusha's wrist. As Edwards stared, the image evanesced, spreading outward and upward, leaving in its wake bright, oily dust motes.

When they were settled in the carriage, Edwards said, "We must have proper introductions. I am Reverend Jonathan Edwards."

"I knew you were a man of God, sir."

"Because I saved you from a beating by that foul innkeeper? Any man with a conscience, Christian or barbarian, would have acted as I did."

"No, sir," replied the girl. "I knew you were a man of God because I saw Jesus standing next to you as you scolded Mr. Welliver."

"You saw Jesus Christ standing beside me?" Edwards did not believe that the Son made personal appearances in filthy Newport barrooms with sputum-coated floorboards.

"Yes, sir. He was touching your shoulder."

"How can you know that the ... person ... you saw was Jesus Christ?" Edwards had spoken many times with the Father, but never with the Son. Edwards could not understand why He would appear to a common sailor's daughter but not to Edwards himself.

In answer to Edwards' question, the girl unbuttoned the top button of her maid's uniform, sliding her fingers into the opening and pulling out the crucifix she wore around her neck. "Because He is always with me, sir, and I know His face."

Edwards frowned. "What is your name, child?"

"Maria, sir."

He had detected an accent—Italian? "And where were you born?"

"My father and I come from Venesia. The English use the name Venice for our city."

So—the girl was a Roman Catholic, with a Papist-sounding name and a Papist fondness for idols, icons, and visions.

"Your name is not well suited to your new home," Edwards said. "Henceforth you will be called Mariah."

"As you wish, sir."

"Please give me the cross that hangs from your neck."

"But, sir, it was a gift from my late father. It has sustained me since his death."

"No, Mariah. Your faith has sustained you, not a piece of wood dangling from a cord. I do not condone such idolatry in my house." No idolatry, with one exception: Jerusha's bracelet, which Edwards insisted she conceal beneath her sleeve.

"I am to live with you, sir?"

"Yes. My wife and housemaid need assistance with the children and the housework, and I sense that you are a good girl. I am not often wrong in my judgments. What is the true reason the innkeeper was whipping you?"

"He ... Mrs. Welliver ..."

"You may speak freely, Mariah. The Bible says we must speak the truth to one another."

"They believed I should earn my keep by ... being with ... men ... who stay at the inn. I refused." She clutched her cross with her right hand. "*He* has told me that my destiny is to aid those in need. That I must live to help others, not become a Whore of Babylon."

The girl's faith impressed Edwards. It was rare to find such conviction in one so young. "Your strength is admirable, Mariah. You do not need the idol you wear around your neck. Now, give it to me, please, and I will hold it for you. You may ask for its return one year hence. By that time, you will not need or want it."

As a tear slid down her cheek, Maria untied the cord from her neck and dropped her father's gift into Edwards' hand.

Upon arriving home, Edwards explained to his wife, Sarah: "The road to Northampton was like the road to Damascus. During the journey, I witnessed a great conversion." He had borne witness to Mariah's conversion to the true faith as she surrendered her crucifix.

Two months later, Mariah was received into Edwards' congregation after the Reverend stated that he had witnessed her personal encounter with God. He did not reveal that Mariah's encounter had been with Jesus, not with the Father, and he swore her to secrecy on the matter. He was aware of the whisperings and the gossip, the *sotto voce* accusations that Edwards maintained too-rigorous standards for his congregation and less demanding criteria for members of his family.

Now, as Edwards reached for the mug, he saw that Mariah had also left a letter for him. He recognized Bébhinn's handwriting on the envelope.

He hadn't heard one word from her since she departed for Maine, but according to the informal news that reached him, Cape Agamenticus was prospering. Einar Koskinen had returned to the Colonies and had his hands full with the rowdy community, which would explain why Edwards' letters to him had gone unanswered.

Edwards broke the seal and unfolded the parchment. The letter had been written almost a year earlier. Only God knew how many times it had been misrouted on its way to Northampton.

18 Oct 1746

Reverend—

I have not always lived according to God's Will – You know of my transgressions – But I have welcomed the new minister and have served you loyally even as you sought to remove me from your life – I do not complain for these are the seeds I have sown –

You will say I am experiencing the fantasies that accompany old age and lack of sleep but I can no longer deny the Truth – Parthalán serves a father, but not Our Father above –

Because my eyes are weak and my ears clogged he thinks I do not know what happens in the cellars and on the cliff – But I have seen the bodies and I have smelled the blood – I have seen the casks with their etchings and I know what they hold –

There is no greater betrayal than for a Mother to expose her Child but it must not be permitted to continue – A slashing bloody thorn grows here and it is our son –

If you care a whit for the mortal souls of this town, you will act – For myself, I care nothing – My time approaches –

For the night we once shared I tell you — You must not come – Parthalán is your sworn enemy and you will return to Northampton a charred corpse – if you return at all —

I sign the name newly and forcibly given me –
Vivian Forde

Edwards was tempted to rip the letter to bits and toss them into the fireplace. He had fulfilled his obligations to Bébhinn. His blackmailer was no longer his responsibility, her son no longer a constant reminder of his infidelity. But Bébhinn's words had the ring of truth, and they explained earlier events that had unsettled and worried him. As a man of God, he could not sit on the sidelines and allow evil to gain a foothold in the Colonies. He would conduct his own research, pray for guidance, and act if he must.

13

Kinnawe House
Agamenticus, Maine

As Matthew walked along Agamenticus Cliff Road, gravel turned into dirt, which turned into macadam, which turned into pebbles, which became dirt again. Straggly wild bushes on both sides of the road sprouted gigantic blueberries with an enticing indigo sheen. Matthew was tempted to pluck and eat a few of them, but he remembered an early childhood lesson that Josh's father, Toby Brody, had taught him: If you aren't sure, don't eat it.

The neighbors' houses were much more modest than Kinnawe House, vestiges of an earlier era in which non-millionaires were able to purchase a plot on the coast. The simple Cape Cod-style houses sat on stone foundations, each with a back door a few steps up from the ground.

He saw no signs of human life. No cars parked in driveways; no children's toys sitting on the sparse rear lawns; no open windows to circulate the air. Bartholomew Dubh had mentioned that "the season" ended by the last week of September, so most of the summer residents would be gone by now.

At the end of the road, a small, well-maintained house clad in white-painted cedar clapboard sat on a spit of land just a few yards from the water's edge. To the left of the house—land's end—was a stand of lush, healthy evergreens: cypress, white pine, Norway spruce. As he stared at the house, a small brick of alabaster fluttered in Matthew's peripheral vision. Turning his head toward the trees, he saw that a dove—or a seagull, or an erne, or another ocean bird—had settled on a high branch of the tallest spruce. Its soft coos were the harmony to the Atlantic's melody.

As he turned to face the house, he realized with a start that a woman stood next to him.

"Sorry. Didn't mean to sneak up on you," she said. With her small, almost prim mouth, almond-shaped eyes, salt-and-pepper hair swept up into a bun, and ample bosom, she was straight out of Central Casting, Sweet Old Lady Division. In her speech Matthew heard a slight New England accent, vaguely reminiscent of his mother's Yankee twang. Matthew warmed to her instantly.

"Hi," Matthew said, smiling. "I'm Matthew. Matthew Rollins. I'll be living at Kinnawe House until the spring."

"I'd heard that the Fordes hired a caretaker. Pleased to meet you. I'm Helen Crowe." She grabbed Matthew's hand and shook it firmly.

"I just arrived, about half an hour ago," Matthew said, "and I wanted to explore before the sun sets. I've never been in Maine before."

"Not much to see on the cliff, unfortunately. Just the ocean and some rocks."

"I live in New York City. My bedroom window overlooks an alley filled with rats and garbage. The ocean view will be a nice change."

Helen smiled. "I've been here so long, I guess I take it for granted."

Their conversation was interrupted by three loud bangs that sounded like the backfiring of a 1920s jalopy. The dove fluttered off the bough of Helen's spruce and took wing over the Atlantic.

Helen huffed. "Those damned hunters, and calling the police doesn't do any good. They say this is a 'private community,' we don't pay their salaries, and we have to handle it ourselves."

A private community. That would explain why he hadn't been able to find Agamenticus on any map. It was a neighborhood, a housing development, a beach community—not a town.

"It seems pretty insane to go hunting where people *live*," Matthew said. "Besides, what's there to hunt on a beach?"

"Wild goats. You'll see them hopping from rock to rock at low tide. They're difficult to shoot, and they attract every gun-toting male within a hundred miles. You said this is your first visit to Maine? Do you have any experience with the ocean?"

"I've been to the Jersey shore, but that's it. I'm originally from Pennsylvania, outside of Philadelphia."

"Then you need a primer. Tonight, you'll see how dark the cliff gets. When the moon is waning, it's almost pitch black out here. You won't be able to see your hand in front of your face. So stay indoors at night. You don't want to get shot by a hunter who thinks you're the local wildlife. You see how close we are to the Atlantic? A couple of wrong steps in the dark and you could get swept out to sea. Always respect the ocean, and don't take chances. During the day, don't climb out on the rocks, because the ocean will hypnotize you, and before you know it, the tide will start coming in. You'll be stranded, and you'll drown. And always leave a window open in the house. If you don't, mold grows and makes you sick. If a window is open, the ocean air gets in, and the salt kills the mold. So always leave a window open, if only a crack, no matter what the weather. And keep a dust cloth handy, because the salt accumulates quickly."

Matthew thanked Helen for the advice and began walking back to Kinnawe House. As he unlocked the door, he realized that the gashes on his right hand, the cuts from the mirror shards still wrapped in gauze, had stopped throbbing. Already Maine was having a curative effect.

He'd made the right decision in coming here.

14

After receiving Bébhinn's letter, Jonathan Edwards spent two weeks asking discreet questions of friends and other ministers. Uncovering reliable information proved impossible. The men who'd left Northampton to settle Cape Agamenticus—Gregory Brautigam, Sebastian Collinge, Michael Ayers, Charles Meer, Samuel Mason, and others—had cut all ties with Northampton. Several months earlier, Brautigam had sent for his sister, Lotte, and his daughter, Emma. Lotte had sold her house, and the two women left Northampton. They were not heard from again.

At inns and taverns Edwards listened to rumors spread by men who'd imbibed large amounts of rum. The Reverend Einar Koskinen, they said, had arrived in Cape Agamenticus a healthy man, but he'd soon grown pale and thin. Due to the minister's failing health, his acolyte, Bartholomew Kinnawe, had begun taking on more responsibilities in the community.

It was rumored, too, that Reverend Kinnawe—yes, he used the title "Reverend" and called himself a minister—conducted services at unorthodox hours. People traveling along the shore road between York and Wells late at night reported circles of candlelight deep in the woods, as well as colored light emanating from the second story of the meeting house. The same travelers reported a strong, unpleasant odor, a mixture of sulfur and rancid mud, permeating the air.

The evidence was suggestive, not damning, as details were sparse. Then Edwards' nine-year-old son Timothy repeated a story his friends had told him: A two-headed goat had been born in the Maine district, in a town named for an American Indian, something like Acrigentimus?

As Timothy finished his story, Edwards' body crumpled and his head smashed into the stone floor. As he lay unconscious, bandages swaddled around his bleeding head, Reverend Jonathan Edwards spoke with the Father, who explained what he must do.

• • • •

As soon as Edwards was able to walk through his house without constant attention from his concerned wife and children, he summoned his housemaid, Léana Mac Concradha, to his library.

"Oh, Reverend," Léana said, "it is a great relief to see you back to your routine. We have been so worried."

The sloe-eyed Léana, born in Ballynahinch in Northern Ireland, had worked for and lived with the Edwards family since their arrival in Northampton. The town held not a single soul whom Edwards trusted more than he trusted Léana.

"Léana, God is calling you. Will you heed the call?"

Without hesitation Léana replied, "Yes, Reverend. I am God's servant."

"Then listen well, my valued friend. I have arranged for a house to be built in Cape Agamenticus, a small town on the southern shore of Maine. It will soon be finished and waiting for you. Upon your arrival, become acquainted with the minister, who is my old friend Einar Koskinen, and his acolyte, Bartholomew Kinnawe. I have had disturbing reports of the latter. Without endangering yourself, learn what you can about him, and write to me with details of everything you see and hear. You will become privy to speculation that you cannot substantiate. In your letters, spare no details, no matter how untruthful or exaggerated they seem to be."

"This is rather a coincidence, Reverend," Léana said.

"Léana?"

"The acolyte, Bartholomew Kinnawe. We are well acquainted with someone by that name. He used to live in this very house."

"I do not understand."

"Bartholomew Kinnawe. It is the English version of the Gaelic Parthalán Mac Conshnámha. Bébhinn's son. Forde is another English version of Mac Conshnámha."

"For all the years we've known each other, Léana, I've had no idea that you speak Gaelic." Learning that Léana spoke Gaelic was even more of a surprise than discovering that Parthalán, proudly Irish, had anglicized his name.

"It is the language of my parents and my grandparents, and it flows in my blood, though I do not often speak it."

"What would be the English translation of Bébhinn?"

"The closest would be Vivian, I think."

Edwards exhaled. Bébhinn's letter said that the name Vivian had been forced on her.

"You will not be alone on your journey, Léana. God will be with you, as will our beloved Mariah and Cutler Hauer."

15

After meeting Helen Crowe, Matthew carried his two old suitcases from the Honda into Kinnawe House. He arranged his clothing in the master bedroom in the same places that he'd kept it on West 51st—socks in the top drawer, underwear in the second drawer, T-shirts in the bottom drawer, jeans and button-down shirts in the closet. Then he sat at the piano and played the "Silver Horses" melody line, delighted with the instrument's crystalline clarity and perfect tuning.

He played the song again, singing the lyrics to test his voice. It was a little croaky in the lower range, a bit forced in the upper range as he reached for the notes he'd once hit and held with ease, but Rome was not rebuilt in a day. The former, better Matthew, the pre-breakup, non-exhausted Matthew, whose lively tenor had achieved moderate airplay on NYC Top 40 radio, seemed within reach.

In his peripheral vision, a hazy figure walked down the hallway toward the bedrooms and bathroom. He turned toward the movement.

A door gaped open in the far wall. Neither the door nor the room beyond it had been there during Dubh's house tour.

Entering the room, Matthew stopped dead in his tracks, staring in disbelief at his mother's accommodations at the Bedford Hills Institute.

The room was painted the cerulean blue that Doctor Mavro had recommended as "calming" to disordered minds like Rose of Sharon's. Her rose- and tulip-patterned duvet hugged the brass bed to which she'd been manacled during her final insane years. Her rolltop desk sat in the corner, nestled into an alcove with a view of the ocean. Paintings that Toby Brody had painted hung on the walls, most of them slightly above eye level, as Rose of Sharon would have positioned them.

Among the paintings was the portrait he'd been searching for: the tall, handsome, unsmiling, dark-haired man, clothed in a preacher's robes, clutching a book in his left hand. An ancestor? A relative of the man who hovered over Matthew and his dead twin in the Polaroid he'd found in his mother's jewelry box?

Matthew stepped forward to examine the artist's signature. Someone named "T. Brautigam" had painted the minister's portrait.

Surrounding the minister's portrait were much smaller, square portraits of beautiful young women. All had flawless complexions and long, flowing locks. The portraits were unsigned, but the painter had brush-stroked the models' names in the lower-right corner of each portrait: Mehitabel, Josephine, Bébhinn, Cecelia, Dorcas, Léana, Madselin, Sybilla, Rose of Sharon.

A chill crept up Matthew's spine as he backed away from the painting of his mother as a young woman. The ornamental teakwood table from the Bala Cynwyd house stood in front of the window. On top of the table was the urn containing her ashes, which he'd left in his linen closet on West 51st Street with a note asking the subletters not to disturb it.

His mother and the man who might be his father, or grandfather, or great-grandfather, in the same room. So why didn't it feel like a happy family reunion?

Matthew had been unsure of what to do with his mother's cremated remains. Suddenly he had the answer: He'd sprinkle her ashes in the Atlantic, here in this most beautiful of places, and let the tide wash her out to sea. The waves would carry her to her eternal rest, bringing her the serenity she'd never achieved in life.

Matthew reached for the urn with both hands. When his bandaged left hand touched the urn, the gauze began to unravel.

Matthew felt himself frozen to the floor, paralyzed. The bandage crawled up his arm and looped itself around his neck. As it pulled tighter, Matthew began gasping for air.

As he lost consciousness, his mother whispered in his ear: *You want nothing more than to be rid of me. But I'll always be with you, Matthew.*

.　　.　　.

He awoke on the king-sized bed in the master bedroom.

He pulled his phone from his pocket and looked at the time. He couldn't have been asleep more than five minutes, perhaps as few as two or three. He had no memory of going into the bedroom or falling asleep.

He swung his legs off the bed and lowered his feet to the floor. Walking to the doorway, he poked his head into the corridor and looked to the left.

His mother's room was gone, replaced by a solid wall papered with an abstract pattern that almost, but not quite, resolved itself into images of three-headed beasts chewing on living humans. No door. No room. No paintings. No urn. The bandage that had been on his right hand had disappeared.

In the bathroom mirror, he examined his neck for compression marks left by the gauze that had acted like a boa constrictor.

No abrasions, no bruises, no welts. Nothing.

In other words, another hallucination.

How sharper than a serpent's tooth it is to have a thankless child.

I'll never understand you, Mom, Matthew thought. Why do you want to stay cramped and imprisoned inside that urn when the Atlantic Ocean can set you free? Why would you rather haunt me than find peace? Is punishing me more important than freeing your soul?

But of course the urn sat on a shelf in a closet on West 51st Street in Manhattan, not on an ornamental teakwood desk in a nonexistent room in a grand old house in Agamenticus, Maine.

16

Jonathan Edwards stared at the notes on his desk, bits and pieces of information and gossip he'd heard about Einar Koskinen and the congregation in Agamenticus, Maine. The fact that his daughter lay dying in another room made it impossible to concentrate.

It is too soon, a voice inside his head screamed. *It is not her time.* Jerusha, his second child, was just seventeen years old, a second mother to Esther, Mary, Lucy, Timothy, Susannah, Eunice, Jonathan the Younger, and baby Elizabeth. Jerusha: the most mysterious, the most gifted, of his ten children.

His wife Sarah slept in her chamber upstairs, exhausted by the rigors of caring for her daughter, leaving her husband to receive the dire prognosis.

"You must prepare yourself, Reverend," Doctor O'Hara said.

"I must speak with her," Jonathan Edwards said.

"The fever is contagious. I could not convince Mrs. Edwards not to risk her life, but I must convince *you*. I have three daughters of my own. I understand your pain. But you must not risk your own health."

"You understand *nothing*," Edwards hissed.

"Then enter if you must, and may you bring solace to her final hours."

Edwards pushed open the door to Jerusha's chamber. The girl lay on the bed, her sweat-soaked bedclothes clinging to her wasted body, her head facing away from the door. A rasp like a demon's whisper escaped from her throat as she struggled to breathe.

Edwards took his daughter's hand. "Dearest, I come to express a father's love, but I struggle for words. 'We know that to go to heaven, to fully enjoy God, is infinitely better than the most pleasant accommodation here.' But my own sermons sound empty and meaningless to my ears. Jerusha, can you forgive me? I am weak, more craven and wicked than the weakest member of this, or any, congregation."

As his daughter's pulse thrummed through him, her whooshing heartbeat rose into his ears.

"It has taken me too long to understand, Jerusha. It was God who gave you the gift, and the Devil who made me fear it. You have protected me these many years, and instead of thanking you, I have feared you. I thought you were sent to punish me for my sins."

As Edwards bowed his head, fighting tears, Jerusha squeezed his hand. A rush of memories flashed through Edwards' brain like a series of thunderbolts—

—*the horse about to throw him, Jerusha's eyes boring into the steed's, the Devil leaving the horse as its gentle temperament returned, Parthalán's unknown tutor a witness to all of it—his hand reaching for the tankard of water, Jerusha appearing as if from thin air to knock it from his hand, the acid spilling onto his vestments and dissolving them—the kitchen on fire, his cloak engulfed in flames, Jerusha's faint, feminine scent as the flames were extinguished, leaving the kitchen in ruins but Edwards unharmed—*

"Dearest, if you can, please look at me."

Jerusha managed to turn her head and meet her father's gaze.

"You have always known about Bébhinn and Parthalán," Edwards said. "Since you were a young girl."

Jerusha blinked her milky gray eyes.

"Word comes to me from Cape Agamenticus. It is said that my son—my son!—serves a diabolical master."

Though his daughter's lips did not move, Edwards heard Jerusha's voice.

There are two sorts of hypocrites: those who are deceived with their outward morality and external religion, and the others who are deceived with false discoveries and elevation.

"You are justified in using my words against me, Jerusha. I have struggled with the desires of the flesh, but the innocent must not suffer for my transgressions. I am sending Léana, Mariah, and Cutler Hauer to the seacoast. Our Father has ordered it."

You know not what you have unleashed in the Maine colony.

"I know the men's souls are in mortal danger."

You sent Gregory Brautigam and the others to protect and expand your own interests, and to keep your deception and infidelity from the people who rely on your good example.

"I do not deny it, Jerusha."

Our Father has spoken: You must destroy what you caused to be created.

"I have given my solemn vow, Jerusha. I devote myself to the destruction of that foul stain on God's Earth. You must help me. Protect the innocent and the good after your death, as you have protected me and your mother, and your sisters and brothers, during your life."

Take the bracelet. Give one stone to each of the travelers. They must wear it at all times.

Edwards released Jerusha's hand and removed the bracelet from her slender wrist. One summer day more than a decade earlier, the six-year-old Jerusha disappeared for two hours, reappearing as Reverend and Mrs. Edwards began to mobilize a search party. Her fingers were caked with mud. In her hand, she clutched three stones, each carved with the same runic symbol. Jerusha had refused to eat or drink until her father commissioned a local artisan to drill a hole through each stone and link them together in a bracelet.

Since that day eleven years ago, the bracelet had not left Jerusha's wrist, and it had remained a source of anxiety to Edwards, who'd spent years inveighing against false idols. In the face of Jerusha's obstinacy, Edwards had corresponded with scholars in the Colonies and in Europe, inquiring about the rune's meaning. All but one claimed not to have seen the rune before and thus to have no knowledge of its symbolism or origin. A solitary monk in Bury St. Edmunds, rumored to study the occult, wrote to Edwards in secret, posting his letter from London. In his forty years of religious scholarship, he said, he'd encountered the symbol only twice: carved on a piece of the True Cross hidden underground in Jerusalem, and daubed in wax on a pillar in the Church of the Nativity in Bethlehem.

Parthalán's strength is increasing, Father. It is he who has done this to me, and eleven years hence he will claim you.

As Jerusha's eyes rolled upward, her last weak breath slid through her lips. The faint exhalation rose to the ceiling, dropped to the floor, and gathered strength as it ricocheted off the walls, morphing into a whirlpool of wind whipping around the four walls of the bedchamber, overturning candles and books. Struggling against the swirling air, Edwards threw open the window sash and set free his daughter's soul.

17

Kinnawe House
Agamenticus, Maine

The mattress was comfortable, the sheets soft and cool, the duvet feathery and light, the pillows divine—(almost) enough to make Matthew forget his earlier hallucination of being choked to death by a gauze bandage. Following Helen Crowe's suggestion, Matthew had opened one of the kitchen windows a crack, and that small chink in the house's armor filled the bedroom with the sounds of the Atlantic. The ocean waves were a soothing lullaby, and the moon emitted a silvery, relaxing glow.

Before the sun went down, he'd inspected the eastern side of the house, where his mother's room had appeared and then disappeared. He'd rooted through the shrubberies, searching for the remains of a foundation that would have pointed to a room that had once existed but had been torn down. But the soil was soft, the bushes well established and unwieldy. The house's siding, though weathered and fading, showed no signs of having been repaired or renovated.

The night birds' calls were comforting, but the house's whines and groans weren't. As he tried to summon sleep by envisioning a blank sheet of unlined white paper, the footsteps on the second floor above him and whispers in the cellar below made his heartbeat accelerate. *The sleep of reason produces monsters*, a demonic voice rasped in his ear as the woman from Goya's painting raised her head, revealed Rose of Sharon's face, bared her fangs, and spat bats and owls at him.

The vision startled him out of the twilight of semi-consciousness. He went into the bathroom and flicked on the light switch. As the Edison-style light bulbs in the ceiling fixture flickered on, he retrieved two Ambien tablets from the medicine chest and swallowed them with a handful of water from the tap. Sometimes they helped; more often, they didn't.

A sibilant hiss reached his ears from the bathroom's far corner. A long, glossy, slithery thing shot up the side of the bathtub and disappeared down the drain before Matthew got a good look at it.

His heart pounding in his tonsils, Matthew used his fist to pound the rubber plug into the drain so that whatever had wriggled in would be unable to wriggle out.

•　　•　　•

The Ambien must have worked because he woke an indeterminate time later to a persistent creaking beyond the deck. Underneath the creaking was a persistent *squeak-squeak-squeak*, like the maddening chirping of a dying smoke-detector battery.

Groggy, Matthew climbed out of bed to find the source of the squeak and to *make it stop*. He grabbed his phone and stabbed at the flashlight app, turning the beam up to full brightness.

The sound came from outside—from the scrub pines that grew on the western edge of the property between the beach and the road. From the kitchen, Matthew stepped onto the rear deck in his bare feet, which the ocean mist instantly coated with a salty stickiness. He walked to the edge of the deck and shone the beam into the darkness.

Rose of Sharon was swinging from one of the tree's lowest branches, suspended in a noose of soiled white sheets. Her eyes were closed, but when Matthew trained the light on her face, the corpse's eyes opened. Matthew heard her words in his head:

You did this to me, Matthew.

No, Mom, he wanted to scream. *You did it to yourself.*

18

Since the construction of the meeting house in 1746, Cape Agamenticus had experienced waves of migration, most inward but some outward. Many of the local families stayed after the husbands—many of them poor fishermen—agreed to join Reverend Kinnawe's community. Other families, more protective of their souls than their property, sold their shanties to the men who came from New York, Boston, Princeton, Philadelphia, Providence, Newport, Charles Town, and New Orleans. Those who wished to remain on their land without joining the church found themselves outcasts. By the summer of 1747, the few people who'd vowed to stay on their land until Judgment Day had packed up and moved inland or north along the seacoast.

On an oppressive, humid July day, Parthalán convened a meeting of his town council to discuss several pressing problems. The meeting was held in the lower portion of Parthalán's spacious parlor. Each chair, hewn by the village's expert carpenters, was positioned on the point of what would have been a five-pointed star if such a star had been burnt into the wide oak floorboards.

"The ocean is more and more uncooperative," said muscular Michael Ayers, who handled matters relating to the sea. "Each day, the fishermen must go out farther. Two men have been lost, and the catch becomes smaller each day."

"The crops have begun to wither," added Sebastian Collinge, master of the land. "And the carpenters complain that the wood smells of piss and will not cure."

"These are natural cycles," Parthalán replied. "The bounty of the past two years has spoiled us. We must be patient until the end of the cycle, at which time the fields and waters will be renewed." But would they? Trees and wood that reeked of urine signaled a deep disturbance in the Earth, an angry hand reaching up from the planet's core to twist and poison the roots—or they were the result of noxious chemical rains falling from the heavens, intended to contaminate the landscape and drive the congregation from the land. In either case, one of the forces—the Protector or the Foe—was sending a strong message.

"The animals are victims to this cycle as well," said weak-chinned Charles Meer, the town's husbandry expert. "The cows give sour milk, the horses are spooked by trifles, and the pigs miscarry. We have no chicks because the roosters will not breed with the hens, which crush their eggs when sitting on them. The goats escape from their pens and throw themselves off the cliff."

"The difficulties extend beyond food and livestock," added Gregory Brautigam, Parthalán's town manager. "We also need books, paper, and ink. We cannot make these items ourselves. The women can sew, but they cannot weave cloth."

"Those are minor difficulties, Gregory," Parthalán said. "The four of you travel and trade for what is needed." The wares crafted in Cape Agamenticus had always fetched good prices. Candlesticks, furniture, cutlery, tools, and other items manufactured before the current difficulties should provide enough revenue to keep the people fed until Parthalán consulted his books, identified the source of the problem, and determined the best solution.

"That is yet another hindrance, Parthalán," Gregory replied. "Merchants and tradesmen between here and Boston deny us entrance to their shops. The shopkeepers in York Village will not even speak to us on the street."

"Have you attempted to sell the catch and the harvest at lower prices to the poor of Falmouth?" Parthalán asked. "The poor would rather eat rancid meat and rotting corn than starve."

"Yes, but to no avail," said Gregory. "Nobody will buy from us."

"Have any of you men shown your mark in public?" Parthalán asked. Despite the acknowledged hysteria surrounding the witch trials, many devout Christians continued to interpret odd marks and moles, an affinity for animals, and the tendency to dream as indicators of Satanic influence. Even in Northampton, a progressive city, women avoided braiding their hair and touching pig carcasses for fear of being accused of sorcery. "You—Collinge—you like your drink. Have you rolled up your shirtsleeves in a public house?"

"I have not," Collinge replied. "I know the law and abide by it."

"In Concord, a drunkard called me the Devil's own," Meer said. "He pointed to my beard and said that only Satan's spawn have beards of this color."

"And the women?" Parthalán asked. "Do they share our secrets with outsiders?"

"They do not," said Ayers. "They leave town only to market, and their marks are hidden beneath many layers. And no woman would endanger her children. My Abigail worries herself sick over our boy, Calvin. He is not thriving. He refuses his mother's breast, and when he does suckle, he spits out the milk, as if it is tainted."

Knowing that Calvin Ayers' chances of survival were slim—Mrs. Feeley, the town's nurse-midwife, had told him so—Parthalán considered how to use the boy to his benefit. The relief might be temporary, but it would keep the town loyal to Parthalán.

"We must start stocking provisions for the winter," Brautigam said. "But we have barely enough to sustain us now."

"I will think on all of this," Parthalán said, "and consult with the Protector."

"We ask you to request not only an end to these difficulties, but also additional protection," Ayers said. He explained: The fishermen had witnessed several ominous portents of a brutal winter. Seagulls, formerly harbingers of good luck, had attacked fishermen at sea. Huge floating ice chunks had materialized out of the mist and almost destroyed two boats.

"There is one additional matter, Parthalán," Brautigam said. "The women sometimes see Vivian wandering the cliffs. They fear she comes to take their children, or to take revenge on us."

His mother! An omnipresent millstone around his neck. Parthalán found woven strands of red hair in his bath, underneath his pillow, and in his food. A week earlier he'd been awakened by a choking sensation as he dreamt. Gasping for breath, he'd bolted out of bed, rammed his fingers down his throat, and pulled out the clump of red hair lodged in his windpipe.

"Tell your wives she is nothing more than a harmless wraith," Parthalán ordered. "I give you all strict orders: No-one is to acknowledge her in any way. Anyone caught speaking with her, or looking in her direction, will be punished. The sooner Vivian learns she is unwelcome here, the sooner she will throw herself into the ocean and dissolve into sea foam."

Parthalán rose from his chair to indicate that the meeting was over.

·　　·　　·

After spending hours poring over his books, Parthalán could not deny the facts. When the last original resident left Cape Agamenticus, the force in opposition to Parthalán had begun its effort to destroy the village. The sun hid itself behind a perpetual veil of thick charcoal-colored clouds, as if attempting to deny Cape Agamenticus its benefits. The sources of the troubles came from above, not below.

Parthalán had hoped to convert Einar Koskinen, the same way he'd converted Brautigam and the other men who'd abandoned God as soon as it was convenient to do so. A former holy man might have been a powerful ally in Parthalán's search for a solution. But Koskinen had proven obstinate, and it had been his undoing.

Parthalán called for his maid, Lotte, and asked her to summon Michael Ayers.

Three evenings later, on a moonless midnight, all the townspeople older than sixteen gathered in the meeting house.

Parthalán stood at the altar. "Give me the child," he said to Abigail Ayers.

Weeping, the diminutive Abigail handed a swaddled bundle to Parthalán. It was always thus, Parthalán thought. Women were raised to understand that they might be required to make such a sacrifice at any time, but they never expected their child to be the one taken.

19

The vision of his hanged mother burned into his brain, Matthew hurried into the house, wiped the salt off his feet, returned to the bedroom, and lay on the bed, his heart pumping wildly. Sleep was impossible as his mind raced from trauma to trauma: his mother's death, his break-up with Kellyce, the apparitions in the apartment on West 51st Street and here at Kinnawe House. The hissing sounds emanating from the bathroom and the scratching in the attic, like sharp talons on the floorboards of the second story, didn't help, either.

Giving up on sleep, he examined every square inch of the house for a snake's nest. Using his phone's flashlight app, he shined the beam into the four corners of the bathroom and its linen closet. He checked the walls for holes through which a snake might slither and found none. The space underneath the kitchen sink was dusty but otherwise clean and dry. In the utility room, no viper's nest was anywhere in sight.

The pantry, too, appeared to be snake-free. When Matthew shined the beam behind the shelves, he saw only a dozen + signs stuck to the wall. He touched one of them with his index finger. As the soft, dark wax yielded to the warmth of his finger, the stone around his neck sent a tiny jolt of electricity into his chest. Suddenly, inexplicably, he felt energized.

There was still the attic to be checked. Though Bartholomew Dubh had said the second floor was off limits, Matthew used a ballpoint pen and a paper clip to pick the lock on the attic door. Reaching beyond the doorway, he found a light switch and flipped it on.

The attic was a perfect little studio apartment with its own bathroom. The bed faced the large picture window and the upstairs balcony, ensuring an ocean view upon wakening. The portrait of the handsome minister sat on an easel near the window. Matthew took a few steps backward and snapped several pics with his phone. Perhaps the local parish, or the York County historical society, would have more information about him.

Matthew searched every corner of the attic space for snakes' nests and animal droppings. He found no spoor, no hair, no nests, no feathers, no sign of anything alive in that attic.

He found no library, either. So Dubh had been right; Kinnawe House didn't have a library. But the photo on the realtor's website had shown the minister's portrait hanging in a library, not displayed on an easel in an upstairs bedroom. What was the explanation for *that*?

Matthew shivered. Rose of Sharon would have said a goose was walking over his grave.

20

Gregory Brautigam returned home from a meeting with Parthalán shaken to
the core.

Naomi greeted him at the door. "Has he made his demand?"

Brautigam nodded, unable to speak. A year earlier he'd been grateful for
Parthalán's promise that Emma need not join the church. Now Parthalán's
reason was crystal-clear, and again Gregory was powerless to interfere.

Naomi stroked Gregory's cheek. "It is for the best, dearest. The alliance
will strengthen our positions. She must be made to see reason." Without
another word Naomi grabbed her cape and left the house.

Gregory's first wife, Eliza, had teased him for his inability to couch harsh
reality with soothing words. Incapable of circumlocution, Gregory entered
his daughter's chamber without knocking and presented the fait accompli.
"Emma, you will become Reverend Kinnawe's bride. The ceremony will take
place one month hence."

Emma, seventeen years old, rose from the chair in which she was reading
a book rented from the town's book-lender. "Papa, you cannot be serious."

"I *am* serious, Emma. You will be Parthalán's wife." *And, God help us, the*
mother of his children.

"No, Papa. I am frightened of him."

"He is the leader of our community. And you will have your Aunt Lotte
with you for company, perhaps a more pleasant arrangement than you now

have with your stepmother." He did not add: And you will be allowed to live, rather than suffer the gruesome tortures experienced by those chained to the walls of the crypt.

"I would rather stay here with *her* than marry *him*. I will not do it."

Gregory struck a blow across his daughter's face. Emma crumpled to the floor, too shocked to weep.

Brautigam removed his belt and folded it into a strap.

"Do not make me use this, Emma. Give your consent now, or I will beat you until you do." Gregory averted his eyes from his daughter's face. Once again, he was doing what he must, instead of what was right, as Eliza rained curses down on him from heaven. But Eliza was free from pain, sin, and the cruelties of fate. Eliza was not forced to choose between Emma's death or her marriage to Parthalán.

A shocked and frightened Emma nodded her assent, and Brautigam left her whimpering on the floor. With Naomi out of the house, Gregory entered his own bedchamber, locked the door, and wept silent tears, covering his nose and mouth with his hands to prevent any sound from escaping. Parthalán's hearing was excellent, and the faintest whispers traveled like shrieks along the cliff.

21

Kinnawe House
Agamenticus, Maine

The morning after his arrival, Matthew sat at the dining room table, tapping his shopping list into his phone's Notes app: coffee, wine, milk, cheese, orange juice, corn flakes, cinnamon bread, cream cheese, microwavable dinners, chicken, turkey, bottled water, fresh fruits and vegetables, protein bars and shakes.

On his way to the Civic, he examined the tree from which his mother had swung in his dream the night before. No empty noose swayed in the ocean breeze.

Matthew felt the mixture of relief and self-ridicule that most adults feel after they've looked in the closet and discovered no bogeyman or ax-wielding murderer. Daylight revealed the impossibility of the terrors that the dark had suggested. There was no way that anyone, including his already-dead mother, could have hanged herself from that tree. The tree's lowest branch was more than twenty feet from the ground. To hang herself from that tree, she'd have needed a ladder. Or she'd have needed to climb the tree like a bear and then shimmy along the limb, maintaining her balance as she secured one end of the noose to the branch and the other around her neck before taking the drop.

As for the disappearing library—*Just don't think about it, Matthew. Don't think about the snake, either.*

Inside the Civic, he fastened his safety belt and glanced at the moss-covered sundial near the back door. The shadow indicated 6 o'clock, though Matthew's phone said 8:38 A.M.

Driving south on Route 1 in search of a supermarket (he couldn't get a WiFi signal in the house, which meant no internet search for "local grocery store"), Matthew took in the local color. Roadside chalkboards announced end-of-season discounts at antique shops that had once been houses. A red, barnlike building caught his eye: Julie's Bar & Restaurant. A portable sign on wheels at the edge of the parking lot enticed patrons with food, booze, and upcoming events:

FRI – SAT – SUN
CLAM BAKE – LIVE MUSIC – $2 BEERS

A few miles south he spied a Hannaford supermarket in a mini-mall. He wandered the aisles, piling prepackaged, low-nutrition foods into his cart and marveling at the size of the place. It was at least twenty times bigger than the largest grocery store in Manhattan.

Before choosing a checkout line, Matthew scanned the cashiers, a motley mixture that ran the gamut from teenagers to the Social Security-eligible. Sometimes older people made him feel self-conscious about his wispy beard and thrift-store clothes. However, there were people with whom he shared an obvious or not-so-obvious affinity, and they tended to dress in a certain way, or to display some other indicator of a shared worldview: a tattoo, a piece of junk-store jewelry, a retro belt, a hairstyle. He selected a twenty-something cashier with thick, shiny auburn-brown hair shaved close on the right side of her head.

Loading his groceries onto the belt, Matthew attempted to interpret the six earrings tracing the outer rim of her left ear: an eighth note, a fermata, a bird, a Greek psi symbol, a G-clef, the letter P.

She was PRISCILLA S, according to her nametag. He smiled at her, and she smiled back: an invitation to conversation.

As Priscilla slid mass-produced foodstuffs across the scanner, Matthew asked, "Can I guess the meanings of the earrings?"

"You're assuming they *have* meanings," Priscilla S said. "Maybe I just like them."

"No, body adornment always means something," Matthew replied. "I took a course on it in college."

"Then go for it."

Matthew began with the earring at the top of Priscilla's ear. "First, you love fast, upbeat music with lots of eighth notes. The fermata says you pause and think before you act. The G-clef means you're more of a woodwind or string person. The bird matches the dove tattoo on your wrist, so you're into peace and love, which is cool. The psi symbol—it was on the cover of my psychology textbook, so I'm guessing you were a psych major. As for the P, my spidey-sense tells me it stands for Priscilla."

"Not bad, for a stranger in these parts."

Matthew laughed. "And why do you think I'm not from around here?"

"First of all, you're thin. The guys around here aren't thin. Even the ones who *are*, aren't as thin as you. And nobody wears those sneakers. Up in Portland or down in Portsmouth, but not here. New York?"

Matthew nodded. "Guilty. I'm Matthew."

Priscilla pointed to her nametag. "Priscilla."

"This is going to sound like a pick-up line, but I'm a musician, and I like writing for the female voice. You wouldn't happen to be a singer, would you?"

"As a matter of fact, I would. A 'classic soprano,' according to my choir director."

If he'd consulted his Magic 8-Ball, gathering dust in the closet on West 51st Street, it would have said, "Outlook Good." He plunged ahead. "So, you up for singing some songs with, or by, a skinny guy from New York?"

"Oh, Priscilla, just give him your number," said a stocky, gray-haired woman in line behind Matthew. "The two of you are cute, but I'm late for work."

Priscilla used a Sharpie to scribble her name and number on the back of an errant receipt.

"Text me," Priscilla said, handing Matthew the slip of paper. "And that'll be $44.85."

With two twenties and a five, he also handed Priscilla his "business card," which included his email address and his phone number, and promised to be in touch soon. As he pushed his grocery cart to the Honda, the sun felt warm and welcoming on his neck.

Priscilla Sargent knew something fishy when she saw it.

As Matthew left the Hannaford, pulling his shopping cart behind him, a bald muscleman dropped a brown-wrapped bundle into one of the paper sacks in Matthew's cart.

"If you see something, say something." Or so the saying went. But *should* she say something? Priscilla wrestled with the question on her drive home to Rye, New Hampshire. She wasn't a fan of the hard-to-get strategy that her mother was forever espousing, but she also didn't want Matthew to think she was looking for an excuse to jump his bones.

By the time she pulled into the driveway of her house, she'd made up her mind. Something about that bald musclehead seemed off. She climbed the stairs to her bedroom, retrieved the card Matthew had given her, and tapped a text message on her cell phone.

Hey Matthew. I think some guy purposely dropped a package into your grocery bags. It seemed odd. Maybe I was imagining it. But FYI. Priscilla (from Hannaford)

She hit the SEND button. Two seconds later, the message came back as undeliverable. She tried resending the text three times with no success. When she tried to call the number on Matthew's card, a mechanical voice told her it was not in service.

Juggling his grocery bags, Matthew glanced at the sundial, which showed 6 o'clock, just as it had before he'd left the house in search of groceries. He wondered if a sundial had to be placed on a specific compass point, or oriented in a certain direction, to show the correct time. When the WiFi signal came back, he'd do a Google search and find a better location for it.

After storing his provisions and arranging the fruit—oranges, grapefruits, apples, bananas, lemons—in a large wood bowl on the dining room table, he checked the time on his phone. 11:25.

Like most musicians, Matthew needed inspiration to write. Priscilla had provided that, with her shy smile, her upturned button nose, her quiet edginess, the dove tattoo on her wrist. And there was something about her voice, the way she spoke. The command voiced by the woman in line behind him looped through his mind: *Just give him your number*. It was the hook, the chorus, the title.

Josh had advised him to forget Kellyce. Easier said than done, but that didn't mean he couldn't embrace inspiration from a woman who'd reminded him how much he missed having someone in his life.

There would be time to compose later, though. For now, he had to work within the constraints of government business hours. But he still couldn't get an internet connection on his laptop, and his phone had no bars. Taking his laptop and phone out onto the deck didn't help.

He'd passed a Starbucks several miles south on Route 1. Surely it had a WiFi connection. He slipped his laptop into his backpack and drove to the coffee shop, where his computer linked up with the network almost instantly.

First he typed "Priest Minister Kinnawe Agamenticus Maine" into Google's search box. The search engine returned page after page of Maine tourist sites but no relevant matches. After conducting unproductive searches for "Maine preachers 18th century" and "Agamenticus minister 1700s," he researched birth certificates for an hour. It seemed that every U.S. municipality, county, and state had different types of birth records, with the format varying from decade to decade and even from year to year. But almost all of them included fields for "mother's name" and "father's name."

It would be like finding a needle in a haystack, but ... He pulled up the homepage for the local government of Bala Cynwyd/Lower Merion Township, Pennsylvania. Scanning the phone directory, he found a listing for Doris Graff, township clerk, then tapped the number on his cell phone to dial it.

"Clerk's office, Doris speaking."

"Hi, my name is Matthew Rollins. I grew up in Bala Cynwyd. I'm looking for some information, and I thought town hall might be a good place to start."

"Matthew Rollins? Are you ...?"

The accident had been all over the news, his hospital room filled with flowers and balloons and stuffed animals from strangers praying for him and wishing him a speedy recovery. He didn't like talking about that night, and he'd become an expert at evasion.

"Yes, that was me. Everything's OK. I'm totally fine now," Matthew said.

"How can I help, Matthew?" Doris Graff's voice, pleasant to begin with, had become even softer, warmer.

"I'm trying to find a copy of my birth certificate. My mother was a hoarder, and after she passed away, it was impossible to find anything in the house. I was wondering if the town has a copy of it."

"We would, if you were born here."

"Unfortunately, I'm not sure where I was born." He didn't remember anything before his life in the Bala Cynwyd house. "Is there an easy way to check?"

"Well, I wouldn't say it's *easy*, but I have certain methods for cutting through red tape. Give me a couple of minutes. Hold on. I'll be back."

Could it be that easy? Sitting in a Starbucks on Route 1 in Kittery, Maine, would he learn his father's name? And if he did, what would his next step be—use the Web to locate the man and then call him on the phone? *Hi, I'm your son, Matthew. It seems that you vanished after getting my mother pregnant. Oh, you didn't know you have a son?*

Doris returned to the line. "Matthew? There's no record of you being born in Bala Cynwyd or in Montgomery County. But do you have a driver's license issued by the state of Pennsylvania?"

"Yes."

"Then the DMV should have a copy of your birth certificate. There will be paperwork. Lots and lots of paperwork."

As a birthday gift to Matthew, Rose of Sharon had volunteered to wait in line at the DMV for him, even though she didn't like leaving the house or talking with strangers. You could sit for hours in the dirty, smelly waiting room, she said. Thrilled to avoid the long hours of boredom, Matthew had happily accepted his mother's uncharacteristically generous offer. He hadn't known a birth certificate was required to get a driver's license. Another of Rose of Sharon's secrets revealed: She'd gone to the DMV office not because she wanted to do something nice for him, but because she didn't want him to see his father's name on his birth certificate.

"That's OK," Matthew said. "I'll do whatever I need to."

"They'll give the request a higher priority if it comes from my office. Give me your number, and I'll call you after I shake it loose."

Matthew gave the clerk his number. "Before you go, Doris, can I ask one more question?"

"Shoot."

"I think I had a twin who died at birth. Would there be a record of that anywhere?"

"Well, if the baby was stillborn, or if it died soon after birth, there wouldn't be a birth certificate."

"What about the baby's remains?"

"Until the 90s, the baby likely would have been placed in a casket with an adult. That practice is changing, because some bereaved parents want to buy a cemetery plot and gravestone. You *might* able to trace your twin's remains through the hospital where you were born, but that's probably a long shot. A lot of hospitals don't keep those kinds of records."

He spent the next hour on the websites for genetic testing that he'd bookmarked. The disclaimers, in a tiny font, said that the results were not guaranteed to reveal the information that one hoped to find, and they might even reveal something completely unexpected. Or unwelcome.

22

Cape Agamenticus, Maine
Mid-Fall 1747

Gregory Brautigam and Charles Meer sat behind Brautigam's house, facing the road, enjoying an after-supper pipe stuffed with Virginia tobacco. In recent months, men and women from other congregations in the Colonies had emigrated to Cape Agamenticus, more merchants had followed, and the privations of the previous season were forgotten.

His nose attuned to the odors of stables and barnyards, Meer was the first to catch the scent of nervous horses. Minutes later, two men approached on foot. If they'd been townsmen, their horses wouldn't have refused to turn off the shore road.

The newcomers nodded in greeting. "I am Roger Cavendish," said the short, squat man with a large paunch. "This"—he nodded toward his tall, broad-shouldered, bearded companion—"is Cutler Hauer. We and our friends have come to build a house at the end of this road."

"Does Reverend Kinnawe know of your plans?" Brautigam asked, surprised.

"We are not obliged to ask permission of anyone," Cavendish replied.

Brautigam and Meer exchanged a glance. The new residents, they knew, would soon face a horrible choice: death or damnation. *Turn back while you can*, Brautigam wanted to, but dared not, say.

• • •

When Parthalán engaged the newcomers on their way to or from the cliff's edge, they provided the same bare-bones information, in more or less the same words: They were building a house for a family who wanted to live alongside the ocean.

"Why would anyone wish to move here now, when a difficult winter is expected?" Parthalán asked Roger Cavendish. The Protector had not deigned to answer Parthalán's questions. Perhaps the strangers would provide insight.

"'Tis not our place to ask, or answer, such questions," Cavendish replied curtly.

Uneasy and concerned, Parthalán charged Sebastian Collinge with monitoring the workers' daily activity. The men, Collinge reported, arrived at the building site at sunrise, lunched at noon, and worked until sundown. As darkness fell, all of the workers, except one, returned to a boarding house in York Village. The man who remained onsite at night lit a small fire that burned until morning. After sunup, the workmen arrived from York, extinguished the fire, and began the day's labors.

A week after the builders' arrival, Parthalán summoned Meer and Ayers and gave his orders. Ayers, the strongman, would hold the night watchman while Meer slipped the noose around his neck. When the builders arrived in the morning, they'd find their friend hanging from a spruce and their week's work destroyed.

That night, Meer and Ayers crept toward the fire on the beach. They were unable to locate the man guarding the site. He was whistling—or was it snoring?—but he was invisible in the night. Furious, Meer picked up a thick, dry chunk of driftwood and tried to set it aflame with embers from the pit fire. Each time he attempted to transfer the flame to the lumber that the workmen had carted to the site, the flame extinguished itself.

Meer and Ayers went back to their houses and returned with axes. The interlopers would be unable to construct a house from timber that had been hacked to pieces.

It was as if their axe blades had turned to rubber. The petrified lumber resisted any attempts to chop it.

Bewildered, Meer and Ayers went home, fearful of reporting the evening's failures to Parthalán. The splitting and sawing of timber awakened them a few hours later.

· · ·

Parthalán listened to the report and said not a word. He feared no man, but intercession from above could challenge and damage him in the eyes of the townspeople. Unlike the members of his congregation, the newcomers did not fear him. Indeed, they spoke to him with condescension bordering on scorn. And he was powerless to prevent the construction from moving forward. The spit of land at the end of the cliff was not included in the town's original land grant, for reasons Parthalán had never wondered or thought to ask about. Until now.

The following day, as Parthalán approached the building site on foot, the air became thicker and heavier. Struggling for breath, wheezing to draw the clotted air into his lungs, he looked down at the ground. Late-blooming goldenrod surrounded him. He'd suffered from an intense allergy to the weed since childhood. Once, it had almost killed him.

Parthalán flashed back to his miserable early years. One of Reverend Edwards' daughters had picked wildflowers and crafted small bouquets for everyone in the house: her mother and father, her brothers and sisters, and the servants, including Léana, Mariah, Bébhinn, and Parthalán. His mother had brought their bouquets in a small vase into their tiny attic room. He'd begun gasping and sputtering, and within seconds flesh-burning hives had erupted on every part of his body. Bébhinn immediately tossed the flowers out of the window. The next day, after the excruciating itch subsided and his breathing returned to normal, Bébhinn went outdoors to examine the discarded blossoms. Mixed among the anemones, daisies, asters, and buttercups were sprigs of goldenrod: a weed that would look like a flower to any child, and to many adults.

To test her theory, his mother had waited a few days and then placed a sprig of freshly plucked goldenrod in her apron pocket. She then called for Parthalán and observed his reaction. His breathing became labored as soon as he entered the kitchen, and as he approached her, two hives formed next to his right eye.

"Stop! Come no further!" Bébhinn had cried. "Go outside now, and breathe the air." She then spoke with Reverend Edwards and requested that the weed not be permitted inside the house. An allergy to woundwort, or Aaron's rod as it was called in the old country, ran in her family. As Bébhinn later told her son, one of her uncles, unable to cope with encroaching dementia, had decided to end his own life by removing all his clothes and running naked through a field of goldenrod. Two days later, the family found his body, stripped of its flesh by carrion eaters.

Now Parthalán backed away from the building site and rested against a boulder to catch his breath. He looked at his hands. Welts had sprung up between his fingers, and an intense itch tortured the tender skin between his toes.

He looked up. Roger Cavendish stood in front of him.

"You're not welcome here, 'Reverend,' so you'd best keep your distance," the short, rotund man said. "Now go."

It had been years since Parthalán Kinnawe had taken orders from anyone. Furious but powerless, he hastened up the road. As he looked back over his shoulder, sprigs of green shot up from the earth. As he broke into a run, the sprigs matured, and tiny clusters of goldenrod petals pushed themselves forth from the stems. On the verge of collapse, Parthalán stumbled across the long-filled-in trench that had been dug around his house. As his lungs began taking in air again, he turned to face the road. A sea of goldenrod ended at the trench's edge.

Enemies had arrived, and they knew his vulnerabilities. Parthalán limped into his house and locked himself in his study. Somewhere in the hundreds of books he'd collected from the four corners of the globe, he would find a way to destroy Cavendish and the others. He liked the idea of turning them into pigs and roasting their carcasses over an open flame. But they were men with a God, so their flesh would be inedible.

•　　•　　•

Late 1747

From his cave on the cliff, Parthalán watched Roger Cavendish, Cutler Hauer, and the others put the finishing touches on the house. He'd spent weeks poring over thousands of pages written by occultists from ancient Babylon, Assyria, and Mesopotamia. They'd provided no solution, but he now understood that the new house was a fortress from which its occupants would wage war on his town.

In recent months, the men, women, and children of Cape Agamenticus had become ever more loyal to and fearful of him. After the sacrifice of Calvin Ayers, the ocean had become prolific again. The fishermen caught fish larger and more succulent than any available in the markets of Boston,

Portsmouth, and Falmouth. The animals had begun mating, and their young grew fat on little feed. The town was thriving under Parthalán's leadership.

He had nothing to fear, he told himself. The house on the spit, and its occupants, would be nothing more than a minor inconvenience. Nevertheless, he felt a frisson of unease as he looked at the house, which rose from the earth like something alive.

Perhaps he might use the weather to his advantage. To delay the inevitable. To buy some time.

23

Kinnawe House
Agamenticus, Maine

Last night's Ambien-induced dreams/hallucinations and house search had been the opposite of restful or restorative. Tonight Matthew would try a different approach. He'd bought a bottle of Jack Daniels at the supermarket where he'd met Priscilla. At bedtime, he'd mix the Jack with caffeine-free Coke and drink until he passed out. But bedtime was still twelve hours away, and the refrain *Just give him your number* played on a continuous loop through his head.

He needed a bottle of water at his side if he was going to sing as he composed. He pulled open the refrigerator door and stared at its contents like a hard-to-please and indecisive adolescent. The milk, cheese, Aquafina, and OJ he'd bought at the Hannaford sat on the top shelf, where he'd put them before his trip to Starbucks in search of a wireless signal. On the middle shelf, resting on a dinner plate, was a small package wrapped in brown waxed paper. Blood had seeped through the creases and pooled on the plate.

He remembered buying the pre-packaged chicken breasts and ground turkey in the Styrofoam platters next to the plate. He *didn't* remember asking the butchers for any special cuts.

He found a pair of scissors in a kitchen drawer and snipped the thin string that bound the package. Inside was an acrid hunk of muscle and gristle. Gizzards? A liver? Some other disgusting animal organ? Whatever it was, it looked revolting and smelled nauseating. He'd dump it in the compost heap later.

He grabbed a bottle of water, returned to the parlor, and booted up Ableton Live on his laptop. Time melted away as he worked on "Just Give Him Your Number." The creative juices, so long dormant, coursed through his veins. The song almost wrote itself, and the three verses were damned near perfect. One friend telling another not to play hard to get: a simple idea, relatable, ideal for radio and possibly for Priscilla's voice. Catchy as hell. It felt like a worthy follow-up to "Silver Horses."

Delighted with the hooks and the chorus, he hit the playback button and listened to the song from start to finish. The playback wasn't as clean as he expected it to be, which was odd, because Live sanitized everything, removing the dirt and grime that all good musical instruments, including the human voice, have. He isolated the sounds he hadn't intended to include in the song—a repetitive scratching, as of someone dragging heavy shoes along floorboards, and two high-pitched screeches that sounded like prolonged wailing. The background noises somehow lifted his vocal, giving the song more depth and moving it several steps away from bubblegum pop toward something darker.

He clicked on the JUST GIVE HIM YOUR NUMBER folder in which he'd placed the song files. It contained all the files he'd created plus three that he hadn't. The first, the dragging footsteps, was titled Vivian.alc. The first wailing sound was in a file labeled Lucinda.alc, the second in a file labeled Dante.alc.

The scar nearest Matthew's heart split open. As his heart thumped, the bloodstain on his T-shirt expanded rapidly outward from the center. He didn't know who Vivian was, but Lucinda and Dante were the names that he and Kellyce had agreed on for the children they might someday have.

Light-headed from the loss of so much blood in so little time, he ran to the bathroom for a roll of gauze. He wrapped it around his chest as the earworm of the babies' wailing burrowed into his brain.

The blood flow staunched, Matthew returned to the parlor and hit the replay button to study the track again. Hearing those cries was the closest he'd ever get to holding his child. He wondered if the baby had been a boy or a girl. Dante or Lucinda.

While he'd been tending to his scar in the bathroom, the song had been sanitized. The wailing was gone. The Vivian, Lucinda, and Dante files had vanished. The song sounded annoying, cloying, and corporate without them.

But the sounds had been there. He'd seen the files and heard the audio.

Unless he'd slipped into and out of a fugue and had imagined all of it. He'd been alternating between thinking and not-thinking about his mother and father, thinking and not-thinking about Kellyce, thinking and not-thinking about the house's oddities, trying to reason rationally and clearly after the dreams, psychoanalyzing himself to explain the hallucinations. But thoughts were like weeds in the brain; you sprinkled weed killer on one, and another popped up. Rose of Sharon, his father ... Kellyce, the baby. Variations on a theme, going round and round in his head.

Enough was enough. Tomorrow, after a good night's sleep, he'd purchase one of the genetic testing kits he'd researched on the Web. Maybe the results would reveal something he didn't know, or something he needed to know.

Bedtime, and those Jack-and-Cokes, couldn't come fast enough. In the meantime, a bit of human companionship might help. He exited through the rear door of Kinnawe House and went in search of his helpful and kindly neighbor, Helen Crowe.

24

Northampton, Massachusetts
January – April 1748

Winter ravaged the eastern coast of the Colonies, destroying seaside towns from Maine through Georgia in the first months of 1748. Warm winds from Africa traveled west across the Atlantic, and as the Earth spun, the rains started rotating, whipping up ferocious gales as the whirling storms drew heat and energy from the warm ocean waters. Between December and March, storm surges inundated waterside communities, drowning hundreds of people and thousands of animals. Inland rivers crested, wiping out settlements downstream. Old-growth trees toppled like dominoes.

Following the hurricanes came snowstorms that dumped three feet of snow on New England. The temperature plummeted and froze the landscape into a sea of icebergs. Poor families froze to death in their unheated cabins, and commerce crashed to a halt as the roads became impassable. In Western Massachusetts, the relentless brutality of the season caused many people to question their faith in God.

Although God was angry at His people's lazy faith and Reverend Edwards' congregation was on the verge of revolt, Jonathan Edwards knew that the Lord had not sent the winds, rains, snows, and floods. No. The Foe had sent them, and his purpose was clear: to prevent Edwards' missionaries from reaching their destination. Léana and Mariah were resilient, but they would not survive a violent blizzard descending on a lonely stretch of icy, untraveled road. In such conditions, he could not in good conscience send them to the house on the spit.

Searching for other options, Edwards wrote to Boston sailors, attempting to persuade them to take the travelers by boat to Cape Agamenticus. He had no success. No sailor was willing to risk his boat—his livelihood—in the vicious waters of the Atlantic, not during a season in which one bout of deadly weather followed another.

So Léana, Mariah, and Cutler remained in Northampton after Roger Cavendish and Cutler Hauer returned to report that the house was ready to be inhabited. Cavendish told Edwards about a dove that had made a nest in the tallest spruce on the property. The men had considered the bird a good omen and grown fond of it. They'd named it Bán, Gaelic for *white*. Those not of Irish heritage had anglicized the dove's name to Whitey.

Edwards knew the bird's true name: Jerusha.

• • •

As the endless winter stretched into April, and the winds and waves continued to wreak havoc on the shore towns, the houses and businesses of Cape Agamenticus remained unharmed. Indeed, the town experienced only one snowfall the entire winter of 1747–1748. It produced just enough snow to kill all the goldenrod.

25

Agamenticus Cliff Road
Agamenticus, Maine

As Matthew walked along Agamenticus Cliff Road toward Helen's house, the blur of a hunter's tan camouflage gear flickered in his peripheral vision. The hunter seemed to be following him, but each time Matthew turned to face him, the man disappeared.

The hunter may have been a paranoid hallucination, but the hostile faces staring at him through his neighbors' rear windows weren't. His next-door neighbor, as best Matthew could make out through the house's dirty windowpanes, was frighteningly pockmarked. The man pointed a finger at Matthew and mouthed: GO HOME NOW. As Matthew picked up his pace, a weak-chinned man with receding fiery orange hair glared at him from the rear window of the house next to the pockmarked man's.

Helen was in her garden, harvesting the last cucumbers of the season.

"Hi, Helen," Matthew said. "Am I crazy"—though, increasingly, it was not a question to be asked lightly—"or are the neighbors extremely unfriendly?"

Helen dismissed them with a wave of her hand. "Ignore those old cranks. They were slightly, and I do mean *slightly*, more pleasant before their wives died. Now they're just miserable."

Matthew issued his invitation as a dove cooed from a Norway spruce. "I have some wine and cheese at the house. Care to join me?"

"I'd love to," Helen said, pulling off her gardening gloves. "There's enough daylight left, and I haven't been inside that house in decades. The Fordes have never been particularly friendly with the neighbors." She tossed the gloves into the cucumber patch, and the two began the brief trek to Kinnawe House.

Helen stopped suddenly a couple of feet from the staircase that led up to the deck. "I'm not good with stairs," she explained.

"Let me help you," Matthew said, remembering that he'd had similar difficulty the first time he'd tried to climb the deck stairs. He took Helen's hand and led her to the staircase, which she ascended slowly, one step at a time.

"Oh my," she said as she entered the kitchen. "The smell in here ... the air is so thick ..." Helen put her hand on her chest as she fought for breath. The air she drew into her lungs seemed to choke her, and the blood drained from her face. Her skin turned almost translucent, revealing her cheekbones, her chin, her teeth, and her jawbone.

As Matthew helped her into a chair, Helen grabbed the stone that dangled from the cord around his neck. Within seconds her breathing returned to normal.

"Should I call 911 or get you to a hospital?" Matthew asked, alarmed.

Helen shook her head. "Damned asthma. I shouldn't have left the house without my inhaler."

"I'll go and get it for you."

"No, I'm all right now. The attacks usually don't last long. I never know what's going to set one off."

As Helen followed him into the parlor, Matthew glanced at the bowl of fruit on the table. Like most fruit purchased at supermarkets, it had been hard and unripe. He'd assumed it would need to sit for a few days before it was ready to eat. And yet—the juicy citrus scent of the oranges mixed with the heady aroma of ripe bananas, crisp Granny Smith apples, tangy-tart blueberries, and sour-sweet lemons to tickle Matthew's nostrils.

As Helen made herself comfortable on the overstuffed couch, Matthew disappeared into the kitchen, returning with a tray bearing two glasses of wine, a block of cheese, and two peeled oranges.

"I took this job without knowing much about the house," he said. "I think you said you've lived in your house a long time? Do you know much about the people who've lived on the cliff over the years? I think this house was built for a minister in the 1740s, right? That's what the realtor said."

Helen's fingers traced the rim of her wine glass as her eyes took in the room. "Yes, that's true. There used to be a path that connects the house to the church, but it's long since overgrown. The church has been abandoned since the eighteenth century. It's been condemned, but it hasn't been razed. Things move slowly around here, if they move at all."

"Maybe I'll take a field trip to see it," Matthew said. "I'll cut through the woods."

Helen set her glass down. "Please don't, Matthew. A few years ago some boys broke in. A beam came crashing down and killed two of them. If you want to see the sights, go down to York Village or up to Ogunquit, not to that church."

"Thanks for the warning," Matthew said. "I never would have thought of that." After a moment, he added, "Can I confess something? Somehow I have it in my head that I'm related to the Fordes or the Kinnawes."

"Forde is just the Americanized version of Kinnawe," Helen said. "But why do you think you're related to them? Didn't you say you're from Pennsylvania? The Kinnawes came over from Ireland, and they're New Englanders through and through. I doubt that anyone in the family has ever been south of Boston."

"It's a long story, but my mother was from Maine, though she almost never talked about it. And there's a photo of me as a baby with a man standing over me. The man kind of resembles the minister who built Kinnawe House."

"The minister's name was Parthalán Kinnawe. But how would you know what he looked like? He died 250 years ago."

"There's a portrait of him in the house. At least I assume it's him. He's wearing a minister's garb and holding a book that looks like a Bible."

"I remember hearing that he had his portrait painted, but I've never seen it."

"It's in the attic above us." Matthew pointed to the ceiling. "It's on an easel in front of the window."

"The Fordes had a relative who lived up there for a while," Helen said. "A young man, a recluse. I met him once, a long time ago."

A madman in the attic, à la *Jane Eyre*? The idea was spooky, yet somehow in sync with his hallucinations.

"Did a woman named Vivian ever live here?" Matthew asked. Vivian.alc was the title of the disappearing track that had added the scratching effect to "Just Give Him Your Number." He already knew who Dante and Lucinda were, or would have been.

The question seemed to startle Helen. "Yes. Her Gaelic name was Bébhinn. Vivian is the English translation. She disappeared one night and was never found. Everyone assumed that the ocean caught her off guard and took her."

Matthew had seen that uncommon name—Bébhinn—somewhere. Where? He remembered: in the series of portraits of beautiful young women surrounding the portrait of Reverend Kinnawe, hanging on the wall of the imaginary room at the eastern end of the house that was a carbon copy of his mother's room at the Bedford Hills Institute.

"I'm sorry," Matthew said. "Were you and Vivian friends?"

"We were fond of each other, but it was a long time ago. Do you like living here all by yourself?" Matthew noted the abrupt change of subject. "You seem too young to be isolating yourself on a cliff in Maine with the winter coming."

Matthew considered the question. "Actually, I do like it, even though the house definitely has its quirks. But I'm a musician, and I need to clear my head and write new songs. I'll have plenty of time to do that here. Plus, like I said, I'm trying to learn more about my family history. This seems like a good place to do that."

"Living alone gives you a lot of time to think," Helen said. "Maybe *too* much time. I lost my husband, Cutler, many years ago, and my only child when she was very young. I think about them all the time. If I didn't live alone, I'd have less time to brood."

"I'm sorry, Helen. What was your daughter's name?"

"Fiona." Tears welled up in Helen's eyes. "I had almost no time with her. She had the most beautiful eyes, the color of cornflowers, just like Cutler's."

So he and Helen had something in common, in addition to a lonely life on a cliff alongside the Atlantic: a lost family.

By mutual tacit consent, they moved the conversation away from painful topics, drinking wine and chatting like old friends until the sun began to dip below the horizon, when Helen declared that she must be on her way.

"Before you go," Matthew said, "I bought something by mistake at the supermarket. I don't even know what it is. The only meat I eat is turkey and chicken, and it doesn't look or smell like either one. I was going to throw it out, but I hate to waste it. Maybe you'd like to take it, if it's something you'd eat?"

Matthew retrieved the butcher's package from the refrigerator, and Helen unwrapped it.

"Yes, I'll take it, Matthew. What a treat."

"What the heck is it? I've never seen anything like it."

"I'll spare you the details. Let's just say it's not to everyone's taste."

Matthew smiled. "Thank you for that. I'll walk you home."

"Thank you, but there's no need. It's getting dark, and the hunters have been more active than usual." Helen nodded at the kitchen window. "I'm glad to see that you're leaving that window open. This house needs a lot of fresh air. And don't even think of going out into the ocean in that little boat tied to the dock. I can't imagine why the Fordes would have left it there. The Atlantic would rip it apart."

•   •   •

Helen carried home the conjoined pigs' heart in its brown wrapper. On her beach she made a bonfire from sticks and twigs, tossed the heart onto the flames, and watched it char into dust. Whatever it had been laced with wouldn't have killed Matthew, but it might have made Matthew kill himself.

Unlike the others, he'd begun to investigate his connection to the house. That meant only one thing: Parthalán wanted it that way. He planned to use Matthew's heritage to manipulate him.

And with Matthew dead, the line would cease to exist, and the centuries-long battle would end as Parthalán celebrated by rolling another wine cask into his cellar.

Part III
Goldenrod

26

Cape Agamenticus, Maine
Early Spring 1748

After her marriage to Parthalán, Emma Brautigam had thought she might find an ally in her Aunt Lotte, who'd been Parthalán's housekeeper since Bébhinn's disappearance. But Aunt Lotte made her loyalties clear as soon as Emma crossed the threshold. Emma would live according to the house rules, Lotte said. Any disobedience or disloyalty would be observed, reported, and punished.

The single slap that Gregory Brautigam had delivered to Emma's face had forever estranged a father and daughter who had once adored each other. When Emma was permitted to go to market, she sometimes encountered her father attending to Parthalán's business. She returned his tentative greetings with stony silence.

Parthalán continued to hold meetings with his council in his library, in the parlor, and in the attic. Emma couldn't have cared less about their schemes or the snippets she overheard: "Request denied." "Dispose of his remains in the usual manner." Her own plan was set. Soon she'd sneak out of the house and throw herself from the cliff at high tide. And the nightly, violent ravishing would end.

Before she took her own life, however, she would have her revenge.

She'd known she was pregnant the day she experienced her first bout of morning sickness. Neither Lotte nor Parthalán had been in the house when she'd jumped out of bed and vomited up the chunks of lean beef and tender asparagus she'd eaten the night before. She'd scrubbed the floor with an old rag, which she weighted with stones and tossed into the ocean. But the acrid odor had lingered. Her husband's sense of smell was legendary, except during allergy season, so she sneaked to the far west side of the cliff, where she pinched a sprig of goldenrod from a small patch growing near the house on the spit.

Back at Kinnawe House, she placed the goldenrod in a tiny jar and hid it under a floorboard in the pantry. Parthalán liked to pretend to omnipotence and invincibility in front of an audience, but he was unable to hide his vulnerabilities from a wife who'd devoted herself to discovering them. Emma had experimented with knocking Parthalán off his stride, sometimes successfully and sometimes not, and she'd learned that goldenrod was failsafe, as long as it wasn't overused. The single sprig under the pantry floor, she knew, would affect Parthalán's nose enough to prevent him from catching a whiff of her pregnancy.

Emma's mother, Eliza, had died when Emma was seven years old. Emma remembered her as a sweet, doting woman who'd loved plaiting her daughter's hair and telling stories of her childhood in London. She remembered her mother's advice: "Better tolerant and forgiving than hard-hearted and unyielding." With another man's child, a man she loved or for whom she felt at least moderate affection, Emma would have been an indulgent parent, as Eliza and Gregory were with Emma and her brother, Tobias. That child would have been equal parts Emma and her husband.

She touched her belly. The child inside was none of her; it was Parthalán's seed, pressing against the walls of her womb, sucking the marrow from her bones and the vitality from her blood. She estimated that she'd begun her third month. After the child's birth, Parthalán would have no further use for her. She would be neglected and allowed to die, or perhaps Parthalán would direct Mrs. Feeley, the nurse-midwife, to administer a draught that would kill her. It was the child who mattered, not Emma, and there was no shortage of women in Cape Agamenticus to serve as the baby's wet-nurse.

But Parthalán had underestimated his frail, tiny wife. If she was to be hastened to the grave, so was his child.

She would be unable to hide her pregnancy much longer. Already her clothes were tight and confining. The time had come. Though she was alone in the house, she locked her chamber door. She grabbed her knitting needles from her knitting basket, removed all her clothes, and lay on the featherbed. She wanted it to absorb as much of the blood as possible. Parthalán had commissioned the bed at great expense.

Gathering her resolve and steeling herself against the pain, she jammed one of the knitting needles into her womb. She jabbed until not one but two filthy creatures were expelled from her body. She'd had no idea she was carrying twins.

She faded into oblivion, praying she would awaken in her mother's arms.

•　　•　　•

Somehow Emma recovered. Mrs. Feeley, who served more as a prison warden than a source of comfort, stayed with her all day and all night. Parthalán had hissed "Not a word of this" to Mrs. Feeley, so nobody in Cape Agamenticus, except Parthalán, Mrs. Feeley, Lotte, and Emma herself, knew that the reverend's wife had aborted.

On the first day of spring, Emma rose from her bed and walked into the parlor, where she took in the ocean view. At the end of the road, a tall bearded man climbed down from a horse. He helped two women out of the carriage, and the three newcomers entered the house on the spit, which had sat empty all winter. After months of despair, Emma felt a tiny shimmer of hope. These must be the people whom Parthalán feared, the travelers he'd worked to prevent from reaching their destination.

That evening, Lotte told her that a married couple, Léana and Cutler Hauer, along with their maid Mariah, had taken up residence in the house at the end of the road.

"They will soon realize their mistake," said Lotte, in a tone that almost froze the blood in Emma's veins.

27

Route 1, Maine

Julie's Bar & Restaurant on Route 1 had a "been in the family a long time, the menu hasn't changed much in thirty years" aura. The blackboard in the bar announced the catch of the day—baked sole—as well the daily specials: tuna melt, shepherd's pie. The bar itself, at which Matthew sat sipping a Sprite and awaiting the proprietor, was well worn but polished to a high gloss. So were the tables, where locals sat chatting over lunch.

A tall, lumbering guy approached Matthew.

"I'm Walt. Dave said you wanted to talk to me?"

"Hi, I'm Matthew Rollins. I noticed you have live music. Would you be interested in an opening act? I can play and sing almost anything, and if there's something your patrons like but I don't know, I'll learn it. I'd do it for free, of course." He was tempted to mention the moderate success of "Silver Horses," but that strategy could have backfired if Walt had never heard of it.

"The thing is," Walt said, "we have music only on the weekends after 9, for the late-night bar crowd. Plus I like to support local bands." Walt wasn't rude, but the hint was clear: *You're definitely not local.*

"I understand. In a lot of the places I've played, I've noticed that, um, older people like to come out early. I could play something acoustic and soft for them, here in the bar. You know, background music. Instrumentals and easy listening."

"But what's in for you, man?" Walt asked. "You looking to pick up middle-aged ladies while their husbands are in the can?"

Matthew laughed. "I'm no home wrecker. I just want to get out and play music, and it's not much fun unless someone's there to enjoy it."

Near Matthew and Walt, three women sat at a table, their hands buried in baskets of fried clams. "Give him a chance, Walt," one of them ordered. "He talks nice. He probably sings nice, too."

"All right, all right," Walt said, raising his hands as if the woman were pointing a pistol at him. "Play something for us, Matthew. If these gals give you the thumbs up, you can play on Friday night."

"Any requests?" Matthew asked.

"Clapton. 'Bad Love,'" Walt said. "You know it?"

"Not only do I know it, I've lived it."

The women erupted in laughter. "Who hasn't?" one of them said.

Matthew slung his guitar around his neck and faced the women. As he sang the first verse and the chorus, he noticed a Joe Cocker-type huskiness in his voice. For that he could thank complete exhaustion. Despite drinking almost the full bottle of Jack Daniels the night before, he'd slept only about an hour, maybe less.

As he played the last notes, the room burst into applause.

"That was great," Walt said, only slightly grudgingly. "All right. Get here by 4:30 on Friday to set up, and play from 5 to 7. No Clapton, though. The Carpenters and Air Supply. That shit."

"Thanks, Walt. And thank *you*, ladies." He bowed to the table of clam-eating women.

As Matthew packed his guitar into its case, Walt said, "You look like you could use something to eat. Sit down and I'll have Carol bring you a burger."

Matthew took a seat at the bar. He was sweating profusely, his armpits and groin unpleasantly moist. Audition jitters. As he waited for his burger—Matthew had the sense that Julie's unofficial motto was "Vegetarians NOT Welcome"—he rolled up the sleeves of his long-sleeved T-shirt and flipped through the table tent: daily specials on one page, desserts on another, specialty mixed drinks on a third.

"Where you from?" came a voice from the other side of the bar. The bartender. Earlier, Matthew had introduced himself; the bartender hadn't. But Walt had said, "Dave said you wanted to see me?" Hence, the bartender = Dave.

"Originally from Pennsylvania, but I live in New York now."

"City?" Dave asked.

"Yeah."

"What brings you up here?"

"Taking care of a house and writing some music. That's pretty much it, except for the gig I just landed."

"A bunch of my friends are having a BBQ on Wednesday night. You should come."

Matthew couldn't remember the last time someone his own age had extended the hand of friendship. He'd exchanged phone numbers with Priscilla, the cashier at the grocery store, but that was more of an attraction thing. And Helen was a nice lady, a good neighbor, but he couldn't rap on her window at 10 P.M. and say, "Hey Hel, let's go grab a few beers."

"That would be awesome," Matthew said.

Dave grabbed a pen and wrote an address on a napkin. "Show up around midnight. We all work late."

"What can I bring? Beer? Liquor? Food?"

"There's always plenty of everything. Just bring yourself. I think you're gonna be a popular guy. What with being from New York and all." Was it Matthew's imagination, or did Dave glance at the jagged-star birthmark on Matthew's forearm as he made his prediction?

"Dress like it's summer, not fall," Dave advised. "You know: shorts, T-shirt. We always have bonfires, and it gets really hot."

Matthew was beginning to think that reports of New Englanders' unfriendliness were much exaggerated.

• • •

At a convenience store on Route 1, where he stopped to buy a bottle of decaffeinated iced tea, Matthew picked up a glossy, overcrowded, fold-up pamphlet/map that listed every possible place that tourists might want to visit. With a pen he circled two bars/restaurants: a tavern in Ogunquit and a sports bar in York Village, the two towns that Helen had mentioned as good venues for exploration. It was a gorgeous day, so he drove to the place in Ogunquit to make the same pitch he'd made to Walt, but it was Monday and the tavern was closed.

Still buzzed from his successful audition at Julie's, he took the shore road to the York Bar and Grill, a hole-in-the-wall pub dominated by gigantic big-screen TVs. It was the kind of place where patrons' screams for the Red Sox or the Patriots would drown out any song he played. He didn't bother to make his pitch—the hostess had given him a withering look that seemed to ask, "Do you always carry your guitar into sports bars?"—but to be polite he placed a take-out order for a turkey dinner with mashed potatoes.

The sun was bright but not glaring, the temperature cool, without the autumn New York humidity that sapped his, and everyone else's, strength. After locking his guitar in the Honda's trunk (NYC habits died hard), he strolled along York Street, the main drag through York's historic district. He read the memorial placard outside the Old York Gaol and admired the pristine First Parish Congregational Church, built in the 1740s—around the same time as Kinnawe House. Appreciating York's devotion to and celebration of its history, Matthew strolled through a small cemetery with weathered gravestones dating to the late 1600s. Meanwhile, he thought, a few hundred miles south, Manhattan was busy exterminating its past as it morphed into a playground for the children of the international elite.

While appreciating the ocean-themed paintings in the window of an art gallery that had already closed for the day at 4 P.M., he remembered that Bartholomew Dubh's office was located in the York historic district. While he was here, he should stop in to say hello and give Dubh a progress report ("Everything great so far," he'd say, even if everything wasn't, strictly speaking, great, what with the snake scare, and the scratching in the attic, and the odd dreams and hallucinations). He pulled Dubh's card from his wallet: York Village Realtors, 166 York Road, York, Maine 03909. Matthew glanced at the number over the art gallery's front door: 244. The real-estate office would be no more than a few blocks away.

172 York Road was a private residence. So was the house next to it at 164 York Road. Matthew looked around in puzzlement. There was no building marked number 166, but no real-estate agent worth his salt would hand out business cards with an incorrect address.

He must have looked clueless. A stout middle-aged woman walking her two Labrador retrievers asked him if he was lost.

"I'm looking for York Village Realtors," Matthew said.

"You're several years too late, I'm afraid," the woman replied. "They went out of business during the Great Recession."

• • •

The Labrador retriever lady had to be wrong. Matthew had visited the York Village Realtors website many times. It had to be a going concern. Sitting in his car, he retrieved his phone, searched for Bartholomew Dubh in his contacts, and tried connecting.

The call went straight to Dubh's voice mail. Matthew hung up without leaving a message.

Surfing the Web on his cell phone was maddening, but he opened the browser and searched for York Village Realtors. Google returned about ten pages of hits for realtors and real-estate agencies in York County, Maine, but he found no listing for York Village Realtors.

There had to be a reasonable explanation. Rose of Sharon was a hallucination, and so was the disappearing room at Kinnawe House, but Bartholomew Dubh was not. Matthew had met the man, shaken his cold hand. Perhaps York Village Realtors had gone virtual, office-free, to survive during and after the recession. But that meant that the company should have had *more* of a Web presence, not less.

Odd. Like so many other things in Maine.

He made it back to the house in good time. The odor hit him as he walked in the door—the putrid smell of something once sweet turned sour and sickly. In the bowl on the kitchen table, the fruit he'd bought yesterday sat rotting as flies buzzed around it.

As he retrieved an aspirin from his dopp kit, he wondered briefly why he felt upbeat and positive when he was away from the house, but depressed, confused, and lonely while inside.

28

Cape Agamenticus, Maine
Early Spring 1748

On the long, arduous journey from Northampton to Cape Agamenticus—impassable trails, torrential rains, roads that looped them back to their point of embarkation—something approaching a miracle occurred. The same forces conspiring to prevent Léana Mac Concradha from reaching her new home also allowed her to develop a deep affection for Cutler Hauer, the man whom Reverend Edwards had appointed her protector.

Both Léana and Cutler had reached middle age without marrying, Léana because she was too devoted to serving the Edwards family, Cutler because his natural reserve lent him an intimidating aspect that disguised his generous heart and gentle humor. In Northampton, the two had known each other well; Cutler was one of Edwards' staunchest supporters and a frequent visitor to the Edwards house. Nonetheless, Cutler and Léana's relationship had not progressed beyond friendly greetings, genuine smiles, and mutual respect. On the journey to Maine, the two spent many hours talking and joking, despite the gravity of their undertaking.

Mariah, who would serve as their housekeeper, often joined in the conversations and the laughter. Though she was fifteen years younger than Léana, the two had been close friends since Edwards brought her to Northampton.

"Are we right to be laughing in these circumstances, Mr. Hauer?" Léana asked after the party had howled over one of Cutler's terrible puns.

"I think He would not object," Cutler replied. "As Proverbs tells us, 'A joyful spirit is good medicine. But a broken spirit dries up the bones.'"

Four weeks into their journey, Léana gasped in shocked delight as Cutler went down on bended knee to request her hand in marriage. Léana, who'd expected to die unmarried, dissolved into joyful tears as she nodded *Yes, yes, yes*. The travelers took a brief detour to meet a minister of Cutler's acquaintance. The preacher performed a brief, simple ceremony with his wife and Mariah in attendance. Thus Léana started her journey as Léana Mac Concradha and completed it as Léana Hauer.

•   •   •

Léana felt a change in the atmosphere as the carriage passed the painted wooden sign staked into the ground:

CAPE AGAMENTICUS, MAINE
FOUNDED 1746
Pop. 450

The air, cold and bracing during their entire journey, became engorged with metallic humidity, and the horses protested with a startled whinny as their hooves touched the land incorporated in the town's southernmost reaches. Cutler prodded the horses forward with his usual firm, reassuring hand.

Most travelers would have looked at the bright façades of the houses and shops and seen evidence of a special favor God had bestowed on the seaside village. Up and down the eastern seaboard, the grueling winter had wrecked homes, sheared off roofing shingles, and smashed windowpanes. In contrast, Cape Agamenticus seemed to have enjoyed a mild and long-lasting summer. The pines were sturdy, strong, and upright, with lush, verdant needles; the deciduous trees were budding out; and the earliest flowers of the season—crocus, snowdrops—were in full bloom. And the size of those blooms! Never before had Léana seen such large, dark crocus, nor such a profusion of snowdrops, which, unlike those in Northampton, were a light charcoal gray rather than stark, bright white.

The shop owners' wives and customers stuck their heads out of the shop doors to steal glances at the strangers, their horses, and their carriage. The locals, Léana noticed, did not have the faces of those who'd suffered through a brutal winter. Instead, they looked healthy and vigorous. Salt air purified the lungs, Léana knew, but it also lined the face and grayed the hair. But not in Cape Agamenticus. All the women—from the young wives to the older women holding their grandchildren's hands—had perfect complexions.

At this very minute, Léana thought, someone might be galloping on horseback to Bébhinn and Parthalán's house to alert them to her arrival. She grabbed and held the stone that dangled from a cord around her neck, and the stone's warmth renewed her determination. Then she took Mariah's hand. In return Mariah laid her other hand over Léana's, where it stayed as Cutler coaxed the horses onto Agamenticus Cliff Road, which terminated at their new home.

As the preacher's house came into view, a chill cut through Léana. Soldier, a Quarter horse known for his mild temperament, stopped dead, while Bertha, a high-spirited mare, started to rear back. Cutler dismounted and stroked the horses' necks, talking to them and offering them lumps of sugar.

Despite Cutler's wheedling, the horses refused to move forward. Cutler took two sets of blinders from his pocket and attached them to each horse's head, blocking their peripheral vision and focusing them on the road ahead instead of the minister's house to the right. After a bit more cajoling, Soldier took a reluctant step forward, and Bertha followed suit.

Léana examined the ground as the horses clopped past the Brautigam, Collinge, Meer, and Ayers houses. The winter might have been mild in Cape Agamenticus, but the temperature must have dropped low enough, at some point, to kill the goldenrod that, according to Cutler, had bloomed in such profusion while the house was built. But goldenrod was indefatigable; it would be back. If it didn't spring up from the ground on its own, Léana had a box of seeds at the ready.

Cutler helped Léana and Mariah out of the carriage, and the three stood in front of the white-painted Cape Cod-style house at the edge the Atlantic. The view took Léana's breath away. It was difficult to believe that a place of such beauty harbored such evil.

29

Kinnawe House
Agamenticus, Maine

Kinnawe House seemed to be disarranging itself, Matthew thought, as he wandered the house in his sweats after another night of almost no sleep. In the parlor, the shelf of porcelain figurines, once arranged in descending order by height, now looked like the forgotten corner of a consignment shop. The bookshelves, pristine and well ordered a couple of days earlier, were messy, cluttered. Sleepwalking was the likely explanation. While semi-unconscious in the night, he must have imposed chaos on the order.

Not only had the fruit on the dining room table rotted, the dairy products had spoiled, too, which he realized after pouring congealed lumps of 2% milk over a bowl of corn flakes. He checked the refrigerator, thinking it might require a repairman, but it seemed cool enough, and the ice in the freezer hadn't melted. The corn flakes, which he tried to eat dry, tasted like pencil shavings, as if they'd been sitting for decades in a forgotten storage room. The Pepperidge Farm cinnamon bread was rock-hard, the cream cheese an oily and unappetizing yellow.

And the dust. When he arrived, the house was immaculate, as if a cleaning crew had spent weeks polishing every surface. Now a fine layer of salty dust covered everything—every piece of furniture, every tchotchke, every exposed floorboard. It was as if time sped up on Agamenticus Cliff Road. The dust that built up in one day in Kinnawe House would have required months to accumulate anywhere else. Helen had warned him about it on the day he'd met her.

As Matthew ran his index finger through the dust that had settled on top of the piano, he felt a small tear in the thick, jagged scar that stretched across the top of his right foot. He'd developed a sixth sense for which torn-open scars would bleed profusely and which would seal up quickly. Fortunately, this felt like the latter. At the end of the day he'd use warm water to loosen the blood-encrusted sock from his foot.

From his pocket came the ding of a text message. Finally, the house's WiFi had kicked in. He retrieved the phone, hoping the text was from Priscilla. It wasn't.

Josh

Hope R&R is getting you back on track.

It was Josh's way of saying *Me and Kellyce, it's no big deal. Really.*

Matthew realized with a start that he'd left Manhattan only three days earlier—it felt so much longer. Delighted that Josh had reached out, he hit the REPLY button and tapped a response.

Me

Maine is great. Come up for a visit whenever you want.

He hit the SEND icon, hoping for a quick response that didn't arrive. Having company, if only for a day or two, might be therapeutic. Robinson Crusoe had spent too much time alone on a deserted island (except for the cannibals), and he'd gone insane. There was a lesson to be learned, there.

He needed to practice the 70s and 80s soft-rock ballads that Walt, the owner/proprietor of Julie's Bar & Restaurant, wanted for his early birds, but first he needed to get a few caretaking chores done. He began by dusting the house, remembering his mother telling him that dust is the skin cells of dead bodies carried on the wind from all around the world. She may have been right, but it was a hell of a thing to say to a six-year-old. He poured the sour milk down the drain and ran the hot water to dissolve the pungent chunks. Then he dumped the rotting fruit into the compost heap in the far corner of the yard.

Many of the trees on the Fordes' property were conifers, but a few, including the one from which his mother had dangled in his dream, were deciduous and had begun dropping their leaves. Matthew returned to the house, donned his sunglasses, and retrieved a sturdy metal rake from the storage room.

He hummed as he worked, working out the lyrics for a song that was much too similar to "Dust in the Wind" but would evolve with time. By the time he'd figured out how to rhyme *air filled with silt* in a non-embarrassing way, the pile of leaves was two feet high. The immediate problem was the distance between the pile and the compost heap, which seemed miles away.

His search for a wheelbarrow took him to the stable-turned-garage-turned-hoarder's storage unit. Through the window he saw the old furniture and junk at which he'd peeked on the day of his arrival, but no wheelbarrow.

In the far corner of the garage, beyond an impenetrable mass of *stuff*, stood a small end table, painted midnight blue. It resembled the table that once sat next to his mother's bed at the Bedford Hills Institute. Matthew shifted his gaze to a box piled high with glassware. From his vantage point at the window, it looked like the Depression glass his mother had collected. And those gilt picture frames next to the box ... the junk blocked them, but Matthew thought he discerned bits of Toby Brody's paintings that he'd seen in the phantom room on the day of his arrival.

Cradled in the arms of a moss-covered department store mannequin was the urn containing his mother's ashes. The last time he'd seen that urn, a bandage had tried to strangle him. He turned away abruptly.

The lack of sleep was starting to break his brain. He could dismiss the disturbing visions of the past few nights as the pangs of conscience bouncing around inside his head, but now he was hallucinating while he was awake. Because there was no way a mannequin in the crap-filled garage of an isolated house in Agamenticus, Maine, could be cradling the urn containing his mother's ashes.

He forced himself to look at the mannequin again. Its arms were empty. The Depression glass looked to be nothing more than the cheap glassware sold at yard sales. The paintings all faced the wall, revealing the backs of their canvases and nothing else. So, yes—he'd just experienced a brief but vivid waking hallucination.

He took a moment to gather himself. At least he was able to distinguish between reality and delusion. That was a good thing. Maybe the purifying air of southern Maine needed more time to work its magic. He'd give it another week. If the hallucinations persisted, then he'd find a shrink or a doctor to pump him with tranquilizers, because the lack of sleep had to be causing the hallucinations, and the Ambien and the Jack Daniels certainly weren't doing their job.

Matthew turned the doorknob on the garage door. It was locked. Bartholomew Dubh hadn't given him a key, or told him where to find one.

The basement, he thought, was another likely storage space for a wheelbarrow. Shaking off the sense that his mother was standing near him, just outside his peripheral vision, Matthew followed the foundation of the house to the cellar, wondering if he could figure out how to get into it. The door was secured with a hardware-store combination lock with three tumblers numbered 0 through 9.

What number would he use for the combination if he owned Kinnawe House? His birthday, probably: 8-0-8. But he didn't know the Fordes' birthdays.

Maybe the house number? He turned the tumblers to 0 – 9 – 9, and the lock sprang open.

Matthew flipped up the light switch near the door, illuminating a light bulb dangling overhead. The ceiling was low, so Matthew ducked as he entered, brushing thick, sharp cobwebs from his face. *Sharp cobwebs?* Yes, sharp enough to tear open three of the scars on Matthew's right hand, including the one between his index and middle finger.

He surveyed the cellar, which stank of stale seawater, sweaty armpits, and penicillin. Along the right wall, about fifteen feet from the entrance, was an old wheelbarrow on a rusty frame. The path to the wheelbarrow was clear, but oak barrels lined both sides of the path. Matthew stopped to examine one of the casks. Burnt into one of the staves were the letters AAYERS. A local vineyard? Maybe tons of the region's famous blueberries were fermenting in the casks, to be bottled as blueberry wine and given to friends during the holiday season, or to be sold in upscale bread-and-wine shops.

Guiding the wheelbarrow through the basement, Matthew noticed that one of the casks had sprung a leak. A treacly fluid dribbled down one side of the barrel. Whiskey? Moonshine? Matthew dipped the tip of his index finger into the drop of brownish liquid. As he lifted his finger to his nose to sniff at the drop, the treacle dripped down his index finger and into the scar that the cobweb had ripped open. Matthew howled in pain as the brown glop entered his bloodstream. He hadn't felt such ripping, searing pain since the doctors began weaning him off the morphine drip.

As the scent reached his nose, Matthew began retching. He ran out of the cellar, the cobwebs tearing at his face like razor blades. At the edge of the beach, he dropped to his knees and plunged his hand into the water. A large round blister had formed where the glop entered the scar. Matthew used his left thumbnail to pop the blister. The brown poison that popped out solidified into a jagged cube and dropped to the sand.

His hand dangling in the Atlantic, Matthew looked at Kinnawe House and wondered wildly why the Fordes stored dozens of barrels of excrement in their cellar. He also wondered why he had, for a moment, considered retrieving the chunk of solidified poison from the ocean bed, popping it into his mouth, and swallowing it.

30

Cape Agamenticus, Maine
November 1748

As Mrs. Feeley, the nurse-midwife, entered Parthalán's library, a coiled black rope darted into a dark corner.

"Reverend, I bring good news," Moira Feeley said. "I believe Mrs. Kinnawe is healed."

"You have my thanks, Mrs. Feeley," Parthalán said. "You are free to go."

His wait was over. Now he would exact the vengeance he'd been plotting since discovering his wife bled out and near death on her bed, the remains of his heirs aborted between her legs.

Parthalán entered his wife's chamber without knocking. "Get dressed, Emma. We are leaving the house."

Emma did not respond; did not bother to look up from her book.

"This can be simple, or it can be difficult," Parthalán said. "Either you choose to accompany me of your own free will, or I drag you from this house by your hair while our neighbors, including your father, watch. I will return in thirty minutes."

Parthalán returned half an hour later. Emma sat in a chair, clothed, her chestnut hair gathered into a ponytail.

Parthalán stared at his wife. Her self-mutilation and long illness had dulled her beauty, but he still desired her. He wished that she desired him in the same way that Naomi desired Gregory Brautigam and Abigail desired Michael Ayers, but Emma's willing participation in sexual relations would not give him the child he wanted. Her hatred of him serviced his greater need, but he sometimes felt a twinge of envy when he considered his men's relationships with their wives.

Emma walked ahead of him on the path to the church. She was the only resident of Cape Agamenticus, other than the Hauers and Mariah, who had never been inside. Their wedding had taken place on the cliff, in Parthalán's cave. Parthalán had promised Gregory that he would not require Emma's participation in church rites, and he'd kept his promise. The mother of his heir must be a good Christian woman taken against her will.

Parthalán pushed open the church's rear door and led Emma to a staircase hidden behind a panel. He lit two black candles—one for him, one for her—and motioned for her to descend the staircase ahead of him. Nailed to the walls were the skulls of the men who'd declined to join the congregation in 1746.

"Wait here," Parthalán said, following the basement walls to light candles in the niches. Each candle revealed a different shadowy horror. A table held a corpse in an advanced state of decomposition. The rats that had been chewing on its flesh scurried away as he approached. An iron maiden stood in a far corner, a desiccated skeleton within. As Parthalán lit the next candle, three large snakes slithered across the floor and into the iron maiden's cavity. Next to the iron maiden was a chair covered with spikes. A woman's decapitated and impaled body was strapped into the chair. As Parthalán shone his candle onto the woman's remains, hundreds of long-legged spiders scampered from the floor to the neck and disappeared inside the rotting carcass.

The last three candles revealed a wall on which metal instruments dangled from spikes and rings. Parthalán pointed to a set of tongs with sharpened ends.

"This, Emma, is an Iron Spider." He paused, savoring the moment. Until now, Emma had displayed no more emotion than a sackcloth doll stuffed with sawdust. Now her eyes were round with fear.

"The Iron Spider rips the breasts from women guilty of adultery or self-abortion," Parthalán continued. "That pyramid-shaped seat, there, is a Judas cradle. The ropes suspend the traitor over the pyramid's point. The ropes are pulled tight and she is lowered onto it, ripping open her orifice. Being impaled is a slow, painful death, but it is not as painful as dying from infection while suspended in mid-air."

"Do with me as you will, Parthalán," Emma said. Her round eyes had become angry slits. "Even a lingering death will be better than a life spent with you."

"Brave words from a headstrong girl."

Emma folded her arms over her chest and made no further response.

That this girl, chosen to be the mother of his child, should treat him with such contempt, such disrespect, when any woman in Cape Agamenticus would have welcomed him to her bed! How well Emma knew him, and how well she used that knowledge to infuriate him! Since failing to kill herself, tormenting him had become her sole pleasure. But here, in the basement of his church, where only one entity held more power than he did, he would not be provoked. He was her master. *She* lived to serve *him*.

"You are reticent as always, Emma. You vilify me and my congregation, but you are as empty of your God's love as any resident of this town. There is but one person in my congregation who retains a spark of humanity: your father, who sacrificed his soul to save *you*. But you—not only do you not appreciate your father's gift, you brutalize him with your indifference."

Emma's mouth twitched at the corners. At last, a crack in the façade.

"Ah, so my dear wife holds a shred of affection for her father in the otherwise empty crypt that is her heart? Perhaps that is for the best, Emma, because only you have the power to save him from the rack"—Parthalán pointed to the table with the rats chewing on the body, which was chained by its arms and legs to the rollers at each end—"or the Catherine Wheel"— he pointed to a large wooden wheel with chains to which a man's arms and legs would be attached—"or the Heretic's Fork." From the wall of metal instruments, he removed a short belt to which a metallic fork with two tines was attached at either end. "When your father is suspended from the ceiling and the Heretic's Fork is placed around his neck, one fork will dig into his chin while the other pierces his throat. He will be unable to speak or move his head. As soon as his head starts to sag with fatigue, his throat will be pierced. More men die of madness from a lack of sleep than they do from loss of blood."

"You would torture a man who serves you without question?"

He was on the edge of breaking her with his oratory, honed and polished during his rise to power, as Jonathan Edwards' had been. "Yes. And as he dies, you will sit in that chair and watch. Of course, I will have the spikes removed first. Your head will be held stationary and your eyes pried open with metal rods. You will neither be able to close your eyes nor look away. When the rite is finished, and the community has feasted on your father's entrails, you will live with the knowledge that you, and you alone, are responsible for his death.

"The terms are as follows," Parthalán continued, savoring his wife's anguish. "Each night I will come into your bed, and you will resist me. If I so much as suspect that you are planning to harm my unborn children, your father will be roused from his bed and brought here. I will give you no warnings and no second chances. What remains of Gregory after the feast will be pounded into dust and mixed with pigs' offal. And you will live the rest of your days in this cellar with nothing but the rats, snakes, and spiders for company. And, perhaps, an occasional visit from our Protector, whose physical needs dwarf my own. Now return to the house and give me your decision by midnight."

That night, Emma was so wild in her resistance that Parthalán later joked to Charles Meer that she'd had something of the devil inside her.

Soon he would have his heir.

31

Kinnawe House
Agamenticus, Maine

During his long hospitalization, Matthew had heard the word *sepsis* a hundred times. The staff had been as concerned with preventing infection as they'd been with sewing him up.

He knew not to take chances. Using alcohol and peroxide, he sterilized the scar into which the ordure from the cask had seeped. To his surprise, the scar was sealed tight, rubbery. He poked at the scar with a paring knife but drew not a drop of blood. The scar seemed impermeable.

Popping the blister into the ocean had expelled the poison, but it hadn't washed the stench from his nostrils or the sensation of gelatinous slime sliding down his limbs. In the bathroom, he stripped off his clothes and settled into the claw-foot bathtub while the water ran full blast. Lying in two feet of scalding water, he scrubbed himself from head to toe with a bar of soap, hoping to shed an entire layer of his skin. When he touched the bottom of the bathtub, his fingers sunk into half an inch of dirt, sand, and sediment. He brought a palmful of the mixture to his nose. It smelled of the ocean, of damp seaweed and rotting fish.

The water in the tub was so dark that he could have been bleeding to death and unaware of it. Matthew raised one limb at a time from the water to examine his scars. Even the most active scars on his right and left arms, and on his right leg, remained sealed, thank God. As he lifted his left leg from the water, he wondered why it felt tighter than the rest of him.

A black viper had curled itself around his leg from ankle to thigh. The snake reared its head back, took aim, spat at Matthew's face, and sank its fangs into the meat of his thigh.

What the fuck! Jesus Christ! What the fuck!

As Matthew, panicked, sprang out of the bathtub, his big toe popped the thick rubber plug off the drain. As the last dregs of water drained from the tub, the viper slid down Matthew's leg, darted up the side of the bathtub, and disappeared down the drain. Matthew grabbed the stopper and jammed it into the drainpipe, smashing the stopper into place with his fist.

He fled the bathroom for the living room. Naked, he sat on the couch and examined his left leg. The snake's fangs should have left puncture wounds. But his left thigh looked normal. Pale and skinny.

He found his phone where he'd left it in the bedroom. No bars, as usual, but Helen might have a landline.

He dressed, slipped his phone into his jeans pocket out of habit, and walked slowly to Helen's. He'd read somewhere that running causes venom to spread through the body more quickly.

As he set foot on Helen's property, his phone dinged with a new voicemail message. He pulled the phone from his pocket, saw three bars, and dialed 9-1-1.

"What is your emergency?"

"A snake bit my leg."

"I'm connecting you with Poison Control."

Three seconds later, a male voice asked, "Are there two punctures on your leg, with swelling around them?"

"No."

"That's a good sign. Does your leg, face, or any part of you feel numb?"

"No."

"Any trouble breathing? Nausea?"

"No."

"Salivating?"

"No."

"Then you probably haven't been envenomed. You have a 917 phone number. You're calling from New York City?"

"No, I'm in southern Maine."

"Even better. There are no poisonous snakes native to Maine. But are you near water?"

"Yes."

"Then it was likely a water snake. They can be mean if they feel threatened, and they can deliver a vicious bite, but they're not venomous."

Matthew almost fainted from relief.

Rather than bother Helen, he began walking back to the house, shaking from the adrenaline surge.

He'd already checked the house for snakes, but he hadn't checked the basement—in retrospect, a really stupid oversight. The snake, or snakes, might be coiled in a dank corner near the well pump, waiting for an excuse to slither up through the pipes and have another go at him.

Matthew turned on his phone's flashlight app and pushed his way through the heavy wooden door into the basement. Threading his way through the casks, he shone the flashlight on every square inch of the floor, ceiling, and walls, noticing the letters burned into the barrels: EKOSKINEN, CHAUER, LMEER. He approached the well pump and peeked behind it. No snakes there; only a couple of spiders and a tiny mouse.

In the bathroom, there was no residue left behind in the bathtub. All the silt had followed the snake down the drain.

He heard his mother's recriminations. *How sharper than a serpent's tooth it is to have a thankless child.* And what more appropriate way to punish him than to send a sharp-toothed serpent after him?

His mind zigzagged between sheer terror and cold fury. Why did she blame *him* for what she herself had done? Why was it *his* fault that she'd ended up in an insane asylum? He'd tried to do the right thing. Just because it was right for him didn't mean it wasn't right for her, too.

The WiFi in the house was down again, so he drove to Ogunquit, where he parked in a public parking lot and picked up an errant signal.

Bartholomew Dubh didn't answer, so Matthew left a message in which he tried very hard to explain the snake problem at Kinnawe House calmly and rationally.

He didn't want to flee the house, return to New York. Where would he go? He'd sublet the apartment on West 51st for six months. Besides, he'd made a commitment to serving as the winter caretaker at Kinnawe House, and he'd discovered a few tantalizing bits of information that might help him find the family he'd never had. As he remembered his plans to research Ray Lonegan, the man who'd abandoned him and his mother when he was seven years old, a text blipped in:

Bartholomew Dubh
Rec'd your message. Have not heard of such problems at K House but sometimes there are snakes near the water. We have a service we use. I will get someone there today/tonight. They use bait to draw snakes out of the house. If you see yellow canisters on the property leave them alone. That's the bait. Carrion feeders will eat any dead snakes you see outside. No need to worry. The snakes here are ugly but harmless.

Dubh's message was moderately reassuring. More worrisome was Matthew's fear that he'd hallucinated the snake, the snakebite, and all the rest of it.

32

Cape Agamenticus
November 1748

Léana read the letter she'd written the night before.

> *Dear Reverend,*
> *Word may have reached you that Cutler and I are now husband and wife. Never as we set forth from your house did I expect to find a spouse on my journey, and I thank you for choosing Cutler to accompany me and Mariah.*
>
> *The information-gathering process is frustrating and slow, and I meet resistance at every turn. The shopkeepers will not speak with me, other than to quote prices and the final sum due. Even my neighborly comments about the weather are met with silent nods. However, a few facts are clear.*
>
> *The townspeople call Parthalán "Reverend Kinnawe," but his authority appears to extend beyond a minister's usual sphere of influence. Despite our friendship when we both lived in your home, he does not deign to acknowledge me or Cutler. Parthalán's wife, Emma (Gregory Brautigam's daughter), is an outcast here. Her name is mentioned only rarely, and then with a note of dislike. I have tried calling on the wives of Mr. Brautigam, Mr. Collinge, Mr. Meer, and Mr. Ayers, but their maids say the women are not at home even as they watch me from an upstairs window. Cutler fares no better with their husbands, who took a dislike to him while he and Roger Cavendish built the house.*
>
> *Bébhinn is nowhere to be found. It is said that she went to visit a relative and never returned.*

The meeting house is mostly hidden by trees. However, it does not seem to be the simple building required by our faith. Instead it has large stained-glass windows that glow after dark. We are not permitted to approach the meeting house, and sentries are stationed on all paths leading to it at all times.

There is no worship on Sundays. Rather, the meeting house is most active on Friday and Saturday. On those nights, Cutler, Mariah, and I hear moans, sometimes loud, sometimes faint, carried on the wind.

Though the town seems shiny and prosperous, I cannot help but feel that a heavy rainstorm will wash away the bright façade and reveal the rot beneath. Most days the air carries the scent of salt, flowers, and sunlight, but every so often a westerly breeze brings an odor of decaying carrion that lingers a few minutes before drifting out to sea. The reek is always a forceful reminder of our mission.

I will write again soon. My love to Mrs. Edwards and the children.

Your humble servant, Léana Hauer

Léana addressed the envelope and handed it to Cutler, who slid it into a pocket in his tunic.

Soon thereafter, Cutler and Mariah left for the York Village Inn, at which Cutler planned to leave the letter. It would be carried to Reverend Edwards via a network of inns along the roads that connected Maine to Boston, Concord, and Northampton. The Cape Agamenticus Inn on the shore road was popular, often filled with men drinking at the bar and women nibbling on sandwiches in the dining room, but neither Léana nor Cutler trusted that a letter dropped off at that establishment would leave town.

In York Village, Cutler handed the letter, along with a generous tip, to the innkeeper. An hour later, after Cutler and Mariah had arrived home, the innkeeper handed Léana's letter to Michael Ayers, who delivered it into Parthalán's hands that evening.

●　　●　　●

After Cutler and Mariah left for York Village, Léana lay down for a brief nap. Upon closing her eyes, she heard a footfall inside her chamber. She turned toward the door, expecting to see Cutler.

The person standing in the doorway was not Cutler but rather an overweight, haggard, redheaded woman. Léana blinked and recognized her old friend.

"Bébhinn," Léana said. How weary Bébhinn looked; how insubstantial and ethereal despite her weight gain.

"Now Vivian Forde."

"Not Vivian Kinnawe?"

"My son no longer wishes to share a surname with his mother."

Léana rose from the bed to embrace her friend. Her arms locked around a column of stale air, and her suspicions regarding Bébhinn's disappearance were confirmed. Bébhinn was dead. An important question remained, however. Was she enemy or ally?

"Bébhinn. What has happened? Why are you here?"

"I'm here because I know why *you* are here, Léana. And you'll need my help."

An ally.

33

Kinnawe House
Agamenticus, Maine

The exterminator had already visited Kinnawe House by the time Matthew returned from Ogunquit. Matthew saw the yellow canisters glinting in the sun and thought, *Wow, that was fast.*

Keeping busy was the best way to distract his thoughts from the casks, their contents, and the snakes. Picking up his chores where he'd left off, Matthew piled the raked leaves into the wheelbarrow and guided it to the compost heap, where maggots and junebugs worked at devouring the rotten fruit he'd tossed there earlier. Matthew dumped the leaves on top of the wriggling insects.

Glints of lapis blue, olive green, and red-gold danced in his peripheral vision. Turning east, he saw the source of the colored light: the high stained-glass windows of the church whose grounds, according to Helen Crowe, bordered the Fordes'.

Matthew began walking toward the church. Helen had warned him away from it, but he could check it out without getting too close or setting foot inside it. Maybe he'd find a cemetery, like the one he'd seen in York Village, that served as the final resting place of Fordes, Kinnawes, Crowes, Dubhs, and Lonegans.

With each step Matthew took, the church seemed to recede farther into the distance. It was almost as if he were walking in place, but he knew he was moving because the view beneath his feet kept changing.

He turned around to assess how far he'd trekked, ignoring the throbbing in his thigh where the snake had sunk its fangs into him. Kinnawe House was a distant fleck on the landscape.

Undaunted, Matthew continued trudging along the remains of the overgrown path that had once connected the house and the church. Half an hour later, he was no closer to his destination. The trail had twisted and turned, and he was now walking on a high cliffside path with a hundred-foot drop to the beach.

Weak, foamy waves slapped against the boulders. In his left periphery, a blur of white hopped from rock to rock: a goat, the local hunters' quarry. Matthew turned to look at the goat straight-on. The animal moved so quickly that it appeared to have two heads. As Matthew squinted to focus, it disappeared among the craggy outcroppings.

Matthew walked toward the edge of the cliff, hoping to catch another glimpse of the goat, but it had disappeared. At the end of the path he saw a large opening in the cliff, an entry into what looked like a cave. Normally he'd be a bit more intrepid, but after the snake attack he had little desire to explore a dark, wet cave on his own. Visions of water moccasins danced in his head. Maybe another time.

The sun was starting to set, and he was mindful of Helen's advice to get home before dark. As he turned back toward Kinnawe House, he noticed a man sitting on a small boulder, his back to Matthew. One of the hunters? A neighbor? Either way, it was an opportunity to talk to somebody new, someone who might know more about Kinnawe House and the Kinnawe family.

Not wanting to surprise a man who might be holding a gun, Matthew called out, "Hey. Hi." The setting sun partially obscured the man's bearded face as he turned toward Matthew.

Matthew waved in greeting and approached the man, who spoke not a word. Matthew gasped when he saw the gaping hole where the bearded man's Adam's apple should have been.

"Hey, are you OK?" Matthew asked without thinking. It was a dumb question. The man wasn't bleeding, just missing a part of himself.

The man reached out and grabbed the stone hanging from Matthew's neck. The painful throbbing from Matthew's snakebite vanished instantly.

Removing his hand from Matthew's stone, the man used his index finger to draw a plus sign on his own chest. Then he merged with the setting sun and was gone.

Matthew blinked his eyes and found himself back at the compost heap. He ran into the house and unbuckled his belt, then pulled down his jeans. With his fingers he prodded the area that the snake had bitten. No tenderness, no pain, just pale white flesh.

The bearded man had drawn a + sign on his chest. Matthew had seen that sign before—in one of the storage rooms at Kinnawe House.

In the pantry at the back of the house, Matthew moved the empty shelf to reveal the dozen or so + signs dabbed in wax against the wall. With his fingernail he scraped one off and rolled the wax into a ball until it was soft and warm. Without thinking he applied the wax to the scar between his fingers into which the ordure had seeped. He massaged the wax into his skin until it disappeared, taking the scar along with it.

A minute later, sitting at the kitchen table and staring at the new skin between his fingers, Matthew felt that he'd encountered a force of intense goodness. Kinnawe House and its environs were, it seemed, influenced by spirits both malignant and benevolent. Either that, or he was losing a little bit more of his mind with each passing hour.

Helen might know more about the man on the cliff, he thought. But perhaps she hadn't wanted Matthew to find him, which would explain why she'd warned him to stay away from the church. There was only one way to find out: Ask her.

34

Boston, Massachusetts
Late Fall 1748

Gregory Brautigam's son Tobias lived happily in Boston, where he worked long hours for a bookbinder, setting type and printing pamphlets and books. Fortunately, his employer was a churchgoing man who paid him well and forbade his employees from working on Sundays. At night and after Sunday services, Tobias sat in his small, comfortable rented room in Boston's North End, painting scenes from the manuscripts he'd typeset. Over the past few months, neighbors had begun purchasing them.

In short, Tobias Brautigam was a content young man living in a well-kept boarding house in a major port city, working at a job he enjoyed and nurturing dreams of supporting himself as an artist. Quick to make friends, he spent most Saturday evenings with his drinking comrades, though he was not one to overindulge. In recent weeks he'd begun an understated flirtation with Olivia Updegraff, the daughter of a Beacon Hill merchant who sold art supplies. Silas Updegraff had not given his blessing to a courtship, but he hadn't chased Tobias off, which was as close to approval as Tobias could hope for.

Into this charmed life arrived the unexpected summons. Tobias was to pack his bags and move to Cape Agamenticus. His aging father required his presence.

Tobias read the letter three times, hoping he'd misunderstood his father's wishes. He and Gregory enjoyed a companionable, if not close, relationship, exchanging letters several times a year. Gregory's missives were straightforward narratives, while Tobias's provided newsy and sometimes humorous tales of the city and his trade. At no time prior had Gregory hinted that he would someday expect his son to join him in Maine.

Yet this was not the first surprise that Gregory had dropped into Tobias's lap. Tobias hadn't learned of his sister's marriage until two months after the fact, and then only in a one-sentence postscript. Tobias responded with a letter filled with happy wishes for Emma and her husband. As a wedding gift he sent a painting, a romantic scene of a couple strolling arm in arm alongside a lake. Because he hadn't met Parthalán Kinnawe, he couldn't paint the groom's face, so he'd painted the couple from behind, creating one of Emma's favorite dresses from memory, her chestnut tresses flowing down her back. For all Tobias knew, Parthalán Kinnawe might be short, fat, and unattractive, but in the painting he was tall, slender, and broad-shouldered. Tobias had not received a thank-you note, or any communication at all, from Emma. He was hard pressed to understand why his sister, of whom he was very fond and who returned his affection, did not acknowledge his gift or respond to his letters.

Tobias wrote back to his father, asking if his move might be delayed a few months or a year. Two weeks letter a letter arrived from Gregory stating that he expected Tobias in Cape Agamenticus by the end of October.

Tobias had no choice in the matter. He acceded to his father's wishes—to do otherwise would be the mark of a disloyal and ungrateful child—and corresponded with his stepmother Naomi to make the arrangements.

35

Agamenticus – Kittery, Maine

Helen wasn't at home, which meant that Matthew would have to wait to ask her about the bearded man on the cliff. Maybe it was just as well. He hadn't quite figured out how to ask Helen about a ghost wandering the cliff without coming off as a crackpot.

He tried, but failed, to suppress the thought that maybe he *was* cracking up, walking a path that would end at the Bedford Hills Institute, a tight straightjacket, and weekly electroconvulsive therapy. Why did he keep blacking out and returning to normal consciousness just a few minutes later? Were his past traumas, the hazy history of Kinnawe House, and a lack of sleep blurring the line between reality and delusion?

ECT hadn't helped his mother, so it wasn't likely to help him, either. Genes were everything.

Genes. As soon as he finished his chores, he'd stop procrastinating, drive to the chain drugstore in Kittery, and buy the FamilyTree Kit, whose website had promised it was "available at all major pharmacies!"

First, though, he wanted to use the remaining daylight to trim the vines that surrounded the back door of Kinnawe House, the door facing the road. He didn't like those vines. They scratched against the house at night like the fingernails of tiny demons.

The vines' long, sharp thorns left lengthy scratches on his arms as he hacked away at the overgrowth, but he made good progress, and within an hour the vines lay in an entwined mass at his feet.

The scraping began as the sun dipped under the western horizon. He turned and found himself face to face with his mother, who dangled by the neck from the vines wrapped around one of the willow trees. Her eyes were open. The scratching and scraping came from her shoes dragging the earth as the vine swayed from side to side.

Rose of Sharon looked young and beautiful. This sane version of her had visited him once before, when he was unconscious from his morphine drip. Then, they'd traded fond memories. Feeding the ducks at the pond. Cobbling together a few dollars to buy books at a local bookstore. Heating Chef-Boy-ar-Dee ravioli and devouring the salty, gummy glop. This was the mother he wanted to remember: the quirky, pretty Mom, not the raging paranoiac of his middle school, high school, and college years.

Matthew looked away. When he turned back—to explain, to beg forgiveness, to say something, anything—Rose of Sharon was gone, though the hangman's loop formed by the vine continued swaying left to right, right to left.

He retrieved his laptop and backpack from the house, fired up the Civic, and drove down to the Kittery drugstore, where he paid $98 for the deluxe FamilyTree Kit, which promised not only a full ancestry report but also an assessment for dozens of health risks, including macular degeneration (which might explain the hallucinations), G6PD deficiency (which might cause anemia and explain his increasingly pale complexion), and a slew of other frightening-sounding genetically heritable diseases, such as beta thalassemia, congenital disorder of glycosylation Type 1a, dihydrolipoamide dehydrogenase deficiency, familial dysautonomia, and neuronal ceroid liofuscinosis.

The FamilyTree Kit: A hypochondriac's dream come true, or an objective, scientific analysis of the genes and chromosomes that made him tick, or not tick? Or vague generalities and complete bullshit? Time would tell.

Sitting on a bench outside the drugstore, he checked his phone: four bars. He tapped the icon to retrieve his voice mail.

"Matthew, hi. Doris from Bala Cynwyd. Give me a call. I found it."

Damn: It was almost 7 P.M., and the township offices would be closed. But tomorrow he'd learn his father's name. Then he could take to the Web and start hunting him down. He wouldn't be surprised to find him living in or near York County, Maine.

To pass the time he tried Googling the words burned into the barrels in the basement of Kinnawe House: EKOSKINEN, CHAUER, LMEER. As he scrolled through the results, he learned that Koskinen is a common Finnish surname.

KOSKINEN. Did the barrel belong to someone named E. Koskinen? And did it really contain excrement, or had he imagined all of it? The thick, foul-smelling liquid could have been blueberry wine gone rancid. Did the other barrels belong to C. Hauer and L. Meer? Further Google searches turned up the fact Meer is a common Dutch surname, along with burial records for Hauers in the vicinity of Northampton, Massachusetts.

All of them were connected to Kinnawe House, somehow. More questions to ask Helen.

After searching in vain for information on RAY LONGEGAN + MAINE and LONEGAN RAY AGAMENTICUS MAINE, he retrieved a slip of paper from his wallet and tapped a text message to Priscilla, the cashier who'd inspired his song-in-progress, "Just Give Him Your Number."

Me
Hey Priscilla. It's Matthew from NY. Short notice but wonder if you'd like to hang?

He received a response a few seconds later.

I have a 15 min break in an hour? There are picnic tables behind the store??

Matthew responded:

I'm already in the neighborhood, near Starbucks. Bring you coffee or tea?

Again a response came quickly:

Chai tea would be excellent.

Matthew smiled. Thinking about a pretty girl was a welcome change from sleeplessness and the growing fear that he might be losing his mind.

36

Although bringing Tobias to Cape Agamenticus had been her idea, Naomi Brautigam was not looking forward to the arrival of her permanent houseguest. After Emma's marriage to Parthalán, a blissful peace had descended on the Brautigam house. Gone were the angry glares between stepmother and stepdaughter, the competition for Gregory's attention and affection. Naomi had enjoyed having her husband all to herself. But she knew of Emma's unwillingness to conceive again, and she'd advised Parthalán accordingly.

"Emma will do anything for her brother," Naomi had said. "Bring Tobias here, and use him as a bargaining chip." She loved her husband, but her first loyalties were to Parthalán and her community.

Now Naomi surveyed the chamber that her maid, Patrizia, had prepared for Tobias. It was one of the house's better rooms, overlooking the ocean. A breeze blew through the window, raising gooseflesh on Naomi's arms.

Patrizia entered the chamber. "Mrs. Brautigam, Mrs. Kinnawe is here."

Naomi greeted her stepdaughter with a polite hello. She knew something of Emma's nighttime tribulations, and she imagined they were much like those she'd experienced. Four of her community's elders in New Orleans had initiated her on her twelfth birthday. But her initiation had been a gift, not a rape.

"My husband has asked me to visit," Emma said. Her eyes were two dark hollows in her face.

"Sit, Emma, and I'll ask Patrizia to bring tea. Your father has gone to meet a visitor. He will be home shortly."

Emma sat in a comfortable chair in the parlor at the front of the house, where she and Naomi engaged in weather-related small talk. As Patrizia stoked the fire, Naomi heard the horses snorting behind the house. Naomi rose from her chair, and Emma followed.

Through the window Naomi saw Gregory climb down from his horse. A younger man—fair-skinned, blond, rather handsome—stood beside him. As a rule, Naomi did not find blond men attractive. They seemed less rugged, more delicate, than darker men. There was fortune in that, however. A weaker man was easier to lead and more likely to follow.

Emma burst through the kitchen door and threw her arms around her brother. "Toby, Toby," she cried, sobs racking her body.

Tobias Brautigam hugged his sister in return. "Emma, darling, why cry like this? We should be laughing and celebrating, not weeping."

"I weep because I am so happy," Emma sobbed, extricating herself from Tobias's embrace. As Tobias watched in puzzlement, his sister ran up the road, back to Kinnawe House.

Gregory, standing stone-faced next to the horses, took Naomi's hand. "Tobias, my wife, your stepmother, Naomi."

Tobias's handshake was firm, and to her surprise, Naomi felt a small tingle of sexual excitement. Perhaps father and son had more in common than she'd expected.

As Gregory, Naomi, and Tobias entered the house, Naomi heard boots on gravel. Through the trees she saw Léana Hauer knocking at Abigail Ayers's door, and her heart skipped a beat. She remembered Parthalán's words: "None of the women are to trust Léana. Not for a second. She seeks our destruction."

After settling Tobias, Naomi would visit Abigail. She knew her friend had not recovered from the sacrifice of her son Calvin, though Abigail knew better than to show it. Naomi missed very little, and everything she saw, she reported to Parthalán.

37

Kittery, Maine

Matthew approached the sliding glass doors of the Hannaford, trying not to spill the two chai teas. Priscilla, waiting outside, slipped her phone into her smock, waved in greeting, and rushed to relieve Matthew of his burden.

Priscilla's slicked-back hair lent her a 1920s film-star glamour. Her scent was the intoxicating aroma of grass clippings. Kellyce had been all dark make-up, hair dye, and syrupy perfumes. In contrast, Priscilla appeared to be free of artificial colors and flavors.

"Perfect timing," Priscilla said. "You wouldn't believe the behind-the-scenes drama at a supermarket."

Matthew followed Priscilla around the back of the building, where they sat at a rickety picnic table facing the delivery docks.

Priscilla sipped from her cardboard cup. "So ... Did you find something in your grocery bags that you didn't buy?" she asked.

"As a matter of fact, I did. It looked and smelled gross. It wasn't a gift from you, was it? If it was, I would have had a more open mind about it."

"No, some guy dropped it into your grocery bags," Priscilla responded. "He was walking behind you, so you probably didn't see him. I thought it seemed weird. I tried texting you about it, but the text wouldn't go through."

It had to be a prank, Matthew thought. A local guy, maybe one of Priscilla's admirers, chucking a hunk of tripe into the grocery sacks of a too-skinny obvious out-of-towner.

"I get lousy reception at the house I'm taking care of," Matthew explained. "Texts don't come through most of the time. When I texted you before, I was sitting outside a drugstore a couple of miles up the road."

They made small talk between sips of chai. Priscilla seemed at ease, unencumbered by the neuroses suffered by those living in big, crowded, competitive cities. Getting to this point had been easy, Matthew thought; sitting here with Priscilla was easy. They'd met, texted, agreed to meet again, and done so. No playing hard to get, no acceptance contingent on other possibilities, no looking over his shoulder for someone better looking or wealthier. It was never so simple in New York. Never.

"I like your necklace," Matthew said, pointing to the dove charm dangling from a thin gold chain around Priscilla's neck.

"It matches this." Priscilla rolled up her sleeve to reveal the dove tattoo on her wrist that he'd noticed as she rang up his groceries. "I got the tattoo in college. I was a peace studies minor, and it seemed appropriate, you know? As for the necklace, it's a bit of a mystery. I found it in my jewelry box this morning, but I don't remember buying it or anyone giving it to me. What does your stone mean?" Priscilla pointed to Matthew's neck. "Is it a rune?"

"Honestly, I have no idea. My mother gave it to me. I've done a million Web searches, but I haven't found any runes shaped like it."

"So both of us have mysterious jewelry," Priscilla said. "That's a coincidence."

"And both of us are singers. Another coincidence. Oh. Speaking of music, have you ever been to Julie's?"

Priscilla nodded. "It's been there forever. Everyone's been there."

"I'm doing an early-bird gig on Friday night. Pop and easy listening. Would you like to come as my guest?"

"I'd love to."

Yes!

Priscilla looked at her watch and rolled down her shirtsleeve. "But right now I have to get back to work. The boss-man gets anxiety attacks if anyone extends their break beyond 15 minutes."

Matthew walked Priscilla to the front door. He was tempted to go in for a hug or a peck on the check, but it was too soon.

No venomous bite and a low-key quasi-date with a local girl, who happened to be a pretty, smart music lover. Things were looking up. As Matthew started his car, he chose to ignore the rusty nail scratching at his skull, the one reminding him that the farther from Kinnawe House he was, the better he felt.

38

Cape Agamenticus, Maine
January 1749

Winter had just begun, but the weather was warm and pleasant. On a horse borrowed from Reverend Kinnawe's stable, blonde, petite Abigail Ayers ambled along the shore road toward York Village, waving at her friends and the other townspeople. Women alone on horses were a rare sight in other parts of New England, but in Cape Agamenticus they attracted no undue notice. The men relied on their wives to undertake certain tasks and perform key duties. When they were not busy fulfilling their duties to their families and to the church, the women were free to come and go as they pleased.

In York Village, away from prying eyes, Abigail purchased small amounts of camphor, marjoram, rehmannia, ligistrum, and skullcap. She did not purchase chaste tree berries, because these took too long to take effect: sometimes four weeks, more often six. She needed relief sooner rather than later.

As she left the shop, a wave of nausea hit her. The child—a boy, she felt sure—was large and boisterous, and he was sapping her strength. She bore not an ounce of resentment against the child, but she needed respite from Michael climbing on top of her night after night. The herbs she'd just purchased, steeped with Michael's tea, would diminish his sex drive. For the next several months she needed to focus all of her body's energy on nourishing the child. Already Rebecca Collinge had three little ones, and Leah Meer was pregnant with her fourth, while Abigail remained childless.

Naomi had offered words of comfort after Calvin's sacrifice: "You'll have another child soon enough, Abigail, so enjoy your body, and allow your husband to enjoy it, before babies wear you out and leave you exhausted. Your time will come. Parthalán will make sure of it."

As Abigail approached her horse, she felt a tug at her sleeve. Standing behind her was the almond-eyed woman whom Parthalán had declared an enemy of the community.

"There is a glow about you, Mrs. Ayers," Léana Hauer said. "When do you expect the child? Late March? March babies are always healthy and adaptable, born at the end of one season and the beginning of another."

Maternal pride overcame Abigail's misgivings and Parthalán's warnings.

"Mrs. Feeley says late March or early April."

"He will be a big boy, I think."

"If you'll excuse me, Mrs. Hauer, I must be getting home."

"I would like to talk with you, Abigail. We are not in his town. Here, alongside a consecrated cemetery, we may speak without fear."

Abigail looked around. Léana was naïve indeed if she thought that Parthalán's influence did not extend far beyond Cape Agamenticus.

"You may live among us, Mrs. Hauer, but we are under no obligation to befriend you."

"And what of *you*, Abigail? What will happen when Parthalán wants this child, as he demanded your first?"

Parthalán had forbidden the townspeople from talking with Léana, Cutler, and Mariah, but Léana's mention of Abigail's sacrificed child overrode her fear. The image of her son's butchered body haunted her. "How do you know about Calvin?" she whispered.

"I have been told."

"Nobody in Cape Agamenticus would discuss these matters with an outsider."

"The person who told me no longer fears death or torture."

"Bébhinn." During the summer, Abigail had seen her wandering the cliffs at twilight, her red hair reflecting the setting sun. She'd turned away from the ghost, as Parthalán had ordered.

"Yes. Bébhinn," Léana replied. "She and I were friends, once. Her soul finds no rest."

"She is a traitor who betrayed her son and her community. You would be wise to pay her no heed."

"Would you like to know where your son's remains are hidden, Abigail? We can retrieve them, and then you can give him a proper burial. His soul will fly to freedom."

"Calvin's remains were sprinkled in the ocean."

"No, Parthalán stashes the remains of all who are sacrificed. Your son's heart is in one place, his bones in another. Bébhinn followed Parthalán as he hid them. I can bring you to his heart and his bones, but I cannot cross the barriers without your assistance. You may then come to this cemetery at night and bury Calvin in hallowed ground. God will not punish an innocent infant for his parents' sins."

Abigail's temper flared as she remembered her son's tiny heart being ripped from his chest. "How dare you use my child to tempt me into deceiving my husband and betraying my town? Look around Cape Agamenticus—you will see how healthy the people are, how fertile the land, how prosperous the merchants. It was *my* child who brought that prosperity."

"The sacrifice of a single child is not enough to satisfy a fiend whose hunger never abates. The unborn child you are now protecting from his father—yes, I saw what you purchased from the apothecary—what is to stop Parthalán from demanding *him*? And your next child, and the one after that? Are you nothing more than a breeding ground for children to be taken and murdered? Do you believe the children of your friends and neighbors are any safer? Mark my words, Abigail, someday Parthalán will demand a child from Leah Meer and from Rebecca Collinge, as well as every other woman who has given herself in bondage to him."

Léana's words struck close to the bone. She alone had dared to voice the threat looming over every child in Cape Agamenticus.

"I will report this conversation to my husband, Mrs. Hauer. He will report it to Parthalán. You, your husband, and your maid will be forced to leave, or worse."

Léana stood her ground. "No one in Cape Agamenticus—not you, not your husband, not Parthalán Kinnawe himself—has the ability to remove me from my home. If Parthalán was capable of ridding himself of us, don't you think he would have done so by now? You—and he—may feel protected, but I am protected also. Remember, Abigail, that it is never too late to repent, and to take your baby where he will be safe from harm."

As Léana walked away, Abigail felt a series of hearty kicks in her womb.

39

Kinnawe House
Agamenticus, Maine

Back from his pleasant (and encouraging) get-together with Priscilla, Matthew picked up his guitar to practice for his Friday-night gig at Julie's. Just as he'd strummed the opening bars of "Sweet Caroline"—certain to be requested by the early bird crowd—tires crunched on the gravel driveway and a car door slammed. Then the deep bass of Kinnawe House's rear doorbell reverberated through the house like a death knell.

She'd demanded a permanent break with him. She'd said she never wanted to see or speak with him again. Yet here she was on his doorstep, a vision in black.

Matthew found his voice. "Kellyce. How did you find me?"

"Josh. Can I come in? I have to pee really bad."

Matthew stepped aside to let Kellyce into the house, wondering if, miraculously, her feelings had changed. She wouldn't have rented a car and driven six hours as a lark. But he didn't remember giving Josh the address of Kinnawe House. And his throbbing scars did not portend happy news.

"End of the hall," he said. "On the right."

He was sitting on a chair in the lower parlor, trying to sort through his very mixed feelings, when Kellyce returned.

She didn't look him in the eye as she settled herself onto the couch. Not a good sign. Matthew's abdomen cramped as his gastric juices attacked his stomach lining. First the house resurrected his mother. Then it inserted the cries of his aborted child into the song Priscilla had inspired him to write. Now the house seemed to have summoned Kellyce, too.

"I'm sure you're wondering why I'm here," Kellyce said without preamble. "And before you ask, yes, I had the procedure. Then I spent like a hundred hours on the Net researching whether to be honest with someone who has a terminal illness. I decided you have the right to know."

"The right to know what?"

"The baby had what you have, Matthew. He would have died in his teens. Please believe me, I never meant to hurt you."

Kellyce had said *he*. The baby would have been a boy. Dante.

"Are you saying that whatever the baby had, he got from me?" Matthew sputtered. "Does that mean I have it, too? Is that what the doctor said?"

"The doctor didn't tell me," Kellyce said. "Your mother did."

"My mother? You saw my mother before she died?"

Kellyce blinked back tears. "She warned me. She said I'd lose you first, and then I'd lose the children. You don't know what she did after you were born. She told me I had to do the same thing. She thought I was carrying twins, but I wasn't."

"What did she do after I was born? Did she tell you that I'm a twin? I think I had a twin brother, or sister, who died soon after we were born."

"That isn't what happened, Matthew."

The more they talked, the less he understood. Kellyce had gone to see his mother before she died. Had the meeting been so stressful that Rose of Sharon's weak heart had no choice but to stop beating? But now Kellyce was sobbing, and Matthew couldn't bear to watch her fall to pieces or to acknowledge his role in her breakdown. He still loved her. The idea that being with him had brought her misery shattered his heart. He couldn't keep firing questions at her, not while she was so vulnerable. Secrets had been kept from him for 28 years. One more night of ignorance wouldn't matter.

"Why don't you sleep here tonight?" Matthew said. "There's a spare bedroom. We can talk more in the morning. If you want to."

Kellyce wiped her nose with her sleeve. "I have an overnight bag in the car. I was going to find a cheap motel or something."

"No, stay here. Please."

Kellyce nodded and Matthew went to retrieve Kellyce's tote from the rented Ford Focus, hurrying back inside when he heard gunshots. Kellyce had found the guest bedroom. The door was closed. After tapping on the door and leaving the overnight bag in the corridor, Matthew went into the master bedroom, sat on the bed, and stared at the moonlit ocean.

The last time he'd seen Kellyce, she'd said, "You're broken. Your seed is rotten." Now he knew what she meant: The child's genetic abnormalities came from him. Had Kellyce's tests revealed that his brain circuits would degrade, as his mother's had; that his genes doomed not only him, but also his offspring? Did his mother's fate await him, too—psychosis and imprisonment in the Bedford Hills Institute?

He'd spit into the tubes, and the package was ready to be mailed off to Family Tree's lab in Braintree, Massachusetts. Had Kellyce driven all the way to Maine to give him a preview of the results?

A voice on the other side of the door broke Matthew's concentration.

"Matthew. I know you don't want me to say this, but I love you, and I always will, even if we can't be together."

Matthew listened to Kellyce tiptoe back to her bedroom. History and literature were filled with couples who loved each other but couldn't be together: Mark Antony and Cleopatra, Romeo and Juliet, Tony and Maria, Jack and Rose. None of those stories ended happily, and at least one of the lovers ended up dead.

●

He awoke to Kellyce straddling him, begging him to fuck her harder and deeper. He exploded inside her, not considering the consequences. Then he flipped her onto her back, climbed on top of her, and pounded with abandon as she writhed in ecstasy.

After ejaculating a second time, Matthew rolled off Kellyce and had his best sleep of the year.

As the first glimmers of day filtered through the windows, Matthew's eyes popped open. Kellyce was asleep next to him, curled under the covers. So: The sex hadn't been a wild wet dream. It had been the real thing. He hadn't used a condom. Were they both insane? Their relationship had ended because she'd become pregnant, and she'd had an abortion after receiving catastrophic test results. So why the fuck would they abandon their sanity and have unprotected sex?

Something about Kellyce had changed during the night. Underneath the blanket and duvet she looked smaller, more fragile. The head on the pillow didn't have Kellyce's Goth dyed-black hair. The woman lying there had curly hair the color of a chestnut.

Matthew sprang out of bed as the woman kicked off the covers. Her slender body gaped open at the abdomen. Blood had soaked through the sheets and into the mattress. She held a pair of knitting needles in her right hand.

"Take these, Matthew," the girl, a teenager, said. "Drive one through your eye socket and into your brain. Take charge of your life. Don't die the way your mother did."

Matthew took the needles from the girl's outstretched hand. He saw it all clearly now: A quick death would be better than a slow, agonizing march to insanity and the grave. He didn't deserve to live. He'd abandoned his mother in a psych ward. He'd ignored his best friend when his music career started taking off. He'd brought sorrow and pain to the woman he loved.

He gripped one of the needles in his right hand, bent his head at the neck, and prepared to drive the needle upward through his eyeball.

Behind him—the flapping of wings.

"Matthew! Stop! Stop!" Helen screamed, and Matthew fainted dead away.

40

Cape Agamenticus, Maine
February 1749

Tobias Brautigam had decided to make the best of the situation. Accepting that he would be living with his father and stepmother for the foreseeable future, he set out to befriend Naomi and succeeded. He complimented her often and asked her to tell stories of her childhood in New Orleans, a place that seemed as foreign and exotic to him as the Far East.

Tobias hoped to spend more time with Emma after her recovery. Gregory had explained that Emma had experienced a difficult pregnancy and agonizing miscarriage that had damaged not only her health but also her mind. It was rumored, too, that she was pregnant again. Tobias must be patient, Gregory said.

Now, paintbrush in hand, Tobias stood on the beach trying to capture the hazy late-winter sun on canvas. A graceful silhouette appeared on the horizon. Tobias waved in greeting, and the silhouette waved back. Starved for friendship, Tobias began walking toward the stranger.

The silhouette turned out to be a pretty, dark-haired woman with a flawless complexion, very different from Olivia Updegraff, whom he'd courted in Boston. Where Olivia was thin and upright, this young lady was Rubenesque, olive complected, sensual. "Good day, Miss," Tobias said. Her beauty was more apparent up close. "I am Tobias Brautigam, recently arrived from Boston. Gregory Brautigam is my father, Naomi Brautigam my stepmother."

"Welcome, Mr. Brautigam. I am Mariah Edwards, and this is the house of Mr. and Mrs. Cutler Hauer of Northampton."

Mariah's revelation was not a surprise. All of the Brautigams' other neighbors on the cliff—the Ayers, the Collinges, the Meers—had come from Northampton, too.

"It is a small world, indeed," Tobias said. "My father and sister lived in Northampton before coming here. I, too, lived there before moving to Boston."

Mariah pointed to the paintbrush in Tobias's hand. "I see you are a painter, Mr. Brautigam."

"Yes, or at least I try to be. I sometimes flatter myself that I have some ability." Today he felt his talents were minimal, perhaps nonexistent. All afternoon, he'd tried to capture the sun, but the splotch on his canvas was no more than an orange blob.

"Painting must be like cooking," Mariah said. "Give two cooks the same ingredients. One creates a delicious meal. The other throws together a hash that would make sailors retch. One cook has the talent, and the other—not."

Not only was the girl pretty, she was also clever. "I hope," Tobias said with a smile, "that someday I shall be counted among the great chefs, not among those who make sailors vomit."

Tobias continued, "Miss Edwards—pardon my presumption—would you allow me to paint your portrait? Your face is quite distinctive." He had not seen gray eyes like Mariah's before. Just mixing the color would be a challenge.

"I will ask Mr. and Mrs. Hauer." Mariah ran her hand through her hair. "To sit for an artist and a true gentleman! It is a great compliment, and not a request I would have expected. Not here at the end of the Earth, where the neighbors will have nothing to do with us."

"You have no friends in Cape Agamenticus? Not a one? Has there been a misunderstanding that I can help to put right?"

Mariah rushed to correct herself. "I have misspoken, Mr. Brautigam. It is more that Mr. and Mrs. Hauer are solitary by nature, but they are lovely and kind, and I feel certain they will like you."

Tobias recognized an opportunity to befriend his neighbors, to act as a bridge between them and the community, while basking in Mariah's beauty. The coast was magnificent, but it was stark, chilly, and formidable. Tobias needed, craved the warmth that Mariah exuded. "May I call on you tomorrow?" he asked.

"You may," Mariah said, extending her hand. Rather than shake it, Tobias raised it to his lips. It carried the scent of cinnamon, lemon, and rose petals.

Tobias returned to his canvas as Mariah returned to the house on the spit. He glanced at the horizon, dipped his brush onto his palette, and in three strokes transformed the orange blob into a perfect representation of the setting sun.

•   •   •   •

Rebecca Collinge, whose house was located between the Brautigams' and the Meers', watched the proceedings with interest. As soon as Sebastian arrived home, she reported that Gregory Brautigam's son was striking up an entirely inappropriate friendship with the Hauers' maid.

41

Matthew couldn't take it anymore. Not after last night, not after waking up stuck to the floor in a pool of blood that had seeped from his scars. Not after the dream, or hallucination, of Kellyce showing up, imposing the death penalty, and fucking him as a consolation prize before disappearing.

Dazed, he searched the driveway for indications that a car other than his Honda Civic had been parked there. He found none.

As usual, the WiFi connection was down, so Matthew drove to Ogunquit to connect to the Web. First, though, he stopped at the post office to mail his saliva to FamilyTree, which promised results within a week of receipt. Not knowing how the mail worked in Agamenticus—there were no mailboxes anywhere on Agamenticus Cliff Road—he opted for a PDF report delivered to his emailbox.

A Yelp search turned up a general practitioner in Portsmouth, New Hampshire, who'd received nine 5-star and six 4-star reviews. Matthew called the office, and Doctor Max Ansari's receptionist said the doctor could see him at 11.

Matthew arrived in Portsmouth, a mere stone's throw from Agamenticus, an hour early. *What a gorgeous city*, Matthew thought, strolling the centuries-old elegant streets. On Congress Street he found a health-food market where a helpful guy suggested homeopathic remedies for insomnia: lavender, chamomile, melatonin, ashwagandha, holy basil, valerian root. Matthew threw away $42 on three bottles of pills depicting various men and women with smiles on their faces as they slept on pillows of fluffy white clouds.

At the doctor's office, Matthew ticked the relevant boxes on the questionnaires. Sex: MALE. Race: WHITE. Under primary complaint he wrote INSOMNIA, because IMPENDING NERVOUS BREAKDOWN didn't seem clinical enough.

The family history section was difficult to complete. He had no idea what medical conditions ran in his father's family, so under "Father's Medical History" he wrote UNKNOWN. As for his mother, she'd always enjoyed good physical health. Her mental issues were much less straightforward. He checked the box for "Psychological Issues" and wrote SCHIZOPHRENIA / NARCISSISTIC PERSONALITY DISORDER / DEPRESSION in the blank next to it.

Those were the official diagnoses, but the reality was more complicated. In his late teens and early twenties, as Rose of Sharon's mental health spiraled downward, he'd spent weeks researching mental illness in the Bala Cynwyd public library. His mother had symptoms of almost all the personality disorders. She suffered from the narcissist's all-consuming emphasis on self and the attendant delusions of grandeur. She heard and responded to voices, the defining characteristic of schizophrenia. An obsessive compulsion caused her to scrub parts of herself raw, including her hands and feet. So, SCHIZOPHRENIA / NARCISSISTIC PERSONALITY DISORDER was the official diagnosis, but NOT GUILTY BY REASON OF INSANITY would have been accurate, too.

The receptionist, Sheila, took Matthew's paperwork and said the doctor would be with him soon.

The office had good wireless, so Matthew checked his phone. He signed onto Facebook and was surprised to see himself listed as "In a relationship with Kellyce Kobylarz." Tapping the screen, he reset his relationship status to SINGLE and then typed a text to Priscilla. For now, he had to focus on what was real, and Priscilla was real.

Hey. Sing together tonight or tomorrow? I have some songs that might be great for your voice.

A portly woman wearing psychedelic pink scrubs walked into the waiting room and called his name. Matthew followed her into an examination room, where he stepped on the scale and had his blood pressure taken.

Doctor Ansari—graying, stocky, with a mustache—entered the exam room a few minutes later. After greeting Matthew and scanning his file, the doctor checked Matthew's throat with his fingers and asked Matthew to lift his shirt so he could listen to his heart.

The preliminaries taken care of, Doctor Ansari asked, "What brings you here today, Matthew?"

"It's hard to explain," Matthew said. "It's kind of a combination of insomnia and bad dreams or hallucinations. I think I'm getting some sleep, but I can't be sure of it. I can't remember falling asleep, and then I suddenly wake up, sometimes after only a few minutes that seemed like hours."

"Have you been taking any medications for insomnia? Or any street drugs?"

"Street drugs, definitely not. But I do have a prescription for Ambien. I don't think it works, though. I get maybe an hour of sleep, but it's more like an hour of hallucinating. It's disturbing, not restful. A couple of nights ago I drank a bottle of Jack Daniels to help me fall asleep, and that didn't work, either."

"OK, I'm sure you know that's not the right solution. Are you staying away from caffeine? No naps during the day? No playing on the internet or checking your phone all night long?"

"No. I check my email and social media when I can get a signal, but I'm not addicted to technology."

"How long have you been having trouble with your sleep?"

"I've had problems on and off since I'm about 18, but it started to get worse just before I left New York, where I live." He briefly explained his caretaking arrangement. "That's about a week ago. It's gotten even worse since I got to New England."

"Do you think the scars on your chest, back, arms, and neck are related to your sleep problems?"

"Maybe." It was the most truthful answer. For six months after the attack, he'd experienced flashbacks, panic attacks, nightmares, sleepless nights. But *those* problems were different from *these* problems.

"How did you get the scars, Matthew? Car accident?"

"I got stabbed." Matthew rushed to continue. Nobody knew how to respond after he dropped that particular bomb. "I did go to a therapist for a while, and I do sometimes have nightmares about what happened, but it's different now. I wish I could explain it better."

"Have you been feeling particularly stressed or anxious?"

"The last three months haven't been the greatest, in terms of my career and my personal life. I thought I was coping with it OK. But maybe I'm not?"

Doctor Ansari pulled a prescription pad and a pen from the pocket of his lab coat. "The first thing you need is a good night's rest. I'm giving you prescriptions for two strong tranquilizers. One is called benzodiazepine. It will relax you and help you sleep. The other is an atypical antipsychotic called quetiapine. It usually works on stubborn insomnia."

"An antipsychotic? I'm *not* psychotic." His mother had been prescribed antipsychotics: clozapine, risperidone, olanzapine. When she refused to take her pills, Matthew had pulverized them and mixed them with the fruit juices she liked to sip with chipped ice. The medications had calmed her down, zoned her out. *She* needed antipsychotic medications. He didn't. Kellyce's appearance last night had been a hallucination, but he *knew* she was a hallucination, just as he knew the disappearing room was a hallucination. Unlike his mother, he was able to distinguish between illusion and reality.

"It's a very mild dose," Doctor Ansari said. "I'm sorry, I didn't mean to imply that you have a psychological disorder. Quetiapine is an effective, off-label treatment for insomnia. And you won't be on either of these medications for an extended period. Once you're sleeping at least six hours a night, we'll make a plan for moving forward. A colleague of mine, Dr. Sands, is a sleep specialist in Portland. I'll refer you to him once you're stabilized. In the meantime, drink a lot of water and other liquids. Dehydration sneaks up on you if you're not careful."

Doctor Ansari handed the scrips to Matthew. "Both of these drugs are potent, Matthew, so please respect them. Get into bed as soon as you take them, because soon afterwards you'll be asleep. Do you live with someone who can keep an eye on you?"

"No."

"All right, here's how we'll do it. Each morning, call Sheila with a progress report. If you haven't called us by noon, we'll call you. There's a pharmacy around the block. They'll fill the prescriptions while you wait."

Matthew thought a moment before asking his next question. "Doc, can I ask you a crazy question? Have you ever heard of a scar just disappearing? I had one between my two fingers"—Matthew spread his right index and middle fingers apart, displaying the healthy skin—"but I rubbed some wax on it, and it disappeared."

"Well," Doctor Ansari said, "medicine is filled with stories of spontaneous recoveries that come out of nowhere. Consider a healed scar as a gift and try not to worry. The prescriptions will help with that. Once you're sleeping normally, everything will be better."

· · ·

As Matthew left the office, a text blipped in from Priscilla.

Hey. I'm free tomorrow night. "Let's make some music."

Matthew texted back:

Awesome. My address is 99 Agamenticus Cliff Road 03906. 8 pm?

Priscilla's response came a few seconds later:

I'm always late so 8:30 is more likely. Looking forward.

As he walked to the pharmacy, Doctor Ansari's advice reverberated in his head. "Try not to worry, Matthew." He'd liked the doctor, who'd talked with him, unlike the doctors at the New York clinics who'd asked him one question, sent him on his way with a prescription, and never expected to see him again. Doctor Ansari seemed confident that the medications would help, and Priscilla had seemed enthusiastic about getting together tomorrow night. He'd focus on the positive and hope for the best.

It was always easier to be hopeful when he wasn't inside Kinnawe House.

159

42

Cape Agamenticus, Maine
February 1749

"Use a little wine for thy stomach's sake," Cutler said, quoting 1 Timothy 5:23 and asking Tobias if he'd take a glass of port. Tobias declined, citing the need for a steady hand.

"Miss Edwards," Tobias said, "would you tilt your head back a bit? The stone you wear around your neck must be in the portrait. It is rather unusual."

As Tobias used a fine-bristled brush to capture Mariah's dark eyebrows, he continued to bristle at Naomi's disapproval of his friendship with the Hauers. Unlike the townspeople, who mostly ignored and avoided Tobias, the Hauers had welcomed him into their home.

"The Hauers are not well regarded," Naomi had said the night before. "Your father disapproves of your visits."

"But Naomi, they are our neighbors. We will see them every day until we die. Would it not be best to make peace? It is the Christian thing to do."

"You are better off with friends your own age."

"But there are no people my age on this cliff, and my sister is too ill to receive visitors," he'd replied.

Tobias had wondered whether Naomi thought he should not have befriended a maid. Though Naomi never spoke about her family's wealth or position, she carried herself as a woman of the moneyed class. *What is the import of such distinctions, here at land's end?* Tobias had wanted to ask her.

They were a community of 450 people living on the frontier, where survival and cooperation should take precedence over social class.

• • •

Léana sat mending one of Cutler's handkerchiefs as Tobias worked on Mariah's portrait. As she looked at her husband, an unspoken communication passed between them, similar to their conversation the night before.

Are you certain it is safe to allow this man in our home?

Yes, Cutler. Like Bébhinn, he is an ally.

He is the son of Parthalán's town manager. How can you be sure?

Jerusha, Mariah, and I all sense it. Bébhinn confirms our intuition.

You cannot trust Bébhinn. She is not always sane.

Nonetheless, she retains a vital part of herself that spurs her to help us. And she has promised not to visit while she is overcome by madness. She appears only while she is cogent.

Perhaps it is all a ruse. A trick from the ultimate Trickster. Reverend Edwards warned us to trust no one.

I believe that Reverend Edwards would approve of Tobias Brautigam.

Then I bow to your greater understanding, my angel.

43

Portsmouth, New Hampshire – Agamenticus, Maine

The pharmacist in downtown Portsmouth needed half an hour to fill the prescriptions, so Matthew found a coffee house on Congress Street, the main drag. He ordered chamomile tea and a blueberry scone, which he brought to an outdoor table. It was lunchtime, and Portsmouth was hopping. Everyone, it seemed, was a few years younger than him, and hipper.

His heartbeat accelerated a little as he hit the RETURN CALL icon on Doris Graff's voice-mail message. After the how-are-yous, Doris got down to business. "I've got a PDF of your birth certificate open on my computer, Matthew. You were born in Charleston, South Carolina."

South Carolina? That made no sense at all.

"Are both my parents' names listed?" Matthew asked, tentatively.

"Yes. There's a small anomaly, but an easy explanation, I think."

"My mother is Rose of Sharon Rollins?"

"It says here: Rose of Sharon Pauling."

Pauling, not Rollins. Matthew wasn't surprised. He'd long suspected his mother had changed both her name and his. "But my birth name is Matthew Rollins?"

"Yes. Matthew Thomas Rollins."

Now for the big question. "Was my father's last name Rollins?"

"No," Doris replied. "His name is listed as Jernej Boudreaux." Doris spelled out the name as Matthew wrote it on the receipt from Doctor Ansari's office. Jernej—it sounded Eastern European. Polish? Russian?

"You mentioned an anomaly?" Matthew said.

"Yes, a common one. Your mother signed the birth certificate, but your father didn't."

"Why not?" A stupid question. Doris hadn't been present at his birth. How would she know why his father hadn't signed the birth certificate? "I mean, is there any specific reason why he wouldn't he have signed it?"

"He was probably illiterate. Most illiterate people use an X as their signature, but your father drew a little symbol. It looks like a star."

A star, like the red birthmark on his forearm.

"Can you email me the PDF?" Matthew asked. He wanted to examine how closely his father's scribble matched his birthmark. Among other things.

"I'm not allowed to email personal documents, but I can put a hard copy in the mail to you. Give me your address, and I'll send it out this afternoon."

"I'm living in Maine until the spring," Matthew said. "Can you send it to me care of General Delivery, Ogunquit, Maine?"

"Sure thing."

•

The pills rattled on the passenger seat as he drove north on Route 1. He needed them more than ever, because now he was wound up. Or the opposite—unraveling.

His mother's last name was Pauling. His father's was Boudreaux. So where did "Rollins" come from? Maybe it was his maternal grandmother's maiden name. Or maybe Rose of Sharon had opened a phone book and chosen a name at random. Rollins was neutral. It called no attention to itself. It wasn't ubiquitous, but it was easy to say and easy to forget.

Jernej Boudreaux hadn't abandoned Rose of Sharon and Matthew if he'd stuck around to sign Matthew's birth certificate—or, at least, to make a mark on it.

Matthew pulled into the Starbucks parking lot, picked up the WiFi signal, and typed JERNEJ BOUDREAUX into his phone's Google search box.

The query returned more than 100,000 results. The surname seemed as common in the South as Smith and Johnson in the North. Narrowing the search, he typed "Jernej AND Boudreaux," and Google returned exactly zero results.

He needed an expert's help. He called the reference desk of his local branch of the New York Public Library on West 53rd Street and explained that he was trying to find his cousin Jernej Boudreaux, last seen in South Carolina. The librarian volunteered to check a few databases if Matthew didn't mind holding. Matthew thanked the guy as the perspiration trickled down from his armpits. He double-checked the trickle to make sure it wasn't blood. Fortunately, it wasn't.

The librarian returned about five minutes later. "I'm afraid I can't find anyone with that name in South Carolina, or anywhere else, for that matter. I went back as far as 1900."

Matthew considered possible next steps: calling a university library in South Carolina, searching newspaper archives (did such things still exist?), checking Rose of Sharon's records from the Bedford Hills Institute. Copies of her death certificate and related PDFs were in a folder on his laptop; Patricia Symons had sent them to him after he'd driven to Bedford Hills to collect his mother's ashes and belongings.

He spent another hour researching birthmarks. One of the more reliable medical websites indicated that birthmarks come in many different colors. "Most are not inherited," the website said. "Many folk tales and myths exist about the causes of birthmarks, but none of these stories explain the true causes of birthmarks."

Though some bloggers noted that they had a birthmark similar to their mother's or father's, Matthew couldn't find any evidence to support the idea that birthmarks run in families. Likely, that jagged star on his forearm was simply a random blotch of red pigment.

44

Cape Agamenticus, Maine
March 1749

As Léana and Cutler lay curled around each other, sound asleep, Mariah tiptoed from her room, dressed in black.

The night was as dark as the day had been bright. The full moon had waxed and waned, and the only natural light came from stray moonbeams reflecting off the water.

Cutler and Léana had not been successful in breaching the defenses of the local meeting house. Parthalán's minions guarded the paths day and night, Mariah knew, but even men aided by the Foe did not have supernatural powers and could not see in almost complete darkness. She felt confident in her ability to slip past the guard. Tomorrow morning, she would describe to Léana and Cutler what she'd found on the grounds of, and inside, the meeting house.

Perhaps what she discovered would cause them to return to Northampton. For Mariah, that would be the best possible outcome, though she would miss Tobias Brautigam. She'd slept poorly since her arrival in Cape Agamenticus. Sometimes the air was so thick with rot and stench she found it difficult to breathe. When she stole glances at her neighbors—Charles and Leah Meer, Sebastian and Rebecca Collinge, Michael and Abigail Ayers—she saw glowing red disks reflected in their eyes. Naomi Brautigam's eyes were the most intense scarlet, Gregory Brautigam's a dark brown with a tinge of pink. The one time she'd glanced at Reverend Kinnawe, as he rode through town on a silver-eyed steed, she'd seen two bottomless pits of blackness in his eye sockets. Only in Tobias's eyes did the light of humanity shine. Only when he took her hand, in those fleeting moments on the rocks while the tide was out, did she dare to believe that Léana and Cutler would succeed in their mission.

She suppressed the thought that they might not be welcomed back in Northampton. The Hauers had received not a single message from Reverend Edwards, despite Léana's frequent letters to him.

As Mariah crept toward the dark preacher's house, she felt her progress impeded by an invisible barrier, a rubbery band of air that repelled her with double the force she exerted. Rather than continue fighting it, she skirted the house until she discerned a lantern in the distance. Crouching behind two large boulders that separated the path from the beach, she picked up a stone and tossed it in the direction from which she'd come.

The lantern's light grew brighter as the guard approached. She would slip past him as soon as he moved beyond the boulders that hid her. The guard wouldn't think to look for an intruder between him and the meeting house. Any threat would have to come from outside the perimeter, not within it.

The guard stopped in front of the boulders. Mariah's heartbeat throbbed in her ears.

"Maria, is that you? Have I found you after all these years?"

She had not heard her father's husky voice for more than two decades.

"My darling girl, I thought I would never lay eyes on you again. Where are you? Show yourself."

Mariah peeked over the boulder. The lamplight illuminated her father's face. He'd aged, but there was no mistaking that voice, those eyes, the thick horseshoe-shaped scar on his cheek.

"Papa?"

"Yes, child. Oh, my dearest Maria."

Turn back! Jerusha cried from the bough of a scrub pine. *Mariah. Turn back!*

"Come to me, Maria. Let me hold my own beloved daughter."

Mariah, you must listen to me. Not to him. Mariah, stop. Stop!

Mariah didn't want to stop. Her father was alive! She would not lose this opportunity to embrace the man who'd loved and protected her.

"Maria, what hangs around your neck? What sacrilege?"

"It is not sacrilege, Papa. Reverend Edwards gave it to me."

"Where is the cross I gave you? Your Reverend Edwards has stolen not only your name, but also your faith. He has forced his beliefs on you. He compels you to wear a stone around your neck to remind you that you have no will of your own."

"No, Papa." She wanted her father's approval, but she would not turn her back on Reverend Edwards, would not deny that he'd saved her from humiliation and ruin. All he'd required in return was a conversion to a faith that was not so dissimilar from her own. It had been a small price to pay for survival, for food and a bed in a comfortable house owned by a man of God. "Reverend Edwards saved me from the innkeeper and his wife, who saw me as an orphan to be used and discarded. I accepted Reverend Edwards' offer so that I might live a virtuous life. Now I live with people I love, to whom I am a friend and equal. The stone was a gift from a holy man who was my salvation."

"You must choose, Maria. Do you choose the minister who took your name from you, or do you choose your father, who has loved you since before you entered the world?"

Mariah touched the stone, which had grown icy on her neck.

"That stone holds no good fortune, child. Cast it off and embrace the father who adores you."

Mariah, stop, Jerusha pleaded. *It is a trick! Mariah, do not surrender the stone.*

"Why do you hesitate, Maria? You will obey your father. If you will not, you are no daughter of mine."

"Papa, please don't say that. All these years I have thought you were dead, murdered. To see you alive is to experience a joy I thought impossible." She was aware of Jerusha in the background, but the bird's chattering blended with the sounds of the ocean, rendering her words unintelligible.

"Then rid yourself of that stone and come to me. In exchange, I return the symbol of your faith that your Reverend stole from you."

In the palm of her father's left hand was the cross she'd surrendered to Reverend Edwards on the trip from Providence to Northampton. Mariah, once again Maria, untied the cord that held the stone around her neck and dropped her necklace into her father's right hand. As she was fastening the cross around her neck, she saw that Jesus hung upside down on it.

Léana bolted awake and ran to Mariah's chamber on the second floor. It was empty.

Frantic, she awakened Cutler.

"Cutler, Cutler! Mariah is gone."

"Heaven help us," Cutler said.

45

Agamenticus – Biddeford, Maine

Doctor Ansari hadn't prescribed a party, but a get-together might be just what the doctor ordered. Matthew had considered texting Priscilla and asking her to accompany him to Dave's BBQ, but Dave, the bartender at Julie's, hadn't said "Bring a friend." Besides, going to a party alone would be a better way to meet people. If Priscilla was there, he might stick close to her instead of mingling, bumping fists, and slapping backs.

The address that Dave had given him was 1748 Natas Road in Biddeford. Fearing that he might not be able to get a WiFi signal on his phone, and almost completely ignorant of Maine geography, Matthew had written down the directions in Portsmouth while he waited for his prescriptions to be filled. The route took him due north on Route 1, through Wells, Kennebunk, and Arundel, and then westward. As he headed inland, he crossed over Interstate 95. Almost instantly the well-traveled byways became dark, deserted country roads that required him to use the Civic's high beams.

A large crowd had already gathered by the time Matthew arrived at his destination. In the dark, the not-very-well-lit house looked like a vacation cabin. Matthew parked the Honda on the road—it was the only car among a couple dozen pick-up trucks and SUVs—and followed the glow around to the back of the house.

The heat struck him instantly. The hosts had five fires going, some in metal garbage cans, some in firepits, one in a chimenea. Sweat trickled down his back as he placed a six-pack of beer on the liquor table. Everyone else, it seemed, had brought red wine. A dozen bottles of Egri Bikaver's Bull's Blood sat next to an old-fashioned crystal punch bowl with orange, lemon, and lime wheels floating on top of the punch.

Matthew scanned the crowd looking for Dave. He'd expected the attendees to be about his age, give or take a few years, but they ran the gamut from quite elderly-looking seniors to youngish teenagers. In a far corner, an animal carcass roasted on a spit over a crackling flame. The dripping fat saturated the air with the simultaneously mouth-watering and slightly nauseating scent of roasting flesh.

Dave was suddenly next to him.

"Hey, Matthew. Glad you could make it."

"Hey, Dave. Wow, it's hot."

"I told you to wear shorts and a T-shirt. You're gonna roast your nuts off."

Matthew didn't like wearing shorts and short-sleeved T-shirts around strangers. They inevitably yielded too many questions about the scars, too many sidelong glances from people who wanted to ask but thought it would be impolite to do so.

"There's someone I want you to meet," Dave continued. "He owns this place. Have some punch first, though. It's good."

Using the ladle, Matthew transferred a pint of the punch into a red plastic Solo cup. He sipped at the red glögg tentatively. The punch was heavily mulled with spices, giving it a gritty, almost muddy, texture. He took another sip, and another. The more he drank, the more he liked it. After draining the Solo cup, he went back for seconds.

"Whoa, take it easy, buddy," Dave laughed. "That stuff goes straight to your head."

The warning didn't stop Matthew from refilling his cup to the brim. He sipped on the punch as he followed Dave through the crowd. Matthew seemed to be floating above his own body, watching the crowd as their eyes followed him and Dave. The attention was a bit unnerving but not necessarily frightening. What exactly did he see in their eyes? Delight? Curiosity? Concern?

With each step he felt more woozy. He really should stop drinking the punch so quickly, but those spices, that chewy texture, the heat and the odor ...

The crowd parted to reveal a short, stocky man. Over the man's shoulder, Matthew watched a couple of teenagers turn the spit on which the animal roasted. As the carcass turned, Matthew saw its two heads springing from one neck. Despite being drunk off his ass, Matthew made the connection: The stocky guy was one of the hunters, and he'd shot one of the two-headed goats that hopped from rock to rock on the ocean side of Agamenticus Cliff Road.

Dave made the introduction. "Anton, this is Matthew."

The birthmark on Matthew's arm began to itch intensely. Every scar on his body pulsated. *I have to get out of here*, Matthew thought. *If all my scars open at once, I'll die from the blood loss.*

Anton grabbed Matthew's hand with both of his. Tattoos of barbed wire encircled both of Anton's wrists.

"Welcome, Matthew," Anton said. "We've been waiting to meet you for a long time."

A long time? He'd met Dave just a couple of days ago.

It was hot, so hot. He was drenched in sweat. As he fought to prevent himself from passing out, he was conscious of the crowd drawing closer to him. As the partygoers encroached on his space, Matthew saw a man kneeling in a wooden cage, his hands wrapped around the bars. Triangular face, bushy eyebrows, a widow's peak ... Hair, once blond, now a scraggly and wild gray ...

"I'm ... it's good to meet you, too." Matthew stumbled for words as the memory came rushing back. The man in the cage was Ray. Ray Lonegan. A much older, enslaved Ray Lonegan. "Thanks for inviting me ... It's so hot ... I ... I'm ..." The rotting odor from the roasting animal carcass was threatening to make him vomit. Sweat dripped into his eyes, blurring his view of Ray's face, hands. Those desperate hands, gripping the cage ... That smell of burning hair, as if Ray was roasting on the spit, not the two-headed goat ...

The perspiration soaked through Matthew's clothes. His flesh was burning, his eyebrows and eyelashes being singed. He wanted to kick off his sneakers, strip naked, do anything to cool himself down. As he pushed his sleeves up from his wrists to above his elbows, Anton's eyes focused on Matthew's red, throbbing birthmark.

All hell broke loose. Anton slid backward, away from Matthew, as if a gigantic hand had pushed him. The crowd, which had gathered so close to Matthew, dispersed, attempting to get as far away from him as possible.

Matthew dropped to the ground, unable to speak or move.

"Get him out of here," Anton hissed at Dave.

"What's wrong, Anton? I don't get it," Dave stammered.

"You fool. It's red. Not black. You've brought the Enemy here."

Matthew, unable to move, lost consciousness.

•　•　•

The deck emitted a heavy creak. Matthew's eyes popped open and he sat up in bed, startled. Next to a half-drunk bottle of water, the two pill bottles sat on the night table. He hadn't bothered to screw their caps back on, though he didn't remember taking the pills. The last thing he remembered was being drunk and passing out at the BBQ—

A shadowy figure sat on one of the deck chairs, his back to Matthew. A hunter, with a rifle crossed over his lap. Matthew shifted his eyes to the French doors, which were unlocked and cracked open to let the night air circulate through the bedroom.

Overcoming the near paralysis brought on by stark terror, Matthew lowered his feet to the bedroom floor, planning to drop to his knees, crawl from the room, and flee the house. As soon as his foot touched the floor, the hunter dissipated into the night.

Matthew felt a cold hand on his shoulder.

"I'll be back, son," a voice whispered in his ear.

Matthew tiptoed toward the French doors. Dark figures danced on the beach. Flames from autumn bonfires illuminated the shadows, revealing the faces of his neighbors, the old cranks who'd glared at him through their houses' filthy rear windows. Squinting to focus, Matthew saw that the men were not dancing. One was mounting a ram with long curling horns. Another man, with a heavy red beard, thrust into a beast with two heads, one of a jackal and one of a hyena. A third, over-muscled man mounted a pig covered with the thorny spikes of a porcupine. In the center of the orgy, a woman writhed in ecstasy as a two-headed goat licked her with both tongues. The church bells clanged in the howling wind.

Among the copulating, a woman with frizzled red hair walked in an expanding spiral, sowing seeds from a sack suspended from her shoulder.

A voice called him from the hallway. Sleepwalking, he entered the parlor as footsteps padded behind him. Matthew turned to look in the direction from which he'd come. Behind him, Doctor Ansari emerged from the master bedroom.

"The medication isn't working, Matthew," the doctor said. "You need a much stronger dose." From the pocket of his lab coat he retrieved the two pill bottles that Matthew had left on the bedroom nightstand. He handed the bottles to Matthew. The directions on each read TAKE 60 TABLETS BY MOUTH AT BEDTIME.

"Sixty tablets? That's the entire bottle." He tried to remember his mother's heaviest dose. She'd taken two tranquilizers three times a day. Six pills a day total.

"If you want to sleep, you need to take your medication." Doctor Ansari's tone had hardened. "I'll get your water bottle from the bedroom."

"I do want to sleep," Matthew said, dumping all the pills into his hand.

From the corner of his eye, Matthew saw a dove fluttering on the top of the bookshelf and sensed someone approach him from behind. He turned toward the approaching figure. With a fast slap Helen Crowe knocked the pills out of his hand. They fell to the floor, scattering in all directions.

Doctor Ansari stomped out of the bedroom. As he approached, Matthew saw the face of Bartholomew Dubh.

The dove flew off the bookshelf and alit on Matthew's shoulder.

"Good evening, Léana," Dubh said. "Strike two." He reached into the pocket of his lab coat and threw a handful of dirt into Helen's face.

Helen screamed as the dove flew off Matthew's shoulders, aiming its beak at Dubh's left eye.

"Next time you won't have her to protect you," Dubh said, smacking the bird away and dissolving into a reeking thick liquid that disappeared through the cracks in the floorboards.

"Let's get you back to bed, Matthew," Helen said, taking Matthew's arm.

Matthew felt as though someone had stuffed cotton into his mouth. "Helen, what happened? Your face. It's burned ..."

"I'll be fine." Helen turned to the dove, which had perched on top of the bookshelf again. "Help him sleep, Jerusha."

Helen put her arm around Matthew's shoulders and guided him to the bed. The dove fluttered onto the curtain rod in the bedroom. Matthew was asleep within seconds. His last conscious thought was his father's promise to return.

Good. He had a lot of questions to ask Jernej Boudreaux.

Part IV
The Voice of Silence

46

Matthew picked up his phone from the nightstand. The time was 11:02 A.M. By his estimation, he'd been unconscious more than 13 hours.

He remembered the visions from the night before: the beach orgy, the redhead sowing the seeds, his father's promise to return. It was all psychological detritus, his subconscious chewing on his problems while he slept.

But the BBQ was real—wasn't it? He hadn't imagined that. He remembered driving to Biddeford, getting drunk on the red-wine punch, catching a glimpse of Ray Lonegan, passing out.

He walked to the back of the house and caught a glimpse of his car in the driveway, undamaged. He hoped he hadn't driven home drunk, which would have been beyond stupid. Maybe Dave had driven him home. But how would Dave have known where he lived? And that guy in the cage—he couldn't possibly have been Ray. Could he? Impossible. Matthew had been drunk off his ass. Only a drunk would imagine a man trapped in a cage at a midnight BBQ.

As if fainting at someone's BBQ wasn't bad enough, tomorrow night Matthew would have to face the additional embarrassment of seeing Dave at Julie's Bar and Restaurant, when Matthew sang and played during the early-bird special. He'd apologize profusely, hoping Dave would forgive him for making a complete ass of himself.

In the kitchen, he peeled the foil off a Special K protein bar. The bar, dense and solid when he'd purchased it a few days ago, had become mushy and salty, as if it had been soaked in seawater. Matthew tossed it into the trashcan after one bite.

He decided to go to the gourmet mini-market in Ogunquit Center to get something to eat, along with snacks to share with Priscilla, who'd promised to arrive around 8:30. It was a good excuse to get out of the house, clear his head, and try to enjoy the cool, bright day.

He returned to the bedroom to collect his phone and his wallet. His medications were missing. He thought he'd left the two pill bottles on the nightstand, but they were gone.

He checked the bathroom—the living room—the spare bedroom—the kitchen and dining room—the storeroom with the wax + signs that had healed one of his scars—his backpack—his computer case—the trashcans—the utility closet—but the bottles had disappeared.

He slipped his feet into his sneakers, opened the back door of the house, and caught his breath. The landscape had been transformed into a still from *The Wizard of Oz*. Blooming goldenrod stretched for what seemed like miles in all directions, covering the land beyond the house and crowding both sides of the road. The scudding clouds floated by in heavy relief against the pure, unbroken blue of the sky, their edges sharp, not fuzzy, like the cobwebs in the cellar.

He checked the Civic, but the pills weren't in the glove compartment, the trunk, the door pockets, or anywhere else. He wondered if forgetfulness was a side effect of the medications, which, in retrospect, he probably shouldn't have taken after drinking so much alcohol. He didn't even *remember* taking the medications after his as-yet unexplained return to Kinnawe House the night before.

On the positive side: The night had been bizarre, but he'd slept. Apparently, a benzodiazepine and an antipsychotic medication had worked for him, even if they'd upped the ante on his nighttime visitors. It was tempting to let a doubt niggle through: *I'm psychotic, which is why the pills worked*.

Before driving to Ogunquit, he decided to check on Helen. Somewhere in the back of his mind he was worried that she'd been hurt, somehow.

She was sitting, her back to him, on a low canvas chair on her stretch of beach.

"Helen?"

Helen turned toward him. The right side of her face was mottled, burned, blotchy.

"Helen! Are you all right?"

"My face? It's a rash that comes and goes. Nothing to worry about."

Matthew tried not to stare. Layers of skin had apparently been stripped off Helen's face; the injury looked very painful. He flashed on a dream in which Doctor Ansari (or was it Bartholomew Dubh?) threw dirt at her.

"You were in my dreams last night, Helen. I took a couple of sleeping pills, and you made a cameo appearance." No need to mention the dirt-throwing.

"Aren't you too young for sleeping pills?"

"Yes, but I've had terrible insomnia for the last couple of weeks. I've had hardly any restful sleep, and my brain was starting to go haywire. I got the prescriptions yesterday."

"What medications are you taking?"

Matthew named them, adding, "Somehow I already misplaced them. I searched the house from top to bottom and I can't find them anywhere."

"As luck would have it, I have those same prescriptions. I'll give you some of mine. Forgive me for not inviting you inside, Matthew. The house is a bit untidy."

Forgive me for not inviting you inside. His mother had used the same phrase with anyone who rang the doorbell of the Bala Cynwyd house: meter men, tax assessors, Jehovah's Witnesses. It was the hoarder's mantra, a strategy to prevent the world from looking down its collective nose at the pigsty of your home or, worse, calling the authorities. Helen might be a hoarder, too, Matthew thought. She'd been living here forever, and she'd had decades to fill her house with junk. But no matter. He was happy to have her friendship and her low-key New England kindness. If she was too embarrassed to invite him into her house, then so be it. He was more than happy to chat with her outdoors.

Matthew helped Helen to her feet. She stumbled as she took her first few steps but quickly regained her balance.

As Helen entered her house, Matthew's phone dinged, alerting him to a new voice mail message. It was from Josh, calling to check in.

As Matthew awaited Helen's return, he called Doctor Ansari's office.

"Hi, Sheila. It's Matthew Rollins. I just woke up. I slept all night."

"That's fabulous," Sheila said. "Doctor Ansari wants you to take the same dose every night for a week. Then we'll schedule a follow-up."

Matthew thanked Sheila and broke the connection.

As he accepted a handful of pills from Helen, he asked, "I know this is a long shot, but have you ever heard of a man named Jernej Boudreaux? Or Ray Lonegan?"

"Can't say that I have," Helen replied. "Friends of yours?"

"Not really."

"Oh. Relatives of the Fordes?"

"I was hoping *you* could tell *me*."

Helen shook her head. "Tales of my omniscience have been greatly exaggerated. I'm just an old lady who lives alone by the ocean."

•　　•　　•

As Matthew walked back to Kinnawe House, Helen looked up at the spruce. Jerusha was nestled there, napping after a long and difficult night.

She hated lying to Matthew, telling him half-truths and untruths and withholding information. But he was ill, and adding to his burden might only weaken him further. Sharing her knowledge *might* give him strength, but more likely it would send him into a tailspin, which was exactly what Parthalán wanted.

What was Parthalán up to? Was the profusion of goldenrod intended as a barb? He knew she was unaffected by it, and she knew that goldenrod had almost killed him when he was a boy. Were the weeds Parthalán's way of taunting her with the fact that he was growing stronger while she became weaker?

The pills she'd given Matthew were made of sugar. She'd send Jerusha to the house again tonight to make sure he got a few hours of sleep, though spending another night in the house would sap even more of Jerusha's strength.

But they had no other choice.

47

Rye, New Hampshire

Priscilla Sargent checked her hair and makeup in her bedroom mirror. The acne years hadn't been kind to her skin, but she'd camouflaged their remnants with a light application of foundation.

She opened her jewelry box to retrieve the dove necklace. She'd placed it in the top drawer, but it wasn't there. That was strange, because she was careful about her jewelry, even the cheap stuff. She had two choices: Rip her room apart until she found it and risk being very late to Matthew's, or admit temporary defeat. She chose the latter.

Dressing up for a guy felt good. Most New Hampshire guys didn't expect more than jeans and a revealing top. She'd never visited New York, but reruns of *Sex and the City* had taught her that New York women don't leave the apartment without full hair, makeup, and accoutrements. Besides, she wanted to look her best for Matthew. She'd checked out Matthew's Facebook page and downloaded "Silver Horses," and she loved it.

After stuffing a bunch of sheet music into her backpack and finding her keys, she tried to open her bedroom door. The doorknob was frozen. As she fought with it, she felt ridiculous—a 24-year-old college graduate working at a supermarket while she looked for a full-time job in her field, a woman who wasn't a weakling, struggling with a doorknob.

Frustrated, she banged on the door.

"Mom! Dad! I'm locked in!"

Her parents should have heard her. Her bedroom was at the top of the staircase. The bottom stair ended at the living room, where her father was glued to the TV. Her mother was there, too, curled up with a romance novel. But though Priscilla shouted and pounded on the door loud enough to wake the dead, her parents didn't respond.

"This is ridiculous," Priscilla said, as if someone were there to hear her. She retrieved her phone from her backpack as Henry, her parakeet, blinked at her. The phone's battery was fully charged, and the screen showed four bars.

She dialed the downstairs landline. She tried six times, but the call did not connect.

She decided to resort to a tactic she hadn't used since her teens. Her bedroom was located over the front porch. A decade earlier, when her parents had been uncooperative in terms of curfews and such, she'd sometimes slipped out of her bedroom window onto the porch roof, and then jumped, tucked, and rolled her way to freedom. The same escape method was still available to her.

She attempted to raise the sash, but the window wouldn't budge.

Priscilla took a step back and examined the window. Locked. *Duh.*

She unlocked the window and tried again, but it seemed to be glued shut. She moved to the second window, and the third. All were frozen to their frames.

Her parents couldn't have locked her in. The mere idea was ridiculous. Even when she was a rebellious teenager, they hadn't done anything drastic, just the typical parental yelling, grounding, lecturing, and withholding of allowance.

She peered through the window, wondering if her folks had gone outdoors, but she saw no one in the front or side yard.

She'd been looking forward to her date with Matthew (too strong a word; *get-together* or *hang-out session* was more accurate), and she had no intention of accepting imprisonment in her own bedroom. Fortunately, her father, an aficionado of rescue/reality TV, had equipped every room in the house with a fire extinguisher. She retrieved hers from the closet and used it to smash out the windowpane.

With the butt of the fire extinguisher she pushed the remaining shards of glass from the window frame. She pulled a blanket from her bed and placed it around the bottom of the frame. She didn't need a shard of glass in her rear end.

The ground seemed to be much farther from the roof than it had been during her adolescent dives from parental repression. Thinking "bruises heal," she tossed her backpack to the ground and jumped, tucking and rolling as she'd learned in gymnastics, in the long-ago days when she'd been petite.

The house's front door was locked. She rang the doorbell once, twice, three times, but nobody answered. She retrieved her phone from her backpack: No bars.

Whatever. She'd text her parents later, from Matthew's place. The Sargents had a general but loose policy of keeping one another posted on their comings and goings.

She climbed into her Nissan Versa and pressed the button to start the ignition. *Click.*

"Unreal," Priscilla muttered. Her father had replaced the battery six months earlier. Now it was dead again.

Her father's truck and her mother's car were both parked in the driveway. The family often used one another's vehicles, taking whichever one was closest to the street. It was Thursday night, a work night. Mom and Dad wouldn't be going anywhere, so she got behind the wheel of her mother's Buick, which was old enough to require an old-fashioned key. She turned the key in the ignition. The response was another tinny click. She tried again. Another click, another dead battery. Unbelievable.

Her father's truck wouldn't start, either.

She looked at her watch. She was running late, which she'd warned Matthew about, but now she had no way of getting to Matthew's place. She cut across the lawn to her next-door neighbors' house and rang the doorbell.

Wanda Vernon, a couple of years younger than Priscilla, answered.

"I can't find my parents, all the cars are dead, and so is my phone," Priscilla explained, requesting use of the Vernons' landline. In the kitchen, she dialed Matthew's number, which she'd memorized. She half expected him not to answer.

"Hello?"

"Hey, Matthew, it's Priscilla. I'm calling from my neighbor's house."

"Oh, hey. I didn't recognize the number."

"My phone doesn't work and my car is dead. All of this has happened literally in the last ten minutes. I'm bummed that I can't come. I have the sheet music ready and everything."

"Well, your timing is perfect. I'm at the Kittery outlets, killing some time. The WiFi at the house is super-unreliable, but looks like I can get a signal here. How about I pick you up?"

Priscilla already loved Matthew's speaking voice—resonant, a little raspy—and his chivalrous offer melted her a little more. "But won't that be a pain for you? You'd have to drive me home later."

"It's no biggie. Give me your address. I'll GPS it."

Half an hour later, when Matthew pulled up, Priscilla and Wanda were sitting on the Vernons' front porch. Priscilla sipped a Coke as Wanda, whose parents were the opposite of uptight, smoked a joint.

As Priscilla and Matthew walked to the car, Priscilla turned and winked at Wanda. Despite the obstacles placed in her path by an imprisoning bedroom and non-starting cars, she had very pleasant expectations for the evening.

• • •

As Wanda walked to the front door of the Sargents' house and rang the doorbell, she saw that one of Priscilla's bedroom windows was smashed.

Chester Sargent answered the door.

"Hi Chet," Wanda said. "I'm surprised you're home."

"Why? My truck's in the driveway."

"Yeah, but Priscilla thought you and Lisa were out. She said your truck and Lisa's car have dead batteries. Her car does, too. She tried calling you, but she couldn't get a signal on her phone. She asked me to tell you she'll be home later tonight. A friend came to pick her up."

"All right. Thanks, Wanda."

Chester Sargent removed his keys from the key rack and went out to his truck, which started without a hiccup. Lisa's Buick started right up, too, as did Priscilla's Nissan.

48

Cape Agamenticus, Maine
Late March 1749

"Please, Mrs. Ayers, you must calm yourself." Mrs. Moira Feeley spoke in her most soothing tones. "We will get you through this. Breathe deeply. In ... then out ... In ... then out ..."

Mrs. Feeley's goal was simple: to prevent Abigail Ayers from damaging her womb during labor. As for saving the baby, the case was hopeless.

She poured a small amount of valerian root potion onto a spoon and forced it between Abigail's lips.

"Mrs. Feeley—my baby. Will he live?"

"My dear, you don't do the child any good by working yourself up. You must stay calm."

"He's not alive, Mrs. Feeley. I don't feel him moving."

"The fever will run its course, Mrs. Ayers. Maintain control of yourself and you will live to see another day." Mrs. Feeley was stalling. Within minutes the potion would take effect, and her patient would be unconscious.

"I don't want to live if my baby doesn't. Where is Michael? I need my husband." Abigail clutched Mrs. Feeley's hand, and as sleep overtook her, Abigail's grasp weakened.

Now nature would run its course. Mrs. Feeley readied the tub into which the unborn child would pass.

When it was over, Mrs. Feeley examined the fetus: a large boy with overdeveloped hands floating in blood, guts, and placental fluid.

Five minutes later, the town's two deaf-mutes, James and Elias Featherstone, entered the room without knocking. They donned gloves and transferred the tub's contents into a waterproof satchel. In the blink of an eye, they were gone.

Mrs. Feeley shook her head. Something was wrong. Very wrong. Until two months ago, she'd delivered one healthy, robust child after another. But over the past eight weeks, she'd seen more miscarriages and stillbirths than she'd seen in decades of midwifery. It was as if a poison had entered the water, a toxin that deformed children in the womb and caused them to be expelled with the foulest stench Mrs. Feeley's nostrils had ever encountered. The expectant women of Cape Agamenticus almost always remained robust throughout their nine months. Since February, however, their faces had taken on a greenish pallor.

She wasn't the only one who'd noticed. Nervous whisperings and ripples of fear had spread across the town.

The time had come to discuss the situation with Reverend Kinnawe.

• • •

The men sat in the parlor of Kinnawe House in their usual formation. Parthalán had called the meeting to address Mrs. Feeley's concerns and ask pointed questions, but Michael Ayers spoke before being spoken to.

"How is this to be explained, Parthalán?" Ayers demanded. "Our babes are dying before they are born. Our healthy wives are reduced to skin and bones. Women refuse to be with their husbands for fear of conceiving, and men are spilling their seed into the ocean rather than taking their wives. Meanwhile, the catch decreases by the day, and the waves become more threatening."

Trying to wrest control of the conclave from Ayers, Parthalán directed a question to Sebastian Collinge. "Collinge, how go the fields?"

"Poorly," replied Collinge. "A black blight is killing the seedlings. The flowers in the women's gardens are drooping and losing their petals. At the house of Thaddeus and Thomasina Cornwall, all the early roses have dropped from the bushes and are replaced with thorns the size of a man's hand."

"The animals fare no better," said Charles Meer. "The cows will not eat the grass, and the pigs refuse their slop."

"It is *them*," Michael Ayers spat. "*They* bring this plague. All was well before their arrival. And yet you permit them to live among us, Parthalán."

"The Hauers have no power in this town," Gregory Brautigam said.

Ayers jumped to his feet. "You, Brautigam! You attempt to defend them while *your* son befriends them and consorts with their maid. Did you bring your boy here to spit in our faces, to aid the efforts to kill our children and ruin our wives?"

"Enough," Parthalán said. "Michael, sit."

Ayers stomped to Parthalán's chair, inclining his face to within an inch of Parthalán's. "You cannot deny what is happening. Even your own wife cannot conceive."

"I said *sit*," Parthalán ordered through gritted teeth. The force of Parthalán's breath knocked Ayers to the floor and pushed him into a corner as the asp slithered down the inside of Parthalán's pant leg, darted to the corner, and wrapped itself around Ayers' ankles.

"You must not be too hard on him, Parthalán," Brautigam said. "Abigail is speechless with grief, and the loss of his child weighs on him."

"It is well for you to speak, Gregory," Ayers snapped. "You, whose children are alive."

Parthalán stood, his tight black preacher's robes accentuating his height and physique. "Do you think I am oblivious to what is happening before my eyes? You come into my house and accuse me of permitting the cankers to live among us. Are you so blind that you do not see the forces they represent? Those forces are not dispersed with a snap of my fingers. If you think this situation is not as frustrating to me as it is to you, then you are much mistaken. But I will not be insulted in my own home, Michael Ayers, not after all I have done for you and for the people of this community. It was I who ordered Tobias Brautigam brought here, and no one in this room, nor anyone in Cape Agamenticus, will interfere with him. Is that understood?"

All the men nodded in acquiescence—all except Michael Ayers. "Yes, you have done much for us, Parthalán," he said. "But we too have sacrificed. We have held to our end of the bargain, and we expect him to do the same."

"You are a fool indeed if you think that *we* can dictate terms to *him*," Parthalán replied. "Now, begone, all of you, and await word from me."

It took all his resolve not to lift Ayers by the neck from the floor and choke the life out of him. Killing Michael Ayers might cow the townspeople into obedience, but the murder of one so popular might initiate, or stoke, conversations about rebellion.

•　　•　　•

Parthalán spent the evening in his library, poring over the grimoires he'd collected from libraries and monasteries across Europe and Asia. To quell his fury, he sipped a strong cordial. Michael Ayers, who'd sworn an oath of allegiance, behaving like a spoiled child in counsel! Accusing Parthalán of not protecting the community, when Parthalán was their only mediator with the entity that protected Cape Agamenticus, the entity to whom he'd pledged his soul in Northampton.

He would deal with Ayers in good time. For now, he must set his own plans aside, must restore the town's health as the events he'd placed in motion continued to play out.

He flipped page after page of vellum, looking for a solution other than the one he knew would work best.

In the morning, Parthalán summoned Sebastian Collinge to Kinnawe House. Sebastian's face went white as Parthalán explained the requirement.

49

As Matthew drove along the winding shore road toward Kinnawe House, Priscilla analyzed his profile. *Good bones*, her mother would say.

"Do you write, too, or just sing?" Matthew asked. Priscilla shifted her eyes. Best not to be caught checking out his profile and the scars on his hands and neck. She wanted to know more but didn't want to ask questions.

"Mostly sing, but sometimes write," she said. "At this point, it's lyrics without music. Personal stuff." Ex-boyfriends had asked to read her poetry. Fearing half-hearted praise or—worse—indifference, she'd refused. Matthew was different, though. If he asked, she'd say yes.

"Have you ever sung a duet?" Matthew asked.

"No," Priscilla replied. "And to be totally honest, I'm much more comfortable singing in a choir. That way, there's a bunch of other people to carry me if I'm having a bad day." The adjectives that her choir director used to describe her voice were *strong, distinct, crystalline*. She longed for *magnificent, inspiring, moving*.

"I think you're being modest," Matthew said. "It's refreshing. Every musician in New York thinks they're utterly, absolutely fantastic. Then again, if you don't have high self-esteem, no one's going to have it for you. The business is brutal, to say the least."

As Matthew turned off the shore road, Priscilla noticed the church on her right. She'd dated a guy from Wells, had driven up and down this road hundreds of times, but she'd never noticed the church before. As Matthew parked the Civic on the gravel driveway at Kinnawe House, she commented on the profusion of goldenrod.

"It's sort of pretty for a weed," she said. "But if my father lived here, he'd be spraying it with Agent Orange until it's completely annihilated. He has a bug up his rear end about weeds. Like they're a personal insult."

Matthew chuckled. "Come round the back. The view is awesome."

Backpack in hand, Priscilla followed Matthew around the corner of the house. He bounded up the three steps onto the deck. As she tried to place her foot onto the first step, she felt as if she'd encountered a wall of thick gelatin.

She tried again, lifting her foot and trying to place it on the stair. The resistance seemed to increase as her foot hovered in the air.

A fearful person might have thought the house was trying to repel her, but Priscilla Sargent was not a fearful person.

"Hey, Matthew, little help?"

Matthew reached for Priscilla's outstretched hand. As soon as their hands made contact, the invisible wall dissolved. She ascended the steps and, as soon as she saw the ocean panorama, forgot about the rubbery air block.

As Priscilla admired the view, including the dock and the little rowboat bobbing on the waves, Matthew unlocked and pushed open the kitchen door. The odor of rot and feces almost made Priscilla faint. Retching, she turned away from the house, summoning every ounce of her self-control to prevent herself from upchucking.

The wind shifted, the smell dissipated, and Priscilla's nausea abated. From inside the living room, Matthew threw open the French doors, inviting Priscilla to make herself comfortable while he arranged a tray of munchies.

Matthew *looked* clean and smelled fresh (she was a sucker for Old Spice), but if he was a typical guy, he didn't have much experience with cleaning products. She stepped into the living room, prepared for a bachelor-style pigsty, but the room was immaculate, a combination of opulent and comfortable, the bookshelves lined with dusty and ill-arranged but expensive-looking figurines and leather volumes.

Nonetheless, there was something unsettling about the room. The floorboards were soft and spongy, as if they were rotting and she'd end up in a dank, moldy crawlspace if the wood gave way underneath her weight.

She began scratching her wrist; her dove tattoo had become intensely itchy. All around her, the walls—without a crack or flaw anywhere—seemed to ooze a viscous moisture that clogged her ears, nostrils, and throat. She retrieved two Benadryl tablets from her backpack, swallowed them dry, and scanned the room again, trying to distract herself from the throbbing behind her right eyeball, which felt like an ice pick trying to gouge her eye from the socket.

"Matthew? OK to play the piano?"

"Sure," came Matthew's voice from the kitchen.

Priscilla tapped out "Chopsticks," trying to ignore the welts breaking out on her wrist. The piano's notes were clear and pristine, though she detected an underlying minor chord in that most mindless of bright, major-chord melodies. Maybe the piano hadn't been tuned in a while, or, like everything else made of wood in an oceanfront house, it had warped. Either that, or her allergies were messing with her hearing. Wouldn't be the first time.

Matthew entered the upper part of the living room carrying a tray on which he'd placed cheese, crackers, a bottle of chardonnay, two bottles of Aquafina, and two wine glasses.

Priscilla didn't feel like eating, but her lack of appetite wasn't a female hang-up about not wanting to eat in front of a guy. Something in the house was making her feel nauseated, the Benadryl wasn't helping, and she didn't want to spew all over the black-and-white spotted area rug.

As she scratched at the welts on her wrist, the spots on the rug resolved themselves into an image of a goat's head with a five-pointed star in the center of its forehead. When she turned to face the image head-on, the goat's head disappeared.

Dismissing her imagination and not wanting to be rude, she sat across from Matthew and picked up the cheese knife. As she cut a wedge off the blue cheese, bugs crawled from the center of the block. Priscilla dropped the knife with a snort of disgust. Bile traveled from her stomach halfway up her esophagus.

Matthew gave her a puzzled look.

"Sorry," Priscilla said. "I've heard that blue cheese has bugs in it, but I never actually *saw* the bugs before."

"Blue cheese? I thought I bought cheddar."

Indeed, a block of buttery, mite-free Vermont cheddar sat on the cutting board.

Between what had happened at home and what was happening at Kinnawe House, Priscilla was beginning to regret accepting Matthew's invitation. The ice pick continued to gouge at her eyeball. The Benadryl, usually her savior, was not helping at all. Maybe she should admit she was feeling nauseated, or pretend she'd received an emergency text from her mother, and ask Matthew to take her home.

As she looked at Matthew, her escape plan melted away. The dimple in his right cheek was to die for.

"I guess I'm not super hungry," she said. "But it was sweet of you to go to so much trouble."

"I'm just glad you're here," Matthew said, and the delightful buzz created by the compliment almost neutralized her nausea. "You said you brought music? Let's start with what you know, and then sing some of my stuff?"

"I brought some of my choir songs. I thought they'd help you figure out what my voice can do, and what it can't." She flipped through the sheet music and handed a page to Matthew. "Henry likes this one."

"Henry?"

"My parakeet. If he likes the song I'm singing, he sits on his perch and chirps along. If he doesn't like it, or if he thinks I suck, he plays with his toys and pays no attention to me. Then I know I need to practice, or I'm out of my league."

Matthew skimmed the music and the lyrics. "'A Mighty Fortress Is Our God.' My mother was never big on church, so I don't know much about hymns. Let me play it through once to get the hang of it, and you come in the second time. Cool?"

Priscilla nodded as Matthew sat on the piano bench, placed the sheet music on the stand, and positioned his hands over the keys. Priscilla stood next to him, scratching her wrist on the back pocket of her jeans. Her itchy wrist was unbearable, torturous.

"Here we go," Matthew said. "One, two, three, ..." Matthew began striking the keys, but no sound came from the piano.

Matthew looked at Priscilla as if to say, WTF? "Let's give that another try. One, two, three ..." Again Matthew struck the keys, and again the piano made no sound.

"Weren't you playing Chopsticks before?" Matthew asked. As Priscilla nodded, he used his index finger to strike the first few measures of the ditty. The bright, tinkling notes floated through the room.

"I don't know why the piano is wonky all of a sudden," Matthew said, shrugging. "I'll play it on the guitar instead."

His guitar was resting against the couch. Matthew slung it around his neck, turned toward the sheet music, and began strumming. The guitar cooperated, and the hymn's opening notes floated through the room. Matthew got to the end and, without missing a beat, started playing the hymn again.

Priscilla inhaled to fill her lungs with air and started singing. "A mighty fortress is our God, a bulwark never failing; Our helper He, amid the flood of mortal ills prevailing ... For still our ancient foe doth seek to work us woe; his craft and power are great, and armed with cruel hate, on earth is not his equal ..."

She sang the lyrics, but she made no sound. The words were sucked into a black hole as they left her throat.

Her head was pounding. She was having trouble breathing, difficulty expelling the air from her lungs.

Priscilla waved her hand, trying to wipe away their third false start. She felt as though someone with a branding iron was trying to sear the tattoo off her wrist. "Nerves," she said. "Can we try one more time?"

"We've got all night. Try to relax. I know you're going to be great." Matthew tapped his foot three times and began strumming the introduction. Priscilla opened her mouth and began singing, "A mighty fortress is our God," but no sound emerged.

Struggling to ignore not only the itching wrist and the ice pick behind her eyeball but also the signals from the reptilian side of her brain screaming *Get the hell out of here*, Priscilla shuffled through the other sheet music. "How about this one instead?"

After skimming the melody line and lyrics for "How Great Thou Art," Matthew strummed the intro, and Priscilla began singing the first verse. Her lips formed the words, she vocalized through her vocal cords, but she made no sound.

Fighting back tears, Priscilla began gathering her sheet music and stuffing it into her backpack. "Matthew, can you take me home? I'm not feeling so good ... I'm breaking out in hives ... I think I'm going to throw up ..."

As Priscilla zipped up her backpack, she glanced at the carpet. This time a snake slithered under the couch as the black-and-white dots on the carpet resolved themselves into three words:

GET OUT WHORE

Priscilla shrieked and ran for the closest door. In the driveway, next to Matthew's silver Civic, was her Nissan Versa. She had no idea how her car had gotten to Matthew's driveway, and she didn't care. The key waited in the ignition. She started the car and peeled away from Kinnawe House, gas pedal to the floor.

Thirty minutes later, she ran up the stairs to her bedroom and flipped the light switch on.

On the wall facing her, someone had spray painted in gigantic red letters

DON'T GO BACK

Something chunky sat in the center of the "o" in "go." Henry's head had been nailed to the wall with a thick metal spike.

50

Cape Agamenticus, Maine
Late March 1749

Abigail Ayers lay in bed with the full knowledge that she was to blame for the death of her child. Michael, trying to soothe her, held her hand.

She'd made a mortal error in speaking with Léana Hauer in York Village. Yes, she'd rejected Léana's offer, but she hadn't told her husband about the encounter. Worse, for a few brief seconds, she'd considered accepting Léana's help. Now she was being punished for her betrayal.

She knew why so many women had miscarried in the past two months, why so many babies were born misshapen or missing limbs. The protector was displeased. He had no right to be angry, but she did. She'd sacrificed her son Calvin to ensure the safety of Cape Agamenticus and its people. But He was never satisfied. He was forever demanding more, more, more.

"Where is our baby, Michael? I need to hold him."

"Parthalán has arranged for the burial, dearest. Holding the boy would only increase your grief."

"Please, Michael, I must say farewell to him. To tell him I loved him." She wanted to see him whole, once, before Parthalán cut the heart from his tiny chest. To hold him and offer a silent, secret prayer that his soul would not be punished because of her actions.

"I will ask Parthalán," Michael promised. "Now, rest and regain your strength. Parthalán has said you need not attend Friday services."

On Friday night, as Abigail tossed in bed, stuporous but not unconscious, the screams carried on the wind from the meeting house. The rituals were sometimes noisy, but such prolonged shrieks were rare. She wondered if some traitor was being punished, and she feared the traitor might be Michael himself. If her husband was taken, his death would be her fault, too. She curled herself into a ball, reached for Mrs. Feeley's bottle of liquid sleep, and poured its contents down her throat, hoping she would not wake in the morning.

But she did wake twelve hours later to a bright, clear day. In recent weeks, the ocean had been choppy, disturbed, menacing. Sitting up in bed, she saw a calm, serene Atlantic. Her maid, Bridget, came to check on her and said that Michael was out on the water. He and the other fishermen had gone out expecting a vast haul.

"It does feel as though something has changed," Abigail said.

By noon Abigail felt well enough to get dressed. She moved to the parlor, where she took scissors to the needlepoint pillow she'd been crafting for the baby. Most of her nausea had subsided and her womb had stopped throbbing, no small thanks to Mrs. Feeley's concoctions. But the lack of pain felt like further punishment. Not only had she lost her child, she'd also lost any physical reminder of him.

A long-haired woman sat huddled and shaking on the beach.

Abigail opened the door and ran to her friend. Rebecca Collinge, wailing, threw herself into Abigail's arms.

"Rebecca, my dear, what has happened?" Abigail already knew the answer. A woman cried with such abandon for only one reason.

Rebecca's sobs became wails. "Last night Parthalán took my Hester."

And the sea had calmed, and the fishermen were optimistic.

Rebecca took Abigail's hand. "Abigail, can you forgive me?"

"Forgive *you*, Rebecca? Your loss is unspeakable."

"Forgive me for not comforting you after Calvin was taken. It was for the good of the community, I thought. One must be sacrificed for the benefit of the many. But who will lose a child next, Abigail? We have made a pact with the devil, and we are forever powerless to save our own children."

Abigail thought, but did not say, *No. We are not powerless.*

●　　●　　●

The next morning, Léana found an envelope on her kitchen floor.

She hoped the letter would provide information about Mariah, who hadn't returned home after her disappearance. Léana tore open the envelope and read:

I want to know where my child's remains are kept.
Meet me tomorrow afternoon in York Village.
—A.A.

At last, after months of trying—a breakthrough, praise God. Léana searched the house for Cutler. He was reading his Bible in a second-floor room.

As he read Abigail's letter, a team of horses pulled up to the house, and Gregory Brautigam climbed down from the carriage. Léana ran down the stairs and threw the door open before Gregory knocked.

"Mr. and Mrs. Hauer, will you come with me? There is bad news, I am afraid."

"What? What is it?" Léana asked, trying to remain calm. Cutler, who'd followed his wife down the stairs, placed his arm protectively around her waist.

"Please, come with me," Brautigam said. "You know I am unable to harm you."

Cutler nodded, and they climbed into Brautigam's carriage, where they held hands and rode in silence. From the carriage window, they saw the large group that had congregated near the meeting house.

Léana felt her heart ripped from her chest as the carriage approached the crowd, which stared at Mariah hanging on a cross at the side of the road.

51

Kinnawe House
Agamenticus, Maine

Matthew awoke to the flapping of wings. He was in bed, but he didn't remember crawling onto the mattress and losing consciousness. But he must have taken Helen's pills because he'd gotten, what, six or seven hours of sleep? After Priscilla stood him up the night before, he'd distracted himself from his hurt and disappointment by trying to write. No catchy melodies or hooks had come to him; the lyrics he'd scribbled on a napkin were doggerel that rhymed "eyes" with "paradise." He hadn't had the heart to practice "Just Give Him Your Number."

In his dream, Priscilla had fled the house and zoomed off in her car. Half-remembered delusions tumbled in his head, mixing with hard-to-snatch memories from the last few nights: the two-headed goat on the spit—Anton and Dave—the redheaded woman on the beach—Ray Lonegan—Dr. Ansari, Helen, Bartholomew Dubh, the dove—his father, Jernej Boudreaux—his dead twin.

He must have pigged out after swallowing the pills, because a serving tray on the coffee table held a block of moldy cheese and two wine glasses with a few dregs in each.

As his head cleared, he realized the details weren't adding up. If Priscilla hadn't wanted to hang out, she would have texted him. She probably *had* tried to call or text him, but the house's spotty WiFi hadn't sent the message through.

He looked at his phone on the nightstand. It showed no bars, as usual, but a new text was time/date stamped the previous evening:

6:58 P.M.

Hi Matthew. Sorry for the short notice but I can't make it tonight. My old BF is back in my life. Please don't take it personally, it's complicated. Wishing you all the best. P.

A polite brush-off: better than being ghosted, but still depressing.

To locate a decent WiFi signal, he walked into the field of goldenrod across Agamenticus Cliff Road. There he dialed Doctor Ansari's office and reported that he'd slept through the night. He also left a message for Josh, blathering about the beauty of the Maine coastline and reminding him that he welcomed visitors at Kinnawe House. He didn't mention that he'd prefer them to be living rather than dead.

He walked to the end of the road, hoping to find Helen relaxing on the beach or working in her garden, but she was nowhere to be seen. He didn't want to knock on her door and disturb her if she was napping.

Sitting on Helen's beach chair, he placed a call to the Bedford Hills Institute. After a series of transfers and holds, he got through to the nurses' station. He gave his name and asked to speak with Doctor Mavro. The nurse told him the doctor spent mornings at the Institute and afternoons at his private practice.

"Can I make an appointment to see him tomorrow?" Matthew asked.

"You would need to call his office," the nurse said. "He doesn't see patients at the Institute, unless the patient is a resident here."

"My mother was Rose of Sharon Rollins. She died there a couple of weeks ago. I don't need a lot of his time. Five minutes would be enough. I didn't get a chance to speak with him when I picked up my mother's effects. Please, I would really appreciate it."

Matthew heard the clickety-clack of a keyboard.

"Doctor Mavro gets in about 9 A.M. and leaves around noon," the nurse said, quasi-whispering. Matthew wondered if she'd looked up his mother's file. "He's usually in his office from 9 to 10, so if you're waiting for him at 9, you might get a few minutes with him. Prepare your questions in advance, and don't keep repeating them after he answers them. He's not the most easy-going person in the world."

It would be a ten-hour round trip, but it would be time well spent if he returned to Maine knowing exactly how his mother had died and whether the Institute's records held any information about his father and his twin. He'd already checked the PDF file of the paperwork that Patricia Symons had emailed him. It hadn't revealed much beyond her date of death and its cause: cardiac arrest.

• • •

Around 4:30 that afternoon, Matthew washed his face and rubbed some goop through his hair. He wrapped his entire body, except for his hands and face, in thin gauze. Next he donned black jeans and a heavy long-sleeved black T-shirt. Sometimes scars ripped open while he performed, and he didn't want to ooze blood during his easy-listening set at Julie's Bar & Restaurant.

On the drive to Julie's, he practiced his apology to Dave, the bartender. He had to thank Dave for getting him home and apologize for getting sloppily drunk and passing out. He didn't know Dave well, or at all. Was he the type of guy to laugh it off, to joke with Matthew about being a pussy for not being able to hold his liquor? Or would he think Matthew was a pathetic loser?

Matthew hauled his equipment from the Honda to an empty corner of the bar. As he set up, Dave walked into the bar from the dining room. Matthew inhaled and approached him.

"Hey, Dave," he said. "How's it going?"

Dave didn't make eye contact. "Fine."

"Hey, listen. I'm sorry about the other night. That punch really hit me hard. I hope I didn't make a total ass of myself. I really appreciate you bringing me home."

Dave cocked his head. "Huh?"

"You know, the BBQ."

"The BBQ?" Dave's eyes were two skeptical slits: *What the hell are you talking about, man?*

199

So the events at the BBQ were just another dream, like the orgy on the beach. Just a day earlier he'd consoled himself that though he might be hallucinating, he was able to differentiate between dreams and reality. That consolation was no longer available.

"I smoked some heavy pot—must have imagined it," Matthew lied quickly.

Dave looked at him as if to say, *Back off, freak. This weird conversation is over.*

As Matthew tried to get as far away from Dave as possible while remaining in the same room, the hostess—Julie herself—sat a fifty-something couple at a four-top. Within fifteen minutes, most of the tables were occupied. The crowd was mostly nondescript except for four well-dressed, yuppy-ish guys who sat at a table in the corner.

Matthew picked up his guitar and stepped up to the mike.

"Good evening, ladies and gentlemen. I'm Matthew Rollins, and if someone sang it anytime between 1950 and today, there's a good chance I know it. Any requests, please write 'em on the blackboard."

•　　•　　•

At the end of the set—which had been neither a roaring success nor a dismal failure—the four well-dressed young guys approached Matthew en masse.

"Good set, man," said one with fiery red hair.

"Nice work on 'Light My Fire,'" said the biggest of the guys, a muscular bull with a shaved head. "Morrison isn't turning in his grave."

"Thanks a lot," Matthew said, delighted to have been compared favorably to Morrison.

"Where'd you go to school?" asked the third guy. He had round, hypervigilant eyes.

"Susquehanna," Matthew said. "Are you guys musicians, too?"

"Yeah," said the fourth guy, who had a terrible complexion and seemed older than the other three. "Juilliard."

"You guys live near here?" Matthew asked. "Or just visiting?"

"We're locals," said the redhead. He stuck out his hand. "Chuck."

The other guys introduced themselves: Mickey, the muscleman; Trey, of the deer-caught-in-the-headlights eyes; Greg, the pockmarked.

"We'll be back tomorrow night to hear Carl and the Cavemen," Mickey said. "They play in the back tent on Saturday nights. You should come and check them out."

"That sounds awesome," Matthew said. "I'm living here until spring. I definitely want to catch the local bands."

"Cool," Trey said. "We'll save a seat for you."

As Matthew loaded his guitar into its case, a finger tapped his shoulder. Matthew turned and found himself face to face with Josh, who pulled him into a bear hug.

52

Cape Agamenticus, Maine
Late March 1749

Gregory Brautigam helped Cutler take the girl down from the cross. Mariah's eyes, wide open, had changed from their striking milky gray to a flat, lifeless brown. The protective talisman that had hung from her neck was gone.

The townspeople stepped aside to allow Cutler and Gregory to carry the body to Brautigam's carriage. Léana insisted on riding in the carriage with Mariah's body back to the house on the spit. Gregory left his horses there, promising to retrieve them later. "I am sorry for your loss," he said to Cutler and Léana, who had no words.

Gregory returned to the church grounds; Parthalán would require his help in calming the crowd. The cross on which Mariah had been crucified, made from the trunks of two thin pines, lay hacked to pieces at the side of the road. Charles Meer explained to Gregory that two townsmen had run home and returned with axes, intent on destroying the cross as quickly as possible.

The two deaf-mutes, James and Elias Featherstone, began placing the remains of the cross, along with the metal spikes that had pierced Mariah's hands and feet, into burlap sacks.

"This is a direct insult," said a truculent voice in the crowd.

"Who speaks?" Parthalán asked. "Come forward."

Lucas Pendergast, a purveyor of tobacco and spirits, separated himself from the throng.

"You must explain this, Reverend," said Pendergast, a tall, thin man with white hair and a matching beard. "Sebastian and Rebecca gave their child, but the sacrifice has had no effect. The girl was not accepted."

"You were all present when He accepted the offering," Parthalán replied calmly.

"Then what is the explanation?" asked another man. "No person in this town would crucify the maid in this manner."

The crowd nodded its agreement. Crucifixions had been performed in Cape Agamenticus, but those crucified had been hung upside down.

"It is the new people," said Pendergast. "The Hauers. They sacrificed one of their own."

"That is impossible," Gregory said. "You all saw the woman's reaction. Her husband was no less shocked."

Michael Ayers spoke. "Unless we have a traitor in our midst—"

Parthalán interrupted. "There is no traitor."

"Let me speak, Parthalán. Unless we have a traitor among us, only one person can have done this." Michael pointed his finger at Brautigam. "His son. Tobias, the only person in this town, other than your wife, who does not participate in our services."

Gregory turned toward Michael. "Do not speak nonsense, Michael. My son is not capable of such brutality." He had wondered why Parthalán required him to call Toby to Cape Agamenticus. Here was the beginning of an explanation.

"Everyone has seen him and the girl together," Ayers said. "I myself have watched them climb onto the rocks at low tide so that they may sit side by side."

"If what you say is true," Brautigam said, "then there was an affection between them, not a motive for murder."

"No, Gregory," said Lucas Pendergast. "You must answer for this. You bring your son here but separate him from the community. Have you forgotten your oath? Do you now betray us with the help of a useless dandy from Boston? Was this act intended to undo the offering of Hester Collinge?"

Brautigam surveyed the crowd and sensed a seething rage about to erupt. He wondered if he and Naomi, who stood next to him, would be torn to pieces on the spot. A part of him wished for the release that a quick death would bring. Hell awaited him, but he would no longer have to live on Earth, listening to his daughter's screams at night.

"All of you, return to your homes," Parthalán ordered. "The perpetrator will be found and dealt with. In the meantime, look around you. Except for this unexplained event, the town is healing, not ailing. Men, look at your women. Do you not see the health in their cheeks? Those of you with pigs—go home and feel the sows' bellies. You will feel the new life within. Farmers—go to your fields and note how your seedlings grow."

"We will do that, Reverend," said Lucas Pendergast. "But you must deal with that boy. Either he becomes one of us, or he leaves."

Gregory felt the electricity in the air. Nobody told Parthalán what to do, and no decision was taken in Cape Agamenticus without Parthalán's consent.

As the crowd dispersed, Gregory looked at Parthalán, who stood with his arms folded across his chest, surveying the crowd as if searching for a victim to eviscerate. *They know that Parthalán can hear the beating of a hummingbird's wings five miles away*, Gregory thought, *and yet they whisper among themselves.* He lived in a town populated by fools who would someday receive their just desserts. As he himself would.

• • •

That evening, Parthalán summoned Gregory to Kinnawe House.

"Bring your boy to the service tomorrow night, Gregory. It will be faster and less painful than usual."

"It was at your behest that I brought Tobias here. Was it for this purpose? To scapegoat him?"

"Gregory, you cannot believe that anyone else can have crucified the maid. Nobody would dare to execute a girl in that manner on this land. We know that Cutler and Léana Hauer are incapable of such an act. There is no other suspect. Your son is the murderer."

Gregory lowered his head and stared at the floor. A long, shadowy black tube hissed at him and slinked into a corner.

Tobias—good-natured since birth, the very image of Eliza—a murderer? Impossible. This was Parthalán's doing, part of a larger conspiracy that Gregory could not fathom. But he was in no position to save his own son. Not without forfeiting his own life, as well as Emma's and Naomi's.

"Tomorrow I will bring Naomi and Patrizia to market," Gregory said. "Tobias will be alone in the house. Take him while we are gone. But I beg you, please do not make me witness his torments."

"The people require you to prove you care more about them than you care about a traitorous child. You must attend."

Gregory nodded. "I will do what I must."

When he arrived home, he walked past Naomi and into his bedchamber, where he shed silent tears. As much as Parthalán would enjoy attaching Tobias to the Catherine Wheel and pulling him apart, Gregory knew that Parthalán's greater, unspoken joy was Gregory's continued debasement.

His existence was unbearable.

* * *

As Gregory left Reverend Kinnawe's house, the snake slithered out of the corner, over Parthalán's boot, and up the inside of his pant leg, curling itself around his waist and sinking its fangs into his abdomen. The exquisite venom coursed through Parthalán's veins as he considered his triumph. His plan was coming to fruition. Time mattered to his congregation, but not to him. A few months were but a drop in the ocean of the eternal life for which he'd exchanged his soul.

As he removed a book from a shelf, Emma ran into the library and threw herself onto her knees.

"Parthalán, my brother is innocent. One of your guards murdered the Hauers' maid. I watched him do it through the parlor window."

"Impossible, Emma." She'd been eavesdropping, an activity at which she excelled. "No guard would commit such an act without my consent."

"You know all my secrets and all my lies, Parthalán. You know I am speaking the truth."

"The people demand action, Emma."

"Tell me what I must do to save my brother, and I will do it. You already own my body. Protect my brother, and I will give you my soul as well."

* * *

An hour later, Parthalán entered his wife's chamber. "You heard the commotion above?"

Emma nodded.

"Tobias now lives in the attic. He will be fed and clothed, but you will not be permitted to see him. If you are with child within three months, he will be allowed to leave the house for a short time each night. After the children are born, he will be brought to Boston, where he will live for the rest of his days. He need never return to Cape Agamenticus. His fate rests in your hands, Emma."

As Emma nodded her agreement, Parthalán knew that the child he longed for would soon be his.

Naomi's suggestion had borne luscious fruit. He must find a way to reward her. He considered visiting her in her chamber to bestow the sexual ecstasy that a lustful woman needed. The act would increase Gregory's humiliation. But Parthalán had no desire to diminish his own gratification. Naomi would give herself to Parthalán, as the law required, but she would be thinking about Gregory.

53

Route 1, Maine

As Josh settled himself at a table, Matthew asked Dave for a Sam Adams for Josh and a ginger ale for himself. Matthew pulled a twenty out of his wallet, but Dave waved the money away.

Matthew set the drinks on the table and took the chair facing Josh. It seemed impossible, but Josh looked even more Hollywood-handsome than he had at Café 862 just a week earlier. He'd shaved his beard and let his hair grow. His luxuriant locks now grazed the back of his neck and called attention to his chiseled face and a dimple in his chin that Matthew had never noticed before. Which was odd, Matthew thought. How do you know someone for more than two decades and not notice a not-prominent but not-insignificant facial feature?

Josh took a long swig of the Sam Adams. "I decided to take the day off and surprise you. I have a car, I might as well use it." Josh was looking around the bar, grimacing. Matthew wondered if he was comparing Julie's to the trendy Manhattan dives frequented by Wall Streeters slumming it for an evening, trying to show their dates, and the world, that they were Regular Guys.

"How'd you know I was playing here?" Matthew asked.

"Facebook."

Matthew hadn't posted anything on his Facebook page about playing at Julie's, though, in retrospect, he should have. And Julie's Bar & Restaurant didn't have a website; Matthew had checked. But Dave or another young staffer probably posted to a Julie's Facebook page, and those posts had made their way to Josh's laptop. Given the infinite twisting of Facebook's tentacles, it seemed the most likely explanation.

"So, what did you think?" Matthew asked, hoping for a compliment.

"All good."

Matthew had prepared the questions he planned to ask Doctor Mavro tomorrow morning at the Bedford Hills Institute. The doctor would not be able to answer all of his questions, but Josh and his father might.

"Your timing's good, Josh. There's something I've been meaning to ask you about the day of my accident. I wanted to ask you before I left the City, but that night at Café 862 ended up being a little weird."

Distaste flashed across Josh's face. "Wouldn't you rather forget about it? I mean, it's four years ago now."

"I've tried, Josh, but it never goes away. It just keeps coming back. And each time it comes back, it gets uglier."

"Didn't you work it out with your shrink?"

Work it out—as if it were a knot in his shoelace, or a kink in his neck, instead of getting stabbed 140 times.

"I thought I did, but I didn't," Matthew said. "That's what I'm trying to do now. The day it happened—were you at my house?"

"That's a bizarre question. You know I was in Europe with that girl, I can't even remember her name. We were in Switzerland, or maybe Italy."

"That day ... the day I got home from school ... I thought I smelled your cologne in the house. That cologne you wear all the time. The cologne you're wearing now. I smelled it in my house."

"Maybe your mother had some guy over."

"She never got over Ray leaving. She had zero interest in men after that, and she never let strangers into the house."

"I don't know what to tell you, Matt. You probably imagined it."

"I didn't imagine it. I recognized the smell because it's the cologne you always wear. I've smelled it in Kellyce's apartment, too."

"What are you saying, Matt? That I had something to do with you getting attacked?"

"Of course not. But I need to understand *why* it happened. What I did to deserve it."

"Buddy, I wish I had the answers for you, but I don't. You really have to pull yourself together. You don't look so great. Your skin looks kinda yellow."

"I know. My diet's been terrible, and I think I'm losing weight. I get almost no sleep, and I have zero appetite."

"When Kellyce said you were sick, I thought she was exaggerating. You know how dramatic she is. But now I see that she wasn't."

"How often do you see her?"

Josh started picking at the Sam Adams label. "We've been hanging out occasionally. You and I agreed that it's cool, right?"

"It's totally fine," Matthew said. "What's done is done. I'm over it."

He wasn't over it. If he was over it, would he be dreaming about Kellyce driving to Kinnawe House and fucking his brains out?

"Well, I'm glad you can make peace with it before you die," Josh said.

"Die?" Matthew laughed uncomfortably. "I'm 28 years old. I'm planning to stick around a while longer."

"You'll be dead in a few months, Matt. I thought Kellyce told you."

Matthew remembered: The apparition of Kellyce had made a similar prediction before the bloody corpse handed him a pair of knitting needles, but she hadn't put a time frame on it.

"We talked about it," Josh continued. "We agreed that you deserve to know. I paid for the abortion, Matt. She didn't want that kid, and neither did I."

Though the bar had filled with baseball fans cheering at the big-screen TV, Matthew felt as though he and Josh were alone in a black hole. Scars on his feet, legs, arms, back, and neck popped open, one after another. The blood pooled on the table and on the floor at his feet.

"Are you saying what I think you're saying?" Matthew stammered. "It was you who got Kellyce pregnant?"

"Well," Josh said, "she wasn't sure if it was you or me."

Matthew stood up. He felt light-headed from the blood loss. Not knowing what to say or what to do, he limped into the men's room, where he applied layer upon layer of toilet tissue on top of the gauze to stanch the blood flow. When he returned to the bar, Josh was gone and Dave was mopping up the blood.

"I already moved your equipment into your car," Dave said. "Just go home, all right?"

And don't come back.

. . . .

Matthew heard the gunshots near the end of the road as he was unloading his equipment from the Civic. He hurried inside and locked the door. He'd never felt so unworthy of a heartbeat, not even while recuperating from the attack and wondering if he should let himself die instead of listening to the voice in his brain encouraging him to stay alive.

What a fucking night. A mother who haunted him. An ex-girlfriend who'd told him he was broken, rotten, diseased. A father who'd abandoned him. A dead twin. A caretaking job that made him feel suicidal. And twenty-three years of friendship with Josh, vanished in an instant.

54

The storm clouds over the meeting house did not bode well, Jonathan Edwards thought as he entered the building.

Even at the height of his influence during the Great Awakening, the Foe had found voices in the community. Many of those voices belonged to men and women who felt their livelihood threatened by Edwards' call for austerity and self-denial, but others were equally critical for different reasons. Edwards' grandfather, Solomon Stoddard, had indulged in a liberal interpretation of scripture, and his parishioners had become lazy. Those same soft, pampered members of the congregation chafed under Edwards' unwavering insistence on a return to spiritual purity. His booklet, *A Humble Inquiry Into the Rules of the Word of God, Concerning the Qualifications Requisite to a Compleat Standing and Full Communion in the Visible Christian Church*, was an affront to those who believed that Edwards' inflexibility and intolerance were diminishing the size and prestige of the congregation.

Now the whispers, which had begun reaching his ears in the months before he secured the land in Cape Agamenticus for Gregory Brautigam and banished Bébhinn and Parthalán to the frontier, seemed to be gathering into a well-organized chorus plotting his dismissal. Edwards knew that denying membership to the last two applicants had won him no friends. "We do not need a congregation weakened by the admission of those who lack direct experience with God," he'd lectured those who criticized his decision. Those same critics had also taken him to task for censuring the young people caught reading unsuitable books like those that Edwards had watched Parthalán read underneath the tree.

As he sat on a pew making notes for a sermon, the front door creaked.

Nathaniel Davenport, one of his most vocal detractors, strode up the aisle toward him. Edwards steeled himself for a confrontation.

"Good day," said Davenport. Not "Good day, sir," or "Good day, Reverend."

Edwards stood but made no move to shake the man's hand.

"Good day, Mr. Davenport."

The interior of the meeting house darkened as the storm clouds drifted and blocked the sun. Large raindrops began splattering the windows.

"Perhaps it is not such a good day after all," said Davenport.

"God sends rain to replenish the fields. A day with rain is no better, and no worse, than a day of sunshine."

"It seems that you and I agree on very little, Mr. Edwards."

"We agree that God is great."

"And does not God ask that we gather to celebrate and worship Him? And yet, you reject those who wish to do exactly that."

"God has standards, Mr. Davenport, and so do I. Would you have a highwayman join the congregation simply because he desires it? Would you have me welcome a whore who regrets the life she has chosen?"

"We do not face such decisions, Mr. Edwards, because almost nobody wishes to join this congregation. Or perhaps you had not noticed."

"I have noticed, Mr. Davenport, and I am not concerned in the least."

"Two days ago you rejected two applicants who, with all due humility, sought to join us. Your treatment of them was high-handed and dismissive. The members of this congregation grow weary of your arrogance and conceit."

"You dare speak of arrogance and conceit? You come into the house of God to berate me. When last I checked, Mr. Davenport, you are not the leader of this congregation. I am. And I will thank you, and the persons of whom you speak, to concern yourself with your families and your businesses, and to leave spiritual matters to me."

The meeting house shook as a lightning bolt struck the spire.

Davenport stared at Edwards. "Do not forget, Mr. Edwards, that you remain in your position for one reason only: Until today, you have had more supporters than critics. The scales have now tipped against you. Expect to receive a delegation from the congregation in the coming week."

After Davenport departed, Edwards noticed that the man's shoes had scuffed the floorboards.

He defiles the meeting house, as he defiles the congregation, Edwards thought, taking a handkerchief from his pocket and dropping to one knee to scrub away the scuffs. After eliminating the second scuff mark, he folded his handkerchief and returned it to his pocket.

As he returned to making notes for his sermon, he felt a crawling movement against his chest, as if his handkerchief had taken on a life of its own. He removed the handkerchief and unfolded it. Two locusts sat in the handkerchief, twitching their antennae.

Shocked, Edwards dropped the handkerchief. The locusts took wing and darted at his head as he fled toward the bell tower. They pursued him with the fury of tiny demons, buzzing in his ears and biting at his face.

Edwards threw open the door to the bell tower and stumbled up the staircase. Trying to protect himself from the attack, he climbed the ladder that gave access to the bell, pushed open the trap door, and pulled himself through. He slammed the door shut behind him.

The buzzing ceased. Edwards looked to his right and to his left, running his hands through his wig to reassure himself the insects were gone. Then he doubled over in pain, knocking his head against the bell. He began dry heaving as his stomach prepared to expel its contents. He grabbed his belly and began vomiting a steady stream of locusts, which turned into a buzzing swarm that engulfed the meeting house.

55

The House on the Spit
Agamenticus, Maine

Helen sat on the beach, hoping the sunlight would help cure the gunshot wounds. In the distance, the house that Parthalán Kinnawe had built and defiled seemed to spring up from the land like a fortress, impregnable, eternal.

She'd dug the bullets out of her calf, arm, and shoulder. The bullets were made of bone, pieced together according to the specifications in one of Parthalán's books, and they'd burst into fragments when they pierced her skin. She wondered whose bones they once were—Abigail's, Emma's, Naomi's? Some of the shards had worked their way into her bloodstream, causing nausea, weakness, and blurred vision.

Taking corporeal form was taxing. Flesh was so weak, so easily damaged. Leaving her spit of land at night, when the men were at their strongest, made her even more vulnerable. She'd listened for Matthew's car and walked up the road to ensure he'd arrived home safely. As he brought his equipment into the house, she fled back to her own. If she hadn't already had one foot on her property when the bullets hit her, she would have dissolved into the night, never to return to the cliff.

She was weakening, and Matthew's defenses were slipping, while those intent on destroying him gathered strength.

Two large honeybees buzzed past her and flew into a knot in a pine at the land's edge. The bees did not concern her. If anything, they hinted at the lingering benevolence protecting her. If the insects had been wasps or hornets, she would have seen defeat as imminent.

Bébhinn, you have helped me in the past. You must now help again. Jerusha and I cannot succeed on our own.

A hand touched her shoulder. Helen turned and saw that her longtime friend had answered her summons.

Bébhinn kneeled on the sand and removed the leather pouch that hung around her neck. From it she retrieved a vial filled with a thick liquid the color of verdigris. She rolled Helen's pant leg up and began dabbing the gunshot wound with the liquid.

"You are to blame for these wounds, Léana," Bébhinn said. "You and Jerusha know better than to venture out after dark. Yet you persist in doing so."

"You can do what we cannot, Bébhinn. The unresolved state of your soul does not confine you to either light or dark. You must help Matthew at night so that we may conserve our strength."

"Night often brings madness. A madwoman cannot be responsible for someone so vulnerable."

"The end is near, Bébhinn, and I am not a whit closer to breaking the cycle of destruction and madness that began with your lies."

"The cycle began long before my birth, Léana. You know that full well."

"You brought it to the Colonies. You infected Reverend Edwards' house with it. You killed the wrong child. Now your issue returns to bring about the end of the line."

"Why do you torment me, Léana? There is no way to know which child will move toward the light and which toward the darkness. We must choose in a moment, and then live or die with our decision."

"I do not seek to recriminate with you, Bébhinn. You deceived Reverend Edwards so that you and your son would not live in squalor and misery. Were I in your position, I might have done the same. But Jerusha and I have been fighting this battle for too many years. I long to be with Cutler and Mariah again."

"Yes, and when the battle is over, you will ascend, knowing that you have done good in the world. Meanwhile, I will forever remain in-between and alone. My anguish is only made worse by the occasional sanity that reminds me of my suffering all over again."

"What keeps you tethered here is your unwillingness to break from Parthalán. Your soul will never find peace if you remain his ally. After all this time, you must realize this."

"I am not his ally. No one can accuse me of that."

"But you have not taken arms against him since 1749. Jerusha and I have done all the fighting. We could have ended this battle more than a century ago, were it not for your reluctance to aid us."

"I killed one of my children, Léana. Would you also have me destroy the other? Would you take arms against *your* own child?"

"If Parthalán were my child, yes. It is Parthalán who keeps you imprisoned here."

"I promise you, Léana, I will not permit him to destroy the boy, just as I would not permit him to destroy Tobias. Heed those honeybees, Léana. They may be your salvation."

• •

Later that morning Jerusha came to her. As Matthew slept, she reported, he thrashed and kicked and walked the house, talking to the unseen. His illness was getting worse, and unless they found a solution soon, all hope would be lost.

As Jerusha settled herself for a nap in a high bough, Helen watched the honeybees buzzing past her toward their hive in the pine. Attuned to the rhythms of the ocean and the winds, Helen sensed a change in the atmosphere. The bees' buzzing was louder, higher-pitched, insistent. A dozen bees hovered in the air about two feet from her beach chair. They fluttered their tiny wings to stay aloft and in place.

The bees flew up the road, toward Kinnawe House, demanding she follow them.

Helen paused. She'd been tricked before. She would not be fooled this time. But Bébhinn, whom she trusted, had suggested that the bees would play a role in what was to come.

Helen followed the bees onto the shore road, where they veered off into the woods. She'd been in that section of the woods once before.

A sunbeam penetrated the trees, illuminating the bees as they fluttered near the ground. Helen cleared away the brush on the forest floor. She picked up a rock and used it to break up the dirt and clay. About a foot down, the rock struck something hard. She worked it out of the ground.

She tugged the stone from the earth, turned it over, and saw the rune that had been ripped from Cutler's neck. A fragment of the leather cord remained inside the loop attached to the stone.

Helen clutched the stone in both hands and held it to her heart. As visions of Cutler swam through her head, the bone shards in her bloodstream seemed to dissolve.

Léana followed the bees back to the pine, looked into the beehive, and saw a large honeycomb. At Bébhinn's urging, the bees had given her what she and Matthew needed to defeat Parthalán.

56

Bala Cynwyd, Pennsylvania
Four Years Earlier

Matthew graduated magna cum laude from Susquehanna University, but Rose of Sharon didn't attend the commencement service. Josh's parents, Kathryn and Toby, had volunteered to transport her, but she'd declined, saying she preferred not to leave the house. So Matthew received his sheepskin, along with the Rowland J. Nantes Award for Excellence in Music Theory and Performance, while his mother remained in Bala Cynwyd.

He hadn't spent much time at home during his college years, preferring to live in Selinsgrove, Pennsylvania, through the summer and working as many hours as possible. When he went home for a week during the winter and spring breaks, he spent most of his time putting Band-Aids on the house's most pressing problems: a rodent-infested basement, gutters hanging at right angles to the roofline, a crumbling chimney.

Now Matthew and Josh were ready for their move to the big city, and by "big city" they didn't mean Philadelphia. Josh, who'd been elected senior class president, had landed a job with a Wall Street investment bank. It was tough to map out a New York musical career from Selinsgrove, so Matthew's "plan" was to get to Manhattan, work in some restaurants, develop some contacts, and figure it out one step a time. Musicians advertised for bandmates all over the Web and the underground press. He'd join a band or two, develop his chops before striking out on his own. Bands didn't last more than a couple of years anyway. Too many egos in conflict.

Before moving to New York, Matthew had one thorny issue to resolve: his mother, who seemed to be losing larger chunks of her mind each day.

During his last weeks at Susquehanna, he'd developed a pragmatic strategy for solving the problem. He'd go home to Bala Cynwyd for the summer, and he'd visit every social service agency in Montgomery County until he found the right institution. Rose of Sharon's only valuable possession was her ratty house, but the land, on Philadelphia's prestigious Main Line, was worth a hundred times more than the house itself. The state would take the house and the land, and in return his mother would have a decent room and all the tranquilizers the nurses could inject into her veins.

It was the right decision for him. The best place for her. She'd have full-time care. He'd have the freedom to live his life without a millstone around his neck.

While Matthew sought care for his mother, Josh would be backpacking through Europe with Stephanie, a finance major he'd met in his senior seminar. *What a difference a few years of college makes*, Matthew thought as he drove back to Bala Cynwyd. *Josh used to be the shy one. Now, four years later, aspiring models throw themselves at him.*

Terrence Cierna, the medieval studies professor who'd befriended Josh, had helped Josh come out of his shell. Matthew had sometimes seen the two of them in unexpected places—deep in the library stacks, four or five stories below ground, where works of medieval scholarship gathered dust; walking the streets of Selinsgrove early in the morning as Matthew and his bandmates drove home from a gig; sitting in Josh's car in the sweltering student parking lot. Matthew had found the friendship a bit strange, wondering why a young, handsome medieval studies professor would take such an interest in the non-scholarly Josh.

If Cierna had hoped for something more than an academic relationship, he must have been disappointed as Josh morphed into the most eligible bachelor on campus. Toward the end of their junior year, Matthew looked up from a plate of the cafeteria's nauseating Swedish meatballs and thought with a shock: *When did Josh become so handsome?*

•   •   •

As he pulled up to the house on Merion Lane, Matthew was shocked by its deterioration since his last visit. Two panes of glass were shattered in one of the first-floor windows. The screen door hung askew from its hinges. The driveway, which had been breaking apart for years, wasn't so much a driveway now as nuggets of asphalt. The height of the grass reached the window sashes.

Matthew got out of the Civic, stretched, and made his way through the jungle of the front yard. He banged on the front door to announce his arrival, but his banging went unanswered.

Using his key to unlock the door, he pushed his way inside. "Mom? It's Matthew. I'm home. Mom? Are you here?"

Matthew negotiated his way around the stacks of newspapers—the dirty clothes piled to the ceiling—the canned goods so old they were bursting with noxious gases—and knocked on the door of his mother's bedroom.

"Mom? Are you in there? Did you remember I was coming home from college today?"

The bedroom door swung open. Rose of Sharon wore a white garment that looked like several pillowcases sewn end to end. Her long, stringy black hair framed her face. The stench of rotting food filled the air.

A shadow behind Rose of Sharon receded as Matthew's nose picked up the familiar scent of Josh's favorite cologne.

"Mom? Is someone in there with you?"

Rose of Sharon stepped out of the room and pulled the door closed behind her.

"What month is it?" she asked.

"It's May. Mom, is Josh in your bedroom?"

"No, Matthew, I'm not in the habit of bedding your friends. Did you come home to start arguments with me? I would rather have a *nice* visit."

"I want a nice visit, too, Mom." He wasn't lying. He'd been hoping against hope that they'd be able to laugh and talk as they had when he was in grade school. He wanted to remember that version of his mother when he thought about her permanently institutionalized. Imprisoned. Drugged. Discarded.

Getting her to the care facility was going to be the tricky part. She didn't like to leave the house. If he couldn't trick her, he'd have to crush a few of her tranquilizers, add the powder to her fruit juice, carry her to the car.

Worst-case scenario, orderlies might have to come to the house. Forcibly remove her from her home.

"Mom, are you hungry? How about I order the Hawaiian pizza that you like?"

"That would be lovely, Matthew. It's good of you to think of your mother, for once in your life."

·   ·   ·

After they ate the pizza, Rose of Sharon returned to her bedroom while Matthew unpacked. He hadn't accumulated much during his college years, except for a guitar and a case that he'd bought in a second-hand shop in Harrisburg. He carried the guitar to his bedroom, along with four Hefty bags filled with dirty clothes.

He threw himself onto the twin bed in which he'd slept since he was four years old. He awoke—an hour? two hours? four hours?—later to find his mother sitting on his bed and stroking his hair.

"Hi, Mom."

Rose of Sharon continued to stroke his hair. "Sleep while you can, Matthew. Soon you won't be able to sleep at all."

"Mom, please don't say that. It almost sounds like a curse."

"It's in you, Matthew. It comes from your father. The world stops when you can't sleep. Nothing makes sense."

Matthew raised himself onto one elbow, trying to gauge his mother's lucidity. She'd just said two words she almost never said: *your father*. She wasn't screaming or throwing things. She seemed calm, rational. This was his chance to learn more about the man whose existence she'd always refused to discuss.

"What's his name, Mom? Where is he now?"

"He watches me, Matthew. Every minute of every day. He watches you, too."

"Mom, I'm 24 years old. I have a right to know who he was. *Please* tell me."

"After all I've done for you." Rose of Sharon's voice climbed an octave. "All you care about is *him*."

When Rose of Sharon started getting worked up, it was best to divert her attention.

"Let's talk tomorrow instead, Mom," Matthew said. "Why don't you go back to your bedroom? I'll bring you some warm milk." He'd add a couple of shots of cognac, or a few of her pills, to help her sleep.

Rose of Sharon picked up the Rowland J. Nantes Award from the bookshelf. It glinted in the bright moonlight that filtered through the filthy window.

"I got that award for being the best music student at the university," Matthew said. "I sang at the ceremony, and I got a standing ovation. It's a musical note called an eighth note—my name's engraved at the bottom—"

"I thought you were the good one, Matthew. But you aren't. All these years, you tricked me."

Rose of Sharon used the eighth note to slice Matthew's stomach open.

It wasn't the eighth note. It was a knife with a long blade.

"Mom! Stop! Stop!" Matthew whimpered, raising his hands to protect his face as his mother slashed at it. For the last decade she'd screamed at him, ranted about phantasms and dark forces, but she'd always stopped short of physical violence. Was she punishing him for deserting her, for going away to college and leaving her alone with her madness? Did she know he was planning to commit her, and was she trying to prevent it?

He woke up five days later in a hospital bed.

"140 times," someone whispered.

Part V
What Must I Do To Be Saved?

57

Cape Agamenticus, Maine
Early April 1749

The Cape Agamenticus council found it very difficult to prevent secrets from circulating. One man would confide in his wife, and within hours every woman in town was privy to the details. Thus the information disseminated rapidly after Charles Meer told his wife Leah that he, Gregory Brautigam, Sebastian Collinge, Michael Ayers, and Reverend Kinnawe would soon depart for a three-day convocation in Boston. Leah reported the news to Rebecca Collinge, who passed it on to Abigail Ayers.

After her husband left for Boston, Abigail left a note for Léana on the beach, under the rock that served as their drop point.

The following day, after twilight, Abigail watched through Léana's window as Abigail's maid, Bridget, scurried along the path to the church.

Bridget, whom Abigail had instructed to begin a strong sexual flirtation with the guards, easily convinced the guard on duty, Peter Cowper, to return to the house with her. "Mrs. Ayers won't be back until late tonight," Bridget whispered. "The town council is gone for three days. Now is our time, Peter. You mustn't make me wait any longer."

•   •   •

Léana removed the stone from her neck and placed it beneath her bed pillow. An overwhelming sense of dread struck her, a vulnerability she'd never felt, not even when she'd seen Mariah hanging from the cross. But the stone would not permit her to cross the threshold of the sites she needed to enter.

Arm in arm, like the closest of friends, Léana and Abigail walked along the cliff path. A few hundred feet from the cave mouth, Bébhinn sat on a boulder, the winds whipping long tendrils of red hair around her face.

Abigail stopped abruptly, unlinking her arm from Léana's. "*She* will accompany us?"

"We need her help, Abigail. Unlike you and me, she need obey no one's rules."

"All is clear to me now. You work with her to destroy us."

"You know I am not your enemy, Abigail."

"It is true that you seem to care for my child's soul, but you also seek our destruction. You are using me to achieve your goals, and I am permitting it. But I ask you: How do you know I will not betray you to Parthalán after I lay my son to rest?"

"Because I have seen the pain in the women's eyes, Abigail." The women hid their fear and anger from Parthalán and their husbands, but Léana saw their despair. Often it manifested in a blank stare of hopelessness, but sometimes Léana caught an evanescent flash of black lightning in a mother's eyes as she gazed upon Parthalán. It was that rage that Léana hoped to tap. "No mother can bear to have her children taken, not even a mother who has pledged herself to Satan. You will be the first to reclaim your child's soul. Other women will follow your example. You will be a heroine, not a pariah. In addition, to betray me is to betray yourself, and I am certain you do not wish your remains to end up in a wine barrel in Parthalán Kinnawe's basement, forever separated from your husband and everyone you love."

"So you think us capable of love, not as vile creatures worthy only of contempt?"

"It is not my place to judge, Abigail. I have seen the love that you and Michael share. But I confess that I find it difficult to reconcile that love with the shrieks that emanate from the meeting house and then the casks later brought to Parthalán's cellar."

"None of us—Leah, Rebecca, Naomi, myself—asked for this life. Our parents forced it on us. We cannot desert this community and not look back. Those who stray are disciplined as we witness their punishment. I have seen men and women ripped to pieces by the beast with scarlet eyes."

Bébhinn joined them outside the cave entrance. "You must enter first, Abigail, and then help me enter," Léana said. She retrieved a candle from her cloak as Abigail stared into the darkness of the cave mouth.

"How can I know that something does not lie in wait for me inside?" Abigail asked, trembling.

"I would enter the cave first, but it will not be permitted," Léana said. "You must enter first and grant me access."

Abigail held her ground. "You go first, and I will follow."

"I tell you, I cannot. It is impossible without your assistance."

Léana moved three steps closer to the cave.

"See, Abigail. I can go no farther. Push me as hard as you can. I will offer no resistance."

Abigail shoved Léana toward the cave opening. She felt the springy resistance holding Léana in place.

"We must waste no more time, Abigail. Step into the cave while I light the candle."

Abigail did as instructed, encountering no barrier as she entered.

"Now take my hand, Abigail, so that I may cross."

Abigail grasped Léana's hand. Aided thus, Léana crossed the barrier and walked through the cave mouth. A wave of revulsion hit her, and it took all her self-control not to sink to her knees and vomit.

Within, the cave walls were lined with niches, some containing small wooden boxes. Shining her candle into the niches, Léana found the box she sought. Burned into the wood were a symbol and a name:

C AYERS

The box cover was attached to the box with a hinge. Inside was a small, leathery, salt-encrusted clump.

"What is it?" Abigail whispered.

"It is Calvin's heart. Parthalán keeps it separate from his other remains. A person may stumble upon one hiding place but is not likely to stumble upon both. Without all the remains, the soul cannot be laid to rest."

Abigail glanced at Bébhinn, who had followed them into the cave. "*She* led you here?"

Léana nodded. "She can follow Parthalán where no one else can."

"Give me your candle, Léana," Abigail said.

Léana did as requested. While Abigail examined the wooden boxes in the niches, Léana transferred Calvin's desiccated heart to a leather pouch.

"We must make haste to the meeting house," Léana said.

"Why do you call it a *meeting house*? It is a *church*."

"Abigail, we are not at leisure to quibble over terminology. Hurry, and give me the candle."

The two women locked arms again and began walking the path that Peter Cowper had deserted. With each step, a bleaker despair invaded Léana's soul. As she gazed upon the stained-glass windows for the first time, her resolve weakened further. She was one woman, Cutler one man. How were they to defeat a man—no, not a man: an *entity* that had once been a man—who would build such a church, with such obscenity glorified in its windows?

And after she'd breached the church's defenses, what would she do next? To whom would she report her findings? Reverend Edwards had not answered any of her letters. After Mariah's crucifixion, even Jerusha seemed to have abandoned her.

Fighting the malaise, Léana trudged onward, shutting her nostrils to the fetid odor and swampy miasma that rose from the church grounds.

Abigail opened the church's rear door and helped Léana cross the threshold. Bébhinn followed.

Léana lit her candle and gasped in shock. The church's worship area was inverted. Black candles dripped in pentagram-shaped sconces on the walls.

"We must go to the crypt," Bébhinn whispered.

Abigail led Léana to a staircase that curved down into the darkness. Along one wall of the crypt, a man suspended in the Judas Chain twitched as rats chewed his entrails.

"Who is he?" Léana whispered to Abigail.

"They are not always known to us. Sometimes they are sent from other communities to be punished here. Sometimes they are kidnapped from Boston, Falmouth, or Portsmouth."

Following Bébhinn's instructions, Léana located a panel on the far wall and pressed her hand against the upper-right corner. The door sprang open to reveal a set of alcoves carved into the church's stone foundation. Many held small boxes. Léana held her candle in front of her and searched for the box labeled "C AYERS."

She found it, took it from the alcove, removed the lid, and transferred the tiny skull, bones, and ribcage into the leather pouch containing the child's heart. She replaced the box cover, returned the box to the alcove, and clicked the panel shut.

On the beach in front of the Ayers house, Léana transferred the pouch to Abigail's hand. Returning to her own house, she set about boiling water for a bath to scrub the filth from her body. She knew that swimming in the Atlantic would not cleanse her; would, instead, encrust her with caustic brine.

• • •

Boston, Massachusetts

After the service, Brautigam, Ayers, Meer, and Collinge returned to the Red Boar Inn, where they promptly lost consciousness, exhausted from blood loss and pain. The new marks on the small of their backs had been carved with a blade so large and thick that it had scratched the bone. But the trauma caused by the new marks was negligible compared to the lingering agony of the branding iron that had seared the tender flesh on the top of their left feet. All four men felt as though they'd had a foot amputated.

As his men slept, Parthalán walked to the modest house on Hutchinson Street where a recently widowed merchant lived with his three daughters and two sons. The oldest girl, an Irish beauty, bore a striking resemblance to the young Bébhinn.

On his first day in Boston, he'd watched the girl leave the church in the company of an older woman, a prim, sour-faced Bostonian who carried herself with an air of uncompromising moral rectitude. He'd followed at a discreet distance as they returned to the house on Hutchinson Street. Parthalán's inquiries had yielded the information he sought: The girl was Josephine Alcott, the old prune her aunt, Martha Gardiner.

Josephine had bewitched Parthalán. If her family had joined his congregation, he would have had the girl brought to him the instant her parents' blood was dry on the parchment. But the Alcotts were good Roman Catholics, the father a staunch supporter of his parish.

Parthalán had thought about approaching Mr. Alcott with an offer to move to Cape Agamenticus. In the past, men more devout than Alcott had been unable to resist Parthalán's cajoling. But Parthalán's congregation was thriving; he had no need to conscript new members when families arrived of their own accord every month, and the townspeople were very sensitive to anything they perceived as favoritism.

Still, there was no reason to deny himself the girl.

He scuttled up the rear wall of the house and crept in through the window, where the father slept in his nightcap. In the room next door, the ugly aunt looked even uglier by moonlight. Across the hall the two boys slept like cherubs.

Parthalán climbed the stairs to the third floor. In one chamber the two younger girls—twins—shared a bed. In a separate tiny chamber under the eave, Josephine Alcott bolted awake as she sensed a menacing shadow in the room.

He was on her before she could raise the alarm. As he held her face and stared into her eyes, he said, "Miss Alcott, do not take your eyes off my face as I ravish you. If you look away or make even the tiniest sound, when I finish with you, I will visit your sisters, your brothers, and finally your aunt and your father. For the next hour, think a single thought: 'I exist solely to give pleasure to Parthalán Kinnawe, and I continue to live only because he permits it.' Tonight you may say my name as often as you wish, and then never again."

• • •

York, Maine

After midnight, Abigail took a horse to the graveyard in York Village, where Cutler had purchased a plot. There she covered the horse's eyes with blinders so that he could not witness her actions. Taking a trowel from her pocket, she dug a hole in the loamy earth by the weak light of a lantern.

As soon as she dumped the leathery heart and little bones into the earth, a breeze wafted from the hole. As she packed the earth over Calvin's remains, a firefly struggled through the dirt and ascended into the sky. Its light blinked one, two, three, four times before it disappeared.

At that moment, Parthalán was climbing the stairs to his accommodations at The Red Boar Inn in Boston. He had left Miss Alcott's room an hour earlier.

Parthalán stumbled and fell. His chin hit the stair, splitting open at the cleft and spraying black blood onto the wallpaper.

•   •   •

Cape Agamenticus, Maine

Abigail Ayers woke the next morning to an urgent rapping at her chamber door.

Rebecca Collinge entered.

"Abigail. You were seen consorting with the Hauer woman."

"Sit, Rebecca, and I will explain all, including how you may bring eternal peace to your Hester."

58

The nurse had said that Doctor Mavro arrived at the Bedford Hills Institute by nine A.M. If Matthew left Maine at four in the morning, the drive would take no more than five hours. Better safe than sorry, though, so he left Kinnawe House at three.

He had too much time to think during the drive. His life hadn't been free of disappointments and hurt; few people reached the age of 28 without being raked over the coals at least a few times. But the torment of knowing about Josh and Kellyce was almost unbearable. They'd both driven to Maine from New York City to deliver the blow in person, to see the pain in Matthew's eyes. They were chipping away at his will to live, making insanity and death seem imminent. His 140 throbbing scars were mosquito bites compared to the anguish caused by their cruelty. Meanwhile, his father seemed to hover on the periphery of his existence, always menacing, never loving or caring.

He tried to organize what he'd learned. Though his mother and father had been born in Maine, he'd been born in South Carolina. His father, Jernej Boudreaux, was probably a mixture of Eastern European and French stock; his name suggested his provenance. He couldn't shake the feeling that his family was somehow associated with Kinnawe House, but according to his birth certificate, his mother's last name was Pauling, and he hadn't seen that name associated with the house anywhere.

As the Civic exited the Mass Pike and crossed the state line into Connecticut, Matthew cranked open the window. The rush of oxygen was bracing, strengthening. His mood lifted. OK, Priscilla was getting back with her ex-boyfriend: That had nothing to do with him. The four local musicians—Chuck, Trey, Greg, Mickey—had invited him to meet them tonight to check out a local band, Carl and the Cavemen. The meds he'd borrowed from Helen were helping him sleep, even if they brought on surreal dreams straight out of Hieronymus Bosch.

Perhaps getting away from Kinnawe House, and out of Maine, had been the best idea of the week.

He pulled into the parking lot of the Bedford Hills Institute at exactly 8:30. Doctor Mavro's office was located in the North Wing, which permitted visitors. The South Wing, where his mother had lived, was visible in the distance. It looked less like a psychiatric care facility and more like a prison for hardened criminals. Every window was protected by a latticework of thick metal rods.

In the North Wing, Matthew asked the receptionist for directions, found Doctor Mavro's office, and sat down to wait. As he fumbled with his phone to check his email for a message from FamilyTree, his hands shook so badly that he was unable to enter his password.

The doctor arrived a few minutes after nine. Matthew had spoken with him on the phone a few times, had met him in person once. He didn't remember the doctor being so enormous: Matthew guessed 6'5" and 250 pounds. His handshake was like the grip of a vice.

"Please accept my belated condolences, Matthew," Doctor Mavro said after Matthew re-introduced himself. "I don't think we spoke after your mother passed away. I'm sorry I missed you on the day you came to pick up her remains."

Seated in a visitor's chair at the doctor's desk, his hands still trembling, Matthew said, "Doctor, can you please tell me exactly how my mother died?"

"Didn't we send you a copy of the death certificate? That's our standard procedure. It specifies the cause of death."

"I don't mean the cause of death. I mean *how* she died. Would you please tell me in your own words? I need to know."

Doctor Mavro looked up from his desk. His chin was cleft, like Bartholomew Dubh's. "All right, Matthew. But I need to warn you that it's disturbing."

Matthew nodded, and Doctor Mavro continued:

"She hanged herself. She made a noose from her bed sheets. She attached one end to the radiator and then threw herself out of the window. Unfortunately, the drop did not break her neck. By time we got to her, she'd died of heart failure brought on by asphyxiation."

And there was the explanation for his mother's preferred method of haunting him. At some level, conscious or unconscious, he must have suspected that she'd hanged herself. Perhaps he'd overheard a whisper while he waited in Patricia Symons' office.

A vision of the South Wing flashed through Matthew's mind. "But the patients' windows have bars on them."

"She sawed through both sets of bars, on the inside and the outside. We never figured out when or how she did it."

"Wasn't she restrained all the time, after she attacked the nurse?"

"We use humane restraints here, which chafe less than metal restraints do. A chainsaw wouldn't make a nick in them. But your mother found a way to chew through them. She was very resourceful, in her own way."

His mother: reduced to a wounded animal chewing through the chains that were supposed to protect her. She'd stabbed him, tried to murder him, but she didn't deserve *that*. Nobody deserved that.

"I have one other question, Doctor. Do the hospital's records include any information about my father or siblings? My mother kept a lot of that information secret from me, and now that she's gone, I'm trying to learn more about where I come from."

Mavro tapped on his keyboard and looked at his computer screen. "It says here she was unmarried, one son. I'm afraid that's the extent of the information we have."

As Matthew walked through the parking lot, a shadow fluttered in his peripheral vision. He turned to face the South Wing. A body was suspended from a fourth-floor window, swaying back and forth in its makeshift noose of bed sheets. The window bars were gone. As Matthew stared at the swinging corpse, the noose snapped and the body crashed to the cement, shattering like a ceramic vase on impact. A river of silver blood rushed toward him like molten mercury.

He squealed out of the parking lot, trying to put as much distance as possible between him and the insanity that was his birthright.

Employees in the South Wing of the Bedford Hills Institute received more compensation than those who worked in the East, West, and North Wings. The premium pay wasn't a result of elevated danger levels. Plenty of the orderlies had worked at hardcore men's prisons, and they liked living on the edge. What made the South Wing so nerve-racking was the quiet. Staff whispered, when they talked at all; in recent years they'd taken to communicating via text messages. The patient-inmates, who lived in solitary confinement, had few visitors and were so medicated as to be incapable of speech. Their doctors made no efforts to engage them in conversation. Instead, they monitored vital signs, ensured that medications were taken on schedule at the prescribed doses, and scribbled notes on charts that nobody read.

In the other wings, armed guards accompanied the doctors on their rounds. In the South Wing, patients' arms and legs were manacled to their bedposts. They lived their lives in a spread-eagle position. The restraints allowed male patients to turn onto their stomachs to urinate through a hole in the mattress into a waste-management system. Three times a day, a burly nurse entered each patient's room with a bowl of nutrient-rich, flavorless food. Those who wanted sustenance were fed by spoon. Those who refused to open their mouths were not cajoled. The nurse left the room, returned at the next mealtime, and tried again. Patients who refused to eat were allowed to die.

The guard on duty pushed the buzzer to allow Doctor Mavro into the wing.

Doctor Mavro walked down the silent corridor and waved his key card in front of the scanner to gain entry to his patient's room. He caught her scent underneath the bleach and ammonia. Psychotic people emitted a distinct odor that the trained nose could detect: a mixture of fennel, tar, skunk cabbage, sulfur, and rose of sharon.

His patient was unmoving, but she wasn't asleep. As the doctor approached her, she began writhing in her constraints. Sometimes the doctor unzipped his pants, mounted her, pumped his seed into her, and left without a word. Today he had a different mission.

He removed a key from his pocket. First he released her feet from the manacles, then her hands. Freed, she pulled her knees up to her chest and stretched out her arms, first to the sides and then behind her back. Then she threw herself at the doctor, slashing at his face with a steak knife.

Doctor Mavro wrestled the knife from her grasp and kicked her in the stomach. As she clutched her mid-section in agony, he slapped her face so hard that she staggered backward and crumpled against the wall.

"You've been allowed to live for one reason, Sharon," Doctor Mavro said to the cowering woman. "Because someday you might be useful. That day has come, you filthy cunt."

59

Cape Agamenticus, Maine
April 1749

When Parthalán returned from Boston, Lotte fussed over his chin. A lichen-green, scaly scab had formed over the wound and lent a ghoulish cast to Parthalán's handsome Black Irish complexion.

"Shall I send for Mrs. Feeley?" Lotte asked. "She will have something to speed the healing."

"I have no need for Mrs. Feeley," Parthalán spat. What he needed was to find out who was plotting against him. A conspiracy at home was the most likely explanation for his fall on the stairs at the Red Boar Inn.

Meanwhile, Parthalán's traveling companions returned to wives who fended off their amorous advances with various excuses. Rebecca Collinge was running a fever. Abigail Ayers had eaten something that disagreed with her. Leah Meer was in the middle of a heavy cycle that had kept her bleeding for eight days. The men commiserated with one another the following morning, and Meer mentioned the problem in passing to Parthalán.

Something had happened while Parthalán was gone. And he was going to find out what.

Riding through Agamenticus Center, he examined the town and its inhabitants for signs of treachery. Sometimes those whose faith had been compromised, or who'd begun to doubt, manifested their thoughts in ways that only Parthalán could see. Their hair took on a peculiar oily sheen, or they developed large, festering sores on their necks or foreheads. If their hair did not return to its normal texture, or if their wounds did not heal in a fortnight, they were called to make the ultimate sacrifice for their families and their community.

Though he scrutinized all those he encountered, Parthalán discovered no outward indicators of disloyalty.

At dusk, he watched through his library window as the deaf-mutes, James and Elias Featherstone, rolled two barrels into the cellar. When they emerged, he tapped on his window, using his index finger to summon them inside.

Parthalán told the brothers that he'd collected three street people in Boston. They lay in chains in the church basement. Parthalán would perform the rites on two of them with no one but himself and the victims in attendance. The third would be offered at the Friday night service. The Featherstones were to retrieve the first two bodies from the church two days hence, and the third body on Monday, after the spiders had enjoyed their feast.

"James, stay," Parthalán said. "Elias, you may go."

The men—identical twins whom Parthalán had adopted from a New York City orphanage, and who were eternally grateful to be rescued from a hellhole in which they were repeatedly beaten and raped—were the best spies Parthalán could have hoped for. Both men were indeed mute, but both were capable of hearing. Allowing the community to believe that James and Elias were deaf served Parthalán's purposes. Men and women felt no need to whisper or censor their conversations when the brothers were present. James and Elias then reported every word to their master.

Elias bowed and left the library, pulling the door closed behind him.

"Something is amiss, James. There has been disobedience during my absence. What can you tell me?"

James pointed to his throat with his index finger.

Parthalán nodded, and the snake slithered down from inside his pant leg and across the floor, its tongue flicking as it sought James's shoe. The asp curled itself around James's leg and slithered up his torso, wrapping itself around his neck and burying its fangs in his Adam's apple.

James's lips began to move, and a sibilant voice emerged. "I have seen the women whispering."

"That is to be expected. Gossip is exchanged in a whisper, not a shout."

"This was an exchange of information, not idle gossip."

"What was said?"

"They were facing each other. I could neither hear them nor read their lips."

"Name them."

James hesitated.

"Explain your reluctance to speak," Parthalán said, "when you so rarely have the ability to do so."

"I have no proof of ill intentions, Reverend. Only observations of women whispering as if conspiring."

Parthalán knew that those who had lost one of their senses often developed compensating abilities. The Featherstones could not speak, but they knew when someone was lying, withholding the truth, or speaking ill of Reverend Kinnawe. They could smell it, see it, taste it.

"I will not ask you again, James."

"Leah Meer. Abigail Ayers. Rebecca Collinge."

The snake tightened its coil around James's neck.

"Reverend," James croaked. "I cannot breathe."

The viper loosened its hold.

"Do they conspire with the witch, Léana Hauer?"

"I do not know. She is not often seen."

Parthalán had understood the Hauers' mission since their arrival. Léana Mac Concradha, who'd shown him only kindness when he was a boy, was now his sworn enemy. It was one of the cruel, teasing twists of which the Protector was so fond. But Parthalán was powerless to set foot on the Hauers' property, and thus far he'd managed to dispatch only their maid, whose bones soaked in offal in his cellar. The Featherstones had exhumed her body from the cemetery in York Village.

Parthalán could post sentries on the land under his control—the entire tract on which Cape Agamenticus was built—but not on the Hauers' property. Nonetheless, the Hauers had to be monitored, and chances had to be taken. Perhaps Léana Hauer had become emboldened after Mariah's disappearance; perhaps she had managed to sow seeds of discord in his absence.

"Keep watch on the women you have mentioned, as well as their husbands, and report anything you learn to me immediately," Parthalán said. "Interrupt a ceremony if you must."

"Yes, Reverend."

"Relieve Peter Cowper from duty and send him to me."

"You may find that he is not trustworthy, Reverend."

"Explain."

"During your absence, he deserted his post to bed the Ayers' maid, Bridget. Elias saw them running to the Ayers house. Mrs. Ayers was not at home, and Mr. Ayers was with you. We know what a single man and a wench do while the master is away."

Parthalán spread the fingers of his left hand and examined his fingernails. Peter Cowper should have asked him for the maid. He would not have denied a loyal servant the woman he wanted. Parthalán had no argument with lust. It came from the Devil, so he encouraged it. But he would not tolerate a lustful man choosing to bed a woman over protecting his church.

"Relieve him from duty and tell him to meet me at the cave."

The snake released its fangs from James's throat, slithered down his back, and returned to its favorite corner. James, once again deprived of speech, bowed and left.

The following morning, Bridget opened the Ayers' kitchen door to sweep crumbs from the floor. A wrapped package sat on the step. The card was addressed to "Bridget, my dearest, a gift for one so deserving." Bridget exclaimed with delight and took the package into the kitchen, where she unwrapped it. Inside were Peter Cowper's head and penis.

· · ·

Parthalán declined to enter Emma's chamber that night. In the morning, as he annotated the margins of one of his books, Emma knocked on the library door.

"Welcome home, Parthalán," Emma said. "Did all go well in Boston?"

"The trip served its purpose, but it has had a disturbing aftermath." He did not worry that Emma would use confidential information against him. Getting pregnant and saving her brother's life were her only priorities.

"I had hoped to make a request of you," Emma said, "but I will return when it is more convenient for you."

"Tell me what you seek."

Emma perched herself on the chair next to Parthalán's desk.

"I know you wish for children. As do I. I am doing everything in my power to conceive. I have done everything Mrs. Feeley has advised. You know I am trying."

"Yes."

"Mrs. Feeley says that I must be in good spirits for the seed to take root. But I cannot be happy when I hear my brother crying in the night. My heart cannot bear it. Until he was brought here, Tobias had many friends. Now he is alone, imprisoned in an attic."

Breaking Tobias, Parthalán knew, was the key to breaking Emma. "And how do you think it would reflect on me, Emma, if the community learned that I harbor your brother, the murderer, in my home? As far as they know, he has been drawn and quartered, his body parts dumped into the ocean."

"I am grateful for all you've done, but my brother's soul is shriveling and dying, and after I have conceived, his misery will be a burden on me and, more importantly, on the children. Tobias needs activity. He cannot sit in the attic all day long, staring at the sea, with nothing to do. He will go mad."

"You consented to our agreement, Emma. You will not see him until you have conceived."

"I am not asking to see him. You know Tobias is an artist. I ask you to have my father bring Toby's paints, easel, brushes, and canvases to him. And, when those materials run out, to purchase more. We can order the supplies from Boston so that nobody in town knows. Please, Parthalán. This plan will have a positive outcome for you."

Everything was going according to plan. "I will grant your request, Emma, but you must return the favor."

"Whatever you wish."

"You have never been friendly with Rebecca Collinge, Leah Meer, or any of our neighbors. Nor with your stepmother."

"It is true."

"You must behave more as a minister's wife, befriend the women of the community, and gain their trust. Do you agree to do so?"

"Yes."

"Then you may go to your father's house and make your request. Upon your return, slip a note under the attic door telling your brother to paint his host's portrait before he begins anything else. I will also provide charcoal sketches of several women. Your brother will paint their portraits as well. I will leave it to his imagination to fill in the details."

Parthalán knew that all the portraits would be flattering.

·   ·   ·

After midnight, as Tobias worked on the portrait of his jailer, Elias Featherstone took up his post as sentry on the bluff overlooking the Hauers' house. The brothers had received their orders a few hours earlier. They were to stand twelve-hour shifts to monitor the house and its occupants. While one brother watched, the other would make his usual rounds, collecting the townspeople's waste and delivering the casks to the Reverend's basement.

In York Village, Rebecca Collinge climbed down from her horse and hastened to the cemetery. Not a living soul was on the streets. Using a trowel, Rebecca dug a hole. From a pouch she removed her daughter Hester's heart and bones, which Abigail and Léana had helped her retrieve while Parthalán and his men were in Boston. She placed her daughter's remains, one piece at a time, into the ground.

As a firefly flew up to the heavens, Parthalán, who was pacing in his library, tripped and fell face-first into his desk. Its sharp edge ripped open his left cheekbone. The books open on the desk absorbed the blood that spurted from the gash.

60

Ogunquit – Agamenticus, Maine

Matthew wanted to get to the Ogunquit post office before it closed at 3:00. That gave him five and a half hours to get back to Maine from the Bedford Hills Institute. He kept his foot on the gas while scanning the highway for hidden police cars.

He wasn't hungry, but he was tired. An infusion of protein and sugar might give him a boost. In the dining area of a Wendy's off I-84, he called Doctor Ansari's office to report that he was fine. The fast-food joint was filled with friends, most of them teenagers, laughing and joking and acting stupid. At a tiny table for two, Matthew took a bite of his chicken sandwich before deciding that he wasn't hungry after all.

He got to the post office at ten minutes to two. The clerk scrounged under the counter and found a letter sent to him care of General Delivery. It was postmarked BALA CYNWYD, PA.

Matthew unfolded the document and scanned it from top to bottom. The certificate recorded the month and date of his birth—August 8th—but not the year. He recognized his mother's signature. And there was his father's name, Jernej Boudreaux, typed in the Courier font common on old typewriters.

As Doris had indicated, his probably illiterate father had signed with a star.

The star was not a perfect match of Matthew's birthmark, which was a solid blotch. In contrast, Jernej's scribble was not fully inked.

When he was a boy, Matthew liked to interpret the birthmark as a sign that he'd been born under a lucky star. But Jernej's signature made him feel anything but lucky. As he traced the scribble with his finger, a chill crawled up his back.

He found himself driving north on Route 1, into Kennebunk and beyond, until a sign welcomed him to Wiscasset. Matthew shifted his eyes from the road to the dashboard clock and found that he'd been driving north for more than two hours. The car, it seemed, had wanted to take him away from Kinnawe House, not toward it.

Since arriving at Kinnawe House, he'd suspected that he walked in his sleep, but he'd never sleep-driven before. He looked at his face in the rear-view mirror. Heavy purple semicircles formed crescents under both eyes. His hair was mussed, his wispy beard more unkempt-looking than usual. A faint, sour odor emanated from his armpits.

He made a U-turn in a McDonald's parking lot and began the long trek south. As he drove, he tried to prevent his worries about his sanity from gaining the upper hand. Twiddling the radio knob, he found a station that played heavy metal, an underappreciated genre that made all thought impossible.

Twilight had fallen by the time he arrived home. He had a couple of hours to kill before meeting the guys at Julie's. He retrieved the envelope from the Civic, planning to go over his birth certificate with the magnifying glass that he'd found in the kitchen's junk drawer.

The envelope was thicker than it had been when he left Ogunquit. He lifted the flap to investigate. Someone had confetti'd the document into millions of tiny pieces.

Someone? He must have done it, though he couldn't remember doing so.

Which meant he was definitely blacking out. Further losing his grip on reality.

Had all his experiences in Maine been delusions? Maybe he was so lonely, so isolated, that his sleepless mind had conjured burgeoning romantic relationships and friendships—first Priscilla, then Dave and the BBQ, then the guys from Juilliard. Maybe the pill bottles, the object of his frantic search, hadn't existed because he hadn't seen a doctor in New Hampshire.

The people he'd met and talked with: They all filled a need. Doctor Ansari was the antithesis of the doctors he'd seen in New York, who'd kept the conversation to a minimum. Sheila, the smiling receptionist at the doctor's office, was a welcoming face in a new place. Helen was an archetype, too: the grandmother who would have baked cookies for him and sent him presents on his birthday.

He would *not* end up like his mother. He would *not* lock himself in Kinnawe House, as she'd locked herself in the Bala Cynwyd house, growing more insane and homicidal by the day.

He'd go to Julie's Bar & Restaurant, as he'd planned. If the Juilliard guys waved him over to their table, he'd continue taking his medication, make a follow-up appointment with Doctor Ansari next week, and cope with the dreams and delusions until he'd had enough medication-enabled sleep to recover normal brain function.

If the Juilliard guys weren't at Julie's, he would drive to the nearest hospital and check himself in, before he hurt himself or anyone else.

• • •

Rye, New Hampshire

Priscilla had found a burial place for Henry, her parakeet, between two massive oak trees in the backyard. She'd put the little bird into an old plastic jewelry box, reuniting Henry's body—which lay on the floor of his cage— and his head, which she'd extracted from the wall by prying the spike loose.

Now two cops were at the house, investigating. Their best guess, the older, fatter cop said, was that the broken window had allowed someone to get into the house, kill Henry, and spray-paint the warning on the wall.

"Where are you not supposed to go back to?" the slightly thinner cop asked.

"I have no idea," Priscilla said.

Though Priscilla wasn't fond of cops (small dicks, and everyone knew it), she wasn't being evasive. She wasn't sure that the events of the previous evening had *happened*. One minute she was fleeing that creepy house on the coast, and the next she was running up the staircase to her room. The cops were already acting like she was a bit of a flake, giving her the look that cops give edgy young women who might be lesbians.

After the cops left, Priscilla walked to the Vernons' house and rang the doorbell. Wanda answered and hugged her.

"You doing OK, Priss? This is pretty fucked up. I mean, here, on this boring street in this boring town."

"Wanda, did you think there was anything strange about Matthew?"

"Who's Matthew?"

Priscilla didn't miss a beat. "The guy from New York."

"I'm not sure who you're talking about. I know a guy who moved *to* New York, but his name's not Matthew."

Priscilla thought: *She doesn't remember anything. Why am I not surprised?*

61

Stockbridge, Massachusetts
Spring 1749

The revolt, long in coming, finally took place, removing Jonathan Edwards from the pulpit in Northampton. Edwards moved his family to a modest house in Stockbridge, where he ministered to a much smaller, but much more supportive, congregation.

Edwards arrived in Stockbridge a changed man. After the visit from Nathaniel Davenport and the experience with the locusts, Edwards had isolated himself and prayed for guidance. The Lord scolded him for his arrogance and presumption, but most of all for his pride.

You will find your mission in your new home, the Father had said. *Only when you have done My work by serving as a tireless advocate for My oppressed children will your vanity and self-importance be forgiven.*

After living in Stockbridge for a week, Edwards understood that the Father's oppressed children were the local Indians, whose land had been stolen from them. To these noble Native Americans, the Mohawks, he began preaching the word of God through an interpreter. Soon the soft-spoken minister became as fiery in his defense of the ill-treated Indians as he'd been during the Great Awakening, when the people of New England had flocked to ask him, "What must I do to be saved?"

Edwards did not know what had become of Parthalán and Bébhinn in the years since he'd sent them away. He'd had no word from Léana, no response to his numerous letters.

He feared he would never learn the truth, and perhaps that was for the best.

On a mild night in April of 1749, as his family and servants lay sleeping, Edwards rose from bed, lit a candle, and descended the stairs to his study. Though he wanted to read his Bible, he would not do so by candlelight. His eyes were weakening, and he did not want to strain them. Natural light was so much better. In his study he sat in his favorite chair, facing the window. A crescent moon and a million twinkling stars lit the sky as a night bird whirred: proof, if anyone required it, of God's existence and His glory.

Edwards lifted the sash and peered out of the window. A milky white dove perched on the branch of an oak tree. One of its wings hung at an awkward angle from its body, and its feathers were speckled, as if a child had flung mud at it.

"Jerusha?"

Yes, Father. Finding you has been difficult. A new family lives in the Northampton house.

"I have been so concerned, Jerusha. Did Léana, Cutler, and Mariah arrive safely? I've had no communication from them."

Mariah is dead. Parthalán crucified her.

Edwards gasped. "What of Léana and Cutler?"

They are married and in mortal danger, alone in a community that wishes death on them. Parthalán has thwarted all their efforts to reach you. Everything you suspect about him is true.

"I shall recall them. They will live here, with us, for as long as necessary."

Parthalán's men will kill them as soon as they leave the confines of Cape Agamenticus.

"What must I do to save them?"

You must not attempt anything on your own. You will be killed upon your arrival. Instead, muster an army and burn the town to the ground. Every person must be slaughtered.

"But how am I to accomplish such a mission? I can do nothing without the congregation's support, and now I am a simple minister in a remote town."

You must find a way. The longer I tarry here, the longer Léana and Cutler remain vulnerable. I must return to them.

"Do they wear their talismans? Those should bring protection."

They do, but Mariah was deceived into removing hers. Léana and Cutler may also be tricked. They are but two people in a town of five hundred in league against them.

"Jerusha, you are damaged. You must rest."

I cannot rest. I must return.

The injured dove flew off into the night.

Never in his life had Jonathan Edwards felt so powerless. He dropped to his knees and prayed for guidance.

62

Rye, New Hampshire

Priscilla said good night to the other members of the choir. They were heading to a local tavern for a drink and a bite to eat after practice, but Priscilla begged off.

She tossed her backpack over her shoulder and descended the narrow staircase from the choir loft. She walked up the nave of the Roman Catholic First Church of the Nazarene and poked her head around back. Sven Koskinen, the pastor, sat at a small desk, flipping through the pages of a Bible.

As Sven looked up from the Good Book, a welcoming smile brightened his bearded face.

"Hope I'm not interrupting, Sven."

"Not at all. I'm stuck on ideas for the homily. I'm trying a trick I learned in divinity school. When you can't find inspiration, you open the Bible to a random page, close your eyes, place your finger on the page, and let the verse inspire you. Unfortunately, this one won't be a crowd pleaser."

"What does it say?"

Sven read from the Bible. "Ephesians 6:10. 'Finally, let the mighty strength of the Lord make you strong. Put on all the armor that God gives, so you can defend yourself against the devil's tricks. We are not fighting against humans. We are fighting against forces and authorities and against rulers of darkness and powers in the spiritual world. So put on all the armor that God gives. Then when that evil day comes, you will be able to defend yourself. And when the battle is over, you will still be standing firm.'"

Priscilla stared at the priest. The verse from Ephesians spoke directly to the nagging unease that had stalked her since her experience at Kinnawe House.

"Sven, I've never really thought about evil before. But a few nights ago, I felt it."

Sven Koskinen closed the Bible. "Tell me what happened."

The story came tumbling out—she'd met a musician named Matthew, he'd invited her to sing with him, but the house tried to prevent her from entering, wouldn't let him play a hymn on the piano, wouldn't let any lyric be sung. The house's tendrils had reached as far as Rye to kill her sweet little parakeet and to ensure her submission to its will. "I'm scared for myself and my parents," she said, "but I can't stop thinking about Matthew, either. I think that house, or something in it, is using him, or trying to destroy him."

"Where exactly is this house, Priscilla?"

"This is where it gets even *stranger*. It's in a town on the Maine coast that I never heard of. Matthew called it Agamenticus. I can't find it on any map. Before choir practice tonight I drove up there to look for the road and the house, and neither of them is there. But it all happened, I swear it. I'm not making it up."

"I know you're not making it up, Priscilla. Oh, Jesus."

"What, Sven? Do you know something about that house?"

Sven didn't know where to begin, or if he should. In the 1750s one of his ancestors, Vikke Koskinen, had emigrated to the Colonies searching for his lost brother, Einar, who'd left Finland to serve as the minister of a town called Cape Agamenticus, Maine, which had flourished for several years before its annihilation.

63

Emma Kinnawe sipped chamomile tea sweetened with honey imported from England. Mrs. Feeley had recommended the beverage as a safe and effective method of calming her stomach. The honey's soothing effects on her digestion reminded Emma of a phrase she'd heard often as a child, one that had become more popular since its publication in Mr. Franklin's *Almanack*: "You catch more flies with honey."

Indeed.

Life had become much more pleasant for Emma since she'd decided to make a virtue of necessity. She'd been forced into a situation in which she was responsible not only for her father's safety but also her brother's. She must bear the children of a man in league with the devil. But she would outsmart them all.

Mrs. Feeley had confirmed that Emma was carrying twins, and Parthalán had received the news with a knowing nod. Multiple births were common in his family, he'd said during her first pregnancy. Most of the time both children were the same sex, but boy-girl pairs were not unknown.

The babies were growing slowly, but Mrs. Feeley counseled Parthalán and Emma not to worry. Certain babies, she said, took longer to develop. Parthalán told Emma that Bébhinn had carried him for eleven months. He'd been a strong, healthy boy, he said—just as he was a strong, healthy man.

He did not mention his goldenrod allergy or his recent tendency to stumble and fall.

It is so much easier to play along, Emma thought, scolding herself for not doing so from the beginning. In recent weeks, she'd begun inviting her neighbors for lunches and teas. She welcomed Abigail Ayers, Rebecca Collinge, Leah Meer, and her stepmother Naomi with smiles, giving small trinkets to Rebecca's toddler son, Luke, and to Leah's girls, Ruth and Jane. She sent Naomi home with a pair of socks she'd knitted for Gregory, and to Abigail she gifted a tin of Belgian rum-laced cakes that were difficult to find in the Colonies. After each visit, Emma recounted the details to Parthalán.

As she chatted and gossiped with the other wives, Emma wondered if they were playing a part, as she was. Had they decided to accept her peace offerings for the sake of their families and their community? Or were their smiles sincere? Emma sensed Abigail and Rebecca warming to her, which meant that Leah's affections were sure to follow. All three women deferred to Naomi, who would be the last domino to fall. Naomi chatted but did not gossip; she smiled but did not laugh. When Leah, Abigail, and Rebecca poked fun at Mrs. Feeley's duck-like walk and long, disapproving face, Naomi remained silent.

"I am fortunate to have you as friends and neighbors," Emma said as her guests prepared to take their leave on this bright spring day. "I know I shall rely on your advice and experience after my children are born. I feel so unprepared, so ignorant, not only regarding childbirth, but also about what comes after."

Rebecca tucked a wisp of hair into her cap and patted Emma's arm. "It all comes naturally, Emma. You will see."

After the women departed, Emma drank the last few drops of her tea, using a tiny spoon to scoop up the honey at the bottom of the teacup. As she set the spoon onto the saucer, a middle-aged, redheaded woman materialized in the chair opposite her.

"You carry my grandchildren," Bébhinn said without prelude.

Emma had heard the whispers about her mother-in-law, whom Parthalán had banished from the community. "Yes," she replied.

"They will be two boys." Bébhinn's husky voice, Emma noticed, carried an Irish brogue.

"Have you been talking with my brother?" Emma asked. At first, she'd feared that Tobias, locked in the attic, was losing his sanity, engaging in one-sided conversations with imaginary people. But she was almost certain she'd heard another voice, too. Female, husky, Irish.

"Tobias is a sweet boy," said Bébhinn. "He paints all day, every day, on the walls, the ceiling, and the floor. The attic is his canvas."

"His portrait of my husband was received with much admiration."

"Your brother has many talents in portraiture, including the ability to disguise as much as he reveals."

"I hope to see him soon." So far, Parthalán had kept his word. The night after Mrs. Feeley confirmed Emma's pregnancy, Charles Meer had arrived to take Tobias for a ten-minute walk on the beach. As the babies grew, Parthalán promised, Tobias's release time would increase by two minutes per week, and after the babies were born, Emma would be permitted to see her brother one time before his exile to Boston.

"Your brother is tested, Emma, as are we all. But Tobias is strong."

"What is said about you, Bébhinn—is it true? That you betrayed Parthalán?"

"Yes. You understand what he is, Emma. My madness is not always a curse. At times, it has allowed me to see with greater clarity, and I wrote to a good man, whom I once deceived, to inform him of the evil that dwells here. For that I was punished. But if given a second chance, I would do the same again. I betrayed Parthalán, as you must."

Emma, who'd inclined her head toward Bébhinn's, pulled back, suspecting a trap. It seemed entirely likely that Parthalán had sent his mother to test her.

"Parthalán is my husband, and I carry his children," Emma said, placing her hands over her belly. "I will not betray him as you did. I admit I was a difficult, ungrateful wife for too long. But I have embraced my role as wife and mother, and I have pledged my loyalty to my husband and to this town."

Bébhinn winked at Emma. "You are wise to speak in this way. But you need not worry. I have created a diversion. Lotte harbors an intense fear of mice, so I asked several dozen to visit the kitchen. You were too busy chatting with your neighbors—I will not call them friends—to hear her squeal as she ran out of the house."

Emma smiled at the thought of her aunt's discomfort. Once she'd been very fond of Lotte. Now she detested her.

"I have been watching you, Emma, and I know what you plan to do. You are right to seek an end to this. But I am a mother, and I know that you may waver. You must not."

Emma sat in silence, waiting for Bébhinn to continue.

"Parthalán has not yet explained the choice you must make. All women who are made pregnant by the men of Parthalán's line conceive twins. One child will be good and selfless. The other will seek to destroy the first. It is the latter child whom Parthalán will want as his heir.

"Immediately after the babies are born, you must choose one to kill. There is no way to determine which is the good child, and which is the evil. As I did, you must look upon your newborns and decide. I come to give you this information before Parthalán does, as his father's mother gave it to me. If I were alive, it would be my duty to speak with you. But I am not, so Parthalán will explain your obligations in my stead.

"What I have told you has been explained to the victims of Parthalán's forebears for hundreds of years. But what I am about to say, no one knows but me and Parthalán. When Parthalán's father raped me, he did not know that my own family carries a curse in its blood. It is the curse of sleeplessness, and it is the curse that drove me mad. By raping me, Parthalán's father brought my family's illness into his line.

"This is the truth of your situation, Emma: If the good child survives, he will live a normal life until he is a young man, at which time he will lose his ability to sleep, and he will go mad. The evil child, if he lives, also will become unable to sleep, but a demon does not require slumber.

"I planned not to have children, Emma. I did not wish to pass on a birthright of sleeplessness and madness. But, as you know full well, when you are raped and threatened, your rapist steals your will and controls your womb. If you let the wrong child live, that child will someday murder you. He will also murder many others and spit in the face of God. In short, he will become like his father."

Emma stared at Bébhinn. "But, knowing this, why did you not kill both of your babies? Doing so would have been preferable to unleashing a fiend, would it not?"

"Parthalán's father threatened to torture and murder my parents, my brothers, and my sisters if I did so. But there is more to the decision than a demon's threats. You are not yet a mother. After you deliver your babies, you will understand what you do not understand now: If you have the ability to save one of your children, you will do so. But you must resist that temptation.

"Until the day comes, you must be as obedient as you have been these past months. You must agree to Parthalán's terms when he presents them. You will choose the child that you want to survive, and Parthalán will take him from you, promising to protect him. He will then break the child's neck, and in doing so he will attempt to cheat Fate. When you are left alone to bond with your other child, the one whom Parthalán wants as his heir, smother him and end your own life. I have put a bottle of red liquid in your chest of drawers. Place three drops on your tongue. You will go to sleep and never wake up."

Emma feigned horror and disbelief. "Take my own life? To do so is to commit the sin of despair."

"Do you imagine I do not know what I ask of you? You know what this town is. You know about the rites your husband and neighbors perform in the church at night. You know what sits in the cellar of this house. What lies in your womb will extend a centuries-long trail of tears and misery. Do you wish more towns like Cape Agamenticus to spring up throughout this land? If Parthalán has his way, that is exactly what will happen. Only you can end the cycle. Only you can set your father and brother free. As for everyone else in this town, they are not worthy of your care or protection."

Bébhinn rested her hand on Emma's arm. Emma felt warmth where Bébhinn's hand would have been if she had corporeal form. "Resign yourself to your fate, child. I will visit you again."

"In the meantime, will you continue to visit my brother?"

"Yes. Rest assured that Tobias, too, will be released from this hell."

As Bébhinn disappeared, Lotte entered the parlor, her eyes darting to the four corners of the room.

"Who were you talking to, Emma?" she snapped.

"Myself. Don't you do that, Aunt? Earlier you were screaming for no apparent reason."

"An army of mice invaded the kitchen, but they have disbanded." She stomped off in a huff.

That evening, as Parthalán gave Emma his orders—upon delivering the children, she was to choose her favored child, and then give that child to him while she suckled the other baby—Emma nodded her assent.

"As you wish, Parthalán," she said.

"Do not seek to deceive me, Emma," Parthalán said. "I will look into your eyes and know whether the child you have given me is your favored child or not."

Parthalán left her chamber to return to his library, and Emma felt a jolt of triumph. She was certain that neither Bébhinn nor Parthalán suspected her secret.

64

Agamenticus – Ogunquit, Maine

Matthew hoped to get a few hours of rest before meeting the Juilliard guys at Julie's, but a half-Ambien proved useless. He lay on the couch, mourning the loss of his girlfriend, his child, and a friendship that had sustained him throughout his youth, adolescence, and young adulthood. The Brody family had been there through all of it. Josh's father had seen Matthew's car in the driveway and found him lying, near death, on his bed. He'd saved Matthew's life by rushing him to the hospital. Josh's mother, Kathryn, had insisted Matthew stay with them after his release from the hospital. She'd cooked his favorite meals, played Yahtzee with him, and helped him with the exercises prescribed by his physical therapist.

Kinnawe House. It was supposed to be his sanctuary, but over the course of a few days, it had magnified every problem he'd had in New York. He was tempted to pack up and drive back to Manhattan, leaving a vague, bullshittish message for Bartholomew Dubh about an emergency that required him to abandon his caretaking duties. But no; New York would be worse. It was a small city, as everyone who lived there liked to say. He wasn't ready to bump into Kellyce or Josh in a deli or on the subway, or to see the two them holding hands at an outdoor café. And he was determined to unlock the secrets of his past before returning to the insular world of Manhattan and attempting to resume his musical career.

He needed a change of scenery. Wanting to surround himself with fresh air and nature, he walked into the field of goldenrod across Agamenticus

Cliff Road. Hundreds of honeybees crawled over the flowers, collecting pollen and nectar. A dozen of them lifted off and made the proverbial beeline down the road, toward Helen's house.

The fresh air did him some good. He felt a little better. Not quite so hopeless.

His phone couldn't pick up a signal, so he drove to Ogunquit Center, where he sat on a bench and placed a call to Toby Brody.

"Hey, Matt," Mr. Brody said, with genuine warmth. "Josh said you're in Maine for a few months? How are you doing?"

"Doing OK, I guess."

"It's beautiful up there."

"Have you spent much time in Maine?"

Toby Brody hesitated just a moment before answering. "I lived there for about a year in my 20s. It wasn't a great period in my life, to be honest."

"Hey Mr. B., can I ask you a couple of questions? Just some things I've been wondering about."

"Of course, Matt. Shoot."

"I've been thinking about Ray lately," Matthew said. "I've always wondered what happened. My mother never got over him leaving."

Ray Lonegan had come into their lives suddenly and out of nowhere. He'd lived in a rented room somewhere in the country, off the grid, and he'd earned some money doing yard work and household repairs for Rose of Sharon and other helpless homeowners. After he moved in, he'd turned the backyard into a massive garden. The gigantic beefsteak tomatoes, ears of corn, cucumbers, and broccoli had kept them in fresh produce all summer.

He'd treated Matthew kindly, buying him comic books and teaching him how to fish. He'd always said that Matthew reminded him of his baby brother, who'd died before reaching adolescence. Sometimes he'd gently grab Matthew's chin and pivot Matthew's head to study Matthew's face from different angles, usually when Rose of Sharon wasn't present. He'd told Matthew that his birthmark was a sign that great things awaited him. That he'd been born under a lucky star.

Matthew wasn't sure if he'd dreamed the angry confrontation between Josh's father and Ray on the night of Ray's disappearance. From his bed,

Matthew had heard two voices in the backyard, one angry and one placating. Something like:

I don't know who you are, but I know why you're here. I see how you look at Matthew. The angry voice: Mr. Brody's.

The softer voice: Ray's. *I'm not looking at him. I'm watching out for him.*

I don't know whose side you're on, but you're breaking the rules. He must be allowed to mature.

He has the mark. He may be the good child, or he may be the enemy.

We cannot know until he comes of age.

If he is the good seed, he may not reach that age.

I warn you: Be gone by first light. Do not goad me to violence.

You believe your allies are more powerful than mine, Tobias? You are mistaken, and a fool.

When Matthew woke up, Ray was gone. He and his mother never saw him again.

"Ray and I weren't friends," Mr. B. said. "To be honest, I never quite trusted him around you and your mother."

"But we had no money and nothing valuable," Matthew said. Then it hit him. "Wait—you think he was a sicko?" He did not remember Ray ever touching him inappropriately or making creepy suggestions. That didn't mean it hadn't happened, though. He'd been only seven years old, for God's sake.

"I don't know exactly what I was thinking," Toby Brody said. "Something just didn't feel right. Nobody knew who he was or where he came from."

"The night before he left, I heard him arguing with someone. Was it you?"

"I'm sorry, Matt. I know he was like a father to you. But I was afraid he might hurt you."

He did hurt me, Matthew thought. By disappearing without so much as a good-bye.

"Matt, do you forgive me? I only wanted to protect you. You're like a son to me."

"No apology necessary, Mr. B. I know you were looking out for me." *And, unlike my mother, you told me the truth when I asked for it. I didn't dream that conversation. I heard it. It happened.*

259

If you hadn't sent Ray packing, I might not be alive right now. I wonder how many times you've saved my life.

•   •   •

After ending the call with Mr. Brody, Matthew checked his email. His inbox showed a message from SUSAN MCNEIL. The subject line was: YOUR FAMILYTREE® TEST RESULTS. He read:

Dear Mr. Rollins,
Greetings. My name is Susan McNeil, and I am a genetic specialist at FamilyTree®. I have attached the results of your FamilyTree® genetic test.

Thank you for trusting FamilyTree® to bring you closer to your heritage!

Sincerely,
Susan McNeil

Matthew took a deep breath and tapped the attached PDF icon. When the document opened, he scrolled past the blah-blah-blah verbiage until he found the section labeled Geographic Heritage:

GEOGRAPHIC HERITAGE
>>IRELAND 68%
>>GERMANY 14%
>>ENGLAND 10%
>>FRANCE 7%
>>FINLAND/NORWAY/SWEDEN 1%
>>TURKEY 3%

So ... he was nearly three-quarters Irish. Did the 7% from France come from his father, Jernej Boudreaux?

He scrolled to the health-risk information, which began with a disclaimer in boldfaced capital letters: BASED ON YOUR TEST RESULTS, YOU MAY HAVE A GENETIC PREDISPOSITION TO THE FOLLOWING CONDITIONS. YOUR FAMILYTREE® GENETIC TEST IS <u>NOT</u> DIAGNOSTIC. IF YOU ARE CONCERNED ABOUT

YOUR HEALTH, DISCUSS THESE RESULTS WITH YOUR DOCTOR. REMEMBER: A GENETIC PREDISPOSITION DOES NOT MEAN THAT YOU HAVE THIS CONDITION OR THAT YOU WILL DEVELOP THIS CONDITION. NUMBERS IN PARENTHESES COMPARE THE STRENGTH OF YOUR GENETIC PREDISPOSITION TO THAT OF THE GENERAL U.S. POPULATION.

ROLLINS, MATTHEW

>>SLEEP-WAKE DISORDERS (INCLUDING CIRCADIAN RHYTHM DISORDER, NON-24 DISORDER, RESTLESS LEGS SYNDROME, NIGHT TERRORS, PARASOMNIAS, SLEEPWALKING, KLEIN-LEVINE SYNDROME, DELAYED SLEEP PHASE DISORDER, CATATHRENIA, BRUXISM) +508%

>>CREUTZFELDT-JAKOB DISEASE +502%

>>INCONTINENTIA PIGMENTI (GENERALLY BENIGN SKIN DISCOLORATIONS) +260%

>>VASCULITIS +160%

>>WERNICKE-KORSAKOFF SYNDROME +125%

Matthew, who had a good head for math, took in the results. Five times more likely than the average U.S. resident to have a sleep disorder or Creutzfeldt-Jakob disease. And almost three times more likely to have icontinentia pigmenti. Given the insomnia and nightmares of the previous weeks, the possibility of a sleep disorder wasn't a surprise. Doctor Ansari had hinted at it, planned to send Matthew to a specialist once the insomnia was under control.

With each Google search he completed, Matthew grew more panicky. The incontinentia pigmenti in his bloodline wasn't a big deal; it probably explained the birthmark. But Creutzfeldt-Jakob, vasculitis, and Wernicke-Korsakoff were all degenerative brain disorders, often resulting in hallucinations, delusions, and paranoia.

Had he put his mother in a mental institution when she really needed the care of a neurologist, not a psychiatrist? And was he following her down that same road? As his Magic 8-Ball would have said, All Signs Point to Yes.

"Oh God," he whispered, to no one.

65

York Village – Cape Agamenticus, Maine
Mid-Spring 1749

Michael Ayers approached Cutler, who'd traveled to York to place flowers on Mariah's grave. Ayers, unwilling to enter the cemetery grounds, waved Cutler over.

"I wish to speak with you, Mr. Hauer."

Cutler placed his hands in his pockets. "After months of treating my wife and me like bringers of the plague, you now wish to converse?"

"You were not here when we built our church and our town with our bare hands, Mr. Hauer. We have worked hard, and our labors have been rewarded. You come to our town and treat us as the enemy. You behaved thus even as you built the house in which you now live."

"A fine story, Ayers, when we both know that your fondest wish is our death. Your town *crucified* Mariah."

"Tobias Brautigam killed her. We put him to death so that he could harm no one else. Do you think it was easy for us to execute the son of our close friend? Gregory pleaded with us to spare his boy, but we knew that justice must be served."

Cutler made no response.

"If we must be neighbors," Ayers continued, "we should be on civil terms. You may not like us, but you have chosen to live among us. Would it not be better for all if we come to an accord?"

"What do you propose?"

"Join me for a pint at the inn. Let us discuss how to live peaceably as neighbors."

Cutler had no desire to make merry with Parthalán's underlings, but he must not miss this opportunity to learn more about the workings of the town. Léana had made good progress with Abigail Ayers and Rebecca Collinge, but the men held the ultimate power in Cape Agamenticus, not the women.

Cutler followed Ayers to the York Village Inn, where a dozen men sat in the taproom drinking whiskey and cider. One man after another greeted him with a hearty hello, shaking his hand and clapping him on the back. Before he knew it, he held a pint of ale. He sipped from it as the men talked, shouted, and joked. No business was mentioned, but maybe that was the point.

An hour later, Cutler moved to take his leave. Another tankard of ale was thrust into his hand, and he was cajoled into idling a while longer. By the time he left the inn, one day had turned into the next. He returned to his horse, Bertha, tied to a post near the cemetery, and hopped onto the beast's sturdy back.

Cutler heard the heavy panting as he approached Agamenticus Center. The horse whinnied and started to rear up. Cutler clenched the reins and patted her neck. "Now, Bertha, you'll be fine. Stay calm, girl."

But Bertha wanted to gallop, so Cutler let her have her head. As horse and rider passed through Agamenticus Center, Bertha whinnied in terror and began kicking out with her rear legs.

Cutler looked down and saw three wolves biting at Bertha's hooves. More wolves rushed toward him in the moonlight.

Bertha panicked and left the road for the woods, crashing through the trees as Cutler ducked to protect himself from being decapitated by low boughs. With his arms encircling Bertha's neck, he was unable to hold onto the stone that hung from a leather cord around his neck. A sharp twig ripped the leather band in half and the stone tumbled to the ground. Bertha's hoof drove it six inches into the earth.

The horse reared in panic as the wolves approached from left, right, front, and back. Cutler held on as Bertha jumped over the wolves in front of her. She crashed through the trees before stopping short at a massive boulder that was too high for her to clear. Cutler flew from the saddle and sailed over the boulder. The wolves jumped and tore him to pieces before he hit the ground.

•   •   •

In the parlor of her house, Léana was pouring herself a glass of water from an earthenware pitcher. She dropped the pitcher, which shattered into pieces on the floor, and screamed.

"No!" She shrieked. "No! No!"

She slid to the floor, knowing she would never share her happy news with her husband: She had been carrying his child for four months, and she'd been waiting for the right moment to tell him. She herself hadn't been sure until a week ago. Her cycles had been irregular since she was a girl, and she'd experienced no morning sickness and no symptoms beyond a tightening of her clothes as she entered her fourth month.

She was certain the child was a girl.

•   •   •

On the bluff, Elias Featherstone heard the screams coming from the Hauers' house. He wondered if Parthalán had succeeded in doing whatever it was that he planned to do.

A heavy wind blew in from the ocean. The sound was not familiar. Elias surveyed the Atlantic. A large flock of seagulls was rushing inland.

Suddenly the birds were on him, attacking his face, chest, and genitals. As he used his hands to protect himself from their ripping beaks, two birds pecked out his eyes.

Before he lost consciousness, he heard a whisper in his ear: *Now you will no longer be able to watch my house, Elias Featherstone.*

66

Route 1, Maine

Matthew's heart throbbed in his tonsils as he walked into Julie's Bar & Restaurant. He'd blasted the radio at maximum volume on the drive, trying to drive thoughts of Creutzfeldt-Jakob, Wernicke-Korsakoff, and vasculitis from his mind.

Walt, the owner/manager, crossed the dining room, moving toward him.

"Hey, Walt," Matthew said. "I came to check out Carl and the Cavemen."

"They're setting up in the back now. Hey, are you OK?"

It took Matthew a second to understand the question. Walt was referring to the blood Matthew had left on the barroom floor after he'd played his set—during Josh's unexpected visit.

"Yeah, I'm OK. I had surgery a few weeks ago, and I guess I'm not fully healed yet. I feel terrible that Dave had to mop up after me."

Walt shrugged. "He's mopped up a lot worse than that. Listen, take care of yourself, OK?"

Matthew walked along a narrow hallway into the ass-end of the restaurant, where a makeshift dining room jutted into the parking lot at a 90-degree angle from the bar. A thick, clear-plastic overhang kept the rain out. Locals sat at the rickety plastic tables chatting and laughing, their beer bottles and wine glasses within easy reach.

"Hey, Matthew." A hand waved him over. Chuck, the redhead.

Matthew threaded his way through the tables. The Juilliard grads had saved a chair for him. He fist-bumped each of the guys—Chuck, Trey, Greg, Mickey.

All of them were real. He hadn't hallucinated them. Each of them wore a wedding band. He hadn't noticed that when he'd first shaken hands with them.

The conversation was free of content, punctuated with "dude"s and "bro"s and good-natured insults, but to Matthew it was as nourishing and comforting as a home-cooked meal.

As Carl and the Cavemen took their final bow, Trey said, "I hate when Carl talks his way through the high notes. He can hit them when he makes the effort."

"Do you guys sing?" Matthew asked, already knowing the answer. No critic is tougher on a vocalist than another singer. Matthew himself could not listen to the radio without analyzing every vocal performance and thinking about how he would have done it differently.

"If you make us, yeah," Mickey said.

"How about we jam, try some a cappella stuff?" Matthew suggested. "I'm a tenor, but I can go a little lower."

"Baritone," said Greg.

"Bass," said Trey and Chuck simultaneously.

"Countertenor," said Mickey, pointing to himself.

A perfect quintet. "So what do you guys think?" Matthew said. "Do you wanna get something together?"

"Sure, why the hell not?" Mickey replied. "How about tonight?"

"You mean now?" Matthew asked. The drive to and from Bedford Hills had been tiring, and he'd had very little, if any, sleep. But jamming with a group of musicians might take his mind off his troubles.

"It's not like we're not doing anything else," Mickey said.

"It sounds awesome, but there's one thing," Matthew said. "My neighbors are a bunch of old cranks. I wouldn't want anybody to complain about noise."

"Bro," Trey said, "if anyone thinks of music as *noise*, they're not human and we shouldn't worry about them. Right?"

Kindred spirits, right here on Route 1 in southern Maine! "I'm staying in Agamenticus," Matthew said. "Agamenticus Cliff Road, number 99. It's off the shore road, right after the church if you're heading north."

"We know where it is," Greg said. "We'll pay the tab and meet you there in half an hour."

"Awesome." What a fantastic way to end an otherwise massively shitty day. Matthew extracted a $20 bill from his wallet for his share of the bill and tip. "Do you guys want to take my number in case you can't find the house?" he asked the group. "The problem is, the cell service is pretty unreliable."

Mickey waved away Matthew's money and threw a fifty on the table. "Don't worry. Like Greg said, we know where it is."

67

Cape Agamenticus, Maine
Mid-Spring 1749

Léana knew she was alone. Even Jerusha had deserted her.

She slept with her hand coiled around the stone that Reverend Edwards gave her. She felt both its warmth and its impotence. The stone hadn't saved Mariah or Cutler. How would it save her?

She could attempt to flee, to try making her way to Northampton or at least to Boston. She could creep away on Soldier's back in the dead of night, or attempt an audacious escape during the day, and take shelter at the safe houses at which she, Cutler, and Mariah had slept on their long journey to Maine.

She would be taken before she arrived in York Village.

She could travel north instead, beyond Ogunquit and Wells, but Parthalán's allies watched the road for miles in all directions, and her chances of eluding capture were slim to nonexistent.

She accepted the profound irony that she was safest in her house on the spit, surrounded by enemies.

•   •   •

Following Cutler's disappearance, Léana assisted several women in liberating their children's spirits. Much subterfuge was required, and the task was much more difficult now that Parthalán rarely left town. The women used increasingly risky methods to divert the guards as they sneaked into the cliffside cave and the church cellar.

The women had come to Léana's house, always during the day while their husbands were out, always wearing large caps and broad cloaks, always looking over their shoulders. The first two, after Rebecca Collinge, were friends of Leah Meer's. Both had given children to keep the fields and ocean productive and to prevent fierce windstorms from decimating the town.

Léana welcomed the women into her home. She suggested that they enlist Abigail or Rebecca's aid, but they insisted that Léana accompany them. They knew what had happened to Elias on the bluff, and their husbands had refused to take Elias's post. For the sake of their wives and children, the men declared, they needed their eyesight. Nor would the community be well served by having to care for an increasing population of blind men.

"With your help, Abigail and Rebecca avoided detection," the first woman whispered. "We ask you for the same help, the same protection."

Léana examined the supplicants' faces. Just weeks earlier, they'd rebuffed her attempts at conversation. Now they sat trembling in her parlor, terrified for their lives.

Léana prayed for guidance and agreed to help them.

Thus Léana's reputation grew, as did her number of friends. At night, bunches of flowers, jars of preserves, and bolts of cloth were left on her doorstep as tokens of gratitude.

68

Kinnawe House
Agamenticus, Maine

As Matthew was rummaging in the refrigerator, Trey knocked on the kitchen door. Matthew waved the guys in. They had no trouble entering the house. Matthew remembered that he himself, Helen, and the dream-time Priscilla had all needed help to get up the deck stairs the first time. Only Kellyce hadn't needed help to get into the house—but she'd entered through the back door, not from the deck.

"Cool house," Mickey said. "Your folks own it?"

"No, I'm the winter caretaker," Matthew replied, transferring bottles of water from the fridge to the dining room table.

"Getting chilly," Mickey said. "Better close the window." He pulled the sash up and clicked the lock into place.

Matthew respected Helen's admonition to always leave a window open, but Mickey was right. The night had become quite cold, and closing the window for just a couple of hours was unlikely to result in a catastrophe. Matthew would re-open it after the guys left.

In the living room, Greg tapped out the opening notes of Beethoven's Fifth on the piano. Mickey removed the skinny fiddle and bow from the wall. He drew the bow across the fiddle, eliciting a few sweet notes from Mozart's *Eine kleine Nachtmusick*.

"We brainstormed on the way over," Trey said. "How about an *a cappella* of 'Suite: Judy Blue Eyes'"?

"*Yes*! Great idea!" Matthew gushed.

The guys arranged themselves in a circle.

"Here goes," Trey said. "One, two, one, two, three, four ..."

Matthew couldn't believe his ears. All four of the Juilliard guys had perfect pitch. He worried that his excellent, but far from perfect, tenor was ruining the song. But he went with the music, and before he knew it, the Suite was over and the guys were smacking one another on the back, laughing and congratulating themselves.

Mickey threw himself onto the couch and stretched his arms over his head. A rank odor emanated from his armpits, where he'd sweated through his T-shirt.

"Dude, you reek," Chuck said.

"Hey Matthew, where's the bathroom?" Mickey asked.

"Down the hall, on the right," Matthew said, pointing. "That was so awesome. I never do things like this at home."

"What's that around your neck?" Trey asked, pointing to the stone dangling from the leather cord.

"Just something my mother gave me," Matthew said.

"Can I see it? Looks interesting. What is it, a rune?"

Matthew's brain said: *No, don't take it off. Make an excuse.*

From the bathroom came the sound of water rushing into the bathtub.

"It's kind of a good luck thing for me," Matthew said. "I haven't taken it off for a long time."

"Come on, man," Trey insisted. "Taking it off isn't going to kill you."

Unable to come up with another excuse, Matthew reached behind his neck and untied the cord. He pulled the stone from his neck and dropped it, cord and all, into Trey's outstretched hand.

As soon as the stone touched Trey's skin, Trey yelped in pain. Matthew couldn't quite process what had happened. It looked as if the stone had burned a hole clean through Trey's hand and fallen to the floor. As Trey howled in agony, Chuck kicked the stone under the couch.

Matthew felt dizzy. His eyes watered; his nose ran. His lungs filled with a thick, gelatinous phlegm.

Mickey was back. "You've got a real sweet deal here, Matt," he said. "But you don't deserve it."

Matthew wiped his eyes, trying to clear his vision. The four guys had become fuzzy outlines.

"Not after what you did to your mother," Mickey said. "Slipping tranquilizers into her juice when she wasn't looking."

Nobody knew about that ethical lapse except Matthew, and maybe Rose of Sharon herself. Matthew's mind went into overdrive, trying to determine how Mickey could have found out. Maybe he worked at the Bedford Hills Institute, maybe he'd heard Rose of Sharon inveighing against him. But the idea was irrational, wild. Mickey was a Juilliard-trained musician from Maine, not an orderly at a Westchester County mental hospital.

"You didn't care that she was allergic to the pills," Mickey said. "You just wanted her unconscious so that you didn't have to deal with her. Josh visited her at the Institute more often than you did."

The fact that Mickey had worked at the Institute was less shocking than the idea that Josh had visited his mother there. Josh, supposedly Matthew's closest friend, had gone to visit Rose of Sharon after she sliced and diced her own son. But how did four musicians from Maine know who Josh was?

Matthew's shirt was dripping with blood from scars that had ripped open. In the background, the water taps continued to fill the bathtub.

Mickey pushed Matthew onto the couch. "Your mother talked about you a lot," he said. "She told me how you attacked her. How she had to protect herself with a knife."

"No," Matthew wheezed. "You've got it all wrong. *She* attacked *me*." He couldn't think straight. The details of the attack were hazy, confused. He remembered lifting his hands to protect his face, but not fighting back. While convalescing, he'd asked himself over and over: *Why* hadn't he fought back? His answer was always the same: She was his mother. He was incapable of hurting her, even though she was trying to kill him.

"She told me about your disease," Mickey continued. "That's why your girlfriend had the abortion. She didn't want to give birth to a deformed freak."

The words pierced Matthew's heart like a stiletto. Sticky tears sealed his eyelids shut, blinding him. Both Kellyce and Josh had said his genes were defective. Now Mickey was confirming everything in Matthew's DNA analysis. *He* was the sickness. All the people in his life were trying to protect themselves from *him*.

"Everybody sees you for what you are, Matthew. Infected," Trey said. "No family. No friends."

The bald truth he'd fought for so long, and tried so hard to deny.

• • •

Outside Kinnawe House, Helen stared at the closed kitchen window. She ran around the perimeter of the house, seeking a way in, but the house was sealed tight.

In her mind she screamed *Jerusha! Jerusha!*

A mile out over the Atlantic Ocean, the dove began flapping her wings as hard and as fast as she could.

• • •

As Matthew leaned against the couch, Chuck delivered a vicious punch to his head. Matthew toppled to the floor, face first. He struggled to his knees.

"Why are you doing this?" he gasped. "What did I do to you?"

"What did you do? You got our wives tortured and killed. You got us imprisoned. You destroyed our town, our livelihoods, everything we worked to build."

"What are you talking about? I never met you before last night!"

"Don't think about *us*, Matthew. Think about yourself, the way you always do. You know why your mother wanted you dead. You deserve to die, and you know it."

Mickey, Chuck, and Trey advanced on Matthew. Mickey and Chuck each grabbed one of Matthew's arms. Trey grabbed a leg as Greg watched the proceedings.

"Don't just stand there, Gregory," Mickey ordered. "Grab his other leg."

As Greg hesitated, Mickey said through gritted teeth, "I said *grab his leg*, Gregory. You may not want your wife back, but we want ours."

"It's not going to work," Greg said. "He'll find a way to keep us here. We'll never see them again, no matter what we do."

"Spoken like the traitor you are," Mickey spat.

Trey looked at Greg. "You owe us, Gregory."

Greg seemed to come to a decision. He wrapped his hands around Matthew's leg, and the four of them carried Matthew, struggling and writhing, into the bathroom, where they dumped him on the floor.

The bathtub was full. Mickey turned off the taps. "End it, Matthew. Now. Take your own life before you hurt someone else."

"Who would I hurt? I don't want to hurt anyone."

"Maybe Priscilla. Maybe Helen. Maybe Walt. They've all been good to you, and you're just going to get them killed."

"I wouldn't do that."

"You will," Gregory said gently. "You have to accept it, Matthew. It's who you are. So end it now while you have friends here to help you."

•   •   •

Matthew broke—and his heart admitted that he deserved the four guys' hatred. Deserved his mother's attack, deserved to have his child aborted, deserved to be betrayed by his closest friend, deserved to be alone and friendless. He grabbed the edge of the bathtub and pulled himself onto his knees. He felt a hand on his neck—Chuck's? Mickey's? His own?—as he plunged his head into the eighteen inches of water in the bathtub.

He'd heard that drowning was a horrible death, but it wasn't. The water filling his lungs seemed to push every thought of his mother, his father, Josh, and Kellyce from his mind. The release was intoxicating.

He gave himself to the water, grateful to the friends who'd brought him here.

•   •   •

The window shattered as the dove hurled herself through it, breaking her beak and a wing.

It was enough to get Helen in. She rushed into the bathroom and hurled a piece of the stone at each of her neighbors. She'd found it on her doorstep earlier that day, wrapped in a lock of red hair. It was Mariah's stone. Bébhinn had found it deep in the cave, after searching for it for centuries.

Matthew's tormentors—Gregory Brautigam, Michael Ayers, Sebastian Collinge III, and Charles Meer—dissipated in spasms of agony into the night.

69

Cape Agamenticus, Maine
Late Spring 1749

Parthalán spent every night searching his books for any bit of wisdom, any sentence or illustration, that might explain the changes in Cape Agamenticus. He felt himself weakening. He'd been losing his balance after nightfall. One fall had resulted in a painful bruised kneecap. Another had broken the pinkie of his left hand. His right cheekbone had been mashed into a bloody pulp when he crashed to the kitchen floor. The more he weakened, the harder he worked to hide his new vulnerability from the congregation.

Alone in the church basement, he requested guidance, but the Protector remained silent. That was one of the challenges of serving the Protector. He did not always deign to answer Parthalán's questions or provide the guidance Parthalán sought. Sometimes, Parthalán knew, He provided misleading or false information, for no reason other than to enjoy the ensuing conflict.

Emma was aiding him in his quest for information, but she'd uncovered nothing useful. In her quest to free her brother and keep her father alive, she'd succeeded in establishing friendships with her neighbors. She reported every word and every gesture to him, but Parthalán detected nothing suspicious or revealing in Emma's reports.

One of the books on his desk was a codex that had been under lock and key in a Welsh monastery for centuries. It contained pharmacological advice—not for the cure of diseases and ailments but for the creation of them. To inflict gout on a man, rub chicken fat between his toes while he is drunk on strawberry wine. To conjure rheumatism, mix quinine with cardamom and adulterate a dark ale with the mixture. To induce consumption, create a paste of camphor, marigold juice, and sulfur and place a dollop of the mixture under the target's bed.

But none of the recipes would weaken Léana, the only friend he'd ever had.

Returning the codex to the shelf, Parthalán tripped on the Persian rug. Three of his toes snapped like brittle twigs.

As he sat in his chair, his toes throbbing, the snake uncurled itself from his waist, slithered down his leg, and shot across the library.

The seeds do not flourish in Emma's womb, the snake hissed.

Mrs. Feeley says they are safe and healthy.

Both will be weak and unworthy.

They are my offspring. My son will thrive and build another community, as I have done here.

You expect a child born in wedlock to be worthy of serving Him?

The marriage is a sham. She believes us to be married, but we are not.

She sees herself as a married woman performing her duties in the marital bed. A married woman cannot be raped by her husband.

She is not a married woman, and I am not her husband.

Tonight, create a child who is worthy of serving Him.

Explain your words.

Your enemy. You have taken her maid and her husband. She is alone. Take her tonight.

She is protected. I am not permitted within two dozen paces of her.

You were resourceful with the girl and the husband.

Her protection is more powerful.

Meanwhile you weaken. Act tonight, while you can.

The serpent's advice was not always to be trusted, but it plucked at the chord of worry that had plagued Parthalán since his fall at the Red Boar Inn in Boston. He'd taken Josephine Alcott in her own bedchamber. Perhaps an additional back-up plan was called for.

"Lotte! Summon Brautigam, Meer, Ayers, and Collinge at once."

70

Kinnawe House
Agamenticus, Maine

Helen dragged Matthew, unconscious, to the couch in the parlor, where she undressed him, dried him, and wrapped him in blankets.

She sat at Matthew's side until daybreak. As night turned into day, his breathing slowed, and he began trembling. Increasingly harder taps on his cheeks did not rouse him. Under the blankets his skin was a purplish-blue.

No! She would not lose him.

She located Matthew's phone, found Doctor Ansari's contact information, and touched the CALL icon.

"Doctor's answering service."

"I need help. My friend almost drowned."

"I'm connecting you to 911."

"No! They won't be able to find us. We live in the middle of nowhere."

"Is he breathing?"

"Yes, but barely. His name is Matthew Rollins. Please, can you get in touch with Doctor Ansari? I'm afraid Matthew's going to die."

"Please hold while I find a way to assist you."

"Tell the doctor to call me back at this number." She hung up.

Matthew's phone rang two minutes later.

"This is Doctor Max Ansari. Are you with Matthew Rollins?"

"I'm his neighbor, Helen Crowe. I found him unconscious next to his bathtub, soaking wet, with all his clothes on. I can't get him to respond. Doctor, can you come? I don't drive, and we're all alone here."

"He may have hypothermia. We need to get him to a hospital. Give me directions."

Helen did so, adding, "I'll wait for you at the side of the road. What do you drive?"

"A red Volvo sedan."

"I'm wearing a green dress with a hibiscus flower pattern. How long will it take you to get here?"

"About half an hour. In the meantime, don't try to stop him from shivering. That's a good thing. If he starts to come to, ask him if he can swallow. If he can, give him something warm to drink, like coffee or hot chocolate. No alcohol. Don't massage his limbs. I'm on my way."

Helen prayed that Matthew would be alive upon his arrival at the hospital.

• • •

She dragged Matthew's inert body beyond the house perimeter, because Doctor Ansari wouldn't be able to enter the house without Matthew's assistance. She was close to weeping in sorrow, frustration, and anger as she waited for Doctor Ansari to arrive. Despite her attempts to protect Matthew, she was losing the battle. The Foe knew her weaknesses and was exploiting them.

She'd been sitting in that house on the spit of land, waiting for Matthew to arrive, for more than ten years. The illness, Bébhinn had told her, might strike as early as age 18. Matthew was now 28. Jerusha had kept an eye on him in New York while Helen waited for Parthalán to bring Matthew to the house and drive him to suicide.

She couldn't step off her small, protected piece of property without feeling the heat of Parthalán's fury, more than two centuries later. This wasn't Parthalán's first attempt to destroy the last of the good twins, but she was determined that it would be his last. It had been going on for too long. He wanted to end it once and for all. So did she.

And this time it *would* end. Soon, one of them would win. Parthalán Kinnawe or Léana Hauer. Bartholomew Dubh or Helen Crowe. But she was outnumbered. She had the help of only Jerusha and God. Parthalán had his protector and his henchmen, who were driven by their own desire for revenge and their eternal servitude to the man to whom they'd pledged their souls in the 1740s. The balance had tipped in their favor.

As the Volvo rounded the bend, Helen began waving her arms. She climbed into the car, and Doctor Ansari drove her to the house, where he pulled out his stethoscope and checked Matthew's vital signs.

"I'm going to take him to Portland General," Doctor Ansari said. "Do you want to come with us?"

"My husband is bedridden. I can't leave him. I'll keep Matthew's phone with me. Please call me to tell me what he needs."

As Doctor Ansari's car disappeared up the shore road, Helen felt the same fear she'd felt the night that the wolves tore her husband apart. She welcomed the fear. It gave her the strength that had cost Elias Featherstone his sight.

71

Portland, Maine

Doctor Emmanuel Sands, director of the Sleep Disorders Center at Portland General, sat at his desk, examining Matthew Rollins' EEG.

Max Ansari had prescribed a strong slow-on, slow-off benzodiazepine and an atypical antipsychotic. The combination almost guaranteed a good night's sleep. But Matthew had been in the hospital more than 48 hours, and in those two days he hadn't slept for one second. His brain was stuck in the ON position. The EEG readings were downright bizarre. At first Doctor Sands thought that Matthew was a serious drug addict, that all his scars were track marks from botched injections of whatever poison had wreaked havoc on his brain. But a colleague had confirmed that the scars were the remnants of a knife attack, and all the tests seemed to confirm that Matthew hadn't had more than ten hours of sleep over the past two or three weeks.

The head nurse buzzed him. "Doctor, Matthew Rollins went into REM sleep about two minutes ago."

"I'm on my way," Doctor Sands said.

•　　•　　•

Matthew wanted to roll onto his side—to move his legs—to stretch his arms over his head. His ankles seemed nailed to the floor, his wrists to the walls.

He opened his eyes and tried to blink away the gumminess.

He wasn't in the oceanfront bedroom at Kinnawe House, nor his apartment on West 51st Street. This room was painted a soothing blue. Colorful paintings that looked like Marc Chagall or Franz Marc knock-offs lined the walls.

Matthew's heart missed a beat as he recognized his mother's studio apartment at the Bedford Hills Institute. The window, with its shatterproof glass, was protected by metal bars inside and out. Against the wall, on a small end table, sat the urn containing her ashes.

Matthew began to kick and struggle against the restraints that held him tight.

A shadow loomed over him. He looked up. Rose of Sharon Rollins stood over him, her long black hair and the knife blade glinting under the fluorescent light.

• • •

Doctor Sands walked into the room to find Matthew's body twitching and jerking. One of the scars on Matthew's neck popped, ripping open from top to bottom. As Matthew lifted his hands, the scars on his wrists tore open, spurting blood onto Doctor Sands' lab coat. As Matthew kicked the sheets and blanket from the bed, the scars on his legs and feet ripped open one after another. Within seconds his hospital gown and mattress had turned from ivory white to rosy pink to crimson red.

Doctor Sands had never witnessed such a horrifying spectacle. It was as if Matthew's body had decided to use every available scar to rid itself of all its blood.

Doctor Sands pushed the emergency button five times in rapid succession, and the nurses came running.

72

Portland, Maine

The nurses wrapped Matthew in gauze from his feet to his neck to stanch
the blood flow. The gauze bonded to the scars, sealing them shut. Within ten
minutes, Matthew's vital signs stabilized.

Sealing the scars was a temporary solution, Doctor Sands knew. What
Matthew needed more than anything was sleep. But nothing shut down
Matthew's brain: not a double dose of benzos, not knock-you-on-your-ass
antipsychotics, not a hardcore morphine drip.

Doctor Sands hurried from the room to order a complete blood work-up.
Portland General did not have the equipment to perform such a complicated
analysis, so Doctor Sands called a friend at a Boston lab and requested a rush
job.

• • •

Matthew's eyes sprang open, but his body was paralyzed.

He looked first to his right, then to his left. He was restrained in a
hospital bed, but not at the Bedford Hills Institute. The window was not
criss-crossed with bars, inside or out. He was alive, not dead after drowning
in a bathtub. Every scar on his body throbbed, but the pain was bearable.
The last time he'd been in a hospital, he hadn't been able to bat an eyelid
without engaging every pain receptor in his nervous system.

The restraints were disconcerting, but somehow reassuring. He would rather be restrained here in a hospital room, his eyes wide open, than blind on the bathroom floor at Kinnawe House. He attempted to wriggle his fingers and toes. They obeyed the signals from his brain.

"Hello!" he shouted. "Can someone help me please?"

A nurse—according to her name badge, CYNTHIA EUZELL, R.N.—entered the room.

"Where am I?" Matthew asked.

"Portland General Hospital. You were brought in unconscious with hypothermia. We had to restrain you because you kept knocking your intravenous lines out. Let me undo the straps for you. How are you feeling, Matthew?"

"Not great, I guess. How long have I been here?"

"Six days."

"I've been asleep for six days?"

"Well, not really *asleep*. Let me call Doctor Sands. He'll explain everything to you."

Matthew was watching a *Friends* rerun when Doctor Sands entered the room and introduced himself. After some small talk, the doctor said, "Matthew, we need to talk about your test results." The doctor took a deep breath. "I'm sorry to have to tell you that you have a rare, inherited disease called fatal familial insomnia, or FFI. About 25 families in the world carry the gene for it. FFI usually sets in by age 18, but for some people, the onset is later. It starts as regular insomnia, but it quickly progresses until the person can't sleep at all."

FFI: The inherited gene that Kellyce and Josh had hinted at. Not Creutzfeldt-Jakob or Wernicke-Korsakoff, but something just as bad. His mother had said that his father had "it." Finally, Matthew knew what "it" was.

Doctor Sands continued, "The medications that Doctor Ansari prescribed and the sedatives we've given you here don't work on FFI. In fact, they can make the symptoms worse, so we've taken you off them."

"So I haven't slept at all? For weeks? Or months?" Going sleepless for so long explained almost everything: the ghosts, the delusions, the imaginary friends and lovers, the night terrors.

"I can't speak to your condition before Doctor Ansari brought you here," Doctor Sands said, "but by strict medical definition, you've slept only about an hour in the last six days, on your third day here. While you were asleep you experienced a major trauma. Every scar on your body popped open. We thought you might need a blood transfusion, but fortunately you didn't."

"What happens when you go without sleep for so long?"

Doctor Sands frowned. "The body can't function without sleep, Matthew. Neither can the brain. Hallucinations and delusions are common. You've been having them here, talking to people who don't exist."

So it wasn't a mental illness. It was a genetic ailment that took a toll on the brain, which was different. Very different.

"Would you believe this is actually a *relief*?" Matthew said. "I thought I was going crazy. At least now I know I'm not. Or at least that there's a reason for it."

"I can see where that would be a relief," Doctor Sands said.

"You said *fatal* familial insomnia. How much longer do I have?"

"Not long, Matthew. Maybe two weeks. A month at most. I'm sorry."

A month. It should have been a shock, but it wasn't, not after Kellyce and Josh had put the idea in his head.

A month. Enough time, maybe, to find his father. To say a simultaneous hello and good-bye.

• • •

Jerusha nestled high in the Norway spruce near Helen's house, her injured beak tucked under her broken wing. She heard the gunshot and was dead before she hit the ground.

73

Cape Agamenticus, Maine
Late Spring 1749

The whisper came from outside Léana's bedroom window.

"Dearest," said the deep, familiar voice. "I must speak with you."

"Where are you, Cutler?" Léana whispered.

"The remains of my body are in a cask in Parthalán's cellar. My heart is nowhere. It was burnt to cinders."

"Oh, Cutler. Do you suffer?"

"The pain is being separated from you, and being forced to abandon you. Parthalán set wolves on me. I was thrown from Bertha and ripped to pieces. A small bone from my hand lies in the woods across the shore road, unfound by the deaf-mutes. I will bring you to it. Bury it in the cemetery, next to Mariah."

Léana threw open the window and embraced the ghost of her dead husband.

"Come, Léana. We do not have long."

Léana lit two candles and dressed. Cutler led her by the hand out of the back door, up the road, and into the woods where he'd died.

"There," Cutler said, using his candle to illuminate the ground. "There is my bone."

Léana picked up the bone and tucked it into a pocket.

"Now, at last, I may find some peace," Cutler said, taking Léana's hand and helping her rise from the ground.

He reached into his pocket and pulled out a stone attached to a leather cord.

"You must wear this, dearest. It was pulled from my neck as Bertha crashed through the trees. Reverend Edwards gave me the strongest talisman because he believed I would face the most danger and need the most protection. You must wear it, instead of yours, henceforth."

Léana touched her stone. "Reverend Edwards told us not to remove our stones. I have removed it only when doing so was necessary to help the women find their children's remains."

"Please understand, dearest. You must not wear both stones. They might be ripped from you as mine was ripped from me, and as Mariah's was ripped from her. Wear mine and hide yours in a safe place. Not in the house. They will search the house."

"But they cannot enter the house."

"They are becoming stronger, Léana. They crucified Mariah, and they set the wolves on me. Soon they will find a way to invade our home. No, let us bury your stone here—next to the boulder over which Bertha threw me. They will not find it here. But first, place my stone around your neck."

Léana took the necklace from Cutler's hand and tied it around her neck. With trembling hands she untied the knot on her own necklace and let it drop into her hands. Cutler extended his hand, and his wife placed her necklace into his palm.

Four men appeared out of the darkness and pinned Léana to the boulder. Meer and Brautigam pulled up her dress while Ayers and Collinge pulled down her knickers.

Cutler was gone, replaced by Parthalán. He undid his belt and dropped his trousers.

Léana lost consciousness as the snake forced itself inside her.

Part VI
Shatter What Remains

74

Cape Agamenticus, Maine
Late Spring 1749

As she stumbled back to her house in the darkness, Léana knew she would survive. That was the whole point.

He hadn't taken her protective stone. It had been around her neck when consciousness returned. She felt its warmth and knew it was not a fake.

Two weeks after the rape, as her battered body worked to heal itself, a gut-wrenching nausea hit her without warning as she sat in the parlor, staring at the ocean and thinking about Cutler. She threw open the door and flung herself to her knees on the beach, where she vomited up a green, chunky stream that burned her throat like a corrosive acid. She hadn't eaten much since the rape—just broth, tea, and the sweets that were her secret indulgence, the chocolates and caramels that Cutler said were the way to her heart—but her body seemed to expel every ounce of sustenance she'd taken, liquid or solid.

Her stomach empty, she returned to the parlor, where she lowered herself into her chair and considered the grim truth: She was now carrying not only Cutler's child, but also Parthalán's.

•

Bébhinn came to her that night.

Léana felt a hand stroking her hair and imagined the hand was Cutler's. Bébhinn sat on the bed next to her.

"He has ruined you," Bébhinn said. "You, who showed us nothing but kindness when we all lived with Reverend Edwards. This is how he repays you."

"I carry the child of a good man, and the child of an evil one. What am I to do, Bébhinn? Where am I to go? What is Parthalán's plan for me and my children?" Reverend Edwards had assured her that the house on the spit was safe. But for how much longer?

"You do not carry two children, Léana. You carry three. The girl is Cutler's. The two boys are Parthalán's."

Léana gasped. To carry Parthalán's child was horrifying enough. But *two* of his children, alongside her own?

Bébhinn continued, "What I am about to tell you, Léana, is known only to the women who conceive by men such as Parthalán. Listen, and I will explain the choice you must make."

After Bébhinn finished her explanation, Léana said, "So, you chose the wrong child to kill."

Bébhinn nodded. "I was certain I had chosen correctly. I studied each child for an hour, because Parthalán's grandmother said I must wait no longer than that. The boy I smothered had a greenish tint to his skin and a large black birthmark on his tailbone. Meanwhile, Parthalán was so beautiful, it seemed he must be a gift from God. I made my choice when I was young and naïve, before I knew that evil can and does take the form of beauty."

"And now you tell me that, like you, I must kill one boy while allowing the other to live?" When Léana began her journey from Northampton to Maine, she had not considered that doing God's work would mean murdering a child. The mere idea of it challenged not only her faith but also her humanity.

"No," Bébhinn said. "I tell you that both boys must die. It is the only way to end the cycle."

"But you said the good twin, if he lives, becomes a warrior in the battle against the demon. How can I take the life of a baby blessed with God's grace?"

"It is our only option, Léana. I have eavesdropped as Parthalán consults with his master. Emma is pregnant with two children, but her babies grow slowly. They may wither and die before they are born, and he knows this. He must have an heir before he himself is taken. The only progeny who can succeed him must be delivered by a good, God-fearing woman whom he has raped. But do not fear. I will help you.

"When the time is right, I will leave on your doorstep a vial filled with a dark green potion. Drink the entire bottle in one gulp on the day that you begin to feel a scratching in your womb. It contains ingredients that are toxic to Parthalán and will kill his issue. The potion will make you miscarry at least one of the boys. If you are lucky, you will miscarry both."

"But what of Cutler's child? Can you guarantee she will not be harmed?" Léana fought against her tears. "My child was conceived in love. She is all that remains of Cutler. I will not endanger her."

"Reverend Edwards sent you here to plant the seeds of this town's destruction. Long before you arrived, you knew that sacrifices would be required. You must not weaken now."

"But I have already sacrificed my husband and Mariah. Even Jerusha seems not to have survived. I do not have the strength, or the will, to sacrifice not one child, nor two, but three."

"There is no need to act yet. Parthalán permits you to keep your stone because of the protection it affords his children. He believes you will do nothing to harm them while you wear it. You must allow him to continue believing thus while I make the arrangements. Do nothing until we speak again. I swear on my mother's grave that I will liberate the few good people in this town, and you are one of them, Léana."

75

Portland, Maine

After two weeks at Portland General, Matthew was leaving.

He'd told Doctor Sands he didn't want to spend his final days in a hospital, as his mother had. He wanted to play his guitar, write songs, search for his father, and let death come when it would. So Doctor Sands called Doctor Ansari, who called Helen at Matthew's phone number. Helen agreed to care for Matthew during his final days, and arrangements were made for Matthew's return.

In a strange way, he wanted to apologize to Kinnawe House. He'd spun wild tales in his mind about the house's latent evil to explain the manifestations of his fatal insomnia. But there was nothing wrong with Kinnawe House. It was a beautiful, peaceful mansion on a lonely stretch of the coastline. The ugliness was inside him, not inside the house.

Doctor Sands had warned him the disease would lead to complete dementia. Ultimately, he'd become mute and unresponsive to any stimuli. A few days later, he'd take his last breath. He would slip from a living oblivion to a nonliving one. There was no treatment, no cure, no hope. Just as Kellyce and Josh had said.

He wondered how they knew before he did. Rose of Sharon was the only logical explanation. She'd told Josh, and Josh had told Kellyce.

Matthew thanked the nurses and shook Doctor Sands' hand. "Don't forget, Matthew," Doctor Sands said, "keep the restraint on, and use it when you feel yourself starting to slip away."

One end of a PVC restraint dangled from Matthew's left wrist. To prevent him from harming himself or anyone else, Matthew was under strict orders to manacle himself to something solid when he felt himself going under. When consciousness returned, he would determine whether to unlock himself.

The head nurse, Cynthia Euzell, arrived to say that Matthew's friend had arrived. An orderly brought in a wheelchair, and Matthew lowered himself into it, wincing. He'd lost twenty pounds during his stay at Portland General, and his buttocks had disappeared.

Matthew's banged-up Civic waited at the curb in the discharge area. Priscilla emerged from the driver's seat.

"Hi, Matthew," she said. "I'm here to take you home."

He hadn't imagined her. Matthew wanted to drop to his knees, fold her hand in his, and kiss it.

• • •

Priscilla drove down I-95, the quickest route from Portland to Agamenticus.

Matthew tried not to stare at Priscilla. She was real. She was here. She was driving him home.

"When they said a friend was coming to get me, I thought it was Helen," he said.

"She found my number in your phone and called me."

"You know about my condition?"

Priscilla nodded.

"Bear with me," Matthew said, "because I can't always tell the difference between what really happened and what I imagined. I picked you up at your neighbor's house. We tried to sing together, but you were terrified of something and ran out of the house. Your car was waiting in the driveway, and you drove away."

"All of that happened, Matthew."

That wasn't the answer he'd expected, and it raised more questions. "But why did you run out of the house? And how did your car get there?"

"I had written a note to my parents. You texted me your address, remember? My mother drove my car to your house, and my father followed her in his truck. They thought it was super-nice of you to pick me up, and they wanted to spare you the trouble of bringing me home. As for running out of there, the cheese made me sick to my stomach. I was so terrified that I might puke in front of you, I ran out of there like a screaming drama queen. Believe me, I'm not proud of it."

"In other words, nothing supernatural." Just a combination of rancid cheese, a beautiful girl's desire to avoid embarrassment, and fatal familial insomnia.

"Nope. Just an unfortunate confluence of events," Priscilla said, keeping her eyes on the road.

Priscilla's phone, which sat inside the storage compartment between the two front seats, began tinkling a tune Matthew didn't recognize.

"Would you see who it is, Matthew?" Priscilla asked.

Matthew picked up the phone and saw a photo of a handsome bearded man in a clerical collar. The words SVEN KOSKINEN appeared on the screen over his head.

"Sven Koskinen," Matthew said.

"Oh, I'll call him back later. Just let it go to voice mail, please."

As Matthew placed Priscilla's phone back into the storage compartment, he wondered why the man looked so familiar, and why his last name was carved into an oak barrel in the basement of Kinnawe House.

· · ·

Sven Koskinen had told Priscilla the story he'd pieced together about the events in Cape Agamenticus in 1749, when the entire town, established by a devil worshipper named Parthalán Kinnawe, had been obliterated. A branch of the Presbyterian Church, Sven explained, owned the land now but wanted nothing to do with hundreds of acres on which heinous atrocities had been committed centuries earlier. His dreams were haunted by visions of Einar's near-escape, capture, and ripped-out Adam's apple.

Einar wandered the Maine and New Hampshire seacoast, making an occasional appearance in Sven's peripheral vision. Sven's brothers of the cloth had advised him to "let it go," but he couldn't. He'd made it his mission to help his ancestor find peace, but he'd failed time and again. He'd wandered in circles and found not the slightest trace of Cape Agamenticus, though newspapers from the period specified its precise location. And after each excursion in search of Einar's remains, he'd been injured. One morning he woke up with gaping, excruciating puncture wounds in the palms of both hands. Another time he'd risen from bed and fallen to the floor, unable to find his legs. The paralysis had lasted three days.

Following these misfortunes, Sven Koskinen changed his methodology. He now did most of his sleuthing in libraries and archives when he was not attending to his church duties. He had vowed not to return to Cape Agamenticus until he was certain to find Einar's bones, or until he discovered a way to protect himself from the dark forces that remained on the land.

Sven had ended his tale with a piece of advice. "You've had an encounter with evil, Priscilla. Try to forget it happened, and get on with your life."

"But what about Matthew, Sven? How does he fit into your story?"

"I don't know," Sven replied. "But we both know that you've been warned to stay away. Promise me you will."

After learning about Sven's stigmata and three-day paralysis, Priscilla did what any logical, rational person would do: She decided to heed Sven's advice and take care of herself. And not only herself, but her parents, too. They drove her crazy, but they loved her, and she loved them. She wouldn't bring such evil into their home again. The evil lived in Cape Agamenticus, and there it would stay.

She had pangs of conscience when she thought about Matthew, so she tried to think about him as little as possible. She'd kept herself busy for a couple of weeks, and then the caller ID displayed an incoming call from Matthew's phone. She considered ignoring it. But what if it was important, something she should share with Sven?

She tapped the ANSWER icon.

"Hello, Priscilla?" said an unfamiliar voice. "My name is Helen Crowe. I'm Matthew Rollins' neighbor. I found your number in his phone. He's in the hospital, and he needs a friend. I'm hoping you're a friend."

"You said you're Matthew's neighbor?"

"Yes. I live on the same road."

Priscilla shivered. Once again Kinnawe House was reaching south, across the Piscataqua River, to ensnare her, but she remembered her promise to Sven and kept her cool. "That means you can't be real, 'Helen Crowe.' Nobody has lived in Cape Agamenticus for 250 years. The town doesn't exist, and neither does the road you say you live on."

"How do you know this?"

"Because I've already been to Cape Agamenticus once, and I promised my pastor I won't go back."

"Your pastor? Is he a middle-aged blond with a thick beard, looks like a Viking?"

Priscilla's cool evaporated. "Why do you want to know? So you can hurt him again?"

"No, exactly the opposite. I've seen him searching for Einar along the cliff, and I've done everything in my power to keep him away. I'm not some omnipotent being, but I've been able to make him walk in circles to stop him from going places he shouldn't."

"He wants to find a resting place for Einar's soul."

"I lived here in the late 1740s and early 1750s. I know where Parthalán hid Einar's remains. Some of his bones are in a trench that surrounds the house. The others are hidden in the church crypt, and his heart is in a cliffside cave."

If Helen Crowe was telling the truth, she'd be almost three hundred years old. Priscilla felt a movement on her wrist. She looked at her dove tattoo, which flapped its wings once, twice, three times.

"Priscilla, please understand," Helen continued. "I'm trying to save Matthew's life, but I can't do it by myself. You and your pastor may be able to help. If you call Portland General Hospital and speak with Doctor Emmanuel Sands, he'll tell you that I truly am Matthew's friend. If we can protect Matthew, we can also retrieve Einar's remains and bury them in consecrated ground."

"I do want to help," Priscilla whispered.

"Then let me start at the beginning, child. My real name is Léana Mac Concradha Hauer. In the year 1727 I lived in Northampton, Massachusetts, where I served as housekeeper to the Reverend Jonathan Edwards. When the minister was a young man, he hired a young Irish woman to help his wife care for their children ..."

76

Cape Agamenticus, Maine
Late Spring 1749

Gregory Brautigam was traveling from Ogunquit to Cape Agamenticus at twilight. Parthalán planned to move some of his community to the "Beautiful Place by the Sea," with a goal of establishing another church there. He'd acquired several acres on the Ogunquit outskirts. Gregory had been surveying the plots and planning the new houses.

As his horses trotted along the shore road, Gregory reflected on his life's journey. He'd devolved from owning a successful business and adoring his children to doing the devil's work. He'd been lonely after Eliza died. He'd wanted to make a new start, and Lotte's invitation to move his family from Boston to Northampton seemed to promise that. Now his sister, once a good Christian woman, served the minister who tortured his children. He'd thought he was saving Tobias and Emma, but their deaths, and his own, would have been preferable to his daughter pregnant by Satan's minion and his son going mad in an attic prison.

The horses whinnied, ready to bolt. Gregory tightened his hold on the reins.

Bébhinn sat next to him on the box seat.

"I will be drawn and quartered if he discovers that I have talked with you," Gregory said, not making eye contact.

"You grow weary of him, don't you, Gregory? Of all the men, you regret your life most. He continues to wield so much power because you do not break away. When a strong man like you pledges your soul to him, weaker men have the excuse they need to continue living as they do."

Gregory stopped the horses.

"There is no way out for me, Bébhinn. My soul will roast in hell for what I have done to my dear, sweet girl, and my good, happy boy."

"Do you feel the forces gathering? Something will happen when Parthalán's children are born. Neither you nor I, nor anyone else, knows what will happen, but I *do* know you can be absent when it occurs, and you can have your children with you."

"Desert Parthalán?" To do so was to invite swift and barbaric revenge. "We will be tracked down and ripped to pieces."

"Parthalán is neither omnipotent nor omniscient," Bébhinn replied. "He is in league with a devious master who is no more loyal to him than you are to King George of England. Aid me in ending Parthalán's reign of terror."

"But how, Bébhinn?"

"First, you must get Naomi with child."

"She does not want a child. She says she is too old." But her eyes betrayed her lies. Gregory knew her desperation for a child, but she could not bear to make the same sacrifice that Abigail Ayers, Rebecca Collinge, and so many others had made.

"She sees that your heart is heavy with your children's suffering," Bébhinn said. "She knows you do not feel worthy of fatherhood. Because she loves you, her mind overcomes her body, and the seed does not take root. If she believed that you desire a child, she will conceive."

"I do not want another child, Bébhinn. Do you not know the fate of Calvin Ayers, Hester Collinge, and all the others? I have already lost two children to Parthalán. I will not give him a third."

"So instead you allow your friends' and neighbors' children to be taken, and innocent people to be kidnapped, tortured, and murdered? You sicken me, Gregory Brautigam. Parthalán chose well in you."

The accusation cut Gregory to the bone. "How dare you speak thus to me, Bébhinn? You know nothing of my troubles."

"Do not speak to me of troubles, Gregory. Do you pretend not to remember that I gave birth to the evil seed whose orders you obey, or that he murdered me in your presence? I can go where you cannot go, and I can see what you cannot see. You are not the only person in Cape Agamenticus who suffers. The question is: Will you allow the suffering to continue, or will you help me end it?"

Gregory knew: If Parthalán were trying to deceive him, he would not use Bébhinn to do so. The chasm between mother and son was too deep. Perhaps, after these four long years, Bébhinn was offering him an opportunity to escape his personal hell. "I do not understand, Bébhinn. How will getting Naomi with child destroy Parthalán?"

"I will explain."

$$\bullet \qquad \bullet \qquad \bullet$$

Gregory arrived home to find Naomi sitting at the piano in the parlor, playing a sonata she'd composed.

Gregory sat in his favorite chair as the quiet notes rose from the instrument. As Naomi drew the sonata to a close, Gregory unpinned the bun holding his wife's hair. As her tresses fell down her back, he began stroking and kissing her neck. She moaned and turned to kiss him.

As the tender kiss became passionate, Gregory lifted Naomi from the piano bench, carried her to the bedchamber, and tugged at her clothes. She reached for his belt buckle.

"No. I will take you, Naomi."

As he thrust into her, their eyes locked.

"We will make a child tonight," Gregory said. "A beautiful girl, like her mother."

"Oh, yes!" Naomi cried as Gregory exploded inside her.

$$\bullet \qquad \bullet \qquad \bullet$$

In the morning, as Gregory and Naomi lay intertwined, Léana had an unexpected visitor. On her doorstep was a wan, weak-looking girl holding a basket.

"Good day, Mrs. Hauer. I am Emma Kinnawe, the minister's wife. I understand you have not been well. Parthalán asked me to bring food and drink."

Emma Kinnawe: the once defiant wife who, according to Bébhinn, had scored a rare victory over Parthalán by terminating her first pregnancy.

Léana welcomed Mrs. Kinnawe and invited her inside.

77

Kinnawe House
Agamenticus, Maine

Priscilla pulled off to the side of the shore road.

"Here's where I leave you, Matthew," she said. "Call me if you want to talk."

Matthew got out of the Civic and took the driver's seat as Helen, who was waiting for them, climbed into the passenger's seat. Priscilla honked twice as she drove away in her Versa, which had been parked alongside the road.

"Where did the snow come from?" Matthew wondered out loud as he pulled into the driveway. "There wasn't any snow in Portland or on Route 95."

"We had a mini-storm last night."

Matthew looked around. The goldenrod lay dead on the ground, all the tiny golden buds turned black.

Since receiving his diagnosis, he'd been thinking about what would become of his remains. He didn't want to end up in an urn that materialized out of thin air to torture anyone who saw it. He'd decided he wanted to be buried. Being permanently asleep in a comfortable coffin, surrounded by the cool earth, might be a recompense for the ravages of insomnia. As for burial places, Bala Cynwyd was out of the question, and he felt little connection to New York City. A small memorial headstone in a quiet New England churchyard would be just the ticket.

"Helen, I want to ask you a question. Actually, I have a lot of questions that I want to ask you. The first one is: That church over there—does it have a graveyard? I want to be buried in Maine. In spite of everything that's happened, I feel like I belong here."

Helen shook her head. "No, Matthew. There are no burial grounds in Cape Agamenticus. I'm sorry."

"The ghost on the cliff—the man with the beard. Who is he? Do you know?"

"His name was Einar Koskinen," Helen said. "He lived here in the mid-1700s. Why don't you get rested up, and I'll come back a little later and explain more? In the meantime, don't forget to leave a window open."

There it was again. That advice. That warning. She'd been concerned for his safety since his arrival, and she'd stopped him from killing himself more than once. And if Mickey hadn't closed and locked that kitchen window, Matthew thought, he wouldn't have ended up in Portland General.

He'd asked Priscilla point-blank whether his recollections were real or imagined. He'd put the same question to Helen. He'd ask her why a window should always remain open. He'd ask her about the goldenrod, which the unknown redhead had sown in his dream. He'd ask her about all of it. For now, though, he wanted a few hours to himself. The nurses and other hospital staffers had fussed over him, and now he craved solitude. The ocean waves, he hoped, would bring a serenity that beeping hospital monitors made impossible.

As he entered the house, several puzzle pieces fell into place. Priscilla had a friend named Sven Koskinen. The ghost on the cliff was named Einar Koskinen. E KOSKINEN was just one of many names burned into the staves of the casks in the basement. The casks that he'd thought contained excrement.

Helen hadn't lied to him—not quite. Cape Agamenticus had no burial ground, but it did have a cemetery in the cellar of Kinnawe House.

· · ·

In the Civic's hatchback were two bags of groceries that Priscilla had purchased. Matthew unpacked the car and left the grocery bags on the kitchen countertop. It didn't matter if he put the provisions into the refrigerator or the cabinets. They'd all be stale or rotting within a day, regardless.

He looked around the living room. The instruments that the murderous hallucinations had played were mounted to the wall. A thick layer of dust covered them.

He searched under the couch for the stone that his mother had given him, the stone that had burned through Trey's hand, the stone that Chuck had kicked under the couch. He found nothing but a few dust bunnies and the small pile of sand that had been his stone.

• • •

An hour later, Matthew sat at the piano working on the harmony line for "Just Give Him Your Number," the song he'd started to write after meeting Priscilla. He took pleasure in crafting the tune according to his personal definition of "the best possible song" instead of wondering if the song was right for his voice, if its video would get lots of comments on YouTube, if DJ's would remix it and play it at the clubs.

A shiny dust mote glinted in his peripheral vision. Matthew turned toward the glint. During his hospital stay, someone had inserted a key into the keyhole of the door leading to the attic.

Matthew unlocked the door and flipped on the light switch. He climbed the stairs, planning to bring the minister's portrait downstairs, where he'd be able to examine it in better light for more clues to his heritage. Approaching the easel, he saw that the portrait of the minister was gone, replaced by a portrait of a young and beautiful Rose of Sharon. Shocked, he stepped backward into a ceramic tureen—a chamber pot?— and lost his balance. As he stumbled against the wall, his shirtsleeve caught on a protruding nail.

As he disentangled his shirt from the nail, he noticed hints of images swimming hazily beneath the sandy, textured paint. He stepped backward and squinted to focus. Yes, someone had definitely painted over an image on the wall.

Matthew went downstairs to the kitchen, found a flashlight, and returned to the attic. He trained the light beam on the floor, ceiling, and walls. Images, long since painted over, seemed to cover every square inch of the attic.

Returning to the kitchen, he found some rags underneath the sink and filled a bucket with warm, soapy water. Scrubbing the paint off the attic's entire back wall revealed the full panorama of images. Some were impressive copies of great religious paintings, like Lippi's *Madonna and Child* and Leonardo's *The Last Supper*. Another painting showed a young blond man, imprisoned in a cage, being tormented by four men. Matthew recognized the tormentors as Greg Brautigam, Trey Collinge, Mickey Ayers, and Chuck Meer. Next to that disturbing scene was a homey portrait of a happy family: two smiling parents standing behind their children, a tow-headed boy holding a pocket watch engraved with the letter T, and a chestnut-haired girl holding a kitten with an embroidered E on its collar. The father looked like an older version of Greg Brautigam.

Matthew sat on the dusty, plastic-wrapped mattress. Here, in the attic of Kinnawe House, he sensed goodness. Kindness. Humanity.

His pocket vibrated. His phone was ringing. For the first time since his arrival, Kinnawe House sent a phone signal through.

The caller: Josh Brody.

Tentatively, Matthew answered and said "Hello?"

"Matthew, I need to see you. You're my brother. Please say I can come. I can't let you die without apologizing. And explaining."

78

The population of Cape Agamenticus seemed to know that Léana was carrying Parthalán's children. Those who'd formerly snubbed her now called with baked treats, fresh spring water, and other peace offerings. Abigail, Rebecca, and Leah visited often, with the approval of their husbands and Parthalán. When a group of women chatted with her over tea, the conversation was light and airy. In private, Léana's new friends told her their private histories. They'd all been born into families that belonged to different branches of the same church. They'd been raised not to question the disappearance of friends—which occurred when the town fell on hard times, or when the church's sworn enemies came too near—and to conduct all their business, including their marriages, within the community.

Léana did not forget her duty to Reverend Edwards and to God, but her developing relationships allowed tiny doubts to creep into her soul. These women had been born into an unholy church. They hadn't joined of their own accord, as their husbands had. The women might therefore be as innocent as the babies Parthalán had sacrificed, and she suspected that Bébhinn's plan, not yet revealed, might have terrible and unholy consequences for her new friends.

Naomi Brautigam called once a day, sometimes twice, with a breezy hello to "check on her, to make sure she was comfortable and happy." She didn't stay long, and she sidestepped all of Léana's attempts at meaningful conversation. After Parthalán, Léana feared Naomi the most.

One Wednesday afternoon during the third month of her unwanted pregnancy, Abigail stopped by with two blankets she'd knitted. Both were blue. Everyone knew that Léana's children would be boys.

"You are so thoughtful," Léana said. She sidled up to the topic that she feared to broach directly. "May I ask you a question, Abigail? In confidence?"

"You know my secrets, Léana. I vow to keep yours."

"Why does Naomi visit me so often?"

"You have helped many of us, Léana, and we will not betray you," Abigail said. "But Naomi owes you no such debt, and Parthalán has asked her to monitor you. Be assured that she will go to Parthalán immediately if she suspects any danger to his children. You mustn't speak with her as you speak with me. Please say, out loud, that you have no intention of harming the babies in your womb. I will repeat our conversation verbatim to Naomi."

"I am the mother of the children who live inside me. I would do nothing to harm them."

She had just broken the Ninth Commandment, and she would soon break the Sixth. If she ever saw Reverend Edwards again, she would ask him to explain why the Lord's work required her to break the laws Moses brought down from Mount Horeb.

Abigail smiled. "Those are good words for me to hear, Léana. And to repeat."

•   •   •

A week later Léana found a basket containing a small bottle of dark green liquid on her doorstep. She hid it in a drawer and focused on making conversation with the day's visitors, including Mrs. Feeley.

"Well," Mrs. Feeley pronounced with satisfaction, "you're progressing nicely. I suspect the boys will have good lungs. Not much sleep for you in the future, I'm afraid."

Léana smiled and nodded. Already she was not sleeping much. Her maternal instinct was increasing, not weakening, and she doubted her ability to commit the atrocity required of her. And she lived in perpetual terror that Mrs. Feeley would detect a third heartbeat—that of Cutler's daughter.

"Await further instructions from me and Bébhinn," Emma had whispered at the end of her first visit with Léana. Because Parthalán's mother was dead and banished, Emma had explained, the task of informing Léana about the terrible choice had fallen on her.

"In the meantime," Emma said after Léana had agreed to her terms, "I will tell Parthalán you have consented to kill the child whom you would otherwise have chosen to remain alive."

·   ·   ·

Bébhinn had told her to swallow the poison on the day she woke to a scratching inside her womb. A week after Léana's conversation with Abigail about Naomi, Léana rolled onto the right side of her bed—Cutler's side— and felt a scraping inside her, as if a garden claw was raking her uterus.

At nightfall, Léana bolted the doors. She lit a candle and laid three old blankets on the kitchen floor. She removed the stone from her neck; she could not commit such a vile act with it on her person. Then she stripped naked and tugged the stopper from the vial.

The concoction was not bitter, but rather syrupy sweet with an under note of pomegranate. After swallowing it in one gulp, she lay on top of the blankets.

The chills began a minute later. Léana clutched her stomach as fiery knives tore at her womb. She felt one of the babies detach. *Please, Father Above*, she prayed, *not my daughter, please not Cutler's daughter*. Her entire body began to spasm. Placenta and blood burst from her, and in one frenzied heave the child aborted.

She struggled to her feet in the glow of the candlelight and wiped clean her legs and abdomen. She averted her eyes from the floor, unable to reconcile her faith with what she'd done. Perhaps the good seed lay there on the blankets, the child who would have grown into a formidable foe for Parthalán and his brethren. In that case, she, Léana Hauer, was responsible for destroying the angel who'd lived inside her.

She had to look, had to get it over with. There would be time for prayer, time to beg for absolution, time to forgive herself, after Parthalán's defeat.

She held the candle over the aborted mass. The unborn baby was lying on its side, one leg over the other. Léana separated the two legs and shined the candlelight onto its stomach. It was a boy. Perhaps he was the good seed; perhaps the evil one. But it was not her daughter. She heard Reverend Edwards' voice in her head: "You have put your faith in God, Léana, and you have been rewarded."

She curled the bloody blankets and their contents into a tight ball, placed it in a burlap sack, and conveyed the sack to the appointed place on the beach. The final battle had begun, although Parthalán did not know it.

•   •   •

In the library of Kinnawe House, Parthalán reached for a book, and his wrist bone snapped in two.

79

The House on the Spit
Agamenticus, Maine

Helen's neighbors' houses glowed in the moonlight. The men were inside—forever trapped between life and death, forced to serve Parthalán for eternity. She'd managed to hurt them, but as Matthew recovered, so would they.

She felt electricity in the air, as she'd felt that night in 1749. He'd be here soon enough to take advantage of Matthew's weakness, but she knew how to get him here sooner. By striking first, she'd have the advantage.

It was a matter of having the conversation with Matthew, who'd attributed most of his experience to his mind playing tricks on him. She needed to tell him he was the last of the good line, to explain why Parthalán would not relent until he was dead. With Matthew dead, nobody would be left to fight the demon, and Léana's centuries-long struggle would end with Parthalán's victory.

Matthew would ask why Parthalán and his henchmen hadn't killed him, even though they'd had many opportunities to do so. The simple reason was: They couldn't take Matthew's life, just as they couldn't take hers. But if Matthew took his own life, he'd give himself to despair—the sin of *accidie*, or *acedia*. Suicide told God that His child had no faith in Him, and God abandoned those who took their own lives, leaving their souls to wander the earth, forever homeless.

She wouldn't allow that to happen. She'd fought too hard, and for too long, to fail. And now she had the tools she needed to achieve victory: a jar of honey, a sledgehammer, and an army of dead soldiers.

80

Cape Agamenticus, Maine
Late Summer 1749

None of Léana's visitors suspected that her womb had once held three lives. In previous months Léana had wondered why Mrs. Feeley had not detected the presence of Léana's baby girl in her womb. After the events of recent weeks, she understood. A force greater than herself hid the child from Mrs. Feeley.

• • •

Gregory Brautigam knocked on Léana's door. He must be quick about his business.

Mrs. Feeley answered to save Léana the trouble. "Good day, Mr. Brautigam."

"Good day, Mrs. Feeley. How is your patient?"

"Oh, very well, very well. Is Mrs. Brautigam getting along?"

"A bit of morning sickness, but Naomi does not complain. Reverend Kinnawe asks you to call on him."

Parthalán's wish was Mrs. Feeley's command. "If you don't mind, Mrs. Hauer, I'll be on my way."

"Mr. Brautigam," Léana began, as soon as the door closed behind Mrs. Feeley. "Your wife has been so kind to me. And it is kind of you to call on me while she is indisposed ..."

In three rapid strides Gregory closed the distance between him and Léana. "Bébhinn sent me," he whispered in Léana's ear. "Here is what you must do. When next you see Abigail and Rebecca ..."

His plan detailed, Gregory began the walk up Agamenticus Cliff Road toward his house. If all went according to plan, he and his children would be forever free of Parthalán. But there were so many variables, so many unknowns. Those seeking to curry favor with Parthalán were everywhere and would happily watch Gregory, Naomi, Emma, and Tobias roasted over an open fire.

•　　•　　•

"I will be sorry to leave Cape Agamenticus, Reverend," Mrs. Feeley said. "It has been my privilege to serve here."

"We will feel your loss, Mrs. Feeley, but you are needed in Boston. You must help the girl raise the child. Her father has disowned her, but her aunt has taken pity on her and pays for a room. Find her and bring her to live with you."

Mrs. Feeley left Parthalán's library with Josephine Alcott's name and address written on a slip of paper.

According Parthalán's directions, Mrs. Feeley, Josephine, and the child were to live in Boston for a few years before moving to Princeton, New Jersey, where Mrs. Feeley would assist Doctor William Shippen. Mrs. Feeley did not look forward to taking orders from him. She'd never met a doctor who knew more about medicine than she did. In fact, most of them knew a great deal less.

•　　•　　•

Naomi, hands on her belly, sat in her parlor doing nothing. Mrs. Feeley's pills had eased the pressure on her back, which brought some relief. Gregory was away from the house, attending to town business, and the maid, Patrizia, had gone to market. Through the window, she saw the mute twins, one leading the other by the hand.

James knocked on her door.

"James, Elias, good day. Gregory isn't here."

James made a scribbling motion with his finger, his way of asking for a sheet of paper and a pencil.

Naomi invited the brothers inside. Both stood with their hands behind their backs as Naomi retrieved the writing implements. She handed them to James, who sat on a chair and used his lap as a desk. He scribbled a few words and handed the note to Naomi.

EMMA'S BABIES ARE NOT REV KINNAWE'S.

Naomi blinked in disbelief. "It is not possible," she said.

James took the sheet of paper from Naomi and scribbled two sentences underneath the first.

ONE BABY IS MINE. THE OTHER COMES FROM ELIAS.

As Naomi stared at the brothers in disbelief, James again took the sheet of paper from her hands.

EMMA FORCED US.
THREATENED TO TELL REV KINNAWE WE RAPED HER.

An hour later, Naomi had the whole story. Now it was her duty to bring the information to Parthalán.

But how best to convey the information? She needed time to think. She cared not a whit about Emma's fate, but she cared about Gregory's, and she feared that Parthalán would hold him responsible for his daughter's behavior and punish him for Emma's deception and betrayal.

Naomi would need to remind Parthalán that she'd long been his devoted servant. It was she, after all, who'd suggested that he use Tobias to break Emma's will. She hoped her proven loyalty would be enough to save her husband from Parthalán's wrath.

81

The leaders of five neighboring congregations left Jonathan Edwards' home in Stockbridge. Edwards had spent the afternoon laying out all he'd learned and most of what he suspected.

A fuller investigation would have to be launched at an unspecified point in the future, the ministers agreed. Reverend Edwards was making serious allegations. Yes, they admitted, they'd heard rumors that such communities existed—in Virginia, in New Orleans, in New York City—but the allegations had never been proven.

"But, my friends, we are running out of time," Edwards pleaded. "Parthalán Kinnawe's influence is extending further up and down the coastline."

"Reverend Edwards, we cannot rush to judgment," was the consensus. "Not after the hysteria of the witch trials."

In other words: No aid would be forthcoming from his neighbors to the north, south, east, and west of Stockbridge.

He would have to find another way. He feared for Léana and Cutler. He feared for Jerusha. And he feared God's wrath if he did not obey His orders.

82

Parthalán had given Tobias's jailers strict orders not to exchange a single word with him. In addition, they were to walk westward along the beach to prevent Emma, who spent most of her time locked in her chamber, from seeing her brother.

One night in early October, Gregory Brautigam said to Charles Meer, "Parthalán has given me sole charge of Tobias. I'll need your key, please." Meer handed over the attic key without complaint.

Gregory then called at the Ayers and Collinge houses and left with Michael and Sebastian's keys.

•　　•　　•

Rebecca Collinge watched as Gregory returned to his house. As soon as he closed the door behind him, Rebecca slipped out her back door and hurried to the Ayers house.

"Did Gregory take Michael's key?" Rebecca whispered.

"Yes," Abigail said. "And Charles's too. Are Luke, Anne, and Beatrice prepared?"

"Yes."

"Ruth, Jane, Zachary, and Ezra?"

"Leah says yes."

Abigail grabbed her friend's hand. "Oh, Rebecca. Tell me we are doing the right thing. Our torments will be unbearable."

"No. Not unbearable. We will die knowing we saved the innocent."

"What are you two gossips whispering about?" Michael Ayers said, grinning, as he entered the kitchen.

Abigail answered a question with a question. "Is it true that Parthalán is sending Mrs. Feeley to live in Boston?"

Michael placed his arm around his wife's shoulders. "I believe so, but I do not know for sure. He has been more secretive than usual."

"Does it bode ill?" Rebecca asked.

Michael could not give her an answer.

•

At 11:00 that night, Gregory let himself into Kinnawe House. A dim light glowed under the door of the library. Parthalán was within, muttering and scribbling.

Gregory turned the attic key in the lock and ascended the staircase. Tobias sat in his chair, waiting for his nightly respite from prison.

Placing a finger in front of his lips to command silence, Gregory handed his son a note.

Tonight you will have your freedom.
Do not speak a word.
Follow me down the stairs and out of the door.
Walk with heavy footsteps.
I will explain all, later.

Gregory led the way down the staircase, stepping hard onto each stair, with Tobias following. They exited through the parlor door onto the beach and began walking the usual route, past the Brautigams' house, the Ayers', and the Collinges'. On a typical evening, after passing the Meers' they would turn back toward Kinnawe House, but tonight they continued westward.

Léana, heavily pregnant with her daughter and Parthalán's son, waited at the door of the house on the spit. Gregory pointed above his head, directing Tobias to the second floor.

"Give me your cloak," Léana whispered to Tobias, who removed it, handed it to Léana, and climbed the stairs.

Bébhinn entered the parlor from the hallway, her hair under a cap. Léana threw Tobias's cloak over her, and Bébhinn and Gregory began the walk back to Kinnawe House. Gregory walked on the side closer to the house. Bébhinn walked alongside him, stretching herself as tall as possible to approximate Tobias's height and youth.

Inside the house, Bébhinn trudged up the attic stairs. Gregory closed the door and locked it behind her. Bébhinn's footsteps above Parthalán's head would reassure him that Tobias remained imprisoned in the attic until the birth of his children.

In her bedroom, Léana removed the stone from her neck and swallowed a bottle of the same concoction that Bébhinn had given Emma.

83

Kinnawe House
Agamenticus, Maine

Matthew awakened from a fugue, his left arm manacled to the bedpost. It was a small triumph: He'd remembered and followed Doctor Sands' instructions.

Had the call from Josh been real, or had it been a delusion?

His mouth was as dry as a desert. He needed a long drink of cold water. Using the key that dangled from the cord encircling his neck, he freed himself from the bedpost and began walking toward the kitchen.

She was sitting on the piano bench, staring at the wall. Long, snow-white hair fell past her shoulders. The last time he'd visited her at the Bedford Institute, she'd had the long locks that she hadn't trimmed since her adolescence. Only a couple of months earlier, they'd been dark brown, almost black.

She was skeletal, haggard. And dead. She'd been dead for weeks.

"Hi, Mom," Matthew said, accepting, welcoming, hoping to learn from the hallucination. "I didn't know if I'd see you again before I die. I had a horrible nightmare about you when I was in the hospital. I didn't want it to be my last memory of you. What comes after death, Mom? Is there something? Or nothing?"

"I'm not dead, Matthew. Touch me." She held out a bony arm.

Matthew extended his finger and touched cool but living flesh.

"They told you I died, but I didn't," Rose of Sharon said.

"Did you kill yourself so that the fatal insomnia wouldn't? Was it a way for you to control your own death?"

"Your insomnia comes from your father, Matthew. He raped me and forced me to have the children. I was seventeen, living with my family in Presque Isle, Maine. One minute I was sleeping alone in my bed. The next minute he was climbing on top of me. His fingernails were like razor blades shredding my nightgown. He was strong, but he didn't put a hand over my mouth to keep me from screaming. He said if I made a sound, he'd slice my throat open and then rape my sister, my mother, and my father. He made me look at him, at his red eyes, as he ripped me open. He threatened to come back and do it again, so I ran. I ended up in South Carolina. After you were born, I found a job in Pennsylvania as a companion to an old woman with no family. I told her I was a widow. Do you remember her? She used to love rocking you to sleep. She called you her sweet pea. She left us the house in Bala Cynwyd and a little bit of money."

Matthew knew his mother's ghost wasn't lying. Rose of Sharon never lied; she simply withheld the truth. And now he knew why. She hadn't wanted him to live with the knowledge that she'd lived with: that she'd survived a brutal rape of which he was a daily reminder.

Since adolescence, he'd feared that his genes had bestowed on him a familial psychosis, a madness that would warp and destroy him. But what was worse: having fatal insomnia, or being the son of a rapist?

The latter. Definitely the latter.

"I know his name, Mom. Jernej Boudreaux. I found my birth certificate."

"He wanted to claim you as his property, just as he claimed me. I didn't even know he'd signed your birth certificate until I left the hospital with you. He's watched and tormented me ever since you were about ten years old, when he found us. I lived my life in terror for both of us, and it drove me mad. I barely slept a wink during your four years in college. I was terrified he would find you."

Matthew cradled his mother's head in his arms as she cried.

"He tricked me into believing you were the evil one, Matthew. The evil seed always kills his mother. He told me to kill you before *you* killed *me*. As I was stabbing you, he grabbed the knife out of my hand. He said I'd served my purpose."

"Your purpose?"

"To start you thinking about suicide. To make you believe you're worthless, because anyone whose mother tries to kill him must deserve to die."

"So he found you in Bala Cynwyd, and he talked you into trying to kill me?"

"No, I'm not talking about your father. I'm talking about your brother. Joshua. He came to the house to warn me that you planned to sacrifice me. I knew, because the ghost of Jernej's mother told me that the evil twin always sacrifices his mother."

Matthew remembered the night of the stabbing. Earlier that day, upon arriving home from college, he'd heard someone in his mother's bedroom, smelled Josh's cologne. He'd asked Josh about it. He'd asked her about it. They'd both dodged the question.

"You're saying *Josh* is my twin brother?"

"Yes. I let both of you live, which is one of the reasons Jernej continues to punish me. I broke his rules. But I couldn't bring myself to kill a newborn. The idea of murdering my own child—it only made the rape worse. I thought you were the good one, so I kept you. You were so sweet, so happy and adorable. When the doctor spanked your bottom, you giggled instead of crying. I abandoned Joshua at a rural police station in Virginia. When the deaf-mutes came to collect what they thought were his remains, I gave them ashes I bought from a crematorium. I told them I'd smothered him and incinerated the body. Now, after all these years, I know the truth. *You* are the good seed."

"That photo of me and Josh in your jewelry box, Mom. Where did it come from? Why did you keep it?"

"I asked a nurse at the hospital to take it after the two of you were born. He wanted to know which child I'd killed, so I had the photo taken to show him. But he never asked me for it. He thought I was too terrified and obedient to do anything other than obey him. He's never forgiven me. He hates to be outsmarted, but that's what I'm trying to do right now."

On the phone Josh had said, "You're my brother." He wasn't speaking in metaphor. It was the literal truth. But how did Josh know they were brothers?

Suddenly, Matthew knew he was holding a person, not a ghost.

"Mom, how did you get here?"

"Jernej brought me, but he calls himself Doctor Mavro. He's kept me alive to use as a weapon against you. This is his house."

Rose of Sharon picked up a long knife that sat on top of the piano. Matthew looked at the knife with curiosity, not with alarm. He no longer feared her.

"This house has been trying to get me to kill myself since I got here," Matthew said.

"That's why he brought me here, Matthew. He wants me to talk you into killing yourself. He thinks I'm going to, but I'm not. I won't let him use me against you any longer."

Matthew felt a surge of strength and energy. "Tell me how to help you, Mom. Let's fight him together."

Rose of Sharon stroked her son's cheek. "The most important thing, Matthew, is *not* to kill yourself. No matter what happens, no matter what anyone says or does, promise me you will not lose your will to live."

"I promise, Mom. I have only a few weeks left, but I want to live them."

"Stay strong, Matthew. As strong as you've always been. And, Matthew, thank you. Thank you for trying to take care of me. You're taking care of me now. You're setting me free."

Rose of Sharon picked up the knife and plunged it into her heart.

As she collapsed to the floor, her arterial blood spurting onto Matthew's face, her body began to disintegrate: first her skin, then her muscle and her bones. Matthew watched as the last of her blood seeped through the floor into the cellar.

Distraught, Matthew ran out of the house and into the basement cemetery, where his mother's blood dripped into an open barrel. After the *plop* of the last drop, he approached the cask and examined it. Burnt into one of the staves was his mother's name:

R ROLLINS

His mother's cask stood among dozens of casks with other names burnt into them:

E KOSKINEN
E BRAUTIGAM
N BRAUTIGAM
J FEATHERSTONE
E FEATHERSTONE
R COLLINGE
A AYERS

L MEER
C HAUER
MARIAH

All were full and sealed, except the one labeled L HAUER, which was empty.

Matthew touched his mother's cask. For all that Kinnawe House had tried to take from him, it had ultimately given him the gift of a mother who loved him.

He had to talk to Helen. He needed as much information as possible before Josh arrived. Before his brother arrived.

84

Cape Agamenticus, Maine
Early Fall 1749

After sunset, Rebecca brought her three children, Luke, Anne, and Beatrice, to Léana's house. Soon thereafter, Leah arrived with her sons, Zachary and Ezra, and her daughters, Ruth and Jane. The women embraced their children one last time and hurried home as the children ascended to the second floor, where they huddled close to Tobias.

Sitting in his library, Parthalán heard the horses and a carriage, but it was not uncommon for the men to return to the stables late, or to take a horse out at nighttime while performing church obligations. He paid no heed and continued reading the letter that had recently arrived from Philadelphia.

Gregory Brautigam fed sugar cubes to the horses as Tobias and the children left Léana's house and crowded into the carriage.

·   ·   ·

As the contractions came more quickly and painfully, Léana bit onto a thick rag.

Gregory entered the room as Léana's womb pushed out the first child. The girl was a marvelous little thing, kicking her tiny feet, breathing but not crying. A silent baby. A miracle.

Léana asked Gregory to place her necklace around the baby's neck.

"She is so tiny. As Emma was, at her birth," Gregory said, swaddling the child, rocking her in his arms, and placing the stone around her neck. "What is her name?"

"Fiona," Léana whispered, turning her head from her newborn.

"Will you hold your child?" Gregory asked gently.

"No. Nothing must weaken my resolve. Go, and Godspeed. The stone must never leave her neck, Gregory."

"We await Emma's arrival."

"Emma is not going with you. Look in the box there, on top of the chest of drawers. There is a letter for you. She asks you to open it when you reach your final destination, but not before then." Léana had not read the letter, but she knew its contents.

Gregory slipped the letter into the pocket of his cloak.

"Is there nothing more I can do?" he asked.

Léana shook her head. "You are wasting time, Gregory. Every minute you linger brings Parthalán a step closer to preventing your escape."

"I am fortunate to have known you, Léana Hauer. And I thank you from the bottom of my heart."

Gregory rushed to the carriage, handed Fiona to Tobias, and took charge of the horses, turning their heads toward the shore road. The horses clopped northward until they'd passed through Ogunquit and the lower part of Wells.

As the party passed out of Parthalán's sphere of influence, Gregory drew his whip and cracked it. The two horses, the strongest and fastest in Cape Agamenticus, galloped into the night.

Soon after sunrise, the party arrived at the safe house that Bébhinn had found for them. During her frequent absences, she'd wandered hundreds of miles searching for someone willing to shelter the escapees. They planned to remain at the sanctuary for a month, until a hired boat conveyed them to an island off the coast of South Carolina. Gregory had arranged for a house to be built on the island as a home for his new extended family.

Parthalán would assume they'd headed south, toward Boston, and that's where he'd focus his search. Charles, Michael, and Sebastian would have their orders: Bring them all back alive. In the meantime, new casks would be prepared, with the deaf-mutes burning the traitors' names into the staves.

• • •

The second child clawed its way out of Léana's womb, slitting her insides as it wriggled through the birth canal. With a final heave, Léana expelled Parthalán's son. The child writhed on the floor as she mustered her strength.

Bébhinn had said it was impossible to look at the children and determine which was the bad seed. Bébhinn herself had chosen wrong on the basis of her own child's deformed appearance. But the baby on the floor looked almost like a small dragon, with pointy toes and fingers. His grotesque appendages made Léana's task slightly easier.

Thrusting aside all her maternal instincts, she donned a pair of gloves and lifted the boy. This child might be the good seed, but it did not matter. He must die, as his brother had, so that Parthalán and his community might be destroyed.

Like many devout and pious women, Léana did not assume that a place in heaven was guaranteed her. She wondered if this action would count against her in the final tally. But there was no turning back now. She took the boy to a washtub filled with lye and held him against the bottom of the basin while he kicked and flailed. The struggling baby had no chance. Within minutes the lye had dissolved his entire body, and the voice of Léana's conscience said: *You are damned, double murderess.*

• • •

At Kinnawe House, Parthalán collapsed in a dead faint. His forehead smashed into his desk, and blood spurted onto the asp curled in the corner.

Léana dressed and carried the basin to the beach. She waded into the Atlantic and dumped the contents into the water. She dropped the tub and ran back to her house. The ocean boiled behind her, furious.

Now she would wait for Parthalán to come to her.

Within an hour, she would be either victorious or dead.

85

The House on the Spit
Agamenticus, Maine

As Sven Koskinen emerged from the driver's seat of his Subaru Outback, Helen waved to greet the man who'd sometimes wandered the cliffs before Matthew's arrival.

"You seem so real," Sven said to Helen. "So ordinary, I mean. Not what I expected of a ghost."

"I like *spirit* or *soul* better than *ghost*."

"I like *soul*, too," Sven said. "We're fighting for Matthew's soul, and for Einar's. But I need to be sure that Priscilla won't be harmed. You and I are the warriors. She's an innocent."

"Don't underestimate her, Sven. She has extraordinary courage. She *wants* to help us. Come, I've prepared the site."

On the rocky beach, Helen pointed to four rocks, one at each corner of a large invisible square.

Time and tide might wash away the beach cemetery that Einar was preparing to consecrate—the first true, sanctified burial ground in Cape Agamenticus. For now, though, it would be less a place of death than a place of rebirth.

86

Cape Agamenticus, Maine
Early Fall 1749

Naomi Brautigam had wrestled with her conscience for weeks. It was possible that James and Elias had lied, had spun a wild, wicked tale to take revenge on Parthalán for causing, or not preventing, Elias's blindness. She wanted to confide in Gregory, to let him decide whether to repeat the brothers' accusations to Parthalán. But Gregory had been away much more than usual, and on the nights they slept under the same roof he was quiet and aloof.

Then, last night, Gregory stole out of the house after dark. He had not returned. Naomi knew she'd been abandoned, that her beloved husband was a traitor, and that she and her unborn child must now rely on Parthalán's protection.

● ● ●

"Mrs. Brautigam says she must speak with you," Lotte said to Parthalán. "She says the matter is urgent."

As soon as Naomi entered the library, Parthalán knew something was very wrong.

"Naomi. Sit. What is your business?"

The snake that had been coiled on the chair next to Parthalán's desk slithered into a corner. Straightening her dress, Naomi perched herself on the chair's edge.

"Parthalán, what I am about to say will make you very angry. Will you give me your word that you will not punish me as the messenger?"

"I make that promise, Naomi, so long as you are the bearer of bad tidings, and not the cause of them."

"That will have to do."

Parthalán crossed his arms over his broad chest. "Then speak."

"There is a plot among the women who gave their children. It is led by Léana Hauer, who helps them bury the children's remains in a Christian cemetery."

Parthalán had always known Léana was resourceful, but he'd expected a more direct attack on him and his house. He'd underestimated her.

"How far has this plot developed?"

"Five times to date, with plans for additional burials."

Five times. One for each fall he'd taken, which left the recent fainting spell unaccounted for. Despite long hours of research, and despite Emma's and the Featherstones' accounts, he'd been unable to identify the source of his weakness. Now Naomi brought him the explanation that his master had been unwilling to provide.

"To accomplish this treachery," Parthalán said, "they would need to know where the remains are kept. I am the one person with that knowledge."

"Through some means, unknown to me, they have discovered the ossuaries."

"How do you come by this information? Has Léana or one of the traitors taken you into her confidence?"

"No. The women no longer speak freely in my presence. But they take no notice of James Featherstone, assuming that he is both deaf and stupid. He is not stupid, but he *is* terrified to bring you this information, so he brought it to me instead."

"So you know that the brothers have their hearing."

"I have long suspected."

"And why do they confide in you instead of your husband? Why does Gregory not bring this information to me, instead of his wife? His daughter lies pregnant in this house, and his son paces the floor above us. Why does he send you in his stead?"

"He is overseeing construction of the houses in Ogunquit. He has been gone these past three nights. James fears for the town, as I do, which is why I have come here tonight."

Parthalán suspected Naomi was trying to protect Gregory, placing him above the commonweal, above Parthalán himself. He would determine a suitable punishment for her and Gregory later. For now, he needed specifics. "Name the women who conspired with Léana."

"Esther Lacey. Bernice McCauley. Nancy Singleton."

"You said five women are involved. You have named three. Who are the fourth and fifth?"

"This is difficult for me, Parthalán. I count them among my closest friends."

"If they have done what you accuse them of doing, they are neither your friends nor friends of our community. Do not make me coerce you to speak, Naomi." Parthalán's eyes slid toward the snake.

"Abigail Ayers," Naomi said. "And Rebecca Collinge."

The ink bottle on Parthalán's desk shattered, as if a giant fist had descended on it. "Has Leah Meer also participated in this treason?"

Naomi nodded.

"Do you believe James speaks the truth, Naomi? The brothers have acted like ill-behaved children since the birds pecked out Elias's eyes. As if I could have prevented it."

"James's reports accord with what I have seen with my own eyes and heard with my own ears. But you are correct, Parthalán. The Featherstones are resentful. They believe you are losing control over the town, that your power is diminishing, and that you can no longer protect us. They wish for a return to a peaceful and prosperous existence, as we enjoyed before the Hauers' arrival."

Parthalán stamped his boot, splintering the floorboard. "To hell with all of you! None of you appreciate the lengths to which I have gone to rid us of those people. Does anyone thank me for dispatching the first two? No, you complain that the third continues to live."

"Léana's visitors, myself included, understand why she is permitted to live. But they cannot comprehend why you permit her to wear that stone around her neck."

"Now that I have broken the stone's defenses, it is powerless against me, and it helps to ensure that my unborn sons remain unharmed. Léana cannot hurt my children while she wears that stone, and she dare not remove it for fear of her own safety. I expect the people of this town to obey me, not to question me in matters that are beyond their comprehension."

"They have seen your injuries. They wait for you to end these difficulties, as you have always done, but their frustration is growing."

"As is mine."

Naomi took a deep breath before continuing.

"There is another matter. Emma has deceived you."

As Parthalán's eyes glowed silver, Naomi related James's tale. She concluded with, "In my pocket I have the sheets of paper on which James wrote ..."

Naomi did not finish her sentence. The snake darted from the corner, coiling up her legs and torso until it formed three tight circles around her neck, constricting her into unconsciousness.

The Atlantic bubbled as Parthalán stared out of the library window. Steam rose in thick clouds from the water's surface. As the snake loosened its grip on Naomi's throat, the library windows blew out from the inside. Since the night the snake had goaded him into raping Léana, he'd suspected that he was not the father of Emma's children. He'd wondered, with almost grudging admiration, which of his congregation had dared to bed his wife. Now he knew: The men who'd cuckolded him were the twin brothers he'd saved from a brutal New York orphanage.

By the time Naomi regained consciousness, Parthalán's rage had transformed into an icy fury. He would punish the traitors while the entire town, including the children, watched. By conspiring with the witch Léana Hauer, he would declare, the women had endangered their friends and neighbors. The retribution would remind the congregation that their well-being, and the town's continued prosperity, were his only goals, and any further thoughts of rebellion would recede.

"I believe you, and I trust you, Naomi," Parthalán said, as Naomi massaged her throat. "Together we will loosen Cape Agamenticus from Léana Hauer's grip."

87

Agamenticus, Maine

Helen sat on a beach chair, staring at the ocean from her spit of land.

"I just had a visit from my mother," Matthew said without preamble. "I thought she died a few weeks ago, but now she really is dead. She killed herself in front of me."

"I'm sorry, Matthew."

"You're not asking me if she was a hallucination. Because you know she wasn't."

"Did she explain why she attacked you? Did she tell you about your father and your twin brother?"

"Yes, but I need you to fill in the blanks for me." No matter what Helen said, no matter how appalling the truths she divulged, they couldn't be worse than his mother's revelations.

Helen stood and took Matthew's hand. "I didn't know when you'd show up or how he'd get you here. But I knew you'd come. He always finds a way."

"You mean my father? Jernej Boudreaux?"

"That's one of his names. He also goes by Bartholomew Dubh and Perttu Mavro. His given name is Gaelic: Parthalán Kinnawe. He switches up his last name, but he always uses a variation on Parthalán as his first name. In English, it's Bartholomew. In Slovene, it's Jernej. He's also used Bartosz and Barthélemy."

Bartholomew Dubh. The real-estate agent with the phony business card who'd stalked him on the internet and made him an offer too good to refuse.

"After my mother stabbed herself, her blood dripped through the floorboards into a big barrel in the cellar with her name burned into it. 'R Rollins.' The cellar is full of barrels. It's a cemetery."

"I know, Matthew. The remains of my husband Cutler are in one of the barrels. It would be marked C HAUER."

"Isn't your last name Crowe?"

"My birth name is Léana Mac Concradha, which is Gaelic, too. It's Helen Crowe in English. My married name is Léana Hauer. I've been battling Parthalán Kinnawe for more than two centuries. And now I need your help, Matthew."

"I'll do anything you need me to do," Matthew said. He'd made a promise to his mother, and he'd gladly sacrifice his last few weeks of life to help Helen defeat Parthalán. "But who exactly is Parthalán Kinnawe, and why does he want me to kill myself? Is he the minister in the painting?"

Helen nodded. "I'll answer all your questions, Matthew. But the information will be very upsetting. I've been struggling with how much to tell you, and when. But we're running out of time."

Matthew didn't want Helen to hold back a single iota of information that would help him make sense of his life. "What's happening to me ... it's nothing compared to what my mother went through. And I think you've suffered at Parthalán's hands, too. But here you are, ready to fight him again. I know I can be as strong as you and my Mom."

"Then here goes, Matthew. In a nutshell, you are at the center of a battle between good and evil that started in Northampton, Massachusetts, in the 1700s."

88

Cape Agamenticus, Maine
Early Fall 1749

Naomi walked to church with Charles and Leah Meer, Michael and Abigail Ayers, and Rebecca and Sebastian Collinge. The four couples always walked to and from services together. An ill spouse, or a husband away on business, did not change their routine.

Word had come from Lotte that a special rite was to be conducted. Attendance was mandatory for all.

The women entered through the back door and proceeded down the staircase into the cellar, followed by their husbands. A large group had already assembled.

Along one wall, the brazen bull sat on top of a platform. To its right the iron maiden gaped open, its long sharp spikes pointing at the crowd. The Spanish donkey sat to its right, its wedge waiting to rip its next victim in two.

Parthalán entered the cellar wearing a long cloak and carrying a curved staff. He nodded once at the assembly, and the room erupted into chaos. The husbands of Esther Lacey, Bernice McCauley, and Nancy Singleton pulled daggers from their vests and slit their wives' throats.

A group of women grabbed Rebecca and tied her to the inside of the brazen bull as Parthalán lit the fire underneath her. A second group pushed Leah backwards into the iron maiden and slammed the lid shut, impaling her from all sides. A third group tied Abigail's arms behind her back and suspended her above the Spanish donkey. They placed weights around her ankles and left gravity to do its work of splitting her in two.

As the bedlam commenced, the congregation tied Charles Meer, Sebastian Collinge, and Michael Ayers to the pillars that held up the ceiling, with each facing his wife. A heretic's fork was attached to each man's neck. The fork would slice open his throat, chest, or both if he attempted to turn his head.

Their orders carried out, the crowd dispersed, leaving Parthalán and Naomi alone with their cliffside neighbors. Leah died first, impaled on the spikes of the iron maiden, while the brazen bull amplified Rebecca's screams as she roasted to death. Abigail whimpered, first begging for release, then screaming that she would see all of them as damned as she was.

Naomi watched in angry silence as her friends died. Their selfishness had rendered Parthalán and Cape Agamenticus vulnerable to the town's enemies. Those loyal to Parthalán deserved protection from these dying traitors in their midst, as did her unborn child.

"What crime have they committed?" Michael Ayers screamed as the rusty tines of the heretic's fork gouged out a chunk of his chin.

"They betrayed you," Parthalán said. "They betrayed this town, and they betrayed me."

"But how? In the name of Satan, how?"

"You will have eternity to discover the answer, Michael. An eternity to obey, and an eternity to enjoy the fate to which your wives have consigned you."

Parthalán raised his staff and rapped it on the floor three times. Michael Ayers, Charles Meer, and Sebastian Collinge were transported to their houses, which had been stripped of all furnishings and possessions. Parthalán had given the townspeople carte blanche to take anything they wanted from the houses, except for the wives' musical instruments, which were brought to Kinnawe House.

Rebecca's flute, Leah's harp, Abigail's fiddle—Parthalán had told Naomi he would open a window and play the instruments on quiet nights to harrow the men who'd been too blind, too much in love, to control their wives.

•   •   •

As Naomi hurried home, she saw the two cages dangling from the church roof. James Featherstone huddled in one, Elias in the other. They'd been left there to starve to death, the vultures to pick at their bones. The cages would serve as another daily reminder of the end that awaited traitors.

Not a woman who cried easily or frequently, Naomi threw herself weeping onto her bed. Her tears of sorrow became tears of fury as she considered her husband's duplicity. She needed him now, and she hated her weakness. She grabbed his pillow from his side of the marital bed and threw it to the floor. A letter awaited her where the pillow had been.

> *My dear Naomi*
>
> *I have left Cape Agamenticus forever.*
>
> *We have seen Parthalán take the children of our friends and neighbors. He will take our child, too. If you believe otherwise, you are a fool.*
>
> *After you read this letter, take Jasper from the stables. He is saddled and ready.*
>
> *Travel through Ogunquit Center and onto the trail marked with white stones.*
>
> *A friend will bring you to us.*
>
> *If you choose to stay in Cape Agamenticus, I pray God will have mercy on your soul.*
>
> *Your husband*
> *Gregory Brautigam*

The truth of it all descended on her. She'd informed on her friends, who were victims, not traitors. She would not do the same to her husband. She would protect her child. Gregory was right: She'd been deluded in believing that Parthalán would reward her loyalty.

She ran to the barn, climbed onto Jasper, and turned his head toward the shore road.

89

The House on the Spit
Agamenticus, Maine

Matthew listened with intense attention as Helen continued her history not with Parthalán Kinnawe, but with the devil himself.

"You may know that Satan, the devil, was once the angel Lucifer, who rebelled against God. The devil is uniquely evil because he carries the seeds of goodness within him. His seed creates two children in a woman's womb, one good, one evil. For centuries, the women raped by his descendants have sought to destroy the evil child, while his followers have tried to ensure that the good child is killed.

"The good seed is the only person who can defeat the evil seed. The wicked child, being observant and opportunistic, comes to this knowledge before his brother does, giving him the upper hand. In other words, if both children are allowed to live past birth, the wicked child will always seek to destroy the good. Throughout the centuries, the raped women sought advice from their clerics, who passed their accumulated knowledge to the next generation. After many generations, the holy men determined a solution that is now presented to the women who are made pregnant by one of Lucifer's progeny. The rapist's mother visits the woman and explains the choice she must make after giving birth. She must kill one of the twins."

The ghost of Jernej Boudreaux's mother had presented Matthew's mother with that choice. Ruled by a maternal instinct that Matthew believed she didn't have, Rose of Sharon had refused to kill either of her children.

In his days as a lanky, underweight teenager, Matthew had grown accustomed to saying "I'm stronger than I look." Now he knew the source of that strength: his mother.

"But why kill only one of the children, Helen? Léana? Why not kill both? If the raped women had done that, none of this would be happening now."

"That may seem like a simple solution, Matthew, but a mother will do almost anything to save her children. Living with the knowledge that you have murdered one child becomes more bearable if the other child survives. If the woman kills the evil child, then she has saved the good seed and done a service to humanity. But if she kills both babies, she kills the good child along with the evil one. She also knows, because her rapist's mother has told her, that if she kills the good child instead of the evil one, her remaining child will someday murder her. She must therefore act to preserve her own life. This cycle has repeated itself for millennia. Lucifer accepts it because it increases the chances that his evil line will survive.

"In the 1700s, the lineage of Lucifer's descendants became more complicated. Your disease, now called fatal familial insomnia, was the punishment God inflicted on the men who built the Tower of Babel. The afflicted families have vowed not to reproduce. They are trying to end their lines, to kill the disease. However, as the disease progresses and the men's minds become disordered from lack of sleep, some of them have relations with a woman, thus passing the disease onto another generation. Meanwhile, the women afflicted with fatal insomnia confine themselves to a solitary existence in their parents' homes. However, even there, they are not always safe.

"The redheaded ghost whom you may have seen wandering the cliff is Bébhinn Mac Conshnámha. Her English name is Vivian Forde or Vivian Kinnawe, and she is Parthalán's mother. She was born into one of the families afflicted with fatal insomnia. In the mid-1700s, she was raped by one of Lucifer's progeny, thereby mixing two strains. From the father's side came the twins, and from the mother's side, the fatal insomnia. Bébhinn delivered twins, one good and one evil, both carrying fatal insomnia. Now, if the evil child survives, the insomnia does not matter, because he does not need sleep. If the good child survives, the fatal insomnia weakens and kills him, bringing Lucifer that much closer to victory. In Bébhinn's case, the evil child survived, and Parthalán sacrificed her in front of his congregation. In your mother's case, though, both children survived."

The blood drained from Matthew's face. He'd thought that nothing could be more abhorrent than learning that his father had raped and brutalized his mother. He'd been wrong.

Matthew fumbled for words. "So ... the devil is my father? Jernej Boudreaux is the devil?"

"Not Satan himself, but rather one of his descendants. I hope you now understand why I did not share this information sooner, Matthew. The knowledge is too much for most people to bear. It may lead them to suicide, which is what Lucifer wants. But Matthew, you must remember: You are the *good* child, not the evil one. You share your father's angelic side, not his evil side."

Matthew stared at the ocean in shock. The blood of Lucifer flowed through his veins, spurted out of his scars, soaked through his clothes. "This is so much to take in, Helen. I ... I ... I understand why someone would kill himself after hearing that. But why does Lucifer want the good twin to commit suicide? Can't he just make that happen by showing up and saying, 'Hey, I'm your father'?"

Helen explained the sin of despair or *accidie*, its signal to God that His child had no faith in Him. "God abandons those who take their own lives, and it is a great victory for Lucifer to have God disown a child who was to have been His warrior. As for why Lucifer's minions do not appear directly to their children: Despite his bluster and his threats, Lucifer is a coward who maintains his position more through deceit and manipulation than through raw physical power, though he is very powerful indeed, and not afraid to show it. Making the good seed aware of his heritage might not cause the child to kill himself, but rather to embrace the warrior's mantle, as you have. No, Lucifer prefers a series of emotional assaults on the good seed, with the goal of weakening him to the point where suicide seems both logical and sensible."

There it was: the explanation for Kellyce's abortion, his mother's knife attack, Josh's affair with Kellyce. All of it was intended to push Matthew closer and closer to suicide. But he'd resisted, so Jernej had sent the four Juilliard guys. Helen explained, "They've been trapped here since the 1750s. They live, or *exist* may be a better word, in the houses between this house and Kinnawe House. They should be in hell with their king, but Parthalán forces them to remain here, promising to release them when he is victorious. With you, they see the chance to be released from their confinement. You are the end of the line."

"You mean the end of Parthalán's line?"

"Yes. This is where the stone that you once wore comes into the story."

Matthew reached for the stone that had once hung around his neck—the stone that had burned a hole through Mickey's hand.

Helen continued, "I placed that stone around the neck of my daughter, Fiona, on the night that a man named Gregory Brautigam fled Cape Agamenticus with his son and eight innocent children, including Fiona. Somehow that stone found its way from Fiona to your mother. And I believe I know how."

Helen wiped away a tear before continuing.

"I never learned what became of Fiona. I did not want to know where Gregory took her. Parthalán nurses an eternal grudge against me, and in his desire to take revenge, he would not think twice about torturing my child or her descendants.

"Fiona would not have had more than one child, because she would have been unable to bequeath a stone to a second child. Her child would have had no more than one child, and so on. In short, Matthew, I believe that your mother was part of the Mac Concradha-Hauer line. Which makes me your great-great-great-great-grandmother, give or take a few *greats*."

Among the abhorrent disclosures, a jewel. The gift of a grandmother, a strong, fighting spirit who connected his disembodied life to a real history, a real past, a real family.

"As soon as I saw that stone around your neck, Matthew, I knew that one of Parthalán's descendants had found one of my descendants. He *knew* she was my descendant, which is why he chose her. He raped her and threatened to torture her if she did not destroy one of her children—the one she thought was the good seed. That is how the devil's descendants have tried to cheat. By the agreed-upon rules, the minion's mother, not the rapist, must present the choice to the victim. Breaking the rules favors the other party, as Parthalán has learned.

"Instead of killing one of the children, your mother kept the child she thought was the good one, and she gave away the bad one. To an orphanage, or to a convent. As in earlier generations, the evil twin—Joshua—has been trying to destroy the good twin—you. I am charged with protecting you, because you are the end of the line in America. Parthalán understands how strong you are. You've already lived ten years longer than most people who suffer from fatal insomnia. He wants to destroy you, but he can't touch you, and he knows it. As I said, Parthalán has broken the rules in the past, and he's been punished for it. This time, he's been playing by the rulebook, which is how he's gained the upper hand."

"The rulebook?"

"Since coming to Cape Agamenticus from Northampton, Parthalán has pretended to be subservient to his master, and he has tried many times to outsmart Lucifer. Sometimes he has nearly succeeded, but his conceit has always been his downfall. Lucifer has no love of fair play, but he knows his limits, and he dares not circumvent the agreement he made two thousand years ago. Each time Parthalán has exceeded his boundaries, Lucifer has reined him in. Such discipline increases Parthalán's fury, but it has also taught him patience over the centuries."

"Why didn't Parthalán get Josh to convince me to kill myself sooner, while we were in college or high school, or before that? We've been friends since kindergarten."

"It's difficult to predict when the bad seeds will become aware of their birthright. Sometimes they develop the awareness through an intellectual curiosity, but more often their father finds them and begins training them. That's how it happened with Parthalán. As a young man, he was seen in the company of an older man whose identity was unknown to anyone in Northampton. Joshua's father has been coaching him since your college days. Not Toby Brody, but rather his real father. Toby Brody is on your side. He watched over you during your childhood, just as I've watched over you here."

"You know Toby Brody?"

"I knew him as Tobias Brautigam. He is the son of Gregory Brautigam, who saved Fiona from Parthalán. He was dispatched to find your mother's other child, and I was sent here. He couldn't know whether he was adopting the good seed or the bad seed. For years he wouldn't have known whether he was protecting Joshua from you, or you from Joshua. Now, we both know that you are the good seed, and Joshua the evil one. Parthalán needs Joshua to continue his line, and while you are alive, you represent a threat to Joshua.

"That's why Parthalán won't stop until he's driven you to self-destruction, and he's come close to achieving his goal several times since you arrived here. Now *you* have to stop *him*, because you're the last of the line. My friend Jerusha and I have followed that line for years, trying to protect the good seeds and rid the earth of the evil seeds. We thought we'd succeeded in 1749, but at the time we didn't know that Parthalán had raped a woman during a trip he'd taken to Boston. That unfortunate woman sacrificed the good twin, allowing Parthalán's son to come of age in New Jersey and propagate the line."

"Is Jerusha the dove?" Matthew remembered hallucinations, now revealed as reality, in which Helen and the dove were both present. And a lone dove had nested in the maple tree opposite his living room window on West 51st Street.

Helen nodded. "She and I were allies for many years. A few days ago Parthalán succeeded in killing her."

"I want to make the world a better place"—it was the idealist's mantra, the reason people joined the Peace Corps and spent their lives fighting social, political, and personal battles for liberty, equality, and human rights. All he'd wanted to do was write and sing songs. Until now. Ridding the world of Parthalán would give meaning to his life. He'd die knowing he'd made a difference.

"I'm as sick of Parthalán Kinnawe as you are, Helen. Tell me what I need to do and how to do it."

"Bébhinn and I have worked out a plan, Matthew. It may work, or it may not. But it's the best chance we have."

Helen went into her house and returned with a jar filled with golden honey.

"In such mundane things," Helen said, "we may both find our salvation."

•　　•　　•

Their next step was to recruit the army.

Bébhinn awaited them at the cave entrance. Matthew recognized her as the redhead who was sowing seeds on the beach during the midnight orgy.

According to Helen, she and Bébhinn had already visited the church in the woods.

Helen was unable to enter the cave, but Bébhinn's path was not obstructed, and she took Matthew by the hand, helping him inside. For just a moment, as Matthew held Bébhinn's hand, he felt as though his blood mingled with hers. As Matthew shined a flashlight onto the cave walls, she removed small wood boxes from niches in the rock. Matthew placed each box into an individual plastic bag.

Bébhinn melted into the sunlight as Matthew and Helen returned to Kinnawe House. Helen waited outside the house's perimeter while Matthew retrieved a sledgehammer from the storage shed. Then he led Helen into the basement, helping her across the barrier. Finding unexpected physical strength, he used the sledgehammer to smash open each of the barrels. After the filthy sludge had poured out, Helen reached into the noisome liquid to remove the bone fragments at the bottom of the cask, placing each collection of fragments into the correct plastic bag.

As soon as the last barrel was smashed and its remains transferred to the last plastic bag, Helen hurried home with all of the plastic bags in tow.

Matthew entered the living room from the deck, wondering how soon his guest would arrive. Helen believed the smashing of the casks would summon him.

He wore Cutler's stone around his neck, the stone to which the bees had led Helen. He looked forward to receiving his visitor.

90

Cape Agamenticus, Maine
Early Fall 1749

Parthalán placed his hand on the doorknob of Emma's chamber. To determine if he was the father of her children, he'd planned to examine both babies upon their birth, though a strict adherence to the rules would have prevented him from doing so. The Protector had hinted that the children were not Parthalán's, but the Protector would take a sadistic pleasure in tricking his minion into killing his own heir.

Before departing for Boston, Mrs. Feeley had suggested, subtly, that the children were not behaving in the womb as she expected. They did not kick at Emma around the clock, as the children of other minions did with their mothers; nor did they cause Emma to crave spiced organ meat and animal fat. Meanwhile, Léana Hauer had consumed with gusto the gifts of chopped liver and kidney pie that her friends had brought her.

Emma's deceit, her conscription of the deaf-mutes into her service, deserved a fitting revenge. How gratifying it would be to make a public example of her. Last week he'd received a new toy, a simple wood frame from which a heretic was hung upside down and sawed in half. The cut, ending at mid-torso, prolonged the agony. In Emma's case, the gash would pierce her womb and expel the Featherstones' progeny.

But Parthalán wanted the satisfaction of killing Emma with his own hands. He wanted to tear her apart and rip her heart from her chest cavity.

His finely tuned ear caught a nervous whinny as one of the horses, Jasper, carried Naomi toward the shore road.

Another stab in the back. Not by empty-headed consorts, but by Naomi Brautigam, whom he'd hand-picked to become Gregory's wife. The woman who, until now, had been loyal, devoted, and trustworthy.

Her perfidy was worse than the Featherstones'. They were tools, slaves. Naomi was almost a friend.

Parthalán raced to his stable, jumped onto his fastest horse, and rode the animal bareback, whipping him with a crop. Up ahead, Naomi's horse galloped as she fled Parthalán's sphere of authority.

Naomi's hair whipped in the wind as he gained on her. Naomi looked behind her, made eye contact with Parthalán, and kicked Jasper harder.

The horse faltered as he approached a trail littered with white stones. The hesitation was all that Parthalán needed to fling himself from his horse to Naomi's. He knocked Naomi to the ground and rolled with her. Straddling her, he placed his hands around her neck and squeezed until she was dead. Then he tossed her body onto his horse and whipped the animal for the entire trip back to Cape Agamenticus.

Every time he believed he'd mastered the situation, brought the town back under his control, another act of sedition was revealed. All of his chosen men, except Gregory Brautigam, sat locked in their houses, their wives dead. His most trusted men, all banished and humiliated. Soon the townspeople would gossip that their minister's town council had turned against him. It would be said: *Gregory Brautigam fled, rather than continue to serve Parthalán.*

First, he would punish Emma. Then he would determine how best to soothe the community and whom to select as replacements for the imprisoned men. In the meantime, one thought consoled him. The birth of his heir, safe in Léana Hauer's womb, would work greatly to his advantage.

•   •   •

In the north woods of Maine, Gregory Brautigam, smoking a pipe outdoors, snapped to attention.

His wife's voice came to him on the wind. *Gregory*, Naomi said, *I discovered your letter too late, but earlier I saw the notes on Parthalán's desk. You must save your Reverend Edwards, as he is trying to save us. Thus you may begin your atonement. Will you say a prayer for my soul?*

•   •   •

Accompanied by 200 of the strongest warriors of the Mohawk tribe, Jonathan Edwards rode north toward Cape Agamenticus. The party would arrive by early morning after traveling all night.

He'd turned to Chief Theyanoguin in desperation after the leaders of the neighboring congregations refused their assistance. Grateful for Edwards' support of his people, Theyanoguin saw the opportunity to repay a debt.

The Indians' horses were laden with wood for torches. By tomorrow evening, Cape Agamenticus would lie smoldering on the ground.

91

The ceiling creaked as Matthew placed the teapot on the stove. The creak beckoned him to the attic. He climbed the stairs without trepidation, expecting to encounter the ghost of Tobias Brautigam or Parthalán's murdered mother, Bébhinn.

Tobias's attic paintings had become diabolical parodies. Human faces were replaced with the faces of lime-skinned animals with red eyes and multiple heads. On the table at the Last Supper were dishes filled with mounds of dung, animal entrails, and human limbs. The Madonna now had the face of a goat, the baby Jesus the face of a pig. The blond man, whom Matthew now recognized as an eighteenth-century version of Toby Brody, was impaled on spears in his cage while four demons tormented him.

With the smashing of the casks, the house had begun to decompose. The floor sagged beneath his feet. The walls warped, separating from the roofline. Matthew fled down the stairs.

As he stepped into the parlor from the attic staircase, someone rapped on the kitchen door. Bartholomew Dubh stood on the deck waiting for him: the dark preacher modernized as a handsome realtor.

"Mr. Dubh," Matthew said. "This is a surprise."

It wasn't a surprise. Helen had predicted his quick arrival.

"I was passing by and thought I'd check in," Dubh said.

"I'm making a cup of tea. Care to join me?"

"Sure. Why not?"

In the house—of course Dubh had no trouble entering—Matthew said, "Make yourself comfortable," motioning toward the kitchen table. "I'd offer you something to eat, but nothing keeps long in this house. It's all rotten or stale within a day." Helen had instructed him: Keep Dubh talking. Distract him until he's weakened.

"Are you storing everything in airtight containers?" Dubh asked. "Salt air gets into everything."

Matthew poured boiling water from the teapot into two mugs. Earlier, at Helen's suggestion, he'd scrapped the wax + signs off the wall of the storeroom and placed the peelings into the mug intended for Dubh. After dropping a teabag into each mug, he twisted the lid off the jar of honey Helen had given him and added a large dollop to each mug.

"Local honey," Matthew explained. "Is one teaspoon enough, or would you like more?"

"One teaspoon's good."

So Dubh was playing the same game as Matthew. Helen had said Parthalán/Dubh liked to be in control, wanted to wait until Matthew was at his weakest before administering the coup de grâce. Now he was trying to decipher Matthew's actions. Matthew could almost hear an adding machine clicking in Dubh's head.

Matthew placed a mug in front of his guest and sipped from his own mug.

Dubh tasted the tea. As a hive formed near his eye, Dubh's leg jerked upward. He winced in pain as his knee smashed into the table.

"Are you OK?" Matthew asked.

Dubh waved the pain away and continued sipping his tea. "Just a muscle spasm."

"Let's sit in the living room. My mother always said you shouldn't entertain guests in the kitchen."

He enjoyed fucking with Bartholomew Dubh's head. It was nice to finally be the fucker rather than the fuckee.

• • •

Helen had dug a dozen holes in the rocky sand of the oceanside cemetery that Sven Koskinen had consecrated. Alongside each hole, a plastic bag waited.

Helen opened the bag labeled E KOSKINEN and poured its contents into one of the holes. She covered the minister's remains with sand and said a silent prayer.

As she uttered the prayer's final word, a firefly emerged from the sand, beating its tiny wings to hover in place.

In Rye, New Hampshire, Sven Koskinen, brushing his teeth, felt himself embraced and heard the words "Thank you" whispered in his ear.

Helen transferred the shriveled heart and bone fragments of C HAUER into another hole. As she covered her husband's remains, she remembered the nights they'd spent on this beach, gazing at the ocean, her head resting on his shoulder.

As a firefly emerged from the ground, an invisible hand caressed Helen's hair.

Helen placed the remnants of J FEATHERSTONE, E FEATHERSTONE, E BRAUTIGAM, A AYERS, and MARIAH in their assigned graves. Five more fireflies joined the two hovering in the air.

Cutler stood above her, more handsome than she remembered him. As she stared at her dead husband made flesh, Einar Koskinen, James Featherstone, Elias Featherstone, Emma Brautigam, Abigail Ayers, and Mariah Edwards appeared at Cutler's side.

"We will be together soon, my love," Cutler said, leading his army toward Kinnawe House.

The dream of being reunited with him for eternity had sustained her for centuries.

•　　•　　•

Bartholomew Dubh placed his tea on the coffee table. As he turned to sit on the couch, his legs gave out, as if someone had smashed his kneecaps with a pipe wrench. He gasped in pain as Matthew helped him onto the couch.

The honey was working.

Dubh gulped at the tea like a man drawn to a deadly poison. The mug was empty when he placed it on the coffee table.

Dubh doubled over in agony. When he looked up, his face was covered with oozing sores. As Matthew watched, Dubh's head shed its thick curls of black hair, revealing a black star-shaped birthmark on his scalp.

Matthew had never taken pleasure in another person's pain. Until now.

"You're not looking so good, Mr. Dubh," Matthew said.

"Stop playing games with me, Matthew," Dubh hissed. "Ailments do not afflict me for long. What did you hope to gain by smashing those casks? They are none of your concern."

"That's where you're wrong, 'Reverend' Kinnawe. They *are* my concern. You brought me here to make me kill myself. You wanted me where I'd be at my weakest and you'd be at your strongest. Not very fair, is it? Well, I'm sick, and I'm skinny, but I am not *weak*." On the contrary, he'd never felt stronger. Vital blood coursed through his veins. His scars were nothing more than dead skin.

Dubh toppled to the floor, snapping his collarbone and left shin, but he remained defiant. "This is the end, Matthew."

He lunged at Matthew, who stepped out of the way. Dubh lost his balance and crashed to the floor, shattering his right forearm and elbow. Black blood sprayed from the wounds and pooled in large, dark circles on the carpet and the hardwood floor.

Dubh struggled to his knees, grabbed his stomach, and spewed a stream of puke across the room. Post-vomit, he labored for breath.

"What have you done to me?" Dubh gasped.

"Nothing you don't deserve, Parthalán. The honey came from bees that collected nectar from goldenrod. I understand you're allergic to it."

Dubh threw himself at Matthew, who sidestepped his attacker. As Dubh squirmed on the floor, Matthew ran to the storage room and returned with the sledgehammer he'd used to smash the casks in the cellar.

He raised the sledgehammer over his head.

"This is for my mother, 'Reverend.' And for Léana Hauer, Cutler Hauer, Tobias Brautigam, Einar Koskinen, and every other person whose life you've destroyed."

The impact splattered Matthew's jeans with Bartholomew Dubh's gray matter.

Vengeance is mine, sayeth the Lord, Matthew thought. *With a little help from me and Helen.*

At the end of Agamenticus Cliff Road, as Helen placed the remains of R COLLINGE, L MEER, and N BRAUTIGAM into their graves, Cutler and Einar advanced on the Brautigam house.

"Will you join us?" Cutler asked Gregory Brautigam, who stared at them through the window.

Brautigam nodded: *Yes.*

Together Cutler and Einar smashed at one of the windows until it shattered. With Gregory at their side, Michael Ayers, Sebastian Collinge III, and Charles Meer also pledged their assistance.

92

Cape Agamenticus, Maine
Early Fall 1749

Parthalán left Naomi's body draped over the horse as he entered the house built for him three years earlier.

His dark-adapted eyes needed no candle. He pushed open the door to Emma's chamber and entered.

A washbasin on the floor contained two dead fetuses floating in blood and guts, their tiny bodies curled around each other. Emma lay naked and dead on the bed, an empty vial clutched in her right hand.

On the wall, in her blood, Emma had scrawled a final message to the man she believed to be her husband:

YOU ARE DEFEATED

Parthalán laughed. His lying bitch of a wife had gone to her grave believing her pathetic lies had vanquished him. She was gone, and good riddance to her, but now her family would pay for her treachery.

In the living room, he ripped the attic door from its hinges, planning to choke the life out of Emma's simpering brother. He took the stairs three at a time, expecting to find Tobias cowering in a corner.

Instead, he found Bébhinn sitting in the chair facing the ocean.

"Your time has ended, Parthalán," she said.

Parthalán picked up the closest thing to hand, Tobias's chamber pot, and hurled it at his mother. It passed through her and shattered the window.

Parthalán ran down the stairs into the parlor, where he encountered a shivering Lotte in her nightdress. "Reverend, what is happening? I ..."

Parthalán struck her face, killing her with a single blow.

Unlike Emma, Léana would not have taken her own life. No devout Christian woman would renounce her faith in her Lord. Still, he must ensure the safety of his true child. His heir.

In the distance, the ocean waves gathered strength as the winds picked up speed, impeding his progress toward Léana's house. The trees danced in the wind, bending like rubber as they swayed from left to right, front to back. Two giant pines crashed to the ground in a one-two thump.

Léana's house remained undamaged in the center of the raging storm as the angry waves smashed against the shoreline. A heavy pottery jar held the back door open to prevent the wind from slamming it shut.

Léana sat in her parlor. The last time he'd glimpsed her, her stomach had been swollen. Now her distended belly was gone.

"What have you done to my children?"

"They are dead and dissolved."

"And now, Léana, you will pay the price for your interference. You should have remained in Northampton with your beloved Jonathan Edwards, where you belong."

"You don't frighten me, Parthalán. It is *you* who should be frightened. Your community has abandoned you. You have no heir, and you never will. Prosperity that is brought by evil cannot last. Your master grows weary of you. You will not survive this night."

"You filthy whore. You think you will go to your rightful place above, to serve your God? When I am done with you, He will want nothing to do with you." Never before had he been permitted within ten paces of Léana. Now he loomed over her, ready to crush her skull with his bare hands.

·   ·   ·

Léana jumped from her chair and ran through the parlor door facing the ocean, which she'd propped open with an earthenware jar. She ran eastward along the beach and onto the cliff path alongside the ocean, the winds raging at her from all sides. As she ran along the path to higher ground, Parthalán's hands grazed her hair and neck. His stench assaulted her nostrils and almost stole her ability to breathe, but she managed to stay just out of his arm's reach.

In the moonlit distance was the end of the path and the entrance to Parthalán's cave. The path ended at the cave mouth. The only escape was downward, a hundred feet to the rocky beach below.

Perched on an outcropping above the cave opening was a white dove. Jerusha had returned.

Jump, Léana.

Without hesitation, Léana launched herself off the cliff. Parthalán stopped in his tracks, expecting to hear the satisfying crack of Léana's head breaking open on the rocks below. Instead he saw a seagull extend its wings as the roaring winds carried it out to sea.

•   •   •

Parthalán heard the snap as the ocean bed cracked and the wave rushed toward the shore. The tsunami grew taller and more powerful as it approached land. Parthalán ran for the church, planning to take shelter in its crypt.

Trees crashed around him as he fought his way inland. Pine needles and dead leaves, caught in a frantic vortex of air, swirled around him. A roaring wind funnel, its path guided by a massive black-gray cloud, scraped the ground as it approached him, shattering grand old oaks into twigs.

Parthalán reached the church door and struggled to push it open. It was barred from the inside.

"Why do you punish me?" Parthalán shrieked. "I have served you tirelessly and faithfully."

Served me? You are nothing but a disappointment.

"I built this town. Built this church. Built this community. All to serve you!"

No. To serve yourself. You are weak and impotent, so you resort to cheating and trickery. The rules were not made to be broken.

"I have done your bidding without question! My loyalty is complete!" Parthalán screamed through the howling wind.

You were to create a child, an heir. You failed. You were outwitted by a woman who came here to destroy all that I created. You are not worthy to serve me, Parthalán. Nor are the craven gossips, men and women alike, of this town. This church is useless to me.

Parthalán fell to his knees as the savage winds turned his tears into burning drops of ice. "This was your plan all along! You wanted me to fail. You wanted to witness my disgrace!"

Could you have expected any other outcome? You sold your soul to Satan. Did you believe Satan can be trusted?

Thinking only of his survival, Parthalán threw himself behind a boulder as the wind funnel spun toward the church. The twister ripped the church apart, pulling the wood and stone into its increasing circumference. The stained-glass windows blew out from the inside, creating a million little mirrors that reflected bits of colored light inside the vortex.

Parthalán lived to see the tornado continue along the cliff, ripping Kinnawe House from its foundations and causing the structure to explode from within. As the funnel moved toward the Brautigams' house, Parthalán looked toward the sea. A mountainous wave hovered above him. A second later, the wave hit with such force that every house in the seaside community of Cape Agamenticus—except the Hauers'—was swept out to sea, along with the lifeless body of Parthalán Kinnawe.

93

Cape Agamenticus, Maine
Early Fall 1749

As the sun peeked over the horizon, Chief Theyanoguin led the charge. When the war party arrived in Cape Agamenticus, they found nothing but the shattered remains of a once-prosperous community.

Walking through the wreckage, Edwards found a stone sundial that had remained intact and rooted to the earth. He touched it and read the time from the dial: 6 o'clock. He checked the timepiece in his pocket: exactly 6 o'clock.

Edwards dropped to his knees and prayed for Léana Hauer, Cutler Hauer, Mariah, and all the souls sacrificed to evil in this distant outpost of the Massachusetts colony. His desire to be rid of Bébhinn and Parthalán had planted the seeds of this epic destruction.

"May God have mercy on their souls," Edwards whispered.

The Lord had known he would fail and had done the work Himself. He felt God nowhere near this place, nowhere near him. The ministry of Reverend Jonathan Edwards had come to an end.

94

Matthew stared at Dubh's lifeless body, its head reduced to a bloody pulp. Murdering a man in cold blood—that hadn't been on his bucket list, but defeating Parthalán was. And he'd succeeded.

When he'd thought ahead to this moment, he'd expected Dubh's body to dissolve and his fluids to dribble through the floor into the cellar, as his mother's had. But the blood, bone, and brain matter that had pooled on the floor and on the carpet began crawling toward Dubh's neck. An instant later, Matthew was staring at the back of Bartholomew Dubh's intact head, its thick, curly hair unmatted by gore.

Matthew stepped back as the impossibly alive body of Bartholomew Dubh rose to its feet and turned toward him, revealing the face of his twin brother. Josh's olive skin was flawless. The cleft in his chin had become deeper.

Josh placed his arm around Matthew's shoulder and guided him to the couch. Matthew was powerless to resist. In the back of his mind, he remembered Helen's warning that Parthalán would use every trick at his disposal. He'd thought he was prepared, but seeing Josh here, looking like a *Men's Health* cover boy, had almost paralyzed him.

"Matt, I'm so sorry for what you're going through," Josh said.

Josh sat next to him on the couch. Matthew couldn't move, didn't want to. It was comforting to feel his buddy's—his brother's—arm around his shoulder. Like in those photos in their high school and college yearbooks.

"But the truth is, Matt, you deserve it."

No. He didn't deserve it. He was tired of the same old refrain, the house telling him what he deserved and what he didn't. He tried to wriggle out of Josh's embrace, but Josh held him tight.

"Sit still, Matt, and listen to me. You haven't lived a good life. This illness you have—fatal insomnia—it's got to be a punishment, don't you think?"

Matthew shook his head. "No. It's not. I know who you are, Josh. I know *what* you are."

"I hate to see you suffering, Matt."

An opaque orange pill bottle appeared in Josh's hand.

"Take these, Matt. They'll end the pain. It'll be quick. You'll go to sleep, and you won't wake up. You'll get all the sleep you want. Won't that be better than losing more of your mind every day? And knowing you killed an innocent man?"

Josh unscrewed the bottlecap and dropped six pills into his own hand—golden softgel tablets that resembled tiny egg yolks. "They're like candy, Matt. Take two at a time. By the time you take the last two, you'll be half asleep."

Matthew stared at the pills, remembering a similar trick that Parthalán, in the guise of Doctor Ansari, had used to tempt him into ingesting a fatal dose. It had almost worked then, but it wouldn't work now.

Léana was right: Parthalán was nothing but a trickster and a coward.

"I have a better idea, Josh," Matthew said. Anger fueled him as he grabbed Josh's hand and forced it into a fist, breaking the coating on the pills. He walked to the piano, retrieved Rose of Sharon's knife, and offered it to Josh.

"You want me dead, Josh? You think death will be a happy release for me? Then *you* do it to me. Go ahead. One stab right into the heart."

"You want me to kill you because you're not strong enough to kill yourself," Josh spat. "You've always been a coward."

"You're the coward. You want me dead? Then kill me."

"You're a loser whose own mother wanted him to die."

"No, she was a sick woman. You manipulated her and tricked her."

"You're pathetic. You have big dreams but zero talent. I fucked your girlfriend more times than I can count. She aborted your child rather than let him end up like you."

Matthew dropped the knife, made a fist, drew his right arm back, and punched Josh square in the jaw. Josh staggered back.

"*Get out of this house*," Matthew said.

Josh laughed. "You're in *my* house, Matthew. Not the other way around."

In the time it took Matthew's heart to beat once, Josh threw himself backwards, executing a feet-over-head back flip and morphing into a gigantic cobra. Its hood scratched the ceiling as the snake spit two globs of venom into Matthew's eyes.

Matthew was blinded. He fell to the floor with a gasp as the snake slithered over the couch and onto the floor in front of him.

"Did you really believe you can defeat me?" it hissed. "I have the strength of thousands of years. You wanted to die looking at the ocean. Now you will die blind."

Matthew extended his hand, searching for the knife he'd dropped. He grabbed its handle and pulled himself onto his feet, using the piano to steady himself.

"Your time is up, Matthew. Use that knife on yourself. Let your life end with your imagined defeat of me. Choose to die now so that Léana's screams do not torment you in your blindness, as your mother's madness tormented you. As long as you continue to draw breath, I will keep Léana alive and tear her apart, piece by piece."

He had to buy time. He gripped the knife handle. "If I do it, will you promise to let her live in peace?"

"You propose a bargain with the devil," the snake hissed, "as if you have the upper hand. You do not."

"I'm trying to make a deal with you, Parthalán. I'll kill myself right now if you let her live and promise never to go near her again. When I'm gone, she'll have nothing left to fight for. She won't bother you again. I'm the end of the line. She knows it, and so do you."

The cobra's hissing became softer as it lowered its head toward Matthew. "You insult me by mistaking me for Parthalán Kinnawe. But we have an agreement."

Where were the warriors, the revenge-seekers?

"Show me a sign of good faith," Matthew said. "Give me back my eyesight."

The cobra spit into Matthew's right eye. Its sight returned.

"Now," the cobra said, "you must keep your end of the bargain."

Matthew raised the knife, gripping the handle with both fists, and pointed it toward his heart. Then he turned it on the cobra, driving it between the snake's eyes and pulling it down the snake's length until he'd split it in two.

Two miles out in the Atlantic, the ocean floor cracked. The shock rocked Kinnawe House to its foundations as overland winds whipped the atmosphere into a frenzy.

The cobra dissolved into pools of liquid silver that seeped through the floor into the basement. When the last drop had dripped through the floorboards, a massive fist burst through the floor from the cellar beneath, followed by a huge, monstrous half man-half goat with cloven hooves and a pentagram carved on its forehead.

As Matthew stepped backwards to prevent himself from being sucked into the hole in the floorboards, the creature tossed back its head and laughed.

"Behold," it said, sweeping its arm toward the ocean. A gigantic wave approached. "You will meet the same fate as Parthalán."

As Matthew forced himself to look away from the beast's scarlet eyes, all of the house's windows shattered. Millions of shards were swept outward into a vortex of swirling, violent wind.

"Kill yourself now, Matthew," the beast ordered. "Do it, or I will destroy everything within a hundred miles, except Priscilla Sargent. Tonight, she will conceive my heir."

Behind the beast, half a dozen men and women jumped into the house through the window frames. The holy army, the vengeful army, had arrived. A rugged pioneer type with a long, full beard grabbed the sledgehammer and began swinging at the beast. A tall blond Viking grabbed the knife from Matthew's hands and began slashing at the creature's chest and throat. Helen picked up the fireplace poker and in two quick stabs took the creature's eyes out. A muscular man who resembled Mickey, carrying an axe that Matthew had seen in the storage shed, lopped off each arm and leg from the creature's torso as it screamed in agony.

The man-goat would not die. It lay in pieces on the floor, its separate limbs attempting to rejoin its trunk, as the tsunami wave approached.

The bearded pioneer took the knife from the Viking and handed it to Matthew.

"Drive it through his heart, Matthew."

He owed a debt to all of them, his extended family, his brothers and sisters in arms. As one of the creature's eyeballs rolled up its body and toward an eye socket, he plunged the knife deep into the creature's chest.

The beast let out a final shriek. As it drew its final breath, Helen pulled its heart from its chest cavity. Immediately she began to crumple. Her skin tightened around her face, and her thick salt-and-pepper hair started falling out in clumps.

"Take her to the boat," Cutler said to Matthew, "and cut the rope. You are safest on the ocean. Godspeed."

Helen had told Matthew to obey Cutler's orders without question. Matthew scooped Helen off the floor—she was light as a feather—and carried her to the end of the dock, where the little rowboat rode the crashing waves. He laid Helen in the boat, climbed in, and used the knife to cut the boat from its mooring.

"Now we stop the heir," said Cutler.

•   •   •

Joshua Brody drove his Audi at 100 miles per hour north on Route 95. His father needed his help. According to his GPS, Josh would arrive at Kinnawe House in less than half an hour.

As he roared across the Piscataqua River Bridge at dusk, a sudden bright light, like that of a thousand fireflies lighting up, created a dizzying glare off the white box truck in front of him. Trying to maintain control of the car, he skidded across three lanes of traffic. An 18-wheeler slammed into the Audi, sending it soaring through the air and into the Piscataqua River below as a category 5 tornado and massive tsunami wave destroyed Cape Agamenticus and Kinnawe House for the second time.

Epilogue
Swept Out to Sea

95

Princeton, New Jersey
1758

Gregory Brautigam and the children had lived in tranquil solitude on their island for the past seven years. Gregory had married a local woman, Marjorie Pauling, who'd expected to die an old maid. She'd always longed for children, and she loved Fiona Hauer; Luke, Anne, and Beatrice Collinge; and Ruth, Jane, Zachary, and Ezra Meer as if they were her own.

Gregory and all the children had changed their last names to Brodie, and they'd vowed never to speak of Cape Agamenticus. The official story: Gregory, a wealthy Boston widower, had grown weary of the icy northern winters and moved his extended family to the tiny island off the coast of South Carolina.

Gregory embraced Marjorie before setting off for the mainland. He turned and waved good-bye to his third wife, fixing her plain face and bright eyes in his mind. The children were in good hands.

He'd thought about stopping in Philadelphia to visit Tobias but decided against it. In Charles Town, Tobias had become acquainted with the daughter of a Philadelphia merchant, and he'd relocated to Pennsylvania to woo her. They'd married two years earlier, and Gregory had recently received the happy news that he would soon be a grandfather.

Gregory had explained to Tobias the course of events that brought them to the island. "I regret everything," Gregory said, "but nothing more than ignoring my conscience."

Tobias had forgiven him. Emma had not. He carried her letter with him always to remind him of the choices he'd made, the daughter he'd sacrificed. Snatches of the letter rose to his consciousness at unexpected times—while bouncing Fiona on his lap, while sitting with Marjorie, while working the land. *I cannot, I will not continue to live—I have been made the bride of a beast against my will—I go to my death praying for the destruction of this town and everyone in it, including you. Especially you.*

Naomi had informed on her friends, but like her husband she had listened to her conscience in the end. While she sat in Parthalán's library being constricted by Parthalán's asp, she'd read the notes scattered on his desk. She knew Parthalán's abiding hatred for Reverend Edwards and the revenge he planned to exact. She had made it Gregory's mission to stop Parthalán, given him the opportunity to even the score with the man who'd destroyed Gregory Brautigam's family while populating a town with willing servants.

• • •

Jonathan Edwards was now president of The College of New Jersey. His son-in-law, Aaron Burr, had died, leaving the institution without a leader. The college fathers decided that Edwards was the best man for the job.

Since the destruction of Cape Agamenticus, Edwards had been distracted, preaching rambling sermons that confused his congregation. Concerned for his health, his wife Sarah begged him not to accept the college presidency, a position she considered too taxing for an aging and weakened man. She was happy in Stockbridge, she said. She wanted to spend her final years playing with her grandchildren, not serving as a hostess to fussy professors.

Nonetheless, the persuaders achieved their victory, and Jonathan and Sarah Edwards now lived in Princeton. Edwards gave weekly theology assignments to the senior class but held little affection for the rowdy young men from wealthy families who cared not a whit for education, much less spiritual enlightenment or fulfillment.

Edwards met Doctor William Shippen during his first week in Princeton. Most of Shippen's patients were members of the faculty and well-to-do families, and Edwards considered him a very competent, progressive healer.

For decades smallpox had ravaged the Colonies, leaving the few survivors paralyzed and deformed. Though he was, and always would be, a man of God, Edwards was also devoted to science, and Shippen convinced him that inoculation was the best way to combat the disease.

Shippen had persuaded Edwards to set an example for his students and for the entire community. The average man viewed the idea of introducing the virus into one's body *on purpose* as utter madness. By taking the treatment, Shippen argued, Edwards would make a strong public statement about the safety of variolation.

The maid knocked on the door of Edwards' study. "Doctor Shippen is here, sir."

After Shippen and Edwards shook hands, Shippen introduced his assistant, Mrs. Moira Feeley, a long-faced woman with thin ankles.

As Mrs. Feeley began unpacking the doctor's bag, Shippen rolled up Edwards' sleeve.

"You set an excellent example, Reverend Edwards," Mrs. Feeley said, handing the needle to Doctor Shippen.

As the needle broke Edwards' skin, the study door flew open. A sturdy middle-aged man, whose face reminded Edwards of a long-forgotten friend, strode into the room.

"Reverend, you must not submit to this death sentence," the man said. "You are guaranteed to die of the pox."

"I am afraid it is too late, my good man," Edwards said. "I appreciate your concern, but this treatment will prevent me from contracting the pox, not infect me with it. Variolation offers protection from the disease."

"Mrs. Feeley," Doctor Shippen said, "would you please show this gentleman out?"

Mrs. Feeley pinched the man's forearm just above the elbow. Gregory Brautigam winced in pain as she led him out of the study by sheer force of will.

"I admire your concern for Reverend Edwards' safety," Mrs. Feeley said. "You are a true Christian, sir."

As he reached for the doorknob, Gregory felt the pinprick on the back of his hand.

A month later, surrounded by his family, Jonathan Edwards died of smallpox. His last words were, "Trust in God, and ye need not fear."

The symptoms began on his journey back to South Carolina. As the fever came on, Gregory took a room at an inn and spent the entire night vomiting. He noticed the first spots on his hands and arms as he entered Charles Town.

He would not return to his house to infect Marjorie and the children. He wrote a loving letter to each of them, and to Tobias, and left the letters at an inn. He used his remaining strength to paddle his boat to an uninhabited island. By his third day on the island, his face was so ravaged with pox that Marjorie would not have recognized him.

As his heart took its last beats, he wondered where he would wake up.

When he opened his eyes, he found himself in the house he'd shared with Naomi in Cape Agamenticus. Every door and window was sealed shut.

Gregory Brautigam sat on the floor and accepted his punishment.

96

Portland, Maine

As the boat rode the waves, pulled out farther and farther into the Atlantic by the storm, the trees on the mainland snapped like twigs. The church exploded into fragments of wood and glass. Kinnawe House was the next to go, ripped off its foundation and blasted to bits. Matthew held Helen tightly against him. He remained blind in one eye.

A monstrous wave crashed over them, and the impossible happened. He fell asleep.

When his eyes flickered open, he watched Helen lift her hand out of the water. In it she held the beast's salt-shriveled heart. She ground it into dust between the heels of her hands and let the winds scatter the remains into the ocean.

Helen took his hand. "It's time for me to go, Matthew."

"Can't you stay a little longer, Helen? Léana?" He wasn't ready to lose her. His friend. His protector. His grandmother.

Helen shook her head, smiling. "We were a good team, Matthew."

"Léana, you gave me ... everything."

"And because of you," Helen said, "I'll be with Cutler and Mariah again. You're a part of us, a part of our family, Matthew. Never worry about the blood that runs through your veins. It's *good* blood. Mac Concradha and Hauer blood."

Matthew blinked and Helen was gone. A seagull soared up into the clouds. He reached for the stone that dangled from his neck. He loved it, but he didn't need it. He had Helen, and he had his mother, and that was enough.

.   .   .

Matthew left Portland General a week later. He'd been rescued by a ferry-boat captain who had seen his rowboat bobbing in the Atlantic.

During his stay at the hospital, the sight had returned to his blind eye. The test results showed that his FFI gene had disappeared. Doctor Sands, puzzled but delighted, predicted he would live a long time. He used the same phrase that Doctor Ansari had used when Matthew had visited his office in Portsmouth: "spontaneous recovery."

Matthew had purchased a new phone—couldn't live without *that*—so he checked Facebook as the bus merged onto Route I-295. Word had gotten out about his brush with death, and his social media had blown up with health-related memes, song clips, and gushy wishes for a speedy recovery.

People cared.

The bus crossed the Piscataqua River. He'd followed the press coverage. First, the *Portsmouth Herald* reported that a black Audi with New York plates had flipped over into the river 75 feet below. The search party recovered the car but didn't find the driver. After a three-day search, they gave up.

Four days later, the *Herald* ran a follow-up story. A headless body had been discovered on the New Hampshire coastline near Hampton Beach State Park. The bloated body was intact, but the marine life had pecked out its eyes and heart. All its teeth were missing, making dental identification impossible.

Someday he'd forgive Josh. For now, he wanted to remember him as the shy, sweet kid who'd shared his lunch money and baseball cards, long before his real father—most likely Terrence Cierna, that medieval studies professor—found him.

He'd put off making the phone call. Now was the time.

Toby Brody answered.

"Hi, Matthew."

"Toby, I'm so sorry. I don't know what to say."

"You don't need to say anything, Matt. I knew what my son was. Kathryn's a different story, of course. She still thinks he's just missing. Maybe you can stop by sometime? She'd like to see you."

"When did you know for sure?"

"I suspected when his face started changing. The last time he came home, his chin was cleft. It's the final sign."

"And when you saw that, you knew he was the bad seed, and I was the good one?" The good seed: the seed from which good things grow, Helen had said.

"Nobody can know with certainty until the child reaches adulthood. Your birthmark was always red, even when you were a little boy. But the color can change overnight."

"I don't understand."

"The children always have the birthmark. Sometimes it's visible to everyone. Sometimes it's on a part of the body that's covered by clothing or hair. Yours is on your forearm. Josh's was on his left buttock. When the children come of age, the color can no longer change. You're an adult, and your birthmark is red. Josh's was black, and the color never changed."

Matthew flashed back to the barbecue in Biddeford: the spiked punch, the two-headed goat roasting on the spit, Ray Lonegan in a cage, Anton's hiss: *You fool. It's red. Not black. You've brought the Enemy here.*

"And Ray? Who was he?"

"He was on our side, but he was a heretic. Léana and I think he wanted to kidnap you to protect you. But that's not permitted. We're at a disadvantage when we break the rules. And when you're fighting a war, you can't let the enemy gain an edge."

"Toby, I saw Mariah."

Matthew heard only dead air as Toby Brody took a couple of seconds to respond. "She was beautiful, wasn't she? Brave and beautiful. I loved her. I still do."

As he drifted off to sleep, Matthew thought about Priscilla. The dove had fluttered from her wrist into his heart.

• • • •

Park Avenue South
Manhattan

They hadn't intended to get pregnant so soon after getting married, but they'd been having so much great sex it was probably inevitable.

From earlier tests, they knew that Priscilla's womb held just one child. The tests indicated no abnormalities, no ticking time bomb for fatal familial insomnia. Today they'd get to hear the baby's heartbeat for the first time. It was too early to learn the baby's sex, but they wanted to be surprised anyway. The names were already chosen. For a girl, Léana Rose Lisa Hauer. For a boy, Cutler Tobias Sargent Hauer.

Matthew had changed his legal name to Matthew Hauer. Rollins had never felt quite right. Hauer did.

He'd taken a full-time job with an upscale supermarket that provided surprisingly good medical insurance, so Priscilla's OB/GYN was located in a tasteful midrise building. Having the best care for his wife and child was his first priority; the music came second. But he'd asked his manager to put "Silver Horses" into rotation on the sound system during the store's peak hours, and the manager had said: *Yes, of course, I'll be happy to. Everyone who works here has a dream. We're all in it together.*

Sitting next to Priscilla in the waiting room was a raven-haired *anime*-girl tapping away at her smartphone. With her jet-black hair and funky jewelry, she bore a passing resemblance to Kellyce. Her T-shirt, emblazoned with the logo of Satan's Sister, a Brooklyn punk band, stretched across her giant belly.

In the examination room, the little Sargent Hauer was cooperative and energetic. Priscilla thought his or her heartbeat sounded like the galloping of tiny horses. Matthew heard a 4/4 rhythm in the key of C: a steady thump in a bright major key.

As Priscilla and the OB/GYN talked and laughed, Matthew excused himself to use the rest room. As he walked along the hallway, he saw the heavily pregnant *anime*-girl sitting alone in an examination room, crying.

Matthew knew he should mind his own business, but the girl's tears tugged at his heart. Strangers had watched over him and protected him. He would have died without their help. It was time to pay it forward.

"Hi," he said to the girl. "Anything I can do?"

The girl wiped away a tear. "No, I'm OK. Just indulging in some self-pity. Twins."

Matthew smiled. "A double blessing. Twice the work, but I'm sure the dad will help."

The girl sniffled. "He's out of the picture."

"Oh." *Out of the picture* might mean a one-night stand, a boyfriend who split rather than take responsibility, a husband who'd died in a tragic accident.

"Excuse me," said a voice behind Matthew, who stepped aside to let the girl's OB/GYN enter the examination room.

"Don't worry about Ruth," the long-faced, tight-lipped doctor said. "She'll be fine. She has everything she needs."

The girl's face brightened. "I don't know what I'd do without you, Doctor Feeley."

Acknowledgments

I offer sincere gratitude to Christian Alighieri (who was there at the beginning), Bob Costa, Keith Harrington, Linda Konner, Marc Lieberman, Emily Marlowe, Max St. John, Reagan Rothe, and Cheryl Solimini. To all the Pokerinos and my friends from Deadly Ink: Thanks for the laughs, the conversation, the inspiration. And to my dearly departed—Aunt Phyl, Claire, Pam—I know you are with Léana now.

About the Author

Steve Rigolosi is the editor-in-chief of Cambria & Calibri, an editorial services firm, where he specializes in editing psychology, economics, and business books. His published fiction includes four mysteries, including *Who Gets the Apartment?* and *The Outsmarting of Criminals*. Both received the David Award for the Best Mystery of the Year, and Oprah's editors selected *The Outsmarting of Criminals* as one of the best mysteries of its publication year.

He lives in Northern New Jersey, where he plays classical flute with the Ramsey Wind Symphony. He rereads *The Haunting of Hill House*, *Hell House*, *The Shining*, and *The Little Stranger* at least once a year. His other books include *Circle of Assassins* and *The Ocelot Chronicles*.

Note from the Author

Word-of-mouth is crucial for any author to succeed. If you enjoyed *The Haunting of Kinnawe House*, please leave a review online—anywhere you are able, even if it's just a sentence or two. It would make all the difference and would be very much appreciated.

Thanks!
Steven Rigolosi

We hope you enjoyed reading this title from:

BLACK ROSE
writing™

www.blackrosewriting.com

Subscribe to our mailing list – *The Rosevine* – and receive **FREE** books, daily deals, and stay current with news about upcoming releases and our hottest authors.
Scan the QR code below to sign up.

Already a subscriber? Please accept a sincere thank you for being a fan of Black Rose Writing authors.

View other Black Rose Writing titles at www.blackrosewriting.com/books and use promo code **PRINT** to receive a **20% discount** when purchasing.

CPSIA information can be obtained
at www.ICGtesting.com
Printed in the USA
LVHW030256310322
714641LV00004B/12